THE BALIZE

Theo Lemos

Best wishes

Theo

INNER CURRENTS TRILOGY BOOK ONE

Although the inspiration for this novel is heavily influenced by events that took place in the south of Devon in the early 1980s, it is a work of fiction and any resemblance to actual persons is coincidental.

ISBN-13: 978-1508430919
ISBN-10: 1508430918

This novel is dedicated to my wife and children for their love, support and encouragement

CONTENTS

Acknowledgements

My grateful thanks to my son-in-law, Dino Cozadinos, for his book cover design and also to my wife for her invaluable input and support.

Chapter 1: The Moor

8th May 1982

It is the middle of a spring evening, the sky is clear and the moon is swamping the heavens in silvery light so that only the brightest stars are visible. The lush, tightly undulating, sparsely populated farmlands below, crisscrossed by stone walls and neat hedgerows, slumber in the gleam and sigh in the mild south westerly breeze. To the north, amongst the rounded uplands, the wind is stronger and more chilling. These austere moorlands of heather hold their darkness against the pearly light with only the occasional patch of rough grassland giving visual relief from the gloom. Above the gorse-cloaked slopes and on the higher peaks, the dull grey granite tors, with their angular joints and lines, rise defiantly.

This is a bleak, humourless region, with the only mirth coming from the bubbling brooks that emerge from the bogs. These are fringed with hawthorn and rowan and, as they grow, they cut gullies clothed in bracken or ancient stunted trees. Then, plunging down rapids, they leave the desolate moorland plateau to form lush winding valleys of oak woods. Here there is shelter from the wind and the soils are fertile. The clean moist air encourages profuse growths of lichen, liverwort and moss over trees, rocks and exposed ground. In one of these, the vibrant rush of a great river, with its rock-strewn bed, has replaced the gurgling of a juvenile stream, the season's newly sprouted leaves allowing much of the moonlight to filter down to the woodland floor.

The sides of this valley rise steeply away from the riverbanks and within its trees are areas of dense plant growth dissected by paths trodden by man and trails made by animals. Amid the vegetation are the inconspicuous foragings generated by those creatures active at night. Yet in one circular section, several yards wide and set well back from the waterside, such nocturnal activity has ceased. A chill that is not cold, a darkness that is not lack of light, a terror that is indefinable has descended like a mist. Amongst thick undergrowth and in the shade of several mature oaks, a dark four-legged shape has materialised. It was not there a minute ago, nor did it not come from any other part of the forest. It is standing erect with its eyes reflecting images of the moon.

The sights and smells of the wilderness are familiar to this creature from long ago and it desires, once again, to roam and hunt these lands. It tries to move one of its front legs but nearly loses its balance. Despite its muscular body, it is like a new born learning to walk. It realises that in time it will recall its former skills, but for now, it is content just to be. It is acutely aware of the point on which it stands. It was not selected randomly, for beneath its feet lay remains to which it now pays homage. This is a sacred spot, which invokes vivid memories and powerful feelings.

After a few minutes the manifestation loses strength. It is, after all, the first time it has returned in hundreds of years. It will come back to this spot to draw vigour from the significance it held, and in time it will be able to cover its former range, stimulating more memories, experiencing more feelings and thus growing more capable with each effort.

As its consciousness fades, it has a vision of a proud figure clad in a hooded cloak labouring on a night such as this, digging the ground beneath. The rituals performed enshrined it with powers that could be drawn on to this day. But now the presence is losing its hold and within a few more seconds it has vanished, the moss under its paws springing back with the release of weight.

Activity within this area of the forest returns as if nothing had happened.

Chapter 2: The Restaurant

Friday, 25th June 1982

The Italian restaurant, one of his favourites, was a snug basement situated within five minutes' walk of Piccadilly Circus. Its decor was unremarkable: dark wood panelling, dim wall lights, rickety chairs, simple tables laid with white tablecloths and candles set in green wine bottles heavily encrusted in wax. There was no pretentiousness to detract from the enjoyment of the food. An Italian aria was playing in the background, unobtrusively audible below the babble of the diners.

Zen nibbled a breadstick as he observed the waiters. Being Friday evening all the tables were taken, mostly by patrons like him, still in their business suits, having come from their places of work. He heard a soft clink as the ice cubes in his gin and tonic rebalanced themselves. It was a warm, humid evening so he slung his navy blue double vented jacket with the gold buttons over the back of his chair, before removing his tie and unbuttoning the collar of his light blue shirt. He caught the eye of a waiter and signalled for more ice.

His guest had yet to arrive, which was normal. She was always at least half an hour late. This was not a particular trait of hers, rather a Greek thing, but still irritating. He took comfort in the knowledge that this would be their last encounter. After tonight their relationship would be no more. He had tried to break it off before, but this time he was determined to end it.

He rehearsed his announcement, but stopped himself. What he had to say he would say, whether articulate or not. More important was anticipating the repercussions. As the son of prominent members of the London Greek shipping community, his parents had orchestrated this engagement. He should have seen it coming. Both their fathers were friends and such a union would have been their secret wish. Having been spared such proposals in the past from other families, some of which he had heard rumour of from time to time, had lured him into a false sense of freedom.

He experienced a moment of hesitation. This was understandable. To date, everything had been provided for him. He'd never had to make any decisions of his own, certainly not important ones. He'd had his life planned out since birth. What schools to go to, what university, what degree, the inevitable entry into the family business and now, whom he should wed.

He surmised that Sophia had arrived when he saw the waiters' heads turn towards the stairs. She was ushered to his table by the maître d', who could not keep his eyes off her legs. She was wearing a knee-length purple slinky satin dress with batwing sleeves and shoulder pads, and her dark wavy hair was held back with a black and purple leopard print bow. Her narrow face with its dark, seductive eyes bore a minimum of makeup and her olive coloured skin gave her a healthy tone.

Zen stood as she approached. They briefly kissed on both cheeks.

'Sorry I'm late,' she said, as she was helped into her chair. She hung her black Chanel quilted handbag over the back and sat, clasping her manicured hands. 'There was so much to do and I had to queue for the car park.' This was always the excuse, so frequently expressed that it now lacked sincerity.

5

'I'm used to it. But why did you drive?' She lived no more than two miles away and the taxi fare would not have been much more than the fee for the car park.

'Because Mum and Dad want me to pick them up from your parents,' she replied, looking at him incredulously.

'Why didn't they take their car?' he asked, realising there was something he should have remembered.

'Your mind's a sieve. You know Mum has a *venghera* tomorrow; she never drives the day before. She's too nervous, and Dad went from the office.'

He had forgotten about the impending party, to which he was also invited. The waiter brought them menus and took their drinks order. Sophia asked for a tomato juice and Zen another gin and tonic; he was nervous. He hoped she wouldn't notice. 'How are they?'

'Fine, yours?'

'The same,' he replied automatically, without considering the validity of the statement. He had only briefly chatted with his father that morning and hadn't had a conversation with his mum since Tuesday, when she had called to acknowledge his name day.

'So, how's the rest of your week been?' she asked. They had also not spoken since then.

'Same depressing news you must be getting from your father,' he replied. The shipping business was experiencing a sudden decline.

'He says it's the worst since '48 and '49,' she confirmed sombrely.

Sophia had a sharp awareness for commerce and Zen liked talking with her about it. He had to admit that. He wanted them to enjoy their meal before he got

6

down to more contentious matters. 'Looks like our ships may have to lay up,' he said.

'I know. Dad's sending four of ours to Greece. We've men down there who can look after them.'

'We feel laying up in Greece would be a disaster.'

A waiter brought them their drinks and asked for their order. They scanned their menus. Parma ham with melon for Sophia, to be followed by grilled salmon fillet with salad. Zen chose smoked salmon to start, with a medium rare sirloin steak afterwards. Sophia selected a glass of house white and Zen the red.

'Why a disaster?' she continued, clasping her hands again.

'What if this is just the beginning? Just imagine thousands of ships laying up all along the coasts of Greece, all in flotillas. Sure, the outgoings are low, the weather mild with plenty of willing hands. Now, if the crisis lasts for more than six months, they'll have to undergo a dry dock survey before they're allowed to work again. The eastern Med doesn't have enough facilities. It'll be chaos. It'll take months, maybe years, to re-commission them.'

'Better than losing $100,000 a month on a ship that's unemployed.'

'I agree we have to lay up. It's doing it in Greece or anywhere in the Med that's the problem.' Zen became aware that he was gesticulating more than usual.

'Where else is there?' she asked.

'I don't know,' he replied. 'Perhaps you're right. Anyway, as you can imagine, the atmosphere at the office is tense.' The Falklands war had proved an effective distraction, but now that it was over, the name of the recently born royal baby was the focus of attention.

The waiter brought them their starters and they began eating. They did not speak for a while; neither seemed willing to continue the debate.

'Perhaps we should change the subject,' Sophia suggested.

'How was your day?'

'The usual,' she replied. 'Went to an aerobics class, then met up with Chrissy.' Sophia ran an interior decorating business with an ex-school friend from a well-connected Russian family. Most of their clients were from within the Greek and Russian communities. It was a moderate success.

'What about the Hendon job?' Neither girl needed to work for financial reasons. At first Zen thought it was a hobby, to pass the time, until he realized it was an excuse for them to be together.

'We went to the house mid-morning. The owners have changed their minds so often it's ridiculous. But at last we got their agreement.'

'When will you start?'

'End of September. The builders need six weeks, then everybody'll be away. That reminds me; guess who'll be in Halkidiki at the same time as us?'

Zen thought about it as he was finishing his first course. Sophia was talking about the holiday in Greece their families would be spending together to celebrate the announcement of their engagement. He had no intention of going. He feared he would now have to confront the issue sooner than he'd wanted. He wasted time going through a list of random names. 'I give up,

I've no idea,' he said finally, keeping his eyes on his plate whilst trying to hide the tension in his voice.

'John and Niki will be there with their yacht and are planning to stay a week. In fact, I suggested we meet up for coffee after church on Sunday. You going?'

'I'll see what I feel like in the morning. I don't live as close to the cathedral as everyone else and it depends on how long tomorrow night drags on.' He realised he could have referred to her mother's party in more charitable terms.

'That's no excuse,' she said, studying him. 'You're acting a bit strange, what's the matter?'

Zen put the cutlery down on his empty plate. Sophia had also finished. He took a deep breath and a sip of his drink. 'I can't go through with it.'

Sophia waited for the waiter to remove their plates before responding, biting her lip, holding back the torrent that was to follow. 'We've been through this before.' There was frustration in her voice. 'I don't understand the problem. I suppose if I hadn't been open, I could've covered it up and let you find out after the wedding, but I didn't want you to feel deceived.'

He pondered this. Having grown up with Sophia, he had not looked upon her romantically before. When the prospect of marriage arose, he saw her for the beauty and appealing personality she was and began having feelings. When his advances were not reciprocated, the truth emerged. 'I accept that and respect you for it, although it's not something you could keep hidden. You're asking too much.'

'You must see that we get on well. We'd make a great partnership.'

Zen had no doubts about Sophia's competence. She had the potential of being an excellent hostess, efficiently navigating through endless dinner and cocktail parties, entertaining bankers, attending christenings, weddings, balls and more. Under normal circumstances he would have agreed with her. She was everything he was not and did not care to be. He genuinely wished for things to be that way. 'I agree, but I don't want to marry a friend, or worse, a business associate.'

'But it solves so many problems,' she declared. 'Look at your situation. A bachelor of thirty with countless affairs behind you. Every time you acquire a girlfriend, your parents worry that you're going to marry her. I've been hearing about it for years.'

'Well, that's just great,' he broke in. 'Perhaps I should circulate a newsletter.' It was true he'd had a tempestuous love life and, as hard as he tried to keep his relationships discreet, some still seemed to become common knowledge. Saying he'd had countless affairs was an exaggeration though.

'You're just as responsible,' she continued. 'You admitted to me, before marriage was mentioned, that you were worried how you'd settle down. This way, you never have to.'

'I said that a while ago,' he said. 'I was probably boasting.'

'You don't have to be embarrassed. At the time I couldn't tell you that I faced a similar dilemma but, now that you know, you must be able to see that our marriage is the best solution. Our parents won't tolerate us remaining single.'

'I don't share your confidence that the arrangement will work as smoothly as you say,' he retorted. 'And Christina has no problem with this?'

'She accepts it. She knew from the start that I'd have to perform certain duties. She has faith in me.'

'One of the things I have a problem with is people finding out. I'd be a joke.'

'If we weren't careful, it would be out already. The last thing we want is people questioning our relationship. We'd be outcasts.'

'What if she's also forced to marry?'

'She won't be. She doesn't have the same pressures as us. Zen, you're looking for excuses. Who's to say our marriage wouldn't be happier as friends, with separate romantic lives, than more conventional relationships? We'd still have children and in every other way be a normal family. You could've married someone emotionally cold or frigid or someone who lost interest. How long does romantic love last?'

'You have a knack for making the most bizarre arrangements appear logical, I'll give you that,' he said, 'but it still feels wrong, and if there's someone out there for me...'

'Nobody said we wouldn't love each other. Just not in that way. You'll be the father of our children and they'll be like others; loved by their parents. Honestly Zen, you've not made one convincing argument against this.' She was growing impatient and began fidgeting. 'Are you clear about your motives? Are you sure you're not looking for a nice compliant bride who's going to be home moping for you while you're gallivanting round the world with other women?'

'That's just it. I'm not. I want to settle down with one person.'

She looked doubtful and appeared to be on the brink of laughing. 'Perhaps you're just trying to duck your responsibilities.'

Sophia had touched a sensitive spot. 'It's true that I've little love for the social posing that's required by our society,' he replied. In fact he despised it.

'It's not posing. It's the cement that keeps it together.'

'Whatever, I've been through every possible angle with my father.' Zen called these the HYRTSS lectures, his acronym for Haven't You Read The Script, Son. 'The least I could ask is that my marriage be something more than a corporate merger.'

'Don't be dramatic.'

The waiter brought them their main courses and served them salad and vegetables. Another brought the wine. While this was happening, they glared at each other.

'This thing about committing yourself to one relationship's new. It's not what you've said previously,' she said, after the waiters had finished. 'Now you're asking for something few people have. This is an ideal you can't afford. Have you thought of the consequences of breaking this engagement?'

'Of course,' he replied, reflecting on the numerous sleepless nights it had already caused.

'I don't think so. For Christ's sake, our parents have booked a holiday in one of the most exclusive resorts in Greece. Dozens of families have been invited. It's all been arranged around the announcement. Have you no

12

common sense? Who do you think will carry the blame?'

'I will.'

'Do you realise how much face your father will lose? Even if you could give him the reason, which, I remind you, you've sworn not to, he's the one who'll suffer most.'

'At least he'd understand.'

'And I'd have to deny it.'

'I said I wouldn't tell.' He appreciated her reasons. If her father knew the truth, he'd throw her out, and if her clients, all drawn from the community, decided to boycott them, as would be likely, she would be on the street. 'I just think it's unfair. Couldn't we say that we can't stand each other?'

Sophia had a sip of wine and a mouthful of her salmon as if considering his question. 'It would be difficult to explain those years as children.'

'Over-familiarity?'

'Saying that to my father would be meaningless and an obvious lie. Up to yesterday, I've been telling him how much I like you.' Sophia leaned forward. With the help of the candle light he could see the wisps of steam from the hot salmon slithering to her chin and sliding up the sides of her face. Her sensuous lips started to form the next sentence. 'I believe we're perfectly suited. You've the business ability and I've the social skills.'

'I don't doubt that, but I need more.'

'There's something else you should consider. With your name and potential inheritance, how will you trust the motives of women?' she said, continuing to eat.

'I don't know.' This was a good point and one he had often pondered.

'What a let-down that would be, marrying someone who proved to be a gold-digger.'

'True, but isn't that what this is about?' Zen said, putting down his utensils. 'A marriage of financial convenience. Are we therefore not gold-diggers to each other?'

He looked at her expecting a Sophia-style riposte but instead saw something unexpected. For a fleeting moment he thought she was going to cry. Whatever emotion brought that on was quickly suppressed, but she seemed momentarily to have resigned herself. She toyed with her food. 'All I can do is show that I've no hard feelings and give you support, whenever I can. Apart from that, you're on your own. You must realise that our fathers have dreamed of this for years. Your father will take it badly. This isn't something he'll forgive. This'll threaten your relationship. Are you prepared to risk losing that for the sake of a bad feeling or the pursuit of an ideal?'

'Without ideals life would have no meaning.'

'People have ideals,' she said with renewed vigour. 'But if the upholding of one in particular requires too great a sacrifice or causes too much devastation, then one's priorities should be rearranged. Besides, I think you're making this new-found idealism up. You don't seem to be able to make a decision and stick to it. Please make up your mind and do it quickly. You've already left it too late and it can only get worse.'

They fell silent again. Sophia did not eat and looked impatiently around her as if seeking support from the clientele. Despite facing a precipice, Zen's resolve hardened. 'I've made my decision. I know what I want to do.'

'I think you're foolish and pathetic,' she said coldly. 'Don't expect me to tell our parents. You break the news.'

'Look, I'm really fond of you, but want more out of marriage. So let's enjoy this meal together. We're friends, remember? You never know, if you're right, it may be the last expensive one I can afford.' He forced a smile.

'I'd rather sit in the car.' She stood, picked up her handbag and left.

And so it ended. He sat for a few minutes before deciding to finish his steak and explain to the perplexed waiter that his guest had realised there was something important she had forgotten to do.

Chapter 3: John and Semeli Makris

Saturday, 26th June 1982

Semeli Makris woke to find the space beside her vacant. Feeling a wave of unease, she reached over, switched on the bedside light and glanced at her clock. It was three thirty in the morning and she had been asleep for three hours. She looked around the bedroom for evidence that her husband had come to undress, but saw none. The clothes valet stand and easy chair were bare and his pyjamas were still under the pillow.

She recalled the events of the evening. Friday night was cards night and the same friends came at nine o'clock, after supper in their respective homes. Only Spiros, who was running late from work, ate with them on this occasion. They had played until midnight and it was an enjoyable evening, as always. The card games were not taken seriously, although minor amounts of money changed hands. The other couples were also from ship-owning families and it was a chance for the men to talk about business and for her husband to unwind for the weekend.

He was in good spirits to begin with, but something must have happened. She tried to remember if he had received any calls. There were five in all, she recalled. One was from a disgruntled babysitter, three were business-related for the other men and the final one, towards the end of the evening, was after the last of the guests, the Alexandrous, had been picked up by their daughter Sophia. Her husband had answered, but she was too tired to have noticed if his mood had changed.

16

She put on her dressing gown, fearing the worst. Captain John was rarely upset because of business. Besides, things could not get any worse.

She went to the bathroom to comb her hair, give her teeth a brush and rinse her face. By the time she had left it her hands were trembling. She walked down the dim, carpeted corridor to the dining room. From underneath the closed door there was a fan of yellow light and her slippered feet felt a draught. There was the scent of stale tobacco. She held her breath, opened the door and walked in.

She squinted at first, dazzled by the room's central chandelier. When her eyes had adjusted, she found her husband seated where she expected him to be, at the head of the table, facing towards her. He was surrounded by a cloud of blue smoke from a half-finished cigar. His bespectacled face, austere at the best of times, did not register her arrival.

He was wearing a white short-sleeved shirt, open at the neck, and navy blue slacks. The eight-seater dining room table was still draped with the green velvet cover from the night's game and there was a solitary ashtray beside him. The maid had cleared everything else before going to bed. Behind him the curtains had been half-drawn and the nets were gently billowing. She could see the trees that separated their building from the main road and, beyond them, the yellow glow of the street lamps.

Eventually Captain John looked up, but did not speak. She went over and sat beside him. For a moment she reminded herself that this was her happy room. This was the scene of family meals, dinner parties with friends and cosy card games. On the surrounding walls hung her favourite paintings: landscapes from her native part of Greece. She let out a sigh. 'What's wrong, my love?'

'The engagement's off,' was all he said, before putting the cigar back in his mouth.

Semeli paused thoughtfully, then got up and headed for the kitchen. Once out of his sight and back in the darkness of the corridor, she crossed herself and thanked God that nobody they knew and loved had died or was ill. She turned on the kitchen light and set to making tea, moving quietly, aware that adjacent to the kitchen, by the back door, were the maid's quarters.

She needed time to think. In all their thirty-one years of marriage, she knew that this would be her husband's darkest hour.

She recalled the first time they had met and their subsequent courtship. At the time she was living with her parents in the town of Ioannina, in the north west of Greece. Her mother was a teacher in the local girls' school and her father had spent most of her childhood working in Chicago. This was not an unusual arrangement as America was considered the land of opportunity, but too decadent for young girls. They were separated for the duration of the war and, after the liberation of Greece and the end of the subsequent civil war, he sold up his chain of hardware stores for a considerable sum, and returned home.

Her father's journey took him from New York to Naples by steamer and across Italy by train to Brindisi, where he boarded the ferry that would take him to Piraeus. It was during the latter crossing that he met Captain Makris, her husband's father. They became friends and by the time the boat docked, Semeli's father had decided to invest a large proportion of his newly acquired wealth into his latest shipping venture. He was the one and only non-family shareholder the Makris family ever accepted, and held just under half of the total capital of that particular project.

Captain Makris soon came up to Ioannina to meet them. Semeli, the older of two daughters, and her parents listened as he told them about his family, informed them about the shipping business and related tales of travels to different parts of the world. His son, John, at that time, was at sea on one of his ships as a newly qualified First Mate.

After he left they heard no more until 1st May 1950, when her father came home from a trip to Athens and announced to his daughter that she was to go out and buy a new dress. The following Saturday Mr and Mrs Makris were coming with their son John, who was in Greece studying for his Master's Certificate, to meet her. They wanted her for their daughter-in-law.

She was so excited she did not sleep for the next three nights. She was only 22 and John 34. Although she had heard about his life and travels, she had not seen any pictures of him, so when they met, he looked nothing like the dashing hero she had imagined. Instead, he was tall and thin, with a narrow, gaunt face and pale complexion. The addition of a grey suit with navy tie and dark-rimmed glasses made him appear timid; more like a civil servant than an adventurous sea captain. Apart from a few facial wrinkles and white hairs around his temples, he looked much the same now.

Semeli was disappointed at first, but that was before they started talking. Whatever John lacked in outer

19

presence was made up for by what was in his heart: passion, loyalty, dependability and an intense determination.

They fell in love and married in the spring of 1951. During their years together they went through many crises as well as successes. John had to fight for his fortune. They economised severely and he worked tirelessly. But this achievement was dwarfed by the pleasure he experienced from raising their two children.

One of her husband's faults was that he perceived his offspring, especially his son, as an extension of himself. He believed he had a moral obligation to increase and enhance what he had been given responsibility for, namely the family business, and to pass it on to the next generation. Zen did not appear to embrace the same ideals and was therefore a disappointment.

Semeli brought the tray into the dining room. Her husband was still where she had left him. He had finished his cigar so she pushed away the ashtray and laid out the cups and saucers.

'So, tell me what happened,' she said, as she poured.

'It was the last call,' he said, looking down at his lap. 'Zenon said that unfortunately it was impossible for him to marry Sophia.'

'That was it? Didn't he give a reason?'

'He said that they weren't compatible and had nothing they agreed on.' He was still not looking at her.

'Well, that can happen you know.'

'Nonsense, if that was true, how do you explain the hours they spent together as adolescents?' He was engaging her now and she could see the fury in his smoke-reddened eyes. 'Nobody forced them then. No,

Zenon has spent so many years with whores that he can't get on with someone decent.'

Semeli would find it difficult to defend her son on that point. She had met a few of his girlfriends and was not impressed.

'When I was Zenon's age I'd already served twelve years at sea,' Captain John continued, becoming more animated. 'I had purpose; I was part of the Great Contest, which I fought on behalf of my family and Greece. And when we met and got married, you became my family. Zenon, on the other hand, has no vision, no ambition.'

'You lived in a different time. Zenon hasn't had to fight for anything,' she said softly, hoping her husband would lower his voice. She did not want the maid or their daughter Antigoni to be alerted.

'I had the same upbringing,' he said, louder than before. 'We wanted for nothing as children. By the '20s we were a wealthy family and continued to be so till the war. My father was prepared to send me to any university in Europe, had I wanted, but it was my choice to go to sea. My first ship was one of my father's but I realised the captain was giving me special privileges because I was the owner's son, so I left at the next port and embarked on the vessel of an acquaintance. I wanted to prove that I could manage on my own.' Captain John had a few sips of tea, then got up and started pacing. Whenever he got upset about Zenon, he would recount the past. It seemed to be his way of venting his anger. 'During the war, my family lost everything,' he continued predictably. 'I was the only one who kept on working, albeit on convoys for

21

meagre wages. They were financially and spiritually broken. I motivated them back into shipping.'

At that time the Makris family had an office in London as well as Piraeus. The one in England was run by Captain John's Uncle George, who died suddenly in 1938. This precipitated the move of John's family to London, where they remained during the war. 'You mustn't compare Zenon to yourself,' Semeli said. 'I've warned you before. You're bound to be disappointed.'

'No, Semeli,' he retorted. 'It's not just me. Many shipping families lost everything during the war. There were hundreds of men and women like us who went out and took on the sea and conquered it. Now I look around at the other young people of Zenon's generation and what do I see? I see children still loyal to their families and committed to the cause. They're hard working with ambition. Instead of toiling on ships, like we did, they get degrees and learn about finance. But that's as far as Zenon got. After university, nothing.'

'I can't help thinking that it's somehow my fault. I was too soft.' She knew it wasn't in her nature to be firm and assertive, like her husband. 'Maybe it was a mistake to have governesses, perhaps they were a bad influence.'

'We mustn't blame ourselves. Zenon seemed to grow up like any other boy. It was only later that he showed this complete lack of interest in getting to know others of his age from our society. Sophia was one of his few friends. That's what makes me so angry.'

'I was hoping that would change when he started playing basketball,' Semeli said. The community in London was considerable and numbered several hundred families. It ran a basketball team that trained twice a week. 'But he doesn't seem to have made any new acquaintances.'

'Exactly, all the other young men have not only made friends of their own kind but also established contacts that will be useful. Only our son leads a totally pointless life.'

'You must agree, Zenon has a good heart and is trustworthy.' Semeli struggled to find something in her son of which to be proud.

'I admit it, but it's not enough. Loyalty and purpose are just as important. Zenon's crowning achievement, so far, was moving into his apartment. I'm sure everyone was impressed.'

This was a shock, when it happened. Many young men of their society ran apartments for entertaining, but continued to live at home until they married. Zenon was one of the few to move out. 'You've always said he's good at his job and enjoys the work.'

'He is, in a mechanical sort of way, though he acts as if he were an employee, not the potential inheritor. He shows little emotional involvement.'

'Then our son is lost,' she said, dismayed. Behind her husband, through the window, she could see the sky lighting up with the approach of dawn. 'He's too old to change. How could he so thoughtlessly hurt us?'

'Because he's egoistical and only thinks of himself. He could decide one day to marry anyone he finds off the street.'

'Surely he wouldn't humiliate us.'

'Why not? I believe he could. Up to now he's acted irresponsibly. He's our only son and we love him, but we have to face the fact that he may not have what it takes to lead the business after me.' He sat down again and pulled the cup and saucer towards him. He had released his anger for now. 'Fortunately we have a daughter and we should now look to her.'

'And Zenon?'

'Zenon will have to take a lesser role in the future.'

'What if he objects?'

'He'll have no choice and besides, it may be what he wants.

Chapter 4: The Apartment

Saturday, 26th and Sunday, 27th June 1982

After delivering the news on Friday night, Zen felt light and unburdened. The call itself was brief. He told his father of his decision and gave the best reason he could. Captain John's reaction was to put the phone down on him.

Zen waited for a more considered response, but it did not come. Instead there was a barrage of business calls. This was to be expected. They were in the throes of a crisis and every effort was being made to find employment for their idle ships. He was responsible for this task and would only need to consult his father if a final commitment to a contract was about to be made. Fortunately, he did not have cause to make that awkward call.

Realizing he would be housebound during the day, he got up early on both mornings, went for a run on Hampstead Heath, picking up the papers and any shopping he needed on his way home. Otherwise he spent the weekend in track suit bottoms and tee-shirt, sitting by the phone, reading or watching television between calls. He could have gone out in the evenings, and there was no lack of acquaintances to meet, but he felt no desire to do so.

Since the engagement most of his friends had left him alone and he was in no mood for explanations. Besides, he had missed spending time in his flat. Lately, he was always out somewhere with Sophia and, as they did not share intimate moments, he saw no point in inviting her to what was a modest apartment by her standards.

He lived in a block of sixteen units in Crouch End, North London. Being located on the south west corner of the third floor, he was high enough to be above the tree line and have views over the West End and City to the south and Hampstead Heath to the west. All the apartments, apart from those on the ground floor, had balconies, and his only criticism was that these were too small for anything more than a small table, two chairs and a mini barbeque.

Otherwise, everything was perfectly adequate but, as attractive and well-positioned as his home was, his attachment to it was based on the means by which he came to have it. Although his family was wealthy, it did not mean he had access to large sums of money. He received a salary for working in the business and if he wanted a car or something like that he could have it, but living on his own would mean too much freedom. This constriction caused him to feel claustrophobic, stifled; there seemed little room for variations on who he could be and what he could do. As a result, from his mid-teens he was determined to be independent. In addition, he was a careful spender and shunned the profligacy that would normally be expected of those born into affluence.

The eventual acquisition of his flat therefore was the result of several fortuitous circumstances coming together. The first thing was his friendship with one of his father's contacts. Alan Brook was an insurance average adjuster, who had served his time at a large company before starting up on his own. Although a Welshman, his clients were Greeks based in London and Piraeus. If he was working on a case for his father, he would come into their office to look through files. If Zen also happened to drop by after a day at college, they would go for a drink.

On one such occasion Alan revealed that his biggest headache was translating the captains' and chief engineers' logs in order to prepare his claims, not to mention the expense of using a technical interpreter. Zen explained that he could do them in his sleep. They came to an arrangement there and then whereby Zen did the work for cash, while Alan saved tax on cash-flow he no longer had to declare. As a consequence, Zen spent many hours in the university library working for Alan, rather than studying.

He still managed to get a degree, and by the time he joined the family business he had saved most of what he had received as an allowance from his parents and everything he had made from Alan. It all went into his savings account, which had a balance of several thousand pounds. It was far from enough.

The next event was unexpected. When his maternal grandfather, a gentle, loving widower, died at the age of eighty-five, he left his share in the Makris family business to his two daughters, Zen's mother and his aunt. Being prudent, he had also bought an office building in Piraeus and this he gave to his three grandchildren. As Zen's cousin wanted the cash to build a house, they agreed to sell.

It was many agonising months before the affairs of the estate were finalised, the sale completed and they received their money. When it came, he was disappointed. It was a considerable sum, but not enough to buy anything in the areas he was interested in; Hampstead and Highgate.

He could have got a mortgage, but the Building Society would have had to write for an employer's reference, thereby alerting his parents. He wanted it to be a *fait accompli*. He wanted them to find out after the fact and have no opportunity to dissuade him. In any case, as soon as they received their legacy, his parents began to promote their ideas about what Zen and his sister should do with it. These ranged from investing in the stock market to buying building plots in Greece.

Zen had resigned himself to losing his opportunity when the solution presented itself. It happened at the christening of a cousin's son. During the evening meal, at a restaurant in Kensington, he sat next to a young Greek, employed by the chartering department of a shipping company. After spending most of the time exchanging views of where the freight market was heading, Zen asked him where he lived.

He learned that he had a flat in Crouch End, east of Hampstead Heath and Highgate and within reach of both. One of the reasons that the price of properties was more reasonable in that area was because it lacked a convenient commuter service, requiring awkward combinations of buses and trains.

Zen explained that he was looking for something to buy, to which the Greek revealed that the girl in the apartment above him was about to put hers on the market as she had found a job in Hong Kong and was looking for a quick sale.

The following evening he went to see it. The asking price was still higher than he could afford, but, at the end of the tour, having calculated the maximum he could offer, he made his bid, adding that he was a cash buyer with no mortgage to find and she could complete the sale as quickly as the solicitors could do the paperwork. She said she would let him know.

Three days later she called and agreed his terms. Four weeks after that, on a Friday in spring, he exchanged contracts and completed on the same day. The following Saturday morning he drove up to Crouch End and entered his apartment.

Most of the furniture had been left and he decided to keep it. It looked as if it had been bought from second hand shops, but was tastefully restored. He had made minor additions and alterations of his own over the years, mainly consisting of covering the walls in prints of the black and white photos he enjoyed taking, but, on that first morning, he sat at the dining room table wondering how on earth he was going to tell his parents.

There followed a turbulent three months of arguments. Why was he doing it? Who was he going to live with? What should have taken one day to transfer his clothes and papers took until the summer, when his parents went on holiday and he was able to move in peace.

Then, as now, he wondered what the future held.

Chapter 5: Spiros Alexandrou

Monday, 28th June 1982

Zen emerged from the entrance of Moorgate Station and into the sunshine. Despite being the first day of a rail strike, the underground was running well and the trains were not overcrowded. He began the short walk north along Moorfields and Finsbury Street, dodging the multitudes also making their way to work. He rounded the final corner and entered a nondescript building.

Laredo Shipping, the family firm, occupied the fifth floor. When the lift doors opened, he crossed the stairwell landing. Passing through a set of double doors, he was surprised to see their receptionist. Heather lived in Southend with her parents and, due to the strike, could not have travelled by train. She signalled for him to wait while she completed a call.

He sat on the corner of her desk. After Heather, he was usually the next to arrive.

The layout of the rectangular space was simple. From the reception area a dark corridor separated the partitioned offices at the front of the building from those at the back. To his left, as he entered, was the street side and the first office was the chartering department, which housed their brokers, Martin Peters and Charles Nicholls. Their job was to cover the freight market, find suitable employment for their ships and negotiate contracts on the best terms. Connected to that was the telex room, which led to where Ruby, the typist, sat. The last office was the accounts department with Chris Christou and George Lambert.

The right side was the back of the building and overlooked the Honorary Artillery Company grounds. The first entrance led to Zen's office. Linked to this, through an open doorway, was the larger office of the operations manager, George Pittas. Then there was the technical section, which their port captain occupied whenever he was visiting from Greece. The final and largest office along the corridor, and not linked to the others, was his father's.

George Pittas, a former captain, was directly responsible for keeping the ships on the move, with Zen as his assistant.

'How are you today?' Heather, a cute, freckled-faced, fair-haired nineteen year old asked after she had finished her call. A white short sleeved blouse and grey pencil skirt covered her trim figure.

'I'm fine,' he replied, suppressing a yawn. He had fallen asleep on the train and was still not fully alert. 'How did you get in?'

'Stayed with a friend in town. It's also a chance to go out in the evening.'

'Specially with this weather.'

'Here are your messages.' She handed him a wad of slips. Then in a lowered voice, 'You have a visitor. Spiros Alexandrou's in George's office. He came in ten minutes ago asking for you. It's a bit early for him, isn't it? He doesn't usually come till later.'

'That's right,' he said, as his stomach tightened.

'So what do you think of the name?'

'What name?'

'You know. Diana's son.'

'Oh, William. It's okay, I guess,' he said, distracted. 'Let's talk about it later.' He'd realised he would have to

31

confront Sophia's father eventually, but had not expected it so soon.

Zen reluctantly entered his office. It was furnished with a desk, side on to the window and the view of the open field. It had three filing cabinets, a small bookshelf and three chairs. A pile of unopened mail and telexes were waiting for him on his blotter, together with copies of Lloyd's List. Adding his newspaper, he removed his jacket and draped it over the back of his chair before going through to George's office.

George Pittas's desk faced him. Behind it was a map of the world, which took up most of the wall space. It was made of metal layered with enamel, and on it were boat-shaped magnets. Each bore the name of one of their ships and showed its position. Spiros Alexandrou was standing in front of this, inspecting the Caribbean.

Hearing Zen approach, he spun round. 'Morning, Zen. Bet you didn't expect to see me,' he said coming over to him. They shook hands. 'You caught me reminiscing about my youth. Did you know that I crewed several yachts as a young man, before I got into shipping?'

'I think you mentioned it,' Zen replied. It was difficult to imagine. Spiros was short and slight and did not look like he possessed much physical strength. He had a narrow, youthful face and his full head of white hair was immaculately coiffed. He was wearing a lightweight grey suit, white shirt and a tie striped with three different shades of blue. A gold pin kept it anchored to his shirt.

'One time, I was in the Caribbean,' Spiros continued, looking back at the map. 'Spent three months of the summer on the yacht of an American banker. Those were the days. No responsibilities and no ties. But at the same time I decided I wanted to be rich.' Spiros looked at him sternly. 'I bet you think this is the start of a lecture. It isn't, so let's get the difficult bit over with right away and then you can bring me up to date on your ships.' He raised his hand and pointed towards the Pacific.

'Let's sit,' Zen said, indicating the two chairs in front of George's desk. 'Would you like a coffee?'

'Only if it's Greek.'

'I'm no good at making them and Chris isn't here.'

'Then it can wait,' Spiros said as he went to shut the interconnecting door. The wooden chairs creaked as they sat. Spiros drew breath. 'Did you know that Sophia was against a match with you, in the beginning?'

'No, I didn't,' Zen replied, raising an eyebrow in surprise.

'She fought hard against it. She thought you immature and it took a lot of convincing for her to give it a try.'

Zen shrugged his shoulders. If he knew anything about Spiros, then he imagined that Sophia must have received an ultimatum rather than gentle persuasion. He was sorry it did not work out, but had no regrets that Spiros was not to be his father-in-law.

'As a parent who's watched his daughter crying all weekend, I'd like to punch you in the face, even if you're bigger and younger than me.' Spiros's lips had formed a snarl and quivered as he spoke. 'However, I know that out of politeness you wouldn't hit back, so that would be unfair. Tell me, why do you suppose my daughter was so upset?'

33

'I imagine she was hurt by the way I treated her,' Zen replied, puzzled by the question. 'But I can assure you that…'

'Shut up, bastard.' Spiros interrupted aggressively, leaning forward. 'You think I'm here because you insulted her? Now I know you're scum. She fell in love with you, idiot. The only reason I'm here is because she begged me to come. She promised to do whatever I tell her if I'm seen to show you goodwill.'

Spiros waited for this to sink in, still leaning forward, his eyes bulging, searching for a reaction. Zen bent back slightly to compensate for his posture. He could smell Spiros's breath and it was unpleasant. So Sophia had decided to throw him a lifeline after all. But crying all weekend, that must have been a hell of an act, or was Spiros exaggerating? Maybe she was afraid Zen would reveal the truth.

Abruptly the tension seemed to drain out of Spiros and he leaned back in his chair. 'I'm not expecting any remorse and don't want explanations or excuses. Just wanted to speak my mind,' he continued calmly. 'When I meet your father, I'll tell him that I came to see you this morning to say that there were no hard feelings between us and that you in turn apologised.'

Zen cleared his throat. 'Yes, and I'd like to…'

'Don't say anything. It'll just piss me off,' Spiros said raising his hand.

'Okay.'

'Just so that you know, your father broke the news Saturday morning. As a result, we didn't catch up. So why don't you tell me what's been happening here so that when I see him I'll be up to date and can pretend we had a wonderful chat.

Zen felt uneasy that Spiros was being so reasonable. It was not like him. Perhaps Sophia was a stronger influence than he had thought. He turned to look at the map, composing himself. 'The *Jade Trader*'s still unloading in Rotterdam,' he began, remembering that the agents had asked for more money. 'She's due to complete at the end of the week. As yet, there's no follow-on cargo.'

'And there won't be,' Spiros remarked. 'Ten ships for every order on the continent.'

'Fortunately she's on time charter so it isn't our problem but it's no better in the Far East. The *Emerald Trader*'s discharging logs in Japan. She's due to finish Wednesday. We can't even find a cargo to bring her back to Europe at a loss. We'll have to order the captain to proceed to Singapore and hope something turns up.'

'You might get another cargo of logs. The Japanese like dealing with people they know.'

'The *Amber Trader*'s in the English Channel. We've instructed the captain to anchor off Dover and wait.'

'Wasn't she in north Spain?'

'Yes, Santander,' Zen said, anticipating what Spiros was going to say next.

'I'd have gone to Greece and laid up.'

'The *Amber*'s our newest ship. My father believes that whatever happens he'll find something for her, even at a loss.'

'When will your father decide a small loss has turned into an unsustainable one?'

'I don't know, but I agree with him that the *Amber* shouldn't end up in a flotilla.'

'You can always lay her up in northern Europe or even England.'

'England?' Zen was sceptical.

'Yes. Many owners have laid up in the West Country, mostly Falmouth. There are some good estuaries there. I looked into it myself.'

'Why didn't you?'

'As you know my fleet's older than yours, apart from the new-build. It was too expensive. But maybe the *Amber* deserves better. What about the others?'

'The *Opal Trader*'s due here in London on Wednesday,' Zen replied.

'Really? Thought she was going to Hull?'

'Charterers changed to Dagenham Dock. Seems they want to take her down river to Greenhithe afterwards and load cement for the Persian Gulf.'

'What's she discharging?'

'Silver sand.'

'Never heard of it.'

'Apparently it's used in insulation, you know, the stuff that goes in attics.'

'Good time to catch up on some surveys and repairs, eh?'

'Of course.' Zen knew that a considerable amount of work was planned. 'The *Coral Trader*'s just left Italy. She was due for a dry dock survey in Malta, but we've cancelled that and she's heading for Greece. Thankfully…' A rap on the door cut him short. 'Come in.'

'Mr. Alexandrou, Zen, good morning. I'm not interrupting?' George Pittas's voice boomed as he opened the door.

'No, come in,' Spiros said, standing. 'It's your office.' The two men shook hands. George was in his mid-fifties, of similar height to Spiros, but well built. He had

36

wiry, black curly hair with a sprinkling of white around his temples. The arrangement of his round face, pink cheeks and bushy eyebrows made him look perpetually cheerful. He was wearing a loosely fitting beige suit and white shirt. 'Any trouble with the trains?'

'Bit overcrowded, but no delays,' George replied. 'Missed the first two because they were full, but I'm here. Have you had coffee?'

'Chris isn't here,' Zen said.

'He was in the lift,' George said. 'Two mediums?'

They both nodded and George went back out.

'So, have you planned your next diving trip?' Spiros asked.

'Nothing specific. Won't be till September, probably.'

'Still training?'

'Most Monday evenings.' He was hoping to go later, work permitting.

Spiros looked at his watch. 'What time does your father get in?'

'By quarter past. How's the new build?"

'Not due to be launched till spring, but we're looking to arrange a contract from now. New-builds have an advantage, you know. We might get something for five to ten years, maybe longer.'

'So I've heard,' Zen said, although he did not think it justified the initial cost. Captain John used to repeat what a ship owning friend once said, "second hand ships were for dough and new builds were for show". He stopped quoting that ever since Spiros ordered his.

'I've news that came in overnight,' George said when he returned. 'The Japanese have taken the *Emerald* for another trip to Indonesia and back to Japan with logs.'

37

'What did I tell you?' Spiros winked at Zen. 'That'll keep her busy till September.'

'When did you hear this?' Zen asked.

'Martin just told me. You'd already left home so he called your father. We'll have to take a lower rate but I think we'll still break even. Haven't you seen the telexes?'

'Not yet.'

'You'd better go through them, and don't forget to send money to the agents in Rotterdam. Then speak to the charterer's agents of the *Opal* and get some idea how long she'll be in Dagenham and Greenhithe. We need to survey the main engine bearings, provided we have the time. We've a lot of work to cover today and tomorrow. Come Wednesday I won't be in much.'

Zen gladly left George and Spiros to chat. A few minutes later, Chris brought in the coffees. At about nine fifteen, he was aware of his father arriving. The partitioning that divided the offices consisted of cream coloured plaster squares separated by metal strips, and afforded little privacy. He overheard Heather tell him that Spiros was with George, but he didn't come in. Instead he went through to his office. A few minutes later Georges's phone rang. Spiros left shortly afterwards.

Zen opened the window beside his desk. The sweet smell of recently mown grass wafted in. He gazed at the green field for a few minutes and then began his work.

Chapter 6: The Reunion

Zen returned from the bar with two glasses and sat back in his place at the table. There were only the two of them now. The other members had left. He slid the rum and coke across to her and took a sip from his half pint of bitter.

'It's been a while since you've stayed and condescended to speak with me,' she said, with a hint of reproach.

'Sorry it seemed that way, but I had a lot on my mind,' Zen said, feeling a twinge of guilt. The truth was that he could look at her sunny face and listen to her voice, with its hint of a Scottish accent, all night.

Five years ago they'd had a relationship that had lasted nearly eighteen months. It ended when Erika, five years older than him, sought a commitment that was not forthcoming. They'd parted friends and continued seeing each other sporadically, until she met someone and Zen started seeing Sophia.

'You've been distant and distracted, not as involved with the club. Everyone's noticed.'

'You'll be seeing more of me in future.' He regretted the lost time, the missed trips abroad.

'That'll be great, of course, but does it mean something's changed?'

'My engagement didn't work out.'

'Sorry to hear it. You were enthusiastic, at first, but then I detected disillusionment.'

'It's for the best, we weren't compatible.'

'And you knew each other so long.'

'We were great as friends, but when things got more involved...' He let her draw her own conclusions.

39

'Which has only made things worse, as I was the one to break it off.'

'Oh dear and your parents arranged it. Well, if you fall on hard times, I've got a spare room.'

'But I thought...what's your man's name?'

'Tom.'

'I thought he lived with you.'

'We called it a day months ago,' Erika announced.

'My turn to be sorry.' All Zen knew about Tom was that Erika had met him at a scuba rally. He was a professional diver who did contract work for oil and marine companies.

'As you said, it's for the best.'

'What went wrong?'

'Let's just say things got a bit weird, then scary.'

'In what way?'

'It's not fair to go into the details but things came to a head when I got pregnant.'

'Gosh, I had no idea...'

'You mustn't tell anyone at the club, you're the only one who knows.'

'Don't worry.'

'By then I was sure I wasn't going to be staying with him, so I chose to have an abortion.' Erika looked away, trying to hide the emotion.

'If you don't want to talk about it...'

'No, I want to,' she said, putting her hand on his. 'It's just that it was such a decision. On the one hand I wanted the baby, on the other I didn't want to be tied to Tom.'

'You should've told me.'

She squeezed his hand reassuringly. 'Tom tried to dissuade me. That's when things got scary. He wanted

40

me to quit my job, stay at home, that sort of thing. He didn't want me out of his sight. One day he had to go out for an hour, so I packed whatever I could get in the car and fled to Mum's.'

'What an ordeal. How was she about it?'

'She was great, didn't judge or try to sway me one way or the other. I stayed with her till after the abortion and once I'd got that over with, Tom agreed to leave.'

'So you moved back, naturally.'

'Naturally.'

'And since then?'

'He calls every few days, sometimes comes to the door, you know, wanting another chance. I tell him there's no way...'

'He doesn't threaten you.'

'Nothing abusive.'

'Thank goodness. You still working?'

'Oh yeah, changed jobs since we last spoke. Closer to home. Before you ask, Mum still lives down the road.'

'How is she?'

'Same as always.' Erika finished the last of her drink. 'One for the road?' she said, holding up her glass.

'Won't be able to drive if I have another.'

'Think we're past that already.'

'It's okay for you, you can leave the car and walk.'

'Then you can walk me home and burn it off.'

They got their drinks just before last orders and fell out of the pub at closing time. They were unsteady on their feet and before long had their arms around each other, as they spoke of old times. Zen looked across at her. Her auburn hair was tied back and her pale, freckled face showed few signs of ageing. Her buxom figure was still firm.

'Are you coming up?' she asked, when they reached her front door. Her flat was on the second floor above an electrical shop.

'I think under the circumstances...'

'I'd like you to,' she insisted, squeezing his hand.

Inside the common entrance, he looked around him. Erika took this apartment after she had stopped seeing Zen, so he had never been. The communal areas certainly looked and smelt of rented accommodation; old grubby carpets, peeling wallpaper and flaking paintwork. He did not expect a view over London, but knew her home would be tidy and clean.

He followed her up the stairs, visualizing her attractive body beneath the tight jeans. It would be good to be with her, an old lover, an old friend, someone who understood him. The advantages of the familiar, of knowing what to do, sharing the affection they still felt and enjoying the pleasure it would give.

But he did not feel completely at ease. This disquiet was not sufficient to overrule his libido, though. On reflection he concluded that he would have no qualms if they were in his apartment, so the setting was the issue. It was the idea that Tom could turn up at any time.

And what if he did? He didn't care what the chances were, one in a hundred or one in a million, it could happen. Did he still have a key? Would he suspect there was someone else inside? What then? Would he retreat, emotionally wounded or would there be an awkward scuffle? Maybe they would get injured or hurt, maybe they would end up in hospital. What if the police were called? That would look great wouldn't it? What would his parents think? Three days after breaking his engagement, Zen ends up in bed with an old girlfriend. Sophia would turn to her dad and say, 'I told you so, bet he was seeing her all the time', and they would agree he was an immature little shit. 'Good thing I didn't marry that scumbag'.

As they reached the second floor and Erika put the key in the lock, he imagined himself in Erika's bed, in her arms and his desire overwhelmed his hesitation.

His unease did not return until the early hours. They had talked and made love most of the night, before falling asleep. Then he woke with the spine chilling feeling that he was being watched. He sat upright and looked out the open door of the bedroom, into the dark corridor. He saw nothing.

'What's wrong?' Erika groaned, sensing his movement.

'Nothing. Need to go to the loo.'

She turned and snuggled down.

Zen, naked, gingerly walked through the open bedroom door. The shadowy hallway ran to the front entrance, with the second bedroom and bathroom on the left and the kitchen-diner on the right. Half way along its length were two chairs either side of a table on which was the phone. Something about the seat of the first of these caught his eye. The cushion looked sat on, whereas the other did not. Maybe this was the one Erika habitually used when she spoke on the phone. He bent over to puff it up, like he knew she would want him to. When his hand came into contact with the upholstery, he froze. It was warm. He felt the other cushion. There was no question about it, the near

43

cushion was warmer than the other. In a panic he looked about him. He could neither hear, see nor smell anything. He realised that anyone sitting here could observe everything that went on in the bedroom and not be seen.

At the end of the corridor, by the front door, was the bathroom. He stepped into it. He didn't really need the loo; instead he looked round and, after flushing, pretended to wash his hands. Coming out, he stepped across the corridor into the living room. He searched as deftly as he could until he was sure no one was there. Passing the front door he slipped on the chain, before also checking the spare room.

'You took your time,' Erika said when he slid back into bed.

'Had a glass of water.'

'Could've brought me some.'

'I'll get it.' He started to get up again.

'Zen.'

'What?'

'You did enjoy last night?'

'Couldn't you tell?' He saw her smile.

'Do you want to see me again?'

'Very much,' he replied and meant it. 'But I prefer my place.'

'I'd be more relaxed there too.' He could tell from her voice that she also felt unsettled.

'Come and stay the weekend. We can walk on the Heath.'

'Can't wait.' She started putting her arms around him.

'Better get the water first.'

'You might also like to fetch the paracetamol, it's in the bathroom cabinet.'

Zen left early the next morning. He was relieved to be leaving, but felt good about renewing their relationship. As he stepped out onto the street and began the twenty minute walk to his car, he recalled the events of the night and felt warm inside, something he had not experienced for a while.

His revelry did not last. No sooner had he rounded the first corner than he had the sensation of being watched again. He looked about him. The streets were busy, with greengrocers, butchers and newsagents opening up and people making their way to work. He tried to ignore the feeling, tried to think of other things, but it kept nagging at him. He looked around him again. Was it Tom? He had no idea what he looked like.

Zen's anxiety was not relieved until he reached his car and drove off.

Chapter 7: Alan Brook

Tuesday, 29th June 1982

By the time Zen reached the office, his unease had returned. He could not get the thought of that warm cushion out of his mind. As if to reinforce this feeling of foreboding, Heather put through a call from Erika within minutes of him sitting down.

'I'm calling from work,' she said. Her voice sounded weak and subdued.

'Everything okay?'

'He called round.'

'What?'

'Half an hour after you left.'

'And?'

'He asked if I was seeing anyone and wanted to know how long it had been going on.'

'Shit. Does he suspect?' Zen already knew the answer.

'Told him that I'd never seen anyone while I was with him and that a friend stayed with me last night because he'd had too much to drink. I didn't mention you by name.'

'How was it left?'

'Said I had to go to work and he left.'

'What does he know about me?'

'What I told him when we first started going out. Look, what does it matter? I'm through with him.'

'Will you be okay?'

'I'll manage.'

'Do you want to meet up?'

'Love to, but I'm going to Mum's.'

'Would you feel safer if you stayed with me?'

'It's not that bad Zen, besides it's my problem. Leave things as planned.'

'If you change your mind…'

'Sure, I know.'

'We'll speak again, nearer the weekend.'

'Bye, Zen.'

During the course of the morning he managed to concentrate on his work, but when it was close to the end of the day and George had left, his anxiety returned. He did not relish the prospect of going home alone so soon. He thought of contacting some of his friends, whom he had neglected over the past months, but felt reluctant to resume the life he had led before Sophia. In the end he gave Alan Brook a call. Here was someone you could have a few drinks with at short notice. He was married with a young family, efficient at his job and at the same time able to switch off when he wanted. He was unable to meet Zen that same night, but they made arrangements for the following evening.

The next morning, with the underground having joined the rail service in the strike, Zen chose to walk. The prospect of queuing and jostling to get on an overcrowded bus and having to breathe in other peoples' bad breath, body odour or worse did not appeal. It took an hour, but the fine weather made it tolerable. Accordingly, he had decided to forget about a suit and dress down for the foreseeable future.

He found just Heather in the office, his father and George Pittas being on their way to Dagenham Dock where the *Opal Trader* was berthing on the morning tide. The rest of the employees would have to manage their work as best they could from home. In any case, with the immediate destiny of all but one of the fleet's ships having been decided, the pressure had lessened, with only the *Amber Trader* at a loose end. This was her fourth day anchored off Dover with no employment in sight, despite the efforts of the chartering department.

He had observed a change of mood in the city over the last few days. Speaking to his contacts throughout the shipping business, he had noticed that hopeful optimism had changed to pessimistic resignation. Fortunes, careers and jobs were at stake. Some of his Greek contacts were even talking about going back home to live with their parents, even if it meant national service.

He wondered whether his father regretted not sending the *Amber* to Greece when she was still in North Spain and within reach. Would he now consider laying up? He had no way of knowing. The options had to be explored so he decided to follow Spiros Alexandrou's suggestion and locate ports in England that were accessible and had the right facilities. He dismissed northern mainland Europe as too remote from the office. The ideal areas would be the south coast, South Wales and South West England. With the help of a road atlas kept in reception and a 'Guide to Port Entry' from George's bookshelves, he began calling each harbour authority in turn, starting with the ones nearest to London.

It was tedious work and took up most of the day. He was surprised at the lack of facilities and positive responses. Only at the end did Falmouth, in Cornwall, say that they could accommodate the vessel, but, as the Admiralty would be servicing the buoys of the estuary in six months' time, a mooring could not be offered for a longer duration. So much for Spiros's idea.

At six, frustrated with his lack of results, he walked to a pub behind Broad Street station, where he had arranged to meet Alan Brook. This tall, well-built Welshman and ex-rugby player with a goatee beard enjoyed his beer and knew the best places to serve it. The only issue was that Zen had to make sure he drank halves for every one of his pints.

They had a couple of hours together, talking about business, although Zen did touch on the foundering of his engagement. By coincidence, it turned out that Alan was currently working for Spiros, preparing several claims he was making against the insurers of his ships. He was going to be based in his office for the next few weeks. Zen told him about Spiros's idea for laying-up in England and how it had proved to be impractical and a waste of an afternoon.

Afterwards, they stopped off for a curry in nearby Shoreditch High Road before heading home.

It was after eleven when he returned to his apartment. He was getting ready for bed when the phone rang.

'Where have you been?' Erika asked.

'Had a drink with Alan. Why?'

'I've been trying to call.' She let out a sigh of relief. 'I went to visit Mum, like I said. Came back shortly after ten and…'

'Tom was waiting.'

'Yes, by the front door. He wanted to know where I'd been. I said it was no longer his business and he accused me of being with you.'

'Specifically with me?'

49

'He mentioned you by name, yes. I don't know how.... but I told him I was at Mum's.'

'I think you ought to inform the police.'

'What can they do?'

'I don't know…warn him off maybe.'

'Listen, that's not the worst of it. He accused me of lying and said he'd been round to your apartment and you were out too, implying we were somewhere together.'

'He was here? How does he know where I live?' Zen asked. Again, he knew the answer. While he was with Erika two nights ago, his jean jacket was draped over a chair in the living room. In an inside pocket was his wallet with his driving licence.

'I don't know.'

'Look, maybe you should come and stay here. It's more secure.'

'That would only aggravate things and I won't feel at ease. Maybe it's too soon for Tom. Let's give it a few weeks.'

'But…'

'I want to Zen. I so enjoyed the other night, I don't want this to spoil it.'

'I'll worry about you, so if you change your mind…'

'I'm worried about you too; you should be on your guard.'

'How can I be? I don't know what he looks like. Can't you send a photo?'

'I've never had one. He was sensitive about having his picture taken.'

'Are you sure about this? Maybe you should come this weekend and see what happens. It might not be as bad as you think.'

'I really want to, but I'd better not. I'll call you though.'

'Anytime.'

'Bye for now.'

'Bye.'

After turning off his lights he looked out into the blackness of the trees, hedges and bushes that surrounded his building. He imagined the silhouette of Tom hiding in the shadows only a few hours ago, gazing at his windows, spying on him.

Before getting into bed, he went into the spare bedroom and searched through his dive bag. From it he retrieved the serrated knife that was sheathed in an ankle strap and placed it in the drawer of his bedside table.

Chapter 8: The Berth

Zen would not have considered himself paranoid, yet over the next few days he displayed the symptoms. The warm, sunny weather continued and, as was his routine, he went running over the Heath on the morning following his conversation with Erika. His normal route took him through open fields and copses. Avoiding the latter, he gave every clump of trees a wide berth. He was equally suspicious of solitary men who were not walking dogs; and the area was notorious for these. He was sensitive to every noise: a rustle from a bush here, the call to a pet from somewhere else. His heart nearly stopped when he was overtaken by a panting dog, and every parked car heralded a potential ambush.

These anxieties were only partially relieved over the weekend as he could at least go out later when there were more people about. A welcome distraction was the sport on television, which included the Madrid World Cup and the finals of Wimbledon. He particularly enjoyed watching Martina Navratilova play Chris Evert-Lloyd on the Saturday and Jimmy Connors beating John McEnroe on Sunday.

At the office on Monday he was intrigued to find a message from a Captain James Stern of the Tone Harbour Authority. When he returned the call Stern was out, but the individual who answered knew what it was about. Apparently, they had heard that Zen was seeking a lay-up mooring and they in turn were looking for a tenant. Could they have the dimensions of the vessel so they could check the suitability of the berth?

After he had relayed the information and hung up, he fetched the map. Tonemouth had not been on his original list because it did not look like an obvious harbour, being within an estuary. This Captain Stern must have heard about the *Amber* from someone he knew at one of the other harbour authorities Zen had called.

As the prospect of Tonemouth seemed serious he began to research the comparative costs of laying up there as opposed to Greece. The annual expense figure he came up with was $100,000 for Tonemouth, though he still needed to confirm the rent. This was twice the figure for Greece. However, they would need $100,000 worth of fuel, in addition to the normal running costs, to get the *Amber* from Dover to the eastern Mediterranean. The lay-up would therefore have to last for over two years to make the latter more economical.

On Wednesday Zen received another call from Captain Stern. It was good news. They could accommodate the *Amber* and the monthly fee of £6,000 was close to Zen's guess.

Not being able to discuss this with his father, he needed to see George Pittas, who was unlikely to be coming in during normal hours for another two weeks. The *Opal* could be in London for that long. Not only was there repair work taking place on board, but his father was using the ship to host lunches for friends, bankers, suppliers and other business associates.

As he was having these thoughts, George walked in.

'What are you doing here?' Zen asked.

'I'm not well,' George replied, looking uncharacteristically pale.

'What's wrong?'

'Some stomach virus. Last thing I want to do is run round engine rooms and cargo holds, not to mention the daily banquets your father's hosting.' He grimaced at the mention of food.

'You'd think there wasn't a recession.'

'You'd think.'

'You should've stayed at home. I'm managing fine.'

'I know, but my wife's out and I don't like being alone.' George rarely took time off. Zen's father discovered him years ago when he was employed by the Piraeus office as captain for one of their ships. After two years of service he decided his talents were wasted at sea and persuaded him to move to London and work as his second in command.

'Well, while you're here, there's something I'd like to run by you.'

'Give me a few minutes to catch up,' George said, gingerly easing himself into his chair.

'Would you like tea, or something? There's camomile.'

'That would be great. By the time you've made it, I'll be ready.'

Zen went to the end of the corridor to a small kitchen just past his father's office. As he waited for the kettle to boil and the teas to brew, he thought of what he was going to say. When they were ready he took them to George, sat down opposite him and told him the news.

At the end, George looked interested. 'The thought of laying-up on the continent had occurred to me, but I assumed England would be too expensive. Are you sure of your costings?'

'I got them from the harbour master this morning, including the price of diesel.'

'How far's Tonemouth? I've never heard of it.'

'It's in South Devon. According to the map it's two hundred and thirty miles. The drive should take four and a half hours.'

George cringed as he squirmed in his seat. 'How much crew have you accounted for?' he asked.

'I've allowed up to four. That's assuming we want to run a low level maintenance programme. Even so, it'll be on the standard reduced wages for laid-up ships, with no overtime.'

'The way things are there won't be a problem finding crew, but for this to work we'll need at least one trustworthy person on board, otherwise the ship will deteriorate to the point where it might as well have been sent to Greece.' George looked concerned. 'No half-competent captain or senior engineer is going to give up full wages to vegetate in the West Country. No matter how bad the market gets, the good ones will find work or have enough money saved to take several months off.'

'I've thought of that too. It won't be a problem.'

'What do you mean?'

'You must've noticed that my father and I aren't talking.'

'I know.'

'I'll stay in Tonemouth.' Zen was as surprised at this proposal as George. It didn't form part of his original idea, only coming to him as they were talking.

'Look, Zen,' George said after a sip of tea, 'whatever's going on between you two isn't my business. The *Amber* could be laid up for a year or more. Who knows? We need someone who'll stay that long. You're making an emotional decision based on events that have taken place in the last twelve days. In six months the whole thing could've blown over. What'll happen then?'

'I'm serious. I'll stay as long as I'm needed. Besides, soon all our ships will be laid up. Then there won't be enough work for us both.'

'True.'

'Also, I've a feeling that my father will like the idea. I don't think he knows what to do about me and this will give us time apart.'

'Well, if you do go, I'm sure you'll manage, despite lacking the technical knowledge of a captain or an engineer.' George paused to think, sipping more tea. 'Conditions on board won't be comfortable. I'm sure you realise that. You'll have to do without hot water, heating and electricity for most of the time. I should imagine winter will be quite unpleasant.'

'I'm prepared for that,' Zen lied. In truth he had not considered it. On the other hand, the thought of spending the foreseeable future worrying every time he stepped out onto the street seemed worse.

'I don't think your father's decided what to do with the *Amber*. Having gone through the expense of bringing her to the continent, he's clinging to the hope that he'll find something. This may be the way out he needs. Since you can't talk to him, you'll have to trust that I'll bring it up at the right time, okay?'

'Okay.'

'What else is going on?'

'I'm finalising the fuels, lubricants and stores for the *Emerald* in Singapore.'

'After that, call Lloyd's Register, as well as the brokers of the *Coral* and inform them that the vessel is on its way to Greece for lay-up. We need to know what their requirements are for keeping her classified and insured.'

'Okay. Should I do the same for the *Amber*? Just in case.'

'Why not?'

Zen went back to his work. During the day, the possibility of a voyage to South America for the *Amber* was being worked on. He felt disappointed.

Thursday, 8th July 1982

With the beautiful weather, as well as the rail strike continuing, Zen walked to the office and found George already there. Seeing Zen, he waved him into his office.

'Morning, George, still not feeling well?'

'No, I'm much better, thank you. Sit down.' George indicated the chair in front of his desk. 'I spoke to your father last night. You know that inquiry to South America we were so excited about?'

'Yes, I've been following it.'

'It didn't materialise, so he called me. Martin and Charles informed him that the outlook was bleak and deteriorating. I then brought up everything we spoke about.'

'How did he take it?' Zen asked, his excitement reignited.

'By the way, I left out the part about you staying on board, for now.'

'And?'

'He changed the subject and asked about you.'

'About what?'

'Things like how you've been these last few weeks, whether you've spoken about him.'

'What did you say?'

'I said that you were upset that you haven't been talking. He said that he expected you to make the first move by apologising. I said that you probably thought he didn't want you to speak to him.'

'Did he accept that?'

'He didn't say anything, so I added that I thought that, despite your differences, you should be talking in the office, for the sake of the business.'

'And?'

'He agreed. He'll be in later and we'll discuss our options. I think he was avoiding you as much as you were him. This will break the ice. I'll let you know when he wants to see us.'

'Thanks, George,' Zen said, returning to his desk. He gathered his papers on the matter and, after reviewing them to make sure his facts were accurate, placed them in a folder.

Two hours later, file in hand, he followed George into his father's office. This was not particularly fancy, considering he was leading a multi-million pound business. The sole concession to luxury was that his filing cabinets were wood-veneered and the seats upholstered in leather. It was a brighter office as well, as it not only had the window overlooking the playing field but, being in the corner of the building, also had one overlooking an alley. It was in front of this that his father had his desk.

Captain John did not look up as they sat in the two high-backed armchairs in front of his desk but continued to read the most recent market reports. Zen breathed in the familiar scent of leather and cigar tobacco and remembered the time when he was at university and used to drop by at the end of the day to sit at the small table in the corner and do homework or translating.

After an uncomfortable silence, Captain John looked up at his son. Without betraying any emotion he said, 'George tells me you've come up with some idea of laying-up the *Amber* in England.'

'I have,' Zen said, clearing his throat.

'Tell me about it,' Captain John said, leaning back in his chair.

'The only place I've managed to find is called Tonemouth in South Devon. It's 230 miles away, about a four and a half hour drive. The mooring's situated in the middle of a tidal estuary, two hundred metres from either bank. The harbour master assures me that it's surrounded by hills and therefore sheltered from the wind. I've estimated total expenses to be around $100,000 per year, which is twice that for Greece, but we'd need $100,000 to sail the vessel down from Dover. The *Amber* would have to be laid up for over two years for it to be more expensive. We'd also be able to keep her in a better state of maintenance here because of the facilities available in the area. And we'd be better placed geographically to re-commission her and find employment.'

'But re-commissioning would be more costly,' Captain John pointed out. 'The northern European yards are more expensive than those in the Med. Then there's the weather. Here it's cold most of the time and damp all the time. In Greece it's cold only for a few months and dry practically all year.'

'These are disadvantages, but one reason for staying here is the routine maintenance we can do.'

'In a flotilla, maintenance isn't possible, I agree. There'd only be a watchman on board. Here you'd need at least two hands to look after the deck, a good second engineer, someone to cook and maintain the accommodation and someone we can trust to be in charge.'

'In my calculations I took into account only one deck hand. Because of the weather, we wouldn't be able to work outdoors every day. I think it would be more efficient to hire people from the shore on a daily basis, as and when needed. With such unemployment as there is at present, I think it'll be cheap.'

'Fine idea. But we'll still need someone down there who'll make this happen. George can't go because he has a family.'

'And it's too cold,' George added.

'I'll stay on board for as long as the *Amber*'s laid up. The way things are, all our ships will soon be out of commission and there won't be anything for me to do.'

'And I'll relieve him whenever he wants to take a holiday,' George added. 'As long as it's summer.'

'I've got to think about this.' Captain John hesitated, betraying surprise. 'I don't want to give up hope. I'd prefer to keep the *Amber* working, or find a cargo that'll take her to the Med at a loss.' He stood up. 'Okay, that's all for now. I'm going to have a word with Martin.'

Back in George's office, Zen observed, 'My father went cold on the idea of Tonemouth as soon as I mentioned staying.'

'He didn't expect it. What do you think he'll do?'

'I don't know. He certainly wanted to get rid of us,' Zen said, feeling deflated.

Wednesday, 14th July 1982

A week passed and the issue was not mentioned, nor did he see either his father or George. At the same time renewed efforts were being made to find employment for the *Amber*. Despite these, the magnet on the map in George's office remained stubbornly at 49 degrees 58 seconds north and 1 degree 5 seconds east.

When Zen arrived in the office that morning, George was waiting for him.

'What's up, George?' Zen asked in anticipation.

'Your father called last night. He wants to see us as soon he gets in. Is that berth in Tonemouth still free?'

'I don't know, I haven't spoken to them for over a week.'

'Find out and get as much information about the mooring as you can.'

An hour later they were sitting in Captain John's office. 'What's the latest on the berth in Tonemouth?' his father asked.

'I've spoken with the harbour master,' Zen began. 'His name's Captain Stern and the mooring's still available.'

'And the other details?'

'As I've already said, the mooring's in the middle of the estuary, about 200 yards from the Tonemouth bank and 300 yards from the Castlewear side. There's a strong current, which, when combined with heavy rain and spring tides, can reach four knots on the outgoing tide. The *Amber* would be moored lengthways to the bank with the bow facing the entrance, which would be a mile away. Also, the estuary's protected on all sides by hills and only exposed to a south-easterly gale, which is rare.'

'How do we get in?' George asked.

'Two tugs would be needed to bring her in stern first as the currents are particularly strong at the mouth of the estuary. They'd have to come from Plymouth and the earliest they can be arranged, together with the pilot, is Monday. They'd require us to unshackle our port anchor so that the chain can be secured straight onto the buoy. The other anchor will be dropped forward and the stern will be fastened to the aft buoy with another chain and wires.'

'Have you found an agent?' his father asked.

'I spoke to the only one in Tonemouth over a week ago. He sent me a breakdown of expenses amounting to £4,650, including the cost of the pilot.'

'George, give me a few minutes with Zen. I'll call you when I need you.'

After George had left, Captain John leant towards his son. 'Before we go ahead with this, are you sure you want to go?'

'Definitely.'

'Your mother and I spoke about it last weekend. I'm afraid I'm not as understanding as her, or as forgiving. I feel you've betrayed your family and yourself. Worse still, you've embarrassed us in front of our relatives and friends. You seem to have no common sense. How can you expect to inherit all this without being willing to shoulder the responsibility?' His father waved his hands around the office. 'How can you command the authority to run a business when you can hardly manage your own affairs?'

'I don't know what to say,' Zen said, trying to look serious and regretful while masking his excitement.

'And I don't want to talk about it any more. One thing we did agree was that you should go. That'll give us time to think. Besides, you'll gain experience as you've not had the chance to work on ships like George and me. So, for the last time, are you certain you want to go and are you prepared to stay?'

'Yes, I feel pretty much the same as you about it.'

'Okay, before we call George back, there is one more thing,' Captain John said, gathering his thoughts. 'Although the *Amber*'s our most modern ship, she's not the best. The future of bulk carriers is for larger vessels.'

'I know.'

'Added to that, she has problems, which you also know about.'

'I do.' He was referring to the corrosion in the double bottoms and the wing tanks. Although the value of a ship was proportional to its anticipated earning capacity, its age was also a major factor, but a serious corrosion problem like this could reduce her value even more.

'If she's laid up for more than six months she'll need to dry dock to get a Seaworthiness Certificate and that could prove expensive. If I get the chance to sell her at a reasonable price, I'll do so. Your job's to do whatever you can, cosmetically or otherwise, to make her look appealing and well maintained. Do you understand?'

'Perfectly.'

'About my wanting to sell; this is between us. I'll tell George in my own time.'

'I understand.' George was a wonderful person, but struggled to keep secrets.

Zen's father picked up the phone and called for George, who joined them a few minutes later.

'We'll go ahead with the lay-up in Tonemouth on Monday,' Captain John said. 'You'll both have a lot to do in a short time. So, finalise the arrangements with Captain Stern and the agent and send him his money. Send a cable to the master asking him to call me tonight on the VHF after seven. I'll give him his orders. George, you be there on Monday, get on board with the pilot and oversee the entry and mooring. Zen can follow on, say, Wednesday. We'll arrange for the crew to leave in stages. I'll ask the captain to see if any will stay and George can interview them. Zen, you'll arrange with the bank to open an account so that we can send money for expenses. Any questions?'

'Everything's straightforward,' George said. 'I'll take the train on Sunday.'

'I'll drive,' Zen added.

'Okay, let's get things moving,' Captain John said, standing up. 'George and I are going to the *Opal* for the rest of the day.'

Hey, isn't it your birthday Saturday?' Zen asked George when they were back in the latter's office.

'Don't remind me.'

'At least you won't have to leave till the next day.'

'Your present can be to find me a decent hotel for the night.'

Later in the afternoon, after Zen had dealt with the arrangements, he turned to his own issues. The main problem was his apartment. He could be away for months. He needed someone to call in. There would be bills to keep up with as well as other correspondence. He was struggling to think of someone to do this. There was no question of any help from his parents or sister. He had a strangely distant relationship with Antigoni. When they were children they rarely played together as they had separate friends, and consequently they never formed a bond. She became even more distant when he moved out.

He also did not have any other acquaintances to turn to. Erika would, no doubt, have been pleased to do it, but the thought of her having his keys, making them potentially accessible to Tom, put her out of the running, and he was not friendly with any of his neighbours. As the afternoon dragged on he had an idea. At around four thirty he went out to reception, pulled up a chair and sat next to Heather.

'I've got an unusual proposition for you,' he said.

'Oh?'

'You mentioned the other day that you stayed with a friend in London and it was a chance for you to go out,' he said looking into her freckled face with its pale blue eyes. 'Do you do that often?'

'Unfortunately not. She's the only one who has her own place, but it's only got one bedroom, so I sleep on the settee. The others live with their parents.'

'If there was somewhere you could stay, would you?'

'Of course, the last train for Southend leaves too early to enjoy a night out.'

'I have an idea that could help us both. You know I'm leaving for Tonemouth next Wednesday and will be staying for the foreseeable future.'

'So I've heard.' She made a sad expression. 'I'll miss you.'

Zen suspected she had a soft spot for him. 'I need someone to check on my flat once a week or so and send me my post. You could use somewhere to stay in London, on occasions. What do you think?' He did not know Heather that well, but had a feeling that she would respect his property.

'Wow, like the sound of that. Hear your flat's really nice.'

'Why not arrange to see it tomorrow, after work? I'll get a key cut.'

'That's great,' she said, looking poised to leap up and embrace him just as the phone rang. 'Thanks for thinking of me.'

Before leaving that evening he called Erika and gave her the news.

'That was unexpected,' she said.

'The way things go. How are things with you?'

'I'm moving back with Mum.'

'Really? Is it Tom?'

'He's stopped all the aggressive stuff but has gone all slushy, trying to get us back together.'

'Sounds creepy.'

'It makes me sick.'

'Doesn't he work?'

'Hopefully he'll run out of money and take a new contract.'

'When things settle you must visit.'

'You bet. I need a break.'

'Write to me. Send something to my flat and it'll get forwarded.'

'Call me whenever you're in town. You have mum's number?'

'Still do.'

'Take care.'

'You too.'

By Friday evening, Zen had made all the arrangements for getting the *Amber* laid up.

The night before, Heather had been to see the flat. It was agreed she would use the spare bedroom and, after having had a cup of tea, she left. Now he had the weekend and the beginning of the following week to complete his own preparations.

Chapter 9: The Arrival

Monday, 19th July 1982

Ben Earsop stepped through the French doors onto the balcony and surveyed the view he had paid so much for. It was mid-morning and he had just seen the first of his patients out.

There was more activity than usual on the estuary, even for a summer's day. The embankments were lined with people waiting. Many had cameras poised in anticipation of what was about to take place. The sky was cloudless and the sun was warming the air nicely, with only a hint of a breeze.

Perched as he was, high on a steep slope, he had the town at his feet. Looking towards the mouth of the estuary, past the silhouette of the castle and to the open sea, he could make out a dark hulk with three smaller boats surrounding it.

There had been much attention in the local press regarding this event. The harbour master began the controversy some months ago by suggesting that the buoys in the middle of the harbour should be employed to accommodate much larger ships than had previously been the case. To date these moorings had been used by over-wintering Eastern European trawlers. These rusting hulks caused a fair degree of resentment in themselves. After all, Captain Stern argued, Tonemouth was once a commercial port and should retain some vestige of its past and not turn itself entirely over to pleasure craft. Following that, he announced that there was a depression in world shipping with vessels laying-up all over the world. He intended that the river should share in this potential revenue.

Earsop was on the side of the locals who supported Stern. Any initiative that raised money to repair the decaying embankments was welcomed, as was his own involvement.

As the minutes passed it became clear what was happening. One of the smaller boats, probably a tug, was towing upriver from one end. The other was pulling from the other and opposite direction, presumably to keep the ship straight. Ahead of them Earsop recognised the harbour authority launch.

He went inside to retrieve his binoculars, which he kept on the mantelpiece next to his old wrestling trophies, below the print of Napoleon. At the same time, he called down to his housekeeper for a coffee. Back outside he brought the lenses up to his eyes and pointed them downriver. The formless hulk turned into a ship and he could see that she was approaching back end first. Her appearance was striking. Being devoid of cargo she stood unexpectedly tall in the water and her sides were streaked with rust.

A black cloud of smoke intermittently belched from her stack, which was yellow and over-painted with a black 'M'. This coincided with a whirr of her single, half-submerged propeller. He could see a crewman walking along the base of the stack and realised that it alone was taller than his three-storey house.

The first half-mile of the estuary was a narrow S-shape and he appreciated the need for the two tugs as the ship was manoeuvred through. He also observed that the lower ferry had stopped on the Castlewear side and a queue of cars had begun to form.

Once the ship had passed the ferry-crossing, the estuary widened into what was considered *the harbour* and, as she was manoeuvred towards the buoys in mid-stream, she was side-on to him. The white accommodation housing was at the rear and took up a quarter of her length. The decks were painted green and the canopied lifeboats, centred under their davits, orange. The rest of the ship comprised four hatches, covered by tarpaulins. These ran along the centre of a brick-red deck. Between the hatches were mast houses and cranes, all painted yellow. There were groups of men at the front, the back and on both wings of the bridge. They seemed to be engaged in frantic activity and some were carrying walkie-talkies.

As her stern passed what Earsop assumed would be the forward mooring, the ship dropped one of her anchors. This was followed by the sound of the rattling chain echoing within the surrounding hills. Her backward progress then slowed as this involved playing out the links.

She was inched into position between the two buoys, then kept steady by the tugs, while those on the harbour authority launch collected the other anchor chain, dangling from the bow, and took it to the forward buoy. Meanwhile, at the stern, another launch, which had come from the shore, started taking up wires to fasten to the aft mooring. Earsop could now see the ship's name, *Amber Trader*, displayed under the prow.

He checked his watch. It was ten minutes past eleven. He was expecting his next patient at half past. He went back inside, leaving the doors open. Going to the filing cabinet, he retrieved the appropriate patient file and, sitting at his desk, began studying it.

He would not be wasting time worrying about whether the *Amber Trader* was spoiling his view. On the contrary, he would deal with the opportunity its arrival brought in due course. He had more urgent matters to think about now. He felt the anger welling up as he recalled the years of research that were being threatened by his former colleagues. There was a time when they had laughed at his ideas. When his research became too time-consuming, they were more than happy to fatten up their fees by taking on some of his wealthy patients, helping them make enough money to retire in their fifties.

He had heard nothing from them until after the publication of his first book. Now that Earsop was on the verge of recognition, they had re-emerged to claim a split of his earnings, arguing that without their assistance he would not have been able to produce the work, asserting that, as partners, they were entitled to their share. They did not even have the guts to meet him, instead appointing solicitors.

He attempted to call them, but in the one case the bastard put the phone down on him. In the other, the wife answered. She said her husband was out and that their solicitor had advised against speaking. He remembered Veronica, recalling how, in the days when they was still in partnership, and on social occasions, she would eye him when she thought he was not looking. He had sensed an opportunity for mischief and asked her to meet him for coffee, pretending to want to work out a compromise.

She was still an attractive woman and, after the coffee and some flirting, he invited her back to 'see the view'. Rather than look at the estuary, she spent the afternoon staring at his bedroom ceiling. Not bad for a woman in her fifties and they still met at least once a week. He preferred his women younger, but there was always room for exceptions, not to mention the inestimable pleasure of screwing his enemy's wife.

Irrespective of this diversion, there was no way his former colleagues were going to receive any of the credits or money from his efforts. He would do whatever was necessary to fight them. He would resolve the matter before his second book was ready.

His thoughts moved away from his ex-partners and to the patient he would be seeing that evening. This case had been referred to him some months ago and had subsequently proved to be one of the most unusual ever recorded.

With his thick and powerful wrestler's hands he opened the file and, with a great effort, refocused his attention on the patient notes before of him.

Chapter 10: The Valley

Darkness over Tonemouth. The streets are peaceful, having been deserted by their daily influx of tourists and other visitors. In the middle of the estuary, where previously there was a dark void, there is now the presence of a cargo ship, lit by halogen floodlights clustered at the top of each mast. To this is added the invasive, mechanical purring of the diesel generator, emanating from inside the hull, but penetrating deep into the surrounding hills.

The portholes of the ship's accommodation housing glow with pale yellow lights and because of the warmth of the night, most of these are open. Within the metal hull, able seamen, deck officers, oilers and engineers alike are packing. Many of the crew will be leaving at first light, to be taken by coach to Heathrow airport.

Meanwhile, far from this activity, at the mouth of the estuary, the only man-made illumination is the periodic passing beam of a lighthouse several miles to the west. In the starry light, the rocky coast is distinguishable from the sea by being a few shades darker. There is a gentle off-shore breeze and the swells cause the land to tremble as they break against the rocky shore. In places there are pebbly coves, carved out of the cliffs over millions of years, and here the action of the waves makes a rasping sound as they heave and retreat.

Several miles west, where the valley of a water course meets the coast, the cove is sand mixed with shingle. Here the beach is only a hundred yards wide and sits at the end of a finger-like indent. At one time a thriving fishing village, with cellars for salting, all that remains is a popular inn and holiday cottages.

The stream is small but lively as it breaks out across the sands. Up the valley, behind the cottages and derelict cellars, it passes through ash and oak woods as it descends from the inland plateau, collecting smaller tributaries along the way. The woods are surrounded on both sides by sloping fields of sheep and cattle, with the latter coming into the woods at night. From the upper ground the distant tors are visible and ancient trackways connect with the heart of the moor. In daylight these paths are frequented by farmers with their cattle, horses and their riders, ramblers and dog owners. At night, nature's nocturnal creatures take over.

One such bridleway runs from the moor and down to the sea along this valley. At its head, it traverses a road before starting its descent. Here, a few minutes after midnight, a shadow crosses. This creature of the night makes no sound and leaves no scent, but other animals will know that it has passed. In the morning, cattle being moved will be more restless than usual and the farmer will wonder why. Horses will be more hesitant and their riders will feel a passing concern. Dog owners will be puzzled why their pets are reluctant to proceed and lack the usual interest to explore. The occasional walker may believe they are being watched. They will look over their shoulder and then dismiss the impression as atmosphere.

But tonight the route belongs to just the one, as it once did hundreds of years ago. It is being revisited for the first time since then. The creature did not need to walk, for it could have materialised at its destination: close to the sea; but it wants to experience every dark valley, every cold stream, every windswept hilltop and every dank copse. Some things have changed: the tarmaced roads, the street-lighting and the barbed-wire fences; but the feel of the land is as it has always been.

It has killed since coming back, several times, but only small creatures. Now that it is stronger and more confident, it desires larger, stronger prey. It wants to gorge itself with dark flesh and blood. This is its motivation as it enters the wooded valley. The fishing village on the coast is important as well, but a visit there would have to wait.

After a while, the way becomes less steep and the woods broaden. The creature stops, sensing the presence of cattle ahead. It wants to avoid these so it turns left and climbs out of the woods. The tree line forms an edge to a field that rises sharply at first before rounding out of sight. Looking downstream it recognises a tributary that forms another boundary to the field and rises to the top of it. The creature makes its way towards this, all the time keeping within the trees. At the tributary it follows its course up the side. It is thick with undergrowth of gorse, brambles and nettles. It does not mind the discomfort. It is stalking and it feels alive.

Once over the brow it can see into the upper corner, where the tributary meets a hedge and where a small herd of sheep lay huddled in the meagre starlight. It lays on its front, staying still and concealed.

It enjoys renewed excitement and expectancy now that its senses are heightened. It feels the dew settling as the air cools. There is a heady smell to the grass and, as the breeze stirs the air, the coconut scent of gorse adds sweetness. It turns to look behind it and sees the sea.

For a moment it is overwhelmed by memories and emotions, but it quickly turns forward again to the focus of its attention.

It continues to advance a few yards at a time, stopping before it comes too close to agitate the sheep but near enough to observe them and to choose the weakest individual; the one that must give up its life.

Without warning, the beast springs forward and within seconds is upon them. The animals are up and running in all directions. The intended victim is confused and does not respond as quickly. The beast swipes at the sheep's head with a paw and knocks it to the ground, then quickly lies on top of it, biting hard into its neck. There is the sound of bone and flesh being crushed and the beast lies still, waiting until the severed arteries stop pumping warm blood into its mouth.

Chapter 11: On Board

Wednesday, 21st July 1982

Zen set off from the underground garage of his apartment block at five on a bright, fresh morning. Wearing a loose shirt and slim fitting jeans, he drove his blue, nine year old, 3.5 litre Rover Coupé through the deserted streets of the metropolis before joining the M3 motorway at Sunbury.

There was an eerie feel to London after the carnage unleashed by the explosive devices the day before, first in Hyde Park and then in Regents Park, so he was glad to be leaving. This would be a tense city for months to come.

Driving under clear blue skies through the open landscape of Wiltshire, before crossing the scenic Blackdown Hills, then winding through the lush, steeply undulating Devon countryside made for an enjoyable journey, and by eleven o'clock he was descending into Tonemouth. As soon as the view of the estuary opened up, he saw the *Amber*. Then, following the signs for the waterfront, and once on the embankment road, he found the harbour office in a prominent position on a corner. He turned right, along the side of the building, and then right again into the car park behind it.

Having not been to Tonemouth previously, he took a minute to walk to the embankment and take in the surroundings. It was sunny and calm. Before him was the broad sweep of the harbour, which was the widest part of the estuary of the river Tone. To the south it narrowed before winding past what looked like a castle and on to the open sea. To the north, it once again narrowed before curving out of sight to the left. There were yachts and boats everywhere, of every shape and size, either on the move or at moorings.

Steep green slopes, mostly wooded, rose from both sides giving a feeling of security and shelter. In places, deep folds came down to the water's edge to form creeks. Opposite, on the other bank, was Castlewear. Smaller than Tonemouth, it clung to hillsides so steep that the ground floor of each house started above the roof of the one in front. These buildings were painted in such an array of pastel hues that it reminded Zen of the colourful displays of a sweet shop. The centre of Tonemouth, by the water's edge, on the other hand, occupied what appeared to be the only flat ground, and was equally picturesque.

In the middle of this breathtaking, amphitheatre-like setting, on the smooth dark waters, lay the *Amber* at her moorings, a rusting presence that somehow did not belong.

Zen reluctantly turned his back on the view and crossed the road. A few minutes later, after a flight of stairs, Captain James Stern was shaking his hand. The harbour master's office occupied the first and second floors of the building. The lower level was a small open-plan room with four desks. Stern's was beside the window facing south, towards the entrance to the estuary and the open sea. The other two windows looked out over the harbour.

Zen accepted an offer of a hot drink and sat in a chair positioned in front of Stern's desk, while the latter called above to someone to make two white coffees. 'How did it go last Monday?' Zen asked, although he had already received that report from George when he had called the office on Monday afternoon.

'Very well,' Stern replied. He was a slight man, five foot seven, with a narrow face and pale blue eyes. The exuberance of his thick crop of grey hair was in contrast to the sparseness of the rest of his frame. He wore a white shirt with epaulettes and dark navy trousers. 'The weather was like this. Any idea how long she'll be staying? Mr. Pittas was rather vague.'

'That's because we don't know. It could be two months or two years.'

'The longer the better as far as we're concerned,' Stern said, looking into the empty office.

'Good thing Falmouth called you then.'

'What do you mean?' Stern looked at him inquisitively. 'What does Falmouth have to do with it?'

'Didn't they call to tell you about us? They couldn't accommodate us themselves.'

'Hold on a minute,' Stern said. They could hear someone coming down the stairs. A tall, slim, young man with closely cropped red hair brought their coffees. 'Did you take the enquiry about the *Amber Trader*?'

'I did, sir.'

'It was Mr. Makris who called, wasn't it?'

'Yes, sir.'

'You sure?'

'I remember taking the name down carefully, as it was unusual,' he confirmed.

'Okay, Will,' Stern said, as the young man went back upstairs.

'I made so many calls that day to various ports, I must've forgotten,' Zen said, still doubting it was so.

'Anyway, did you know, yours is the largest ship to enter this estuary? Here are some of your predecessors.' Stern indicated the walls of the office, which were arrayed with old black and white photographs of cargo ships navigating the river. He took Zen on a verbal tour. '...and the one behind me was the previous record holder. A passenger ship, also Greek.'

Zen stood up to look at it. 'I don't recognise the position.'

'She was moored near the castle,' Stern said, looking out the window. 'In those days, Tonemouth didn't have the moorings you're now secured to.'

'When was she here?' Zen took a sip of coffee; it was lukewarm and had a bitter taste.

'Forty-nine,' Stern replied. 'The commercial life of the river all but died out in the fifties,' he continued, once Zen had sat down again. 'Since then the policy has been to cater for tourism. Having you here is a departure.'

'Why the change?'

'Most of the yachts are moored at the private marina opposite. Few use our facilities. We simply can't provide them. Eastern European trawlers have mostly used the moorings during the winter months. Consequently our income's too low to fund the improvements we plan to make to the embankments over the next five years. We need something more permanent. Although I must say our decision has caused a lot more controversy than I expected.'

'Her presence is intimidating,' Zen confessed, looking over his shoulder and out the window.

'Only to some, mostly newcomers. The locals want a return to more traditional ways. Your presence will mean revenue for local business as well.'

'I'm sure,' Zen said, glancing at his watch. 'I'm expected at twelve.'

'One of our lads has a launch, which your lot have been using. I suggest you get one of your own as soon as possible.' Stern opened the office door and called upstairs for a man called Richard. A woman replied that he was by the pontoon. 'He's down already,' he relayed to Zen. 'You've parked round the back?'

'That all right?'

'Parking in Tonemouth during the summer's a nightmare. You can use our car park till the end of September. Someone's always on holiday so there's at least one free space. After that you'll have no problem in the town.'

'That's kind of you.'

'You haven't heard the rest,' Stern cautioned. 'We put a chain across the entrance at six every evening and our insurance doesn't allow us to give you a key.'

'Well, if I need it, I'll make sure to move. When do you open?'

'Someone's here by eight. I'll come down with you,' Stern said, following him. 'Do you sail?'

'That's something I've never got into.'

'I like your car,' Stern said as Zen removed everything but the diving equipment from the boot. 'It must be one of the last they made.'

'Yes, 1973's when they phased the model out.'

'Excellent condition. How many miles?'

'76,000. My father bought it new, kept it for five years and I took it off him. It's always been garaged.'

'If you ever want to sell.'

'I've no plans, and there's a queue.'

'What about the cylinder?'

He assured Stern that his diving cylinder was vented and did not contain compressed air. They crossed the road and climbed down the concrete steps from the embankment to a steel pontoon below. This was hard by the passenger ferry landing, which was positioned ten metres from the water's edge and accessed by a covered walkway. At this level it was possible to see that the calm waters disguised a strong, swirling current. The tide was on its way out.

The launch in question was moored next to the harbour authority's own boat and was open-decked. Richard, the owner, a short, burly man with a moustache and sideburns, was wiping down the seats. He wore similar attire to the harbour master.

With Zen's belongings stowed amidships and after a wave to Stern, they began the crossing to the *Amber*. The launch first passed under the ferry walkway before entering the open water. 'Is it always this busy?' Zen asked when they were level with the town square.

'T'is market day,' came the reply carrying a hint of a West Country accent.

'Where's it held?'

'Upriver from the square, behind those trees, is the car park.' Richard, with his left hand on the tiller, pointed with his right. 'On the other side of the road's a row of buildings. One's the police station, by the way. But beyond that's the market square. There's a farmers' market on Wednesdays and Saturdays. The rest of the area has boutiques, antique and gift shops, but also a butcher, a few bakers and a greengrocer. The tourists love it.'

'I expect to visit it too,' Zen replied as his attention shifted to their destination.

As the tide was retreating, the best course was to take the current head on and approach the ship from the bow. He could now appreciate how the *Amber* was moored. The port anchor had been dropped far forward and slightly off the centre line. The starboard chain was latched directly to the buoy. This appeared secure.

Zen was familiar with her statistics. She was five hundred feet long and seventy at the broadest point. She had four cavernous holds, all forward of the accommodation superstructure. Each had its own derrick capable of lifting twenty tons and attached to one of the two mast houses. The main engine, auxiliary machinery and living quarters were aft. Being unladen, all this weight at the back was not counterbalanced with cargo forward. As a result, she not only stood tall in the water generally, but her deck sloped upwards towards the fo'castle, exaggerating the height of the bow.

Passing alongside, Zen examined the hull. The *Amber* had recently crossed the Atlantic twice and encountered bad weather, whose battering accounted for her disagreeably rusty appearance. Below the fully laden line, which now ran half way between the water's surface and the deck, she was coated with a red paint that was resistant to marine growth and above this she was painted black. Both surfaces were flaking, with the worst areas fanning out from the outlets of the deck scuppers.

He could not see the cargo deck, masts and derrick housings, but imagined that they too would be in a poor condition. In contrast, the approaching accommodation decks were a brilliant untarnished white. They had probably been painted whilst the ship was anchored off Dover, as had the yellow and black trimmed stack with its distinct black 'M'. The latter puffed the blue-white smoke of the generator, whose rhythmic rattle, the familiar heartbeat of any ship in port, could be heard through the metal sides.

They were approaching the aluminium accommodation ladder, which descended steeply from the poop deck. Richard manoeuvred the launch so as to come alongside the small square platform at its bottom end. Zen looked up and saw two members of the crew descending to give him a hand with his suitcases. After taking hold of one of the railing spindles and tying the painter to it, he passed on the two heavier items of luggage and left himself the shoulder bag and rucksack.

He bade goodbye to Richard and started his ascent. The two crew, climbing ahead, agitated the ladder so that it wobbled and swayed alarmingly. Zen had to hold on to the side ropes with both hands to maintain his footing. His progress was slow, but once at the top, he stepped onto the sheltered poop deck passage and then on through the door to the interior.

While he waited for his eyes to adjust to the relative darkness, he was greeted by the familiar sounds and scents of a ship. The bulkheads and deckhead of the poop deck landing, lit by cold florescent lights, were painted a duck eggshell colour, which had turned a dirty brown overhead amongst the confusion of pipes, wires and ventilation conduits. The deck underfoot was a darker green. The sound of the generator was more prominent and to this was added the soft hissing of the forced draught ventilation. There was a salty, painty, warm smell of boilers and oil. To his right was a row of six crew cabins facing forward. Some of their doors were open and from within could be heard the muted conversations of men. To his left a flight of stairs led down to the dimly lit passageway of the lowest accommodation deck, occupied by the lesser ranks and from which came the sounds of sharper, more abrasive talk. Beyond this stairwell, emanating from a short corridor that led to the officers' mess, through which was the galley, came the aromas of food on the point of being served.

On the port side, past the ascending central staircase, a parallel passage led to the crew's mess, where similar preparations would be taking place. Within minutes this landing, the central human thoroughfare of the ship, would be thronging with hungry men making their way to lunch.

Chapter 12: The Crew

Stephanos took a respite for a cigarette. He stepped through the doorway that led from the galley to the stern end of the poop. It was pleasantly sunny and still, but the rancid smell from the overflowing garbage bins proved unbearable, although not to the hovering gulls, so he took the external stairs up to the boat deck and found a spot some way forward with fresher air. He leaned against the railings of the starboard side where it was shaded from the sun.

As he dragged on his Marlboro, he could feel his stubble. When you worked on a boat full of men, it was not necessary to shave every day. None of the others did, unless they were in port, and he did not bother then either.

He idly noticed the launch approaching from downriver with its sole passenger and his luggage. He could guess who it would be. He had heard that the owner's son was coming to stay on board. He did not believe it at first; now he was seeing it with his own eyes. He gave him a few weeks, till the end of summer at the most, before he returned to his pampered lifestyle.

This was Stephanos's first break today. The initial contingent of crew had disembarked that morning and, as steward, it was his job to make a bed linen and towel count before their departure. Theft was common and any missing items were taken off the men's wages. At least that was what this captain did. Then he'd helped the cook serve up breakfast and afterwards supervised the cleaning of the vacated quarters whilst there were still enough hands to help. It was amazing what he'd found in the cabins: used condoms under mattresses, hypodermic needles, pornographic magazines, the remains of joints and worse.

The officers and engineers were all right because they were working on ships for a career, but most of the others were the scum of society. Two years ago he came on board with most of the present crew, after a big changeover. It was a boom time for shipping then. Owners were desperate to complete their compliments and had to resort to people who could not get jobs anywhere else.

Stephanos knew about these things. He was educated and read magazines and newspapers. Most of the men, apart from the officers and engineers, were barely literate. He was aware that the economic climate had changed in recent months and that few of those who left today and during the other departure tomorrow would get jobs on ships again.

He surveyed his surroundings. It was beautiful here. The parts of England he had visited before were grey, smelly, industrial ports with oily water. Here the harbour looked clean, the air unpolluted and the surroundings green.

It was whilst they were still anchored off Dover – that God forsaken place where even the smallest waves and swell made the empty *Amber* bob around like a cork – that word came round that they were heading for lay-up. When the captain had asked him whether he was interested in staying, albeit at reduced wages, he'd jumped at the offer. The rest of the crew, mostly those who were not asked, said they would never accept lower wages. They called it exploitation. Proud fools!

Come winter, when they had spent their money and had no jobs, they would see.

Stephanos had no pride left to cause him such conflicts. His had been broken long ago. His priority now was survival. As long as he could send enough money back home to feed his wife, child and elderly mother, he had no further ambitions. He needed little for himself, just enough for smokes, some whiskey, a few books, magazines and newspapers. His cigarette was nearly at its end, but, before flicking it into the water, he used it to light another.

Normally, after two years at sea, he would have felt obliged to return home for a month or two. At least now he had an excuse not to go. He loved his wife and daughter dearly, but being with them proved more painful than staying away.

On board ship people left him alone. He went about his work and during his free time he could retreat to his cabin. Back home there was all his extended family, relatives, friends and acquaintances. There was no peace. He was constantly being reminded of the past. He was poor Stephanos, the unfortunate failure. Here, he was Stephanos, the chief steward and soon to be cook as well. He had a place and a role. No one cared about his past. Hell, no one cared what he did yesterday.

He took one last drag before flicking the stub into the river. It would soon be time to serve lunch.

When Andreas had completed the last stroke, he dropped the brush into the can containing the white spirit and stood up. His joints were stiff from kneeling on the hard metal deck for so long, but he was determined to finish the job. He had managed to paint the whole of the fo'castle in the three weeks since the ship had anchored off Dover. He had others to help him with the initial scraping and undercoating, but the job was his responsibility.

A few days ago, after it was announced that the *Amber* was being laid up, his work crew was pulled from this job to do other tasks. He'd had to complete it himself with overtime. He was particularly proud as this was a difficult part of the ship to maintain, containing mooring bitts, eye holes, the two hawse-holes and the windlass for the anchors.

The sun warmed his shoulders as he gazed across the water to the town from his vantage point. This is a relaxing place, he thought. And there were people about. He had lost track of how many harbours he had seen during his life at sea. Few were memorable. This place was different. He had accepted the offer to stay before they had arrived, without even thinking about it. He had no desire to return home. If he went back to Greece now he would have to go back to his village and collect what was left of his belongings. He would have to see his sisters and brothers-in-law. He still could not forgive them.

He was an only son and had worked at sea from the age of eighteen, after his father died, in order to support his family and save money for his sisters' dowries. This was despite the fact that he was from farming stock and wanted to be a car mechanic. It was nine years before they were both wed. Nine years working for their benefit.

After the second wedding, he went back to sea. This time, despite still supporting his mother, he could save enough to build a house on the land promised him as a reward for his efforts. A few months after he disembarked, his mother was taken ill. His sisters never informed him. Instead, they conspired with his brothers-in-law and talked the confused woman into signing away his birthright to them. He was finally informed of his mother's condition a week before she died and it was after the funeral, when it came to arranging her affairs, that the truth emerged. He could have killed the four of them that very day. Fortunately, he had the insight to pack his bags, to leave without confrontation. He went to Thessalonica and a solicitor friend and dumped the whole matter on his desk. Then he took the bus down to Piraeus where he secured employment on the *Amber* as an able seaman. That was three and a half years ago. The dispute over his inheritance was still ongoing and could drag on for years.

Now he had decided to stay. The pay would be less and there was no overtime, but he was tired and lonely. He needed a rest and some company, especially women. He also hoped he could get on with the others. He liked Steph and often confided in him. Harry was eccentric but seemed nice enough. It was Zenon Makris he was not sure about. He had seen him a few times during port visits. What was the owner's son doing down here though? Was he seriously going to live on board with them? Andreas's past experience with owners' sons was not good. Could he tolerate some spoilt brat bossing him around? He would have to wait and see. He could always leave after a few months if he was not happy.

He began rounding up his brushes and paints. The paint store was just below. That was his responsibility too and he kept it tidy. He looked at his watch. It was time to clean up for lunch.

Harry sat cross-legged on the bed. His back was straight but relaxed and his palms rested on his inner thighs. He was trying to meditate, but thoughts kept intruding.

He usually stepped into his cabin from the engine room half an hour before lunch in order to wash up and have some inner peace, but today something was agitating him. He did not fight the invading doubts, but instead tried to identify them. Was it his decision to stay? He often relied on his intuition and a few days ago his feelings led him to volunteer to remain with the *Amber* when she laid up. He felt there was a need for him here, somehow.

Three years ago, when he was thriving materially in California, his intuition told him he had to go and that was a good call. He had become too settled, too comfortable, corrupt even. He had stopped learning and outside influences were controlling him. So he'd sold up his share of the business he ran, his house, cars, most of his belongings, whatever he could not carry, and returned to Greece and his roots; back to the beginning of his journey.

After a few months sitting at home with his aging parents, doing little, he'd realised that this was only half the answer. So he'd travelled down to Piraeus where he'd signed up on the first boat that would take him. That was the *Amber*. They needed an oiler and that was what he became. This appealed to him immensely. It was the lowest in the hierarchy of the engine room, deep in the bowels of the ship. It was the spell in purgatory he needed.

How he regretted going to California. He had set himself up with two others as self-styled gurus teaching self-awareness. In the beginning he did help people, but when the money came in he began to think he was important. He became a victim of his own success with drugs, alcohol and sex. Now he would stop here for a while and see what happened.

In the years he had spent at sea he had worked hard, managing to raise himself to the rank of third engineer, and was now competent in the engine room. He was rewarded with his own cabin and was one of the few to be asked to stay. As soon as they entered the harbour on Monday and he had seen where they would be based, he had accepted. He needed more balance in his life; being in the sole company of men did not suit him.

He was pleased with his companions too. He liked Steph immensely and enjoyed speaking with him, which was not easy. Andreas also spoke little and seemed to harbour a lot of anger and resentment; maybe he would learn what was behind it. He was looking forward to finding out why a rich, young man like Zenon Makris would abandon the luxury of his home and the good life of London to live like a Spartan.

He took a few deep breaths and got off the bed. It was too late to meditate now. It was time for lunch. There would be plenty of opportunity for mindfulness in the months ahead.

Chapter 13: The Day Room

From the poop deck landing, the men carrying Zen's baggage led him up two flights of stairs.

When they reached the bridge deck they found both the master's day room, which faced forward, and the guest cabin aft of this, locked, so they left the suitcases in the corridor and went to inform the captain of his arrival.

Zen was left alone on the dark landing. Although called the bridge deck, it was actually below the navigation bridge, from which the ship was piloted. It was also the smallest of the accommodation decks with a short corridor running widthways, both ends finishing with heavy wooden doors to the exterior. These had small portholes at eye level, but the glass was smeared with old varnish and let in little light.

Along the passage, on the port side facing forward was the wireless room and the wireless operator's cabin, and aft was the battery room, which supplied emergency power should the generators fail. Amidships forward was the open door of a small bathroom, from which a pale yellow light came from a single encased bulb attached to the deckhead. Overhead was the inevitable array of wire conduits and ventilation ducts, and only one of the three strip lights was working. Not for the first time, Zen reflected on the wisdom of forsaking the cosiness of his home for these soulless metal bulkheads.

Feeling pressed in by the narrow space, he opened the external door nearest him, on the starboard side, and stepped out onto a small area of deck, which was sheltered from above by the wing of the navigation bridge. Having no other access it was more like a balcony. He walked over to the white painted bulwark with its varnished wooden railing to the left of a bracket holding an inflatable life raft in a white capsule. He admired the panorama of Tonemouth that spread out before him. It was twelve o'clock and the sky was cloudless. The air had lost the freshness of the morning and was turning hazy. He was wondering where the nearest beach was when he heard someone call from behind.

Captain Stamatis, a short, round man with black hair and a slick moustache, stood at the doorway, one foot resting on the raised threshold. He wore a light brown polo neck jumper, brown slacks and dark brown shoes. Zen walked over to shake his extended hand and noticed George Pittas in the corridor behind him unlocking the guest cabin door.

'You don't mind staying in the guest room with George tonight?' the captain asked as they transferred Zen's luggage into it. 'As you know, I'm leaving in the morning.'

'I've stayed there before,' Zen replied, 'but never with George. I just hope he doesn't snore like most port captains.'

'My wife still sleeps with me, so it can't be that bad,' George said, indignantly.

The cabin was rectangular, with the deckhead, bulkheads and floor painted in the same greens as the corridors. At each narrow end was a darkly varnished wooden platform bed with drawers underneath. One was behind the door and the other beneath the porthole, which looked out onto the deck where Zen had just been. Both bunks had curtained railings for privacy.

Opposite the door was a grey metal wardrobe and on the near side a basin with a mirror. A grey metal desk and swivel chair were placed between the basin and the outside bed.

'I hope you don't mind sleeping by the porthole?' George asked, 'At my age I'm susceptible to draughts.'

'Not at all,' Zen replied. He preferred that bed when it was warm. The *Amber* had forced draught ventilation and heating throughout but the air-conditioning had broken down.

'We'll have lunch in my cabin,' the captain said from the corridor, reaching into his pocket for his keys. 'There're things we need to discuss which are best not said in front of the crew.'

The captain unlocked his door for them to enter. To the left of it, and taking in the nearside corner, was a three-sided bench settee surrounding a rectangular, formica-topped table supported on two columns fixed to the deck. Between the settee and the opposite bulkhead was a built-in dresser, finished in dark varnished wood. The bottom half had a cabinet containing glasses and was stocked with alcoholic drinks, whilst the drawers above were for cutlery. The top half was glass-fronted and displayed technical books and manuals.

The bulkhead opposite the door had three stainless steel-rimmed portholes facing forward, each with its own set of short red curtains. Below and in front of the portholes were a grey metal desk and swivel chair. These were too large for the room and had to be angled to face the corner with the settee. The internal telephone and two piles of ledgers and papers were on the desk and behind it, in the corner and in the same monotonous grey, was a three-drawer metal filing cabinet. In the centre of the right hand bulkhead was the doorway to the bedroom and bathroom. This had no door, but was screened off by a red curtain. Between this doorway and the bulkhead to the corridor was a recess housing the ship's safe and a fridge, above which were shelves with more ledgers. The bulkheads and deck were finished with a wood-effect veneer.

'What will you drink?' the captain asked, standing behind his desk with one hand on the phone.

'Some of that San Miguel,' George replied.

'The same,' Zen said.

The captain alerted the galley and ordered the lunch and drinks.

They sat round the table, with Zen at the end by the door, the captain opposite him and George between them to his left. The captain placed his cigarettes and lighter next to an ashtray.

'How was the drive?' George asked.

'Uneventful. Your trip?'

'The train was good; so was the hotel, by the way,' George replied. 'The nightmare journey will be tomorrow, on the coach with the crew to Heathrow.' He looked towards the captain for confirmation.

'You can guess what it'll be like,' the captain continued. He had produced a set of opaque, amber-coloured worry beads and was manipulating them with both hands. 'The arguments over final overtime and redundancy started in Dover. They'll end when the plane lands and I get a cab home.'

Zen could imagine. This captain had a reputation for being hard. 'Have you managed to convince anyone to stay?' he asked.

'We had seven altogether,' the captain replied. 'From those I chose the three that gave me the least trouble.'

'One's the steward, Stephanos Georgiou, who can also cook,' George added.

'He used to own a taverna,' the captain continued. 'He's an older man, quiet, reads a lot, well-liked; everyone calls him Steph. The next one's a third engineer, Charalambos Constantinou, or Harry. I know you asked for a second engineer, but neither was interested. This one's nearly as knowledgeable and hard-working. He regularly clocked up the most overtime.'

'I'm surprised he wants to stay,' George said. 'He stands to lose most of his earnings.'

'I advised him to go back to Greece and sit the second engineers' exam,' the captain said, 'but he's adamant.'

'What's his background?' Zen asked.

The captain was about to reply when the steward stepped in carrying a tray. Steph was no more than five foot five inches tall with a slightly hunched back. His greying black hair was swept back over a bald patch. He had large, sensitive, brown eyes with pencil-thin dark brows and black and white stubble. He had the expression of someone who had just received bad news.

He was introduced to Zen before proceeding to serve their beers and starters. The latter consisted of salad, feta cheese, minted meatballs, cheese parcels and a basket with toasted bread. Zen noticed Steph had nicotine-stained fingers on both hands. In a low, soft voice he agreed to come back in half an hour with their main course and more beers.

When he had left the captain continued, 'Steph's a nice guy. All I know is that he married late. They have a young daughter and he's always writing to them and calls as soon as we arrive in port. He's reluctant to go back home though.'

'Maybe he's afraid of not finding work,' George speculated.

'Maybe. But he's competent and would have no problem, in my opinion,' the captain said. 'Cheers.'

They acknowledged his toast and started helping themselves to food.

'You were about to tell me about the third engineer,' Zen said.

'There's nothing to say,' the captain said. 'I don't know anything of his background, except that his father's a priest and that he lived in America for a time.'

'What about the third guy?' Zen asked.

'Andreas Haritsis – likes to be called Andy,' the captain replied; 'an able seaman, early thirties, good worker and never any trouble on board. Unfortunately, the same can't be said for his relationships with women. Whenever we've been alongside he's got tangled up with someone. One woman tried to stow away when we left port and once I had another girl's parents come to me wanting to know if he intended marrying their daughter.'

'He's not the one the Piraeus office complains about, the one who receives all the mail?' Zen asked. He recalled seeing him during a previous visit. He was a good-looking man, tall, slim and well-groomed.

'He gets more letters than the rest of the crew put together,' the captain replied.

'Astonishing,' Zen said. 'I guess we could learn something from him. No wonder he doesn't want to go home. I hope we don't have problems.'

'Keep an eye on him,' the captain cautioned. 'He attracts young, immature girls.'

'When will I meet the engineer?' Zen asked. He couldn't recall ever seeing him.

'Supper time, I should think,' the captain replied. 'All three are busy preparing for the departure tomorrow. After lunch, Steph has to complete an inventory of the stores. This will include food, drinks, cleaning materials, bed linen and towels. Meanwhile the chief engineer will be going over some essential procedures with Harry, especially with regard to the generators and boiler. They'll also have to complete the inventory of fuels, lubricants, fresh water and spares.'

'What's happening with the bonded stores?' Zen asked.

'Customs has allowed us all the beer, but the crew can only have two hundred cigarettes and one bottle of whiskey each,' the captain replied. 'The rest has to stay locked up.'

'That's ridiculous,' George said. 'The cigarettes will have to be thrown away after six months.'

'How are we for paints?' Zen asked, mindful of the work his father wanted him to do.

'Andy will do the inventory,' the captain replied. 'We received a large order six months ago.'

The talk was then mainly between George and the captain and concerned the final accounts and, while they spoke, they finished their starters, the main course and a second beer. By two thirty Zen was struggling to stay awake. Steph brought them Greek coffees and the conversation became more interesting.

'We had Captain Stern on board yesterday,' George said turning to Zen. 'He has a few concerns. After our first night there were complaints about the generator. It seems it can be heard by every house around us. Someone even called in claiming it interfered with their television reception. From tomorrow, it must be switched off at night.'

'I assumed we'd be doing that anyway,' Zen said.

'But what you have to remember to do is to light the navigation lamps by sunset.'

'Where are they?'

'In the paint locker of the fo'castle,' the captain replied, lighting up a Marlboro. 'They're a safety requirement. Andy can do it, but you have to remind him or else you'll be fined.'

'What you'll need to do by tomorrow evening is find lamps for the interior,' George said. 'There's nothing suitable on board, only candles and torches.'

'What about heating?' Zen asked.

'There's nothing on board,' the captain replied. 'Preferably, you should get something that burns oil. We have lots of paraffin.'

'What's it used for?' Zen asked.

'Thinning paints and for the lamps,' the captain replied.

'Your next priority will be to get a boat,' George said.

'Can't we use one of the lifeboats?' Zen asked.

'They're too big and difficult to manoeuvre in these currents and tides,' the captain replied. 'You need something smaller, with an outboard.'

'And as soon as possible,' George added. 'The launch we're using is costing £15 per round trip.'

'Where do we moor it?' Zen asked.

'The answer's tied in with the question of security,' the captain replied. 'At present we can raise the companionway at night but, once you get a boat, you won't be able to do that because the only place to tie it is to the bottom of the ladder.'

'But if we lock the external doors, then the worst an intruder can do is steal the boat,' Zen said.

'Yes, but what if they injure themselves,' George pointed out. 'We could be liable.'

'What about a dog?' the captain asked.

'I'm not keen on that,' Zen replied.

'In the end there may not be a problem,' George said. 'We'll have to see.'

'How are we for diesel?' Zen asked.

'There's 152 tons as of this morning,' the captain replied. 'From tomorrow, with the generator on restricted use, you'll only need a third of a ton a day. So you'll have enough for fifteen months. There's also 150 tons of fuel oil of which you'll need some for the boiler to produce hot water. Unfortunately, you're not so well supplied with fresh water. There's 100 tons in the fore peak, but that's for the engine. The after peak has only 50 tons for domestic use.'

'Can't we use the evaporator?' Zen asked.

'It requires too much power to desalinate and is difficult to keep clean,' the captain replied. 'But I have an idea. Have you seen the boat deck?'

'Not recently,' Zen replied.

'But you're familiar with the problems we're having with it?'

'Indeed,' Zen replied. One of the problems with the *Amber* was that the insulation layer covering the accommodation decks had fractured through wear and tear. Moisture had seeped into the cracks causing the metal below to rust and swell. This had subsequently caused this lagging to blister letting in even more water.

'We've had leaks in some of the cabins,' the captain continued. 'The insulation has to be removed and the deck renewed. It should take Andreas a month to do. Once completed, you can divert the scuppers into the after peak.'

'Seeing how much it rains in England, it could work,' Zen observed.

'As for drinking water,' George said, 'Captain Stern said we can use the fresh water taps of the marina on the Castlewear side. There are plastic containers on board.'

'Anything else I need to know?' Zen asked.

'We've ordered a barge to collect the refuse,' George replied. 'It should come today, but, after that, you'll need to make your own arrangements. Maybe, once you've got the boat, you can dispose of it ashore. Apart from that, I can't think of anything else. What about you, Captain?'

'Just to suggest you could cut the top off an oil drum and burn it. There's plenty of dunnage in the holds and on deck, from the last cargo, and it'll be a good way of getting rid of it.'

The conversation stalled for a few minutes before the captain spoke again. 'I wonder if you'd allow me a few hours. I've hardly slept since leaving Dover, so I'd like a nap as well as time to pack.'

'Wouldn't mind a siesta myself,' George said.

They left the captain as he was calling for Steph to collect the remains of the lunch.

Once they had crossed the corridor and entered their cabin, George complained how he had not slept properly since Saturday, his last night in London, and weren't the bombings in the London parks terrible.

'How was your birthday?' Zen asked, as he sat on his bunk.

'Spent it with the family,' George replied, yawning. 'Had a barbeque.' He stripped down to his boxer shorts and undershirt, unworried by Zen's presence, got onto his bed and pulled the curtain across.

Zen, on the other hand, did not undress, but lay on top of the bunk with the curtain drawn and started on one of his books, retrieved from his rucksack. He only managed one page before his lids felt heavy. He put the paperback down and shut his eyes. He became aware of the gentle breeze that flapped the porthole curtain and carried whiffs of the brackish estuary. In the background was the ever-present grumbling of the generator, which caused everything to vibrate. Closer to hand he could hear the hissing of the forced draught ventilation from the blowers on the ceiling. He drifted off to sleep.

The next thing he was aware of was the rapping on the door.

'Yes?' was the groggy response from George.

'It's six thirty,' came the muted reply from the captain.

'Okay, give us twenty minutes,' George shouted back. Then in a lower voice, 'You awake?'

'Yes, I suppose it's supper at seven,' Zen replied. 'Feel as though I've only just eaten.'

He heard George's curtain drawing open, followed by the running of the basin tap.

There were two dining areas. The more comfortable officers' mess had two round tables, each held up by a single column bolted to the deck, with free-standing armchairs to sit on. The bulkheads had the same veneer finish as the captain's day room. Cutlery, china and glasses were kept in built-in sideboards. Both messes had annexes, comprising a sitting room with television, video recorder and shelves with books, tapes and videos.

Supper was later than usual on this last evening and, as George, the captain and Zen entered, most of the officers were already seated, waiting to be served. Zen took his place at the head of the eight-seater table nearest the galley. George pointed out Harry sitting at the next table. He appeared to be of medium height, well-built with long, dark brown hair, tied back in a ponytail. His face was round with dark brown eyes. His nose was broad and flat and he had a moustache that swept down the sides of his mouth. His complexion was dark, almost Persian.

The first course consisted of small dishes of stuffed vine leaves, humus, taramasalata, tinned crabmeat, salad, feta cheese and bread, followed by chicken breasts in tomato sauce with fried potatoes. At the end, each table had a bowl of fruit accompanied by a hard yellow cheese, which was a cross between English cheddar and Italian parmesan. Zen was not hungry and only nibbled some starters and then fruit.

He tried listening to the conversations around him, but they were mostly to do with Greek politics and sport, of which he knew little and cared even less. This carried on with the serving of coffee and continued after the meal had finished and the remains had been cleared. Most of the men began smoking.

Afterwards, Zen went for a walk on the cargo deck with George. It was nine thirty and, although the sun had set, there was still twilight as well as the bluish white light from the halogen floods. They stood at the prow by the forward flagstaff and took in the view. An off shore breeze moderated the smell of the freshly painted fo'castle.

'Won't there be a problem with immigration for those staying?' Zen asked, leaning on the bulwark.

'I'm taking their passports and will apply to the Home Office,' George said. 'I think we can get six-monthly extensions.'

'That's one less thing to think about.'

'You'll phone if you need anything?'

'Don't worry, I'll be fine.'

Chapter 14: The Departure

Thursday, 22nd July 1982

They were up at four thirty, barely first light, and Zen had slept badly. The sounds of the generator and ventilation, which were no trouble to him during the previous afternoon, had kept him awake. There was also a lot of slamming of doors and shouting from the decks below, and it had not helped that he had to get up during the night to use the toilet down the corridor.

He allowed George, who thankfully did not snore, to dress and shave first before joining him in the captain's day room. The captain had already packed and, before going down for breakfast, he handed over the master keys to Zen, who was now responsible for the *Amber*.

In the officers' mess, the atmosphere was sombre, with none of the lively conversations of the night before. All were tucking into grapefruit segments, then cornflakes, followed by bacon, sausages and eggs. There were baskets of sliced bread, tubs of butter and jars of marmalade and jam. Andy and Harry were taking orders and serving while Steph cooked.

Zen, not the least bit hungry, had a cup of tea while George had the works. Fortunately, the aroma of fresh coffee masked the smell of stale cigarettes and frying.

At six the transport arrived and the scramble to disembark began. The crew formed a chain to pass the luggage down the gangway. The launch needed to make two trips for possessions, followed by another two for the crew itself. George was the last to leave and Zen asked him to instruct the boatman to return at two. He would doubtless have jobs ashore that afternoon.

Leaning over the poop deck railing, he watched George join the others. He followed the launch as it reached the shore and the crew disembarked. He continued to observe as their luggage was being taken up from the pontoon to the embankment, where there was a coach waiting.

Now here he was, responsible for this ship and crew, with no idea what to do next.

Hearing footfalls, he turned to see Steph and Andy approaching from aft, along the poop passage, both smoking. 'We've finished clearing up,' Steph said. 'We're about to have breakfast. Will you join us?'

'Certainly,' Zen replied. He was hungry now and made his way to the mess where Harry was already seated. He had changed into a blue boiler suit, whilst Andy and Steph wore tee-shirts, jeans and trainers. Zen had worn the same clothes as yesterday and felt in need of a shower.

'Hope you like eggs,' Steph said, coming in through the pantry entrance. He had acquired a navy apron.

'In moderation,' Zen responded.

'We have forty dozen,' Steph added.

'At two each a day they'll last two months,' Harry said in a thick, gravelly voice with an accent that was a mixture of Greek and American.

'How long do they keep?' Zen asked.

'Six weeks,' Steph replied, 'I can make cakes.'

'*Galactoboureko* would be nice,' Andy said, joining them. His youthful voice matched his appearance, which was younger than his age.

'Cakes and pastries are my speciality,' Steph said, with the merest hint of a smile.

'It all sounds great, but I don't want to get fat,' Zen remarked, feeling his stomach. He was conscious of having gained weight recently.

'Don't worry, you won't be sitting as much as in an office,' Harry said. 'You'll burn the calories.'

Probably true Zen thought, so he decided to join them in a cooked breakfast. Steph just needed to fry the eggs as there was plenty of meat left over from earlier.

'Thought England was cold and wet,' Harry said, while they waited.

'The best way to describe the English weather is highly unpredictable,' Zen replied.

Harry seemed to mull on this, as if a cherished belief had been shattered. Meanwhile, Andy replenished the bread and a few minutes later Steph brought in their plated food.

'Now that everyone's gone, we need to find our own routine,' Zen said when they were seated. 'There's going to be a certain amount to do to maintain the ship, but I think we can fit most of that into the morning and a few hours in the afternoon.' He was conscious of the fact that they were on reduced wages. 'So I suggest we switch the generator on at, say eight, have breakfast, then work till lunch. We'll switch off after that to save fuel and get the generator going again once it gets dark. Will that give you enough time to cook and clean?' he asked Steph.

'Certainly. It doesn't take long,' Steph replied. 'And I can also do the laundry, as long as there's hot water. We've two washing machines and an ironing board.'

'We only need the boiler for half an hour a day,' Harry said. After a few mouthfuls he carefully dabbed his moustache with his serviette. 'But it's wasteful. It uses a lot of fuel because you have to fill and heat the whole system and we'll only use a fraction of what we produce.'

'I don't think we've any alternative,' Zen said.

'I want to wash after a day's work, especially if I'm going out,' Andy added.

'I hope you know what to do down there,' Zen said to Harry.

'The chief gave me a schedule. It'll be easy to complete in a few hours a day, even for me.'

'What do you want me to do with the dirty sheets and blankets?' Steph asked. 'There are forty sets.'

'We'll send them out; there must be a local laundry,' Zen replied. 'That way they'll be pressed and wrapped for storage. I hear you did the fo'castle?' he said, turning to Andy.

'I organised it, you know,' Andy replied. 'Had help at first, but had to finish it myself.'

'The first thing we'll have to deal with is the boat deck,' Zen said. 'How long will it take?'

'Have you seen it?' Andy asked.

'Not yet,' Zen replied.

'Wait till you see it,' Andy said. 'You know, practically every cabin below has a leak. It'll take months.'

'I was hoping it could be done in time for autumn, so we can collect water,' Zen said.

'It depends what we find when we take the insulation off, how many cracks we have to weld, what the weather does,' Andy said. 'Can't promise anything.'

'Show me later,' Zen said.

'Some of the crew's cabins are in a terrible state,' Steph revealed. 'People show no respect.' Displaying an expression of disgust, he told them some of the damage he had found.

After they had finished, Steph went into the pantry to make coffee while Andy took the dirty plates to the scullery. While they were doing this, Harry described his maintenance schedule for the engine room, most of which Zen could not understand.

'I'll do the shopping and the other outside jobs,' Zen continued when they were seated again. 'Weather permitting, I'll help Andy with the boat deck or otherwise work inside.' The corridors in particular looked awful. The pale green paint had taken on a yellow sheen similar to that of the smoking carriages of underground trains. The contributing factors were not only cigarettes but also the damp, warm, oily air rising from the engine room. To worsen the appearance, the ceilings had turned a dark brown where the ventilation ducts and wiring cables ran. 'Talking about cabins, does anyone want to change?'

Steph decided to stay put, but Harry asked for the chief engineer's cabin and Andy the chief officer's. They would be well distributed, Zen thought. He would be on the starboard side of the bridge deck. Andy would be below him on the boat deck, Harry on its port side and Steph would be alone on the starboard side of the poop deck, hard by the companionway to the mess. As for the cabins of the cargo deck, they would be left to the cockroaches, if there were any.

Having finished their coffees, they dispersed.

Once upstairs, Zen transferred his luggage to the captain's quarters and saw his bedroom for the first time. He had never been past that red curtain. It was small compared to the day room, but cosy with plenty

110

of storage. The double bed was set into the corner and had two full-length drawers underneath. There was a reading strip-light above the headboard and along the forward bulkhead was a bedside table with lockable drawers. All were treated in a dark varnish. Above the table was a single porthole with a red curtain, as in the day room. Aft and a few feet from the foot of the bed was the door to the bathroom, and to the right of this the standard grey metal wardrobe. The bathroom comprised a bath and shower on the left, set against the external bulkhead, and a WC on the right with a basin between them. There was a single porthole with frosted glass above the tub.

Drawing the curtain of the bedroom porthole produced sufficient light for Zen to see. The bed was stripped to the mattress, awaiting fresh linen, so he hoisted his suitcases onto it and began to unpack.

Finishing fifteen minutes later, he put one suitcase inside the other and managed to squeeze them into the space above the wardrobe. There was no bathroom cabinet, just a glass shelf above the basin. Zen was trying to stow his toiletries when there was a knock on the cabin door. He stepped through the curtain to find Harry at the threshold. 'It didn't take you long to move!' Zen observed.

'I only managed to pack. When I got to the cabin, Steph was cleaning it and making the bed. He said he'd do yours next, so I thought this would be a good time to go up to the bridge and cover the electronics. I need the key.'

'I'll come too.'

Chapter 15: The *Amber*

Zen led the way up the single flight to the navigation bridge. The stairs came to a landing with a door, which he unlocked with one of the keys he now kept clipped to his belt loop, before stepping through to the wheelhouse. This, the enclosed part of the deck, consisted of a rectangular space with windows all around, affording maximum visibility. It was warm and stuffy, due to the abundance of glass.

The smell of electronic components, rubber and stale cigarettes brought a rush of memories, of being five or six. His father sometimes took them on business trips, to visit his ships, and this was where he was happiest. He would position himself on a stool while his mother sat nearby reading a book. He would look through the forward observation windows and, whilst holding the hand bar, rock himself to simulate being at sea. He ignored the cranes and men working the cargo and instead imagined waves washing over the deck. He would communicate through the intercom with the engine room, whilst giving orders to the helmsman. Once his mother fell pregnant with his sister, these trips ended.

Before him was the wooden chart table with drawers on two sides containing Admiralty maps. There was a ceiling rail, which allowed a curtain to be drawn round it at night so that the light would not hinder the officers on watch. In front of this were the radar, helm, binnacle, autopilot and engine room controls. Below the forward handrail were cradles for binoculars and, at the back, cupboards storing signal flags.

Hearing movement, Zen turned to find that Harry had crossed to the other side of the stairwell casing and was rummaging within a small room. He came out scratching his head. Behind him, against the staircase bulkhead, Zen spotted the VHF communications equipment.

'Can this be used to make external calls?' Zen asked.

'Only in emergencies. It's rather expensive.'

Harry was shorter than him, Zen noted, but much broader. 'This place needs a clean,' Zen said, turning forward again. There were several ashtrays scattered about, their contents overflowing. The map table surface felt sticky and was covered in coffee cup rings. The surrounding windows were smeared in salt on the outside and a greasy yellow film within. Steph would no doubt get round to it. 'What sort of maintenance can we do?'

'The electronic devices have plastic covers which I thought were kept under the bed in there,' Harry replied, as he stroked his moustache. 'Maybe they're in the radio room. Assuming I can find them, we can keep them covered and run them once a week or so, but I don't know if that'll be enough to stop the damp corroding the wiring.'

'We'll have to open the panelling occasionally to check.' Zen went over to test one of the sliding doors that led to the observation wings.

'Could someone break in through here?' Zen asked, unlocking the starboard one and opening it. 'This equipment could be tempting.'

'It's toughened glass,' Harry replied, making his way over. 'It would make a hell of a racket.'

They stepped outside. Each wing was spacious and surfaced with wooden decking to provide traction in wet weather. They interconnected both forward and aft of the wheelhouse and there were stairs leading up to the flying bridge where the radar and communications antennae were arrayed.

'We won't tire of this view,' Harry said, resting on the handrail and looking aft, upriver. There were boats of every shape and size moored in orderly lines along both banks. Looking round at Tonemouth, Zen noticed that from their vantage point they were higher than the roofs of the buildings of the lower town.

They locked up and returned to the bridge deck landing. Through the open door of his day room, Zen spotted Steph mopping the floor.

At the other end of the passage they stepped into the radio room. It was a mess. Fortunately, the equipment looked intact and they found the plastic covers, coated in dust and grease, on top of a filing cabinet.

'I'm going to have to soak these in some sort of detergent,' Harry said as he carried them outside at the end of an extended arm.

Aft of this was the battery room, consisting of two rows of steel shelves stacked with two-foot square batteries that provided emergency power should the diesel generators fail.

'Couldn't we use these when the generator's off?' Zen asked.

'Unfortunately no. As you will see when we switch off for the first time, they don't power the normal lights but emergency ones on a separate circuit. They're rather dim and you can't select which to switch off or leave on. It's not worth bothering with.'

'So when we switch off, these take over?'

'Yes, together with an annoying alarm. One of us will have to come up every time and turn it off.' Harry opened a small control box on the wall. 'You press the black button. The system resets itself when the generator restarts.'

'In that case I won't lock this door.'

Back in the corridor they found the door of the linen cupboard, next to the battery room, open. Inside Steph was rummaging for sheets and blankets.

In addition to the external sections at either end of the passage, the ones that were like balconies, there was another outside door, to port of the staircase, that opened aft. This led to the narrow area surrounding the funnel. There was not much to see, but Zen wanted to check the insulation layer.

'This deck's okay,' Harry informed him. 'It doesn't get much wear.'

From here there were external stairs leading up to the navigation bridge and down to the boat deck. Behind the funnel was the engine room skylight. With only two panels it appeared too small to be effective for either illumination or ventilation.

'Is there any danger of someone getting in through here?'

'Not without a rope. It's a long way to the first scaffold.'

Back inside, Zen locked the door. Steph, meanwhile, was back in his cabin.

'While you're waiting I could show you a few things,' Harry suggested.

'Sure, but let's start with the boat deck that Andy's so worried about.

The layout of the boat deck below was similar to the level above, consisting of a corridor running widthways, but ending with cabins instead of doors to the exterior. The port one was the chief engineer's and Harry's new quarters. On the starboard side were the chief officer's and Andy's. There were five further cabins facing forward. Leading aft, two short passageways ran to external doors, passing two more outside cabins, one of which was the infirmary. Between these and behind the stairs was the bathroom for that deck, which also housed the two washing machines Steph had spoken about.

Stepping out through the port side exit into the open air, they proceeded around the engine room casing, walking by the spare propeller on the left. There was a lifeboat on each flank, secured in a cradle, and against the starboard bulkhead was the useless air-conditioning plant. Meanwhile, Zen inspected the deck. He saw what Andy meant. It looked like a paved road after an earthquake.

'I've seen enough,' Zen said, 'what did you want to show me?'

'Follow me.'

They came back in from the starboard side. All the external doors from this deck upwards were wooden and warped with age. The locks were stiff and the hinges creaked. After locking up, they went down to the poop deck. Here again was a corridor running widthways, ending in steel weatherproof doors with raised thresholds.

Harry led him down one more flight onto the largest enclosed accommodation area, which took in the full width of the ship. The corridors formed a rectangular shape around the engine room casing. Both passages ended in watertight exits forwards to the cargo deck. It was dark down here, with only half of the florescent lights working.

'A lot of lights have gone,' Zen remarked.

'We ran out of tubes some time ago. We've had them on order, but haven't seen anything yet.'

'I'll chase it.'

'This is what I wanted you to see.' Harry said.

Opposite them, at the aft end of the engine room housing, was another bathroom. When Harry opened the door they were assaulted by the most awful stench, accounted for by the fact that three of the four toilets were blocked. There was something about the combined smell of salt water, used for flushing, and sewage that was unforgettable. In addition, the seats were broken, two of the four cubicles had no shower heads and there were gaps in the tiling. This was the sort of thing that would put perspective buyers off.

'What can we do about this?' Zen asked, his hand over his mouth and nose.

'As far as the showers and tiling are concerned, they're easy to fix. We can find what we need from a hardware store. The same goes for the seats. As for the blocked toilets, I'm not going to clear them. I want to throw up just standing here.'

'Me too. I'll get professionals in. How can things get so bad?'

'You're the owner's son and don't know?'

He did know. This last captain had been on board for three years. After they had taken him on, and it was too late, they heard that he had a certain reputation.

Money that should have been spent on mundane repairs was going into his pocket.

Back outside, to the right of the stairs they had taken, round a corner, was the insulated entrance to the cold rooms.

'Can I have a look?' Zen asked.

'Sure,' Harry replied. He swung open the door, let Zen in, stepped over the raised threshold and, after turning on the light, shut the door behind them.

They were in a small lobby. There were two doors in front and two to the left. On the right hand wall there was a control panel, which housed temperature and humidity dials. It was tolerably cool and there was the hiss of extractor fans. They entered the first left hand door, once again closing it behind them. This was the outer room of the meat locker. There was a wooden butcher's table, crisscrossed by grooves from years of use. Along the walls hung knives and choppers for jointing and boning and, attached to the overhead girders, were hooks for hanging meat to defrost.

Through the next door was the freezer. As they entered they experienced a dramatic drop in temperature. It was so well insulated that the generator was barely audible. From floor to ceiling were sturdy wooden shelves on both sides of a narrow passage.

'There's a lot of meat in here,' Zen observed.

'In January we stocked up in Argentina.'

'I remember.'

On the lower shelf he counted twenty legs of beef. There were two cases of T-bone steaks and three of stewing beef. He spotted a clipboard hanging from a nail in the wooden frame, listing the inventory:

70 kilos pork chops
15 kilos lambs' livers
30 kilos sausages
180 kilos lamb
9 crates chickens
6 crates streaky bacon in tins
Variety salamis and mortadellas
2 cases table butter
85 kilos cooking butter

'How long will it keep?' Zen asked.

'Indefinitely, normally. But I don't know what will happen once we start switching the electricity off. I assume in summer we'll be using the generator even less.'

Zen nodded in agreement. 'Will there be enough running time to keep everything frozen?'

'I don't know. And it's not just about temperature, but also humidity.'

Leaving the meat locker, the next compartment to the left was the fish freezer, which was empty. After that was a chilled storeroom for fruit and vegetables. Zen read the inventory:

150 kilos onions
240 kilos potatoes
4 kilos garlic
10 kilos carrots
3 crates lemons
3 crates tomatoes
1 crate cucumbers
8 crates apples
6 crates oranges
9 crates pears

There were also several watermelons on the lower shelf.

'We'll probably end up throwing most of this away,' Zen lamented.

The fourth and last door off the main lobby contained two separate rooms. The first was kept at a temperature above freezing and contained their eggs, fifty litres of milk and a selection of cheeses. The fifty kilos of Greek feta was kept in barrels of brine and would keep well. However, the twelve kilos of Edam, forty of Gouda, thirty of hard Greek cheese for grating and fifty-three for cooking would not last. The other room contained dried pastas, pulses, semolina and rice.

'We have enough food to host several banquets,' Harry said.

'Perhaps we ought to. We could bribe the locals that don't like us being here.'

Once they were back in the outer lobby, and before leaving, Harry adjusted the thermostat of the meat store to a lower temperature, saying, 'Perhaps this will help.'

Next to the freezers was the bonded store room, which had been locked and sealed by Customs.

The deck had cabins running along both sides. The first to starboard was the crew laundry, with two more washing machines and a drier. It also contained their fifty-six crates of San Miguel lager.

'Hope there's some in the fridge upstairs,' Zen said.

'There usually is.'

The rest of the cabins had three bunks each. The portholes were smaller than on the upper decks, so there was little light. Some of the doors were left open as Steph had not yet cleaned them out. Most had broken wardrobe doors, torn and stained mattresses and basin taps that did not work. The green avocado paint had gone yellow and the ceiling conduits had turned black with dirt. The task ahead seemed overwhelming.

'I don't know where to start,' Zen said. He doubted his father appreciated how bad it was.

At the forward end, between the doors leading outside, was the CO2 locker. In here, supported by metal frames, were dozens of steel cylinders, each six foot tall and containing compressed liquid carbon dioxide gas. A series of pipes and valves led to the engine room and holds. Should there be a fire, the system would be activated, flooding the area and smothering the flames.

'Better go up and move into my cabin,' Harry said.

'Think I'll take a walk round the deck,' Zen said before stepping through the starboard side watertight doors, onto the cargo deck and into the sunshine. The vast surface that lay before him had originally been painted red, with the hatch combings, masts, winch housings and the insides of the railings yellow. Now, from where he stood, all the way to the newly painted fo'castle, it was a sea of flaking paint, rust and dents. The four hatches, with their pontoon covers, were overlaid with weatherproof canvas. Zen surmised that the condition inside the holds would be no better.

He continued forward, whilst examining the deck. At one point he crouched and touched the rough, flaky surface. It felt warm from the sun. As the ship was made of metal, the daily cycle of warming and cooling would cause condensation in the holds. It occurred to him that these had not been opened and aired since the ship left Spain. Weather permitting, this should be done soon and then at regular intervals. It would also be an opportunity to work the deck machinery.

Near the fo'castle, by hold number one, strapped to eyeholes with wires, were several canvas bags full of sweepings from the previous cargo. There were wood chippings, pieces of bark and branches. Next to these were several empty metal barrels. They had the materials for an incinerator. The disposal of the insulation from the boat deck could be a problem. Since it was tar-based, perhaps they could burn it along with their rubbish.

The fo'castle had two doors. The one to port, which was shut, Zen knew was the boson's store and the carpenter's workshop. The one to starboard, which was open, contained the paint, oil and lamp stores. On entering he found Andy, seated on a wooden stool, his back to him, at work organising tins of paint under the light of a single bulb.

'I'm amazed you don't pass out,' Zen said, referring to the overwhelming smell of paraffin and turpentine.

Andy turned and smiled.

'How are we for paints?' Zen asked, looking round at the bewildering array.

'There's quite a bit, you know.' Andy replied. 'I'm grading it. That's the external white.' He pointed into the corner to four thirty-litre cans. 'We won't need it for a while.'

'The accommodation looks good.'

'It was done recently,' Andy continued. 'We also have 230 litres of yellow and 300 of red for the cargo deck. Are we going to do anything about it?'

'I don't know. It might be too big a job.'

'I'd need two people working with me to do the hatches and combings.'

'Once the boat deck's done we'll decide what's next.'

'We can spread fish oil on the deck for now,' Andy said, pointing to some metal barrels. 'We have 120 litres of it.'

'Never heard of it.'

'It loosens the rust and you can then sweep it away. It also inhibits further corrosion.'

'Good idea.'

'I was getting the dark green and its undercoat ready for the boat deck. I'll move what I need today.'

'Do we have any indoor paints?'

'We still have 120 litres of green. It was bought some months ago and never used.'

'Don't we have anything lighter? It makes it so dark.'

'Anything lighter would look dirty more quickly.'

'Hmmm, we'll need that as well. We can be painting cabins and corridors when the weather stops us working outside.'

'I'll move those over too. Do you want to start from the top or bottom?'

'We'd better start from the bottom, that lower deck's the worst.'

'One more thing. We've two electric grinders, but only one's okay. I need spare parts for the other, but if we get two sets then we won't be left without one working.'

'Give me the details and I'll send off for them. How much lamp oil do we have?'

'Forty litres.'

'That's less than I thought. Where are the lamps?'

'Over there,' Andy replied, pointing to a dark corner where they were hanging from hooks attached to the bulkhead. 'Are they for the evening?'

'Yes, do you know where to put them?'

'Leave it to me. I'll have them cleaned and filled.'

'What about torches?'

'They're in the chief officer's office, next to my cabin. I'll get them later.'

'I'm going back now, is there anything you want me to take?'

'You could take this to the boat deck,' he said, pointing to a bucket of brushes and scrapers.

'See you later,' Zen said. He walked back along the deck, heading for his cabin, via the boat deck.

Chapter 16: The Town

The day room smelled clean, the stale cigarette odour had gone and, through the opening to his bedroom, he saw that the bed had been made.

Walking round the desk and looking through the drawers, he found an assortment of stationary given to the captain by the suppliers and agents he had met on his travels. He would need to keep a log, recording the work that was being done, the times the generator was used, the ship's expenses and weather conditions. He chose a dark green diary from a Singapore chandler that was note-book size with one page per day. Taking this, he turned to yesterday's page and, after choosing a pen, began writing.

The circular table nearest the galley was set for four. In its centre was a stainless steel holder with dispensers for oil, vinegar, salt, pepper and toothpicks. Surrounding this were plates of black olives, taramasalata, tsatziki, and a basket with lightly toasted bread. Zen stopped to pop an olive in his mouth on his way to the galley. Harry and Andy were already there, bottle of beer in hand, watching Steph give the chickens and potatoes a final basting before returning them to the oven.

This stainless steel range was amidships and at the forward end of this sprawling space. With its dark elements and extractor fan above, it sat in a recess. Against the surrounding bulkheads were an assortment of stainless steel sinks, work surfaces and cupboards. Dozens of different sized pans hung from hooks attached to the girders of the deckhead. In the centre, was a waist-high table used for preparation, with a shelf underneath containing chopping boards and other utensils. The starboard aft corner contained the scullery. Forward of that, adjoining the officers' mess was a pantry, which housed a fridge, sink and storage cupboards.

'You rarely see a galley this clean,' Zen commented.

'Steph and the cook were excellent. We're lucky to have him.' Andy said, loud enough for Steph to hear.

Zen went and took a beer from the pantry before they sat at the table to share the starters.

'The launch is coming at two,' Zen said, dipping bread into his helping of taramasalata. 'Do we need anything and does anyone want to go out?'

'I've prepared a list,' Steph replied.

'I'll speak to the harbour master about getting a boat,' Zen added.

'How do we stop intruders if we have to keep the gangway down?' Andy asked.

Zen had already had this discussion with George Pittas, but went through it again and, despite spending most of lunch on the subject, the conclusion was the same. There was no convenient way to stop anyone coming on board, since the boat would have to be tied to the bottom of the ladder.

'Are we ready to switch off?' Harry asked, after they'd had watermelon with cheese.

'Wait till I wash up,' Steph replied as he cleared the table.

'Can you get a newspaper so we know what's on TV?' Harry asked.

'I hope there'll be more to do than watch TV,' Andy said.

'I'm going to join a diving club, if there's one nearby,' Zen revealed.

'You dive?' Harry asked.

'Yes, since university. You?'

'Whilst I lived in California I dived most of the coast as well as the Caribbean.'

'I've done mostly the Med, Red Sea and Maldives,' Zen said.

'What's it like round here?' Harry asked.

'I've never dived in England. I hear it's cold and murky, but good for wrecks.'

'I'm interested,' Harry replied. 'I've got my log book.'

'I dive too, you know,' Andy said. 'Before I went to sea I worked with a diving school in Halkidiki.'

'As an instructor?' Zen asked.

'Nothing like that, I crewed the boats,' Andy replied, 'but we were expected to be competent.'

'Are you interested?' Zen asked.

'Not really, it was only a job.'

'You can turn the generator off,' Steph said as he stepped through from the galley. I'll make the coffees with the gas.'

'I'd better go,' Harry said.

Zen made his way upstairs to the battery room. Within a minute of his arrival the main lights went out and the emergency ones took over. At the same time, a high-pitched siren sounded. Zen disengaged the system. He made a quick visit to his cabin to get what he needed for his trip ashore and was on his way back downstairs when the generator died away.

They continued chatting over coffee, sitting in the subdued light of the mess. With the generator silent, the

127

cries of seagulls could be heard in the background. They discussed small mundane things like having a bucket of water by their toilets for when there was no pressure to flush.

'What about heating?' Andy asked.

'We can't use the ship's system even when the generator's on,' Harry pointed out.

'Why not?' Andy asked.

'Because we'd need the boiler on continuously for that, which would use too much fuel,' Harry replied.

'Which wouldn't go down too well,' Zen added.

'Talking about the boiler, I've been thinking about the best time to produce hot water,' Harry said, pinching his chin. 'If we make it late in the afternoon, it'll still be warm the next morning.'

'Sounds reasonable,' Andy said.

'I wouldn't worry about the fuel oil,' Harry said. 'We have well over 300 tons. I estimate we'll only be using two tons a month.'

'Talking about heating, we have two choices,' Zen said. 'Either gas or oil heaters. The gas ones are variable and can produce fast or slow heat while the oil ones are slow but steady. I prefer gas, but the heaters are big and the cylinders heavy.'

'Surely our cabins don't need gas?' Steph said. 'It's only in here we need something more powerful.' He was referring to the mess.

'I agree,' Zen replied. 'Oil heaters will be more convenient. They're small, light and safe to leave unattended. The only problem's the smell.'

'We live with smells,' Harry said. 'We'll have the oil heaters for the cabins…'

'…and the bathroom,' Andy added.

'…and the communal bathrooms,' Harry continued. 'And have a gas heater in here and one in the galley.'

'The galley won't need it,' Steph said. 'I can use the oven.'

'But what about when we've switched off?' Harry asked him.

'Have you seen how big it is?' Steph said. 'It retains heat for hours.'

'Okay, sounds like the best plan,' Zen said. 'I'll get the oil heaters as soon as possible. It can get chilly in the mornings, even in summer. But we won't need the gas one for a while yet.'

'What about light?' Steph asked.

'I'll get us a torch each for this evening,' Andy said.

'But we can't use torches all the time,' Steph said.

'What about oil lamps?' Zen asked.

'They're too weak to read with and will just add to the smell and condensation,' Steph pointed out.

'Then I'll have to see what's available,' Zen said.

'You'll notice that I've put candles in each room,' Steph said.

They heard a call from outside. It was the boatman who had come for Zen.

He started with the harbour master, to ask his advice. He was told where to find oil and gas heaters. '…and for up to a grand you could get a second-hand, rigid-hull inflatable with a fifteen horse power engine. It's all you need round here, easy to maintain and in reasonable weather you can even go out along the coast.'

'Where do I find one?' Zen asked.

Captain Stern took Zen to one of his windows and pointed to the opposite bank. 'Behind the marina and the railway line, there's a basin where the owner has his offices and a maintenance yard. He usually has a few boats for sale. When do you want to go?'

'Won't be till morning.'

'I'll give him a call and tell him to expect you. Whatever you buy may be more expensive, but it'll be good.'

'By the way, I need someone to clear some drains.'

'I'll make some calls,' the harbour master said. 'When should they come?'

'Any morning, just let me know when I come by for the post.' The harbour office was their mailing address.

After dropping into the bank to confirm his new account was open, he set about familiarising himself with the town and was impressed with the sloping, narrow streets, some cobbled, the brightly coloured cottages, the hanging baskets and tubs of flowers outside many houses and shops.

There were pubs, cafés and tea places. There were greengrocers – he bought salad ingredients from one, which was off the market square – butchers and shops selling cream, toffees and fudge. There were two delicatessens and an adequate supermarket from which he bought bread. Added to this variety were yacht chandlers, boutiques, antique and gift shops and an interesting selection of restaurants.

Following the harbour master's instructions, he made his way towards the southern end of the town. Next to the road for the lower car ferry landing and occupying a corner position was an ironmonger. Inside was the largest variety of contents in a small space he had seen, with some items dangling from hooks attached to the ceiling. By just browsing he found much of what he needed, including a blue boiler suit. In one corner were the oil heaters. He particularly liked the Valor paraffin ones as they were compact. He decided to buy nine, two each for Harry, Andy and himself, one for Steph and two for the bathrooms.

In another section, he found camping equipment mixed in with yacht stores. He was interested in the gaslights. They had a gauze-type material for a wick, over which was a round opaque glass diffuser. He decided to buy one to try out.

After paying for his purchases and arranging for them to be delivered to the launch at five, he was back outside. He walked along the quayside towards the centre of town, passing the pontoon where the launch would be waiting. On the near corner was a newsagent, where he bought a paper before returning to the pontoon.

Andy, who was preparing for tomorrow's start on the boat deck, spotted him approaching with his purchases and was waiting at the bottom of the ladder. The others were in their cabins so he left everything in the dining room, just taking his own two heaters to his cabin.

Once inside he shut the door. He was tired after his sleepless night and early start. It was five twenty so he went to his bedroom, took off his shoes, pulled the curtain of the porthole to and lay on top of the newly made bed. The room was dark but warm. The sun was still high on the starboard side and had been heating the metal for hours. The bathroom door was open and a shaft of yellow sunlight poured through the open porthole, spotlighting the tiled floor. From the porthole beside his bed came the sound of passing boats and the cries of circling gulls.

For the first time in weeks, he felt safe and unthreatened. Even the problems with his family and the economic crisis felt remote. He compared his new *offshore* status with living in a castle surrounded by a two hundred yard wide moat. The air carried the brackish scent of the estuary. He relaxed and drifted off to sleep.

The sounds and vibrations of the generator starting up woke him. He was cold. The light in the bathroom had faded. The sun must have set behind the hills and the warmth had dissipated. He switched on the reading light above his bed and looked at his watch. It was eight thirty.

He got up stiffly and pulled on a jumper. In the day room he turned on the light and closed all but the end porthole before going downstairs.

He found Harry and Andy in the mess while Steph was busy in the galley. Fetching a box of matches from the pantry, he demonstrated the gaslight. Everyone decided to have one.

'I've filled a plastic container of oil for each of us to take to our rooms,' Andy said, 'and I've put out the navigation lights.'

'Great,' Zen said.

Steph had prepared a supper of vegetable rice with left-over chicken and salad. Afterwards, Andy helped him clear up while Harry tried tuning the television.

Zen went outside to raise the accommodation ladder for the night. It was dark now, the breeze had dropped and there was a chill in the air. Tonemouth shone in the distance and its near-perfect reflection reached out to them on the calm waters, which otherwise enveloped them in an inky blackness. He could see cars and people milling around, but the generator masked any sounds. Looking forward, along the poop deck passage and across the expanse of the cargo deck, he could just make out the light from the oil lamp that Andy had placed by the flagstaff of the fo'castle. There was another aft and one for each wing of the bridge. The ship's floods, on top of the masts, could be used only as long as the generator was on, but Zen saw no point in doing so from now on.

Beside the break in the bulwark at the top of the companionway, in the shelter of the metal railing, was a box housing the control panel for the ladder. He opened it and switched on the power. When a green light came on he pressed the 'Up' switch. With the whining of the electric motor, the base of the gangway began its slow ascent. When, after a few minutes, it was horizontal with the deck, he switched the power off and came back inside, locking the door behind him. He then went round to check that all the other external doors were also secure. He had an idea. Harry would have made hot water this evening, so he went to his bathroom and filled his tub.

After watching the ten o'clock news, Harry switched off for the night. Zen went to the battery room first to wait for the lights to go off. When they did, he reset the emergency system and went to his room, using the torch to find his way. The generator died away as he lit the gaslight. He sat down and, after making a note of expenses, completed the diary for the day.

133

When he went into the bathroom, he found the water still very warm. He lit one of the candles, which Steph had inserted into an empty beer bottle, and placed it on the shelf above the basin. Then, getting undressed, he slipped into the water. He had left the porthole above his head open. There was little breeze tonight and, with no ship's noises, all he could hear were the sounds coming from the town: cars accelerating, motorbikes, even the occasional raised voice.

Later in bed, with the gaslight beside him, he read until his eyelids became heavy. He turned the light off and soon fell asleep.

Chapter 17: The Boat

Friday, 23rd July 1982

The start-up of the generator woke Zen at eight. Getting up, he went into the bathroom and shaved while running the shower. It was nice and hot, as Harry had promised, but he wondered if the same would hold true in winter. He was the furthest from the engine room and there would be many yards of pipe for the water to travel through.

In the mess, the others were already eating. Zen managed bacon, eggs, toast and a coffee before the launch came to collect him at nine. He dropped by the harbour master's office for the post before making his way to the lower ferry.

The landing stage was a sloping ramp in the gap between two buildings, and the ferry, a square pontoon with railings and an observation bridge, had a tug lashed to it for propulsion. As it began crossing, Zen could view his surroundings from a different perspective. The morning had started grey and overcast, but now the clouds were breaking and blue sky was visible. The forecast must have been fair because a procession of boats and yachts were heading for the open sea, perhaps for a day's sailing or a trip to a favoured beach or cove.

There was activity on shore too, shoppers and tourists milling about pointing cameras in every direction and cars coming and going. In the midst of it all, the *Amber*, commerce in its rawest form meeting pleasure at its most ethereal.

There was a jolt as they ground to a halt. At the top of the ramp Zen turned upriver, following Captain Stern's directions to the Castlewear Marina Company.

Inside the reception area, Zen found a man with a Birmingham accent on the phone. He was of medium height, well-built, with a short, thick neck and fair hair. His skin was a ruddy red and flaking, as if scrubbed with a wire brush. His oversized hands looked able to crush the receiver. He was wearing a blue, open-neck shirt tucked into navy shorts. His desk was one of two in the room and piled with files and papers.

When his conversation ended, he replaced the receiver and came to shake Zen's hand. 'I assume you're Mr. McKee?' he said.

'Makris,' Zen corrected him.

'I do apologise, I must've misheard, although I didn't think McKee sounded Greek.'

'That's quite alright.'

'Your English is good!'

'I'm not one of the crew. I'm from the London office.'

'Ah, excellent, I'm Joe Sayer,' he said, letting go of his hand. 'Jim said you're looking for a tender for your freighter and gave me an idea of the specs. If you follow me I'll show you what I've got.' He led Zen out to a circular basin by a creek, in which was an assortment of tenders chained to spikes cemented into the ground.

'I mainly run a marina providing services for yachts. This is where we keep our small craft. I must warn you, this is the worst time to buy. Everyone's got their boat for the season and they don't tend to upgrade till the end of September.'

'So this is the stuff nobody wants.'

'True, but that's because some of these are dated.'

'I like that one over there, the one with the back-to-back seats.'

'That's three years old and in great condition.'

Zen had a closer look. It was a black inflatable encompassing a cream fibre-glass hull. It had a covered bow section for stowing shopping and other cargo and looked robust enough to take them diving. It could accommodate four, excluding the one manning the engine. 'What about an outboard?'

'We keep those separate.' Sayer walked him to a store behind the offices. 'Is it just for the estuary?'

'Might take it out, weather permitting, but don't need speed.'

Sayer unlatched a padlock, switched on a light and let him in. 'We've several reconditioned ones. Fifteen horsepower should do.'

They were arranged against the walls. 'How much?'

'How long will you be keeping it?'

'I don't know,' Zen said, wondering difference it made. 'Say anything from six months to two years.'

'Do you need a trailer?'

'Not really.'

'Hmm, okay, the one you saw, together with the engine, say £750.'

'Is that the best you can do?' The price was less than he had expected to pay, but he thought he would ask anyway.

'For sure mate, I don't rip people off, especially if Jim calls me. You won't find this anywhere else for less than a grand. If you'd like to wait till September, you'll find plenty at better prices.'

'Can't wait that long.' It seemed to be what they were looking for. 'The boat and engine are a bit dirty.'

'No problem. I can have them cleaned and ready in a couple of hours.'

'It'll have to be tomorrow afternoon.'

'Fine.'

'Do you mind cash?'

'Whatever suits you.'

They shook hands and Zen was on his way.

At one thirty he struggled up the gangway with two carrier bags of food plus four more gaslights. He stepped into the galley where Steph was mopping the floor. 'Your lunch is in the oven,' he said. They had already eaten and the generator was off. Zen left him the shopping and lamps and told him about the boat, adding that he would be back in a few minutes for his meal.

He went out aft from the galley and climbed the stairs to the boat deck. He could hear shovelling and found that Andy had started lifting the old insulation and putting the rubble in canvas sacks. Beneath it was a thick black sludge of dirt, stagnant water and rust.

'I've found a boat,' he told him, 'I'm collecting it tomorrow.'

'Great, we're free to go out. I was getting claustrophobic.'

'Of course, none of you have been ashore since Spain,' Zen realised. 'Are we burning this stuff?'

'Yeah, Harry's preparing a barrel.'

'Where is he?'

'Near the fo'castle.'

Climbing up to his cabin, he had a look out of one of the portholes and could see Harry on the starboard side of hold number one, punching holes in a barrel with a hammer and chisel.

Zen had lunch alone in the mess while reading the local paper. On the front page was a photo of the *Amber* at its mooring and a write-up about its arrival.

Afterwards, he found the others forward of the accommodation, on the port side of hatch number four, tending a roaring fire in the newly prepared drum, throwing in the broken-up insulation and other rubbish. The thick, black smoke drifted off the port side and had a tarry smell. They were discussing the imminent arrival of the boat and all but Steph agreed to go out the next evening and celebrate.

Saturday, 24th July 1982

Their third day started at nine. After breakfast, and with the good weather continuing, Andy resumed work on the boat deck. Having already lifted the insulation on a good half of it on the port side, he was curious to see what the surface was like under the rust. He started removing it with the electric grinder. This made the most terrible noise, easily masking the generator. There was no escaping it. Harry could hear it in the engine room. The galley and mess were the worst places, being just below, and Steph could not cook without ear defenders.

Zen decided that this was an opportunity to air the holds, so, changing into his boiler suit, he fetched Harry from the engine room. It took both of them to partly peel back the tarpaulins from each hatch. This revealed the oblong steel covers that ran widthways. Each hatch had six, apart from the smaller number one hold which only needed four.

It was a simple matter for Harry to sit at the controls, on their raised platforms on top of the mast houses, and work the derricks, but Zen needed Steph to help him secure the lifting chains and manoeuvre each cover once it was raised and placed on the deck. They removed two from each hatch and the whole job took an hour. The bearings and pulleys of the cranes, though, were stiff and squeaky, probably needing more greasing. They would close the holds in the evening.

After they had finished it was lunchtime. They had Greek-style meatballs in an egg lemon sauce with rice followed by a selection of cheeses and watermelon. They discussed their plans for the evening and decided to switch on again at six to give themselves time to seal the hatches, have supper and get ready to go out.

Meanwhile, the launch came at one thirty to take Zen ashore. He dropped into the harbour office for the post and to ask where they could moor the boat. He was assured he could use the harbour authority pontoon. From there he went to the bank to withdraw the cash he needed and then on to the ferry.

Their tender with its fitted engine was unrecognisable from what he had seen the day before. Both had been cleaned and a black hose attached the engine to a red, two-gallon fuel tank. Joe Sayer convinced him he needed a spare, so this, together with petrol to fill them, cost a few more pounds.

They placed the spare tank within the covered bow section, where he also found an anchor connected to a short run of chain, which in turn was fastened to a coil of rope. There was another length of line tied to a steel ring on the bow.

Zen had not handled a boat in years, so was wary at first, especially manoeuvring out of the basin, through the tunnel under the railway line and out of the marina. By the time he was crossing the estuary and had passed the stern of the *Amber*, he had got the hang of it. He tied up to the harbour authority pontoon, and went to do the shopping. He was back on board by four.

Everyone came down to inspect the boat.

That evening they assembled at the top of the gangway at eight thirty for their first night out. Andy insisted on taking control of the boat as they left Steph to look after a lifeless ship about to be enveloped by the gloom of night. Andy also wanted to choose the pub, as the ambience, according to him, had to be right.

They stopped outside each one within the vicinity of the embankment while he checked it out inside. In the end he picked what seemed to be the noisiest. It was not hard to see why. It was bursting with young people, some still in their teens, so Zen and Harry overruled him.

Walking through the town they eventually settled themselves in the bar of the hotel that overlooked the inner harbour. It was an attractive four-floor, timber-framed building and the one Zen had booked George into just a week ago. They sat in armchairs round a table and near to a group of four men who were having drinks whilst reading the restaurant menu. They were wearing navy tops with the initials TSAC embroidered on the left side. Zen overheard their conversation and it soon became obvious they were talking about scuba diving. Zen introduced himself and explained that they were looking for a local club. It turned out that they were members of the Tonebridge Sub Aqua Club, just twelve miles away. They invited Zen and Harry to speak with the club secretary any Thursday evening, which was the club's training night.

'That's one problem taken care of,' Harry observed.

A further surprise for Zen was that the bar had an excellent selection of locally brewed beers, but it took a lot of persuading to convince the other two to try them rather than the lager they were used to. 'Tell me what you think,' he said when he had brought them to the table.

'This is going to kill me,' Andy said, after he'd had a sip.

'It's bitter,' Harry added, 'but tastes more wholesome than lager.'

'So, what are your impressions of Tonemouth?' Zen asked.

'I like it,' Andy replied. 'It's not like other ports where everyone's trying to exploit the seamen.'

'There are real people here,' Harry said, 'and from all over. I could hear different languages and accents when we were walking.'

'The area's popular with tourists,' Zen said.

'Are there any beaches?' Andy asked.

'Sure, I can show you the map,' Zen said, referring to the Ordinance Survey he had bought before leaving London, 'but the water temperature won't be like California or Greece.'

'The sea in California's colder than you'd imagine,' Harry said.

'And you can enjoy the beach without getting wet,' Andy added.

And so they carried on until it was Andy's turn to buy, giving Zen a chance to learn more about Harry's diving experiences. When Andy did not return, they looked round and found him trying to talk with a group of girls sitting near the bar. Once they got up to leave, Andy returned with their drinks.

'Are you going to do this whenever we go out?' Harry remonstrated.

'No, but they looked wanting,' Andy replied.

'Wanting? What does that mean?' Zen asked.

'I don't think we want to know,' Harry said. 'I hope they didn't leave because of you?'

'No, they're eating in the restaurant,' Andy said. 'And for your information, I got the blonde one's phone number.'

'In that case I concede you have some balls,' Zen said. 'But how did you do it? You hardly speak English.'

'I speak well enough,' Andy said. 'I said what I always say, that I'm a foreigner in a strange country and need help.'

'I see you decided to have another English beer,' Zen commented.

'I'd better get used to what men drink round here,' Andy said.

A few minutes past eleven, having bought two rounds each and after much idle talk about times at sea, Greek politics and sport, they were ready to leave. Zen waited in the foyer while Harry and Andy visited the cloakroom. Lying open on a wooden side table was the Guests Book, so to pass the time he started leafing through the pages. It would be useful to know what the diners thought of the food. Most of the entries were from visitors from within Britain but there were foreign ones too. The comments went back to the beginning of the year, but before Easter they started running thin and Zen was about to close the book when he was surprised by a familiar name. There for 12th February was an entry by Ralia Alexandrou, Sophia's mother. There was no doubt about it, it was her handwriting. She commented on the wonderful view from their room and the excellent meals. Zen recalled that earlier that year Sophia's parents and younger sister had gone away for a weekend. He was still thinking about this whilst they were walking back to the pontoon. It was no surprise that the Alexandrous should visit here; it was an attractive place after all. The curious thing was that Spiros, with his wealth, should stay in a hotel well below his standards. Nearby Torquay was more suitable as well as popular with London Greeks.

Soon they were in their boat and cutting through the silky waters with Andy at the tiller, Harry shining a torch forward and Zen sitting beside him. Returning in the dark for the first time was daunting. The new moon had set and once away from the shore, they were cloaked in darkness. Only the navigation lights of the *Amber* were visible to guide them, the rest of the ship a silhouette.

Andy cautiously piloted them through the maze of boats and moorings into the middle of the estuary before turning upriver. Progress was slow, but they did not mind. It was a beautiful night and, once away from the lights of the town, they could see hundreds of stars.

They lashed the painter to the bottom of the gangway and climbed the stairs with Andy taking the petrol can, to be left inside the poop deck door beside the spare. To the left of the entrance Zen saw the yellow glow of Steph's porthole. The camping gas lights were one of his better ideas.

Once inside and with the outside door closed, it was dark. They had not thought to have their torches handy and had to feel their way up the stairs and to their cabins.

It was a still, mild night. All his portholes were open, and in the distance he could hear the traffic of Tonemouth winding down and the occasional shout or laugh. The fresh, brackish scent was always present.

He was enjoying this peaceful end to the day. Here were all the benefits of being at sea: the detachment from the mundane, the unreachability, no noisy neighbours, coupled with the advantages of being in port: human contact and the carnal comforts as and when required. Added to this was the growing sense that his fellow crew were proving to be good company.

Chapter 18: The Gull

The blood on its furry face has dried in the breeze. It belongs to the disembowelled sheep that now lays a few yards away.

Having satisfied its blood lust, it gazes across the dark fields at the distant lights, at what was once its home. How it has changed over the centuries.

At the time that it lived there, in a different form, there were no artificial lights and fewer, less substantial dwellings. In those days the estuary was populated by wooden and masted cargo boats.

It watches from the height of one of the surrounding hills. It has travelled out of its way to come to this spot. It has come here, not from any sentimental desire to revisit its birthplace, but because it is being directed to new prey.

It has made good progress since its first materialisation a few months ago. It now remembers its identity and is recalling more about its past. It has not, as yet, materialised into its human form; that pain is still too great to bear.

It is happy and content as things are, although it never anticipated this diversion. It does, however, appreciate to whom it owes its reappearance and what it will have to do in order to be allowed to reach its full expression.

It focuses on a shape in the estuary. It reminds it of the sailing ships of old, but this vessel is much larger and it guesses that it is the modern equivalent. Here, on board this boat, is the other, the prey. It can sense its presence, but it needs to make a stronger connection. It needs to establish a bond so that it can influence and manipulate.

Under a star-spangled sky, it begins the trek through the fields, bounding over hedgerows, slipping through copses, woods and along creeks until it reaches the water's edge at a silty bank.

The boat is closer. It feels the presence more strongly but it is still not enough. It has to get on board. It remembers what it was once capable of doing. Can it do it again? Is it strong enough?

It begins by clearing its thoughts and focusing its mind on its intention. Minutes pass without result, but eventually its eyes glaze over and become unseeing. The breeze that was ruffling its fur no longer has this effect as the boundaries of its form become undefined. It begins reshaping, collapsing in on itself, initially into a smaller, ball-like shape, black on top, white underneath, then bouncing back into focus as a black-backed gull.

Taking time to enjoy its new manifestation, it surveys its surroundings briefly before walking purposefully up the mud and shingle beach to a stone boundary. Then it charges into the breeze and, stretching its wings, becomes airborne, flapping strongly to gain height. It soars into the sky, at first forgetting the purpose of its flight and enjoying its own sense of power, crying defiantly at the surrounding hills.

It experiences euphoria as it wheels in ever-decreasing circles, first around the harbour, then close to the dark boat, eventually gliding down and alighting on its highest point.

Stretching out its feelings, it locates its goal and, jumping down two levels, it settles on a small area of sheltered deck.

Inside the metal hull, all is quiet and dark. In the engine room several decks below, the generator and its surroundings have not yet cooled after several hours of disuse, and continue to make faint tapping noises.

Forward of the accommodation housing, the much larger spaces of the holds are dark and damp, still smelling of rotting timber despite the airing they had received during the previous day.

In the cabin on the poop deck, on the starboard side, Steph's in bed having an anxious night, as always. On the boat deck above, Harry and Andy are also restless, but in their case this is due to having had more alcohol than they are used to.

One deck above, on the starboard side, Zen has woken. He has come out of sleep with a feeling of anxiety. He is convinced that someone is in the cabin with him. It reminds him of the time he was with Erika. Despite being terrified and breaking into a cold sweat, he throws off the sheet, gets out of bed and steps through the curtain into the day room. It is empty and the door is still locked. All three portholes are open and a breeze agitates the drawn curtains. Filtering through them is the barely discernible sound of fast current rushing past moored boats.

Reassured, he goes into the bathroom to rinse the taste out of his mouth. The porthole above the bath is open, but here there is no curtain and the breeze starts to dry the sweat on his back, causing him to shiver. When he has finished, he gazes out towards Tonemouth. He is inexplicably overwhelmed by a fear that someone or something is about to appear on the other side. He shuts the porthole and tightens the nuts, the frosted glass blurring the town, obscuring most of the light. Still in a panic, he rushes into the day room and does the same with the other portholes, even though he is a good twenty-five feet above the cargo deck.

He gets back under the covers, shaking with cold, and it is a long time before he feels warm enough to fall asleep.

The black-backed gull settles once again on the top deck. It had got as close as it could, within feet in fact. It found no difficulty making contact and would have no trouble carrying out whatever was required of it. It had encountered such odious beings before in its previous existence and would take much pleasure in hurting this one, if it was commanded to do so.

But this encounter has also released unwelcomed memories, which in turn stoke feelings of anger and resentment.

It feels the need to leave this place. It soars skyward, heading upriver, towards the moor.

Chapter 19: The Walk

Sunday, 25th July 1982

Zen was woken by the generator at nine. As he lay in bed and remembered the events of the night, he felt foolish at having reacted in such a way to what was nothing more than a mild nightmare, probably brought on by too much alcohol. He shaved and showered, taking his time going down to breakfast and, when he did so, found Steph and Harry. The former was having a Greek coffee and the latter eating fruit, with a pile of peelings before him. He wished them good morning and asked after Andy.

'He's got a hangover,' Steph said, shaking his head. 'He was banging on my door at six thirty asking for aspirin.'

'I don't understand,' Zen said. 'After the first drink, which was a pint admittedly, the rest were halves. He should've been fine.'

'My head's heavy too,' Harry said. His voice was deeper than usual and his eyes red.

'Do you want me to get you something?' Steph asked Zen.

'No thanks, I'll help myself to fruit.' Zen took an orange from the bowl and sat down.

'Coffee?' Steph asked.

'Later maybe,' Zen said.

'Looks like a nice day,' Harry remarked. 'Thought I'd take a walk after lunch. Might clear my head.'

'I'll join you, if you don't mind,' Zen said.

'Good,' Harry said. 'Do you want to come too?' he asked Steph.

'No, I'm not much for walking, I've got flat feet.' Steph excused himself and headed for the galley. At the doorway he paused, 'I'll go to the post office tomorrow and walk round the shops, if that's okay.'

'Be glad to take you,' Zen said.

Harry finished another orange and stood. 'I'd better get back to the engine room. I'm making hot water for Steph to do the laundry and don't want to leave the boiler on too long.'

When Zen had finished, he took the remains of breakfast into the galley. Steph was peeling potatoes. Zen offered to assist.

'If you help I won't have enough to do,' Steph said.

'Since you don't need me, I'll go and sort my washing.'

'Place your clothes in the wicker basket in the laundry room and I'll put the washing machine on when I finish here.'

'How will you know whose clothes are whose?'

'After I've ironed them I'll leave them out and it will be up to you to collect.'

'That's great. Thanks.'

After doing this, he went back upstairs but, before entering his cabin, he opened the door to the outside deck to let in light and air and latched it to the bulkhead. He squinted with the brightness and went and stood by the railing. It was warmer outside than inside. It was ten o'clock and the pleasure cruisers had already started plying the estuary on their tours. He could hear the muffled voices of the guides as they spoke to their passengers over their PA systems. One in particular came close by and for the first time he heard the *Amber* included in the narrative. The only part he caught was '... and it is the largest cargo ship to...'

It was when he turned round to go back inside that he noticed the marks on the deck. The metal of the ship would collect dew, much like any other surface, during the night. Added to this, the *Amber* was still covered in a layer of salt from its time at sea and there had not yet been any rain to wash it off. Anybody or anything that had walked on the deck at night or during the morning would leave an impression as the sun had not yet come round to that side to dry it. Indeed, he could see the prints he had just left coming out. The ones he noticed to the right of these appeared to belong to a large wading bird. They were the size of his hand and all over the deck, but particularly concentrated underneath his bathroom porthole. It had probably been a gull, black-backed most likely.

He recalled the events of last night and the fear that drove him to shut the portholes. Perhaps he had heard something subconsciously. At least now he had an explanation for what had spooked him, and for the second time he dismissed the event.

After catching up with the diary and some reading, he went back downstairs and found Steph outside the galley on the poop deck smoking a Marlboro. He made his way aft, round the windlass, stepping over the criss-crossing ropes and wires, wrapped around the bitts, which held the *Amber* to its aft buoy, and sat on an adjoining bollard. A waist-high, steel railing encircled the stern and nearby was the aft flagstaff with the Greek flag flapping gently above them.

'Lunch will be ready at one,' Steph said.

'What are we having?'

'Braised beef with tomato and potatoes,' he replied, exhaling blue smoke. 'I woke Andy before coming out for a cigarette.'

'How is he?'

'Better, he's gone for a shower. Claims he met a girl.'

'Yes, I know. This intrigues me; can he speak English?'

'He knows some,' Steph said, with a smile. 'Anyway, he didn't realise how strong the English beer is compared to Greek lager. He's sensitive to alcohol and we rarely drink on board.'

'That explains it, but he seemed all right on the way back.' Remembering the boat, he glanced over the side to check that it had been lashed properly. Its stern was pointing upriver, indicating that the tide was coming in. 'I wonder how well he got on with her?'

'Says he got her phone number but can't remember her name.'

'She'll be impressed.' They laughed.

'Andy tells me most things. Says I look like his father, from what he's seen of him from photos.'

'Didn't he know him?'

'He died when he was young.' Steph took a final drag and flicked the stub over the side. 'I'd better make the salad. There's beer in the fridge, if you want some.'

'Best to give it a miss today.'

Later at lunch, Andy looked dishevelled. He ate little and spoke even less, which made the whole meal rather sombre. The others respected his need for silence.

It was one forty-five by the time Zen and Harry tied the boat to the pontoon and began their walk. The day continued warm and sunny and they wore short-sleeved tee-shirts, jeans and trainers. Zen had the strap of his Pentax camera over his shoulder. They took the road along the estuary towards the castle.

'Can you satisfy my curiosity?' Harry asked with a smile, in his gravelly voice.

'If I can.'

'What's the son of the owner doing here, living aboard a laid-up ship?'

'It's a long story.'

'Never heard of anything like it so it must be interesting.'

Zen started with his parents and how they came to be living in London. He told him of his upbringing and how the strains on his relationship with his father began to build over the years. Then he went through the events of the last few months. Harry asked a few questions and agreed that their way of thinking may be outdated but was by no means unusual. When Harry confessed that he was unconvinced this was sufficient grounds, Zen went on to relate the incident with Erika and how this had proved to be the clincher.

'Sounds like your past is catching up with you,' Harry remarked.

Once they had left the town, they walked through woods that ran along the water's edge, before coming to the castle, owned by English Heritage, for which there was a small fee to walk the ramparts and explore inside.

Afterwards they continued along the narrow track, which followed the coast up a slope and, after half an hour, led to a row of cottages overlooking a cove. Here the paved road ended and became a footpath following the cliff edge. It was dry underfoot so they continued, walking south west facing the afternoon sun. Every now and again Zen stopped to take a photograph.

'So what's your route to the *Amber*?' Zen asked.

'Well, I was born in Sparta and lived my early years during the civil war. They weren't nice times as you may have heard or read but, fortunately, I don't remember much. We were lucky. My father was a priest and well-respected and my mother a school teacher. Both were educated in music and literature and so my sister, two brothers and I received a good grounding in the arts. As I grew older I started to believe I had a calling, like my father, to be a priest.'

'How do you have a calling?'

'It's difficult to explain, but in my case it meant experiencing the presence of God or the spiritual and wanting to learn about it. Of course the only route to that knowledge that I knew of at the time was the priesthood.' Harry paused for a minute as if remembering something and then continued. 'So I started training. Then, during my early twenties, my uncle, a wealthy merchant from Thessalonica, died. He'd never married and left his money to us, his nephews and nieces. This coincided with my becoming disillusioned.'

'What were your reasons?'

'I don't know. I just decided it wasn't for me. But I didn't know what I wanted to do so I went in to do my military service.'

'That must've been a change.'

'It wasn't actually. I rather enjoyed it. I liked the discipline, which I'd already got used to. The fact that your day's planned gives you time to think. When I left

155

two years later I knew I wanted to travel and, having the financial means, went to North Africa, Palestine, India, Japan, then down to Australia. During that time I met people from all walks of life and searching for different things. My religious background gave my travels a spiritual significance.

'Anyway, when I got tired of Australia, I did a quick tour of New Zealand and then made a trip to California to visit a particular group of friends I'd made in India. What I found was a hotbed of New Age thinking and teaching. I decided that this was where I wanted to stay and, thanks to some wealthy and influential contacts, I got a green card. In the meantime I went on dozens of courses and retreats. Eventually, three of us started our own practice, which I ran.'

'Impressive,' Zen said, as they reached the head of a sandy cove with a steep path leading down to the beach. Some people were sitting on the rocks or on towels draped over the flat stones around the fringe. A few children were running with buckets and spades. 'Would you like to sit or shall we carry on?' he asked.

'Let's sit.'

They had to descend in single file so they could not speak. On the beach there were boulders imbedded in the coarse sand. Finding a flat one to sit on, they took off their shoes and socks. Sheltered from the breeze, the sun and sand were warm. The surrounding cliffs echoed with the sounds of excited children. There was the scent of freshly exposed seaweed, which mingled with the salty air.

'So what did your practice do?' Zen asked.

'Basically, we helped people develop their intuition so that they could get in touch with their life's purpose.

156

Then we trained them in the skills of focusing on and achieving their goals.'

'I never even got the chance to ask those questions. My life was decided for me.'

'Your purpose may not be what you do, rather how you do it.'

'Hmm, you say you ran it.'

'Basically, one of my colleagues was an astrologer, the other a numerologist. I taught the time management and goal setting side but also dealt with the practicalities of running the business.'

'So you covered the more pragmatic angle. Was it successful?'

'Very. We had private and corporate clients. But in that success lay the seeds of our failure. Seven years later one of my partners was an alcoholic, the other on drugs and I was going to end up down one or both those paths. I pulled the plug and left the country. Went back to stay with my parents. After a while, I decided I wanted to try something that combined the discipline of the army and also allowed me to travel, so I went down to Piraeus and embarked with the first company that would have me. Found I had an aptitude for engineering so that's how I came to be here.'

'But with your qualifications you could be on another ship making three times the salary.'

'True, but I don't need the money and my real purpose for travelling was to find interesting places to stay, a sort of random role of the dice. I'll try this for a while and see what happens.'

'Do you know much about the others?'

'Some. Steph's from a coastal village, can't remember which. Has an older sister who lives in Patras. Their parents owned a grocery with what we'd call a bed and breakfast above. After they'd left school they worked in it. It was a successful business. Steph was twenty-one, I think, when his sister married and the brother-in-law joined them in the shop. It was the early '50s and there weren't many jobs around. Anyway, one day Steph was told that the priority for work went to his brother-in-law, as he had to support his sister, and there wasn't room for him as well.'

'Ouch.'

'Get the impression that he was okay with it as he wanted to spread his wings. He decided to go to Athens and started to work in restaurants. He proved a good cook and became a chef. By the age of thirty he'd saved enough to start up a taverna of his own on one of the big islands, Rhodes or Crete maybe.'

'Sounds like he caught the start of the tourist boom'.

'Exactly. Then, when he was thirty-five he was called back home because his sister and brother-in-law had left to set up a grocery in Patras and his mother was now too old to work. Steph didn't see any problem with that. He sold up his taverna and invested the profits and most of his savings in the hotel and grocery, adding a small restaurant. This made perfect sense as he knew that one day the business would be his.' Harry took out a tissue from his pocket and wiped his brow. 'It's warm down here.'

'I know, I'm beginning to sweat too,' Zen said, looking out over the water. It was calm with hardly a wave. Several adults and children were swimming. It looked inviting.

'Once again, the business thrived,' Harry continued. 'After more years of hard work and at the age of forty-one, he was found a bride and married in 1972. She was an older spinster and, after two years of trying, they managed to have a daughter; Sophia's her name, I think. By now Steph had also built them a house not far from the business. Then in 1978 things began to go wrong. First his mother fell ill and nearly died. Six months later his father, who still worked at the hotel, accidentally started a fire while making coffee. The hotel burnt down and he died. Fortunately it was winter and there were no guests, but Steph lost everything.'

'Wasn't he insured?'

'Yeah, but the insurance company rejected the claim citing that it was arson that backfired and, after months through the courts, he was forced to accept a minute settlement. After his legal costs, he was left with little.'

'That's tragic, to lose your father and your livelihood at the same time.'

'He didn't have the means or the will to start again and jobs in Greece were scarce owing to an economic depression. A relative told him that there was good money on merchant ships so he ended up where you find him.'

'I suppose he's staying because he's worried he won't find another job.'

'Exactly, good engineers, for example, are always rare. Cooks and stewards are two a penny in these times.'

'What about Andy, what's his story?'

'Don't know so much about him. He's not as stoical or forthcoming. Think he's having a dispute with his family over inheritance.'

It was approaching six o'clock when they decided to walk back. For most of the return journey Harry was showing off his knowledge of plants and herbs and their culinary and medicinal properties.

'How do you know so much?' Zen asked.

'From my father. He picked it up from the older women of the village.'

As they approached the pontoon they saw that the harbour side café was still open so they decided to have a cup of tea.

As they acquired their drinks and sat down, Zen picked up a discarded local paper, an older edition of the one he had bought on Friday, and started leafing through it. On page three a strange article caught his eye. "Black Beast of Dartmoor strikes near Hexworthy" the headline read. 'Hey Harry, look at this.'

They were seated opposite each other at a table overlooking the estuary. Harry was facing upstream towards the *Amber*. He took the paper and studied the article. 'This attack took place last Tuesday night,' he said before reading on. 'It says there are black beast or dog legends throughout the UK going back hundreds of years. They attack pets and livestock but there's no evidence such animals exist. The legend developed from occasional sightings. The recent spate of incidents on Dartmoor started in the beginning of June. It also says that Exmoor, further to the north, and Bodmin Moor to the west, have had incidents and sightings going back many years.'

'At least we've some local excitement,' Zen said, taking back the paper and continuing to leaf through.

They arrived back at the *Amber* at seven thirty and found Andy waiting at the top of the stairs, sitting on a swivel chair from one of the cabins and smoking a cigarette. There was a pile of magazines on the deck beside him.

'Anyone going out?' Zen asked.

'I'm going back to the hotel to see if I can find the girl I met,' Andy replied, shielding his eyes from the sun.

'Doubtful she'll be there again,' Zen speculated.

'I think she said they worked there.'

'What? As barmaids?' Zen asked.

'No, in the restaurant,' Andy replied. 'Anyway, we'll see. What about you?'

'Staying in.'

'Me too,' Harry added.

'What time are you switching on?' Andy asked. 'I'd like a shower.'

'I'll do it now,' Harry replied. The sun was close to setting behind the hills.

'Good,' Andy said. 'I'll put out the lamps.'

'Where's Steph?' Zen asked.

'Aft somewhere,' Andy said, as he gathered up his magazines.

Zen walked along the poop deck passage to the stern and found Steph sitting on a bollard doing something unexpected. He had a cigarette in the corner of his mouth and resting on his legs was a tray on which were a pad of plain paper, a wooden box and a jar of black ink. They nodded to each other and Zen went and stood behind him to see what he was up to. He was sketching Castlewear across the water, framed on the right and bottom by the stern of the ship. He was using different pens for everything from the fine details of individual houses and trees to the more diffuse water and sky. Zen asked if he could see the finished work

161

and any others he had done. Steph looked back and smiled at the inferred compliment.

Chapter 20: Life on board

During the following week, the last in July, they fell into a routine that was to remain largely unchanged throughout the summer. After breakfast, Andy would work on the boat deck, which needed to be finished as soon as possible so they could collect water. In the morning, while the generator was on, he used the electric chipper to clear an area of rust of about one square yard. If necessary, Harry would come up with his welding equipment and deal with any cracks. After lunch, Andy would paint a protective undercoat on the morning's work and a top coat on the previous day's section. Afterwards he would have a nap before going out in the evening, often not coming back until after midnight.

Steph's main morning function, after clearing up breakfast, was to prepare the lunch, which he did in the galley wearing ear protectors to muffle the sound of Andy's electric grinder. He also found time to maintain the stores, give their cabins a clean once a week, change the bed linen and wash and iron their laundry. After the generator was turned off in the afternoon, he would mop the floors of the galley and mess. At the end of lunch he would often present Zen with a shopping list and on two occasions came out with him to post a letter, make a call and walk around the town. He spent his free time reading, letter-writing and occasionally, when the mood took him and the weather was favourable, sketching. Zen was later to discover that these drawings were sent with his letters to his wife and daughter. In the evenings after they had switched on again, he would make a simple supper, usually with leftovers, and prepare his ingredients for the next day.

Harry worked on the maintenance schedule he was given for the engine room. After lunch he would take up a pot of grease and treat wires, derrick pulleys, door hinges and any other moving parts. Every other day he started a fire in the oil drum and they burned deck insulation and refuse. The rest of the afternoon he either spent in his cabin or went out on his own after Zen had come back. On one of these occasions he had his hair cut and no longer sported a pony tail.

Zen would be the first up at seven thirty. He would put on his swimming trunks, running shorts and top, take the boat to shore and go for a thirty-five minute run. He followed the route that he had walked with Harry. When he reached the cove, he would strip down to his trunks and wade in for a few minutes before dressing and running back. Not once was there anyone else in the cove at that time.

At around eight thirty he would buy a newspaper and return to the ship. After a shower and breakfast he spent the morning with whoever needed him. He would either clear up after Andy, hold tools for Harry or help Steph tidy a freezer or store room. After lunch he would go ashore again. There was always shopping to do, post to collect, drinking water to top up, paraffin and petrol to buy and other jobs, like going to the bank to supplement their cash. He called the office and spoke to George every few days. When he rang on the first Monday, he had a word with Heather, who had spent Saturday night at his flat and was about to send the first envelope with his post.

He would return late afternoon and spend time in his cabin updating the accounts, writing the diary and reading before the evening switch-on.

On the Thursday morning they had their first problem. After breakfast, Steph reported that the extractor fan of the vegetable store was not working when he went to fetch ingredients. Harry had a look and decided that the motor had burnt out. Fortunately they had a spare, but it took all morning to replace it.

At around ten o'clock, Zen was sweeping up after Andy on the boat deck when he heard the accommodation ladder rattling. Looking over the side, he saw a man in uniform climbing up from a harbour office launch. His first thought was that they were in some kind of trouble with the authorities, but it turned out to be an officer of the Royal Air Force who wanted to know the dimensions of the *Amber* because of an aerial display being planned by the Red Arrows at the end of August. Zen took him to his day room and they looked up the information over a cup of coffee. After taking some pictures, he left.

Later that morning the launch came again, this time bringing three men from a local drain-clearing company. It took them an hour to clear the crew accommodation toilets.

Over lunch, Andy revealed that he was seeing the girl he had met on Saturday evening. Apparently she hung out with the same two friends and he was having problems getting her on her own. He tried to convince Zen and Harry to pair up with the other two. They unanimously declined. Instead they planned to pay a visit to the Tonebridge Sub Aqua Club.

There was some discussion regarding what they would do about the generator while Harry was out. He was happy to switch on before they left and show Steph how to switch off if there was a problem, but Steph did not want the responsibility and did not care if he had no power. Andy would be out anyway, so they only switched on for an hour so that Steph could prepare supper and Andy have a shower.

When Zen went out in the afternoon, he removed his car from the harbour master's car park so that it was available when they left the *Amber* at eight. Andy took them across in the launch and arranged to meet them at the pontoon at eleven thirty. The drive to Tonebridge took twenty five minutes and they arrived just after eight thirty.

The pool was well signposted and on the outskirts of town. After parking, they entered the building, reporting first to the reception counter. They were directed to the back of the lobby where a grey-haired woman sat beside a trestle table covered with brochures, newsletters and other diving publications. Behind her was a display board pinned with posters promoting the club and the exciting sport of scuba diving.

They approached and asked for the club secretary. She replied that he was currently in the pool training and enquired if they were the two gentlemen from Tonemouth she had been warned about.

When they said that they were, she asked them to sit while she filled out forms with their personal details. She examined their log books and asked for their medical certificates. As Harry's had expired, he would need to be re-examined and both of them would have to take a pool test. She suggested they watch the rest of the training from the gallery before going to the pub where the members would be meeting afterwards.

After mounting a flight of stairs, they entered the top of the observation balcony, finding a seat near the front row. In and around the pool were two dozen men and women wearing wetsuits and varying amounts of scuba gear. They were in clusters of three or four, engaged in a range of exercises. The surrounding area was scattered with equipment.

'Have you done any underwater photography?' Harry asked.

'To be honest, it doesn't appeal to me. I like taking black and white landscapes. I'm intrigued with the prospect of doing the same with the sea and coast.'

When the training had finished and the members went to change, they walked to a nearby pub, an old-style building with beamed ceilings and open fireplaces. In the lounge bar they bought a beer and sat at a table from which they could observe the entrance.

Soon the members began arriving. The woman who had manned the desk was the last to appear. She went up to a tall, grey-haired, bespectacled man sitting at one of the tables with two others, and who had a drink waiting for her. Without sitting and after spotting Zen and Harry, she bade her colleague follow her. They came over with their drinks, sat next to them and introduced themselves as John and Eileen Colburn. John was the membership secretary. They showed him their logbooks and he in turn was impressed with their experience.

He said that provided Harry passed his medical and they did all right in the pool test, they could be enrolled by the end of next week. Zen asked about a local doctor qualified to give such examinations and was given the names of two, both in Plymouth.

John and Eileen then spoke about the dives the club was planning for the rest of the season. This was the part Zen was interested in but, during the conversation, when he idly glanced across to the bar, his eyes fell upon a woman he had not noticed earlier, but who looked familiar. Her dark brown hair, with some lighter highlights, was swept back in a ponytail. He was looking at her profile and when she turned to speak to someone on her left, he remembered that he had seen her in and around Tonemouth. Such an attractive woman would not fail to make an impression on him.

She had almond shaped brown eyes and a small but cute nose. Pronounced cheeks and jaw gave her a sculptured look and her mouth was mischievous, her smile disarming. She had a clear complexion with a faint olive tint, and was shapely and athletic-looking. He guessed she was about five foot six. She wore a salmon pink blouse tucked into jeans. At one point she looked at him. Did she recognise him too? He resisted the temptation to look away and held her stare. He thought one of them was on the verge of a smile.

The moment was interrupted when Harry nudged him. 'Are you still with us?' he asked. 'John and Eileen want to know whether you can manage to take me for my medical by next Thursday. If so, they have spare equipment in a locker and we can have our pool test?'

'Don't see why not,' he replied. When he looked back, the woman had turned away and was talking to her friends.

Chapter 21: Alex

Alex drove up the hill and out of town at eleven fifteen. At this time of night her journey home would only take thirty minutes. She did not usually go to the pub after training but today she felt she had something to celebrate. Tim, her boyfriend of the last eighteen months, had left to return to Australia. He had finally given up trying to get her to marry or move in together.

Everyone in the club loved Tim. He was tall, fair-haired, had a good physique, and was caring but, like all the men who had come into her life, after the initial excitement, she had become bored. She reproached herself for taking pleasure in his departure and was careful not to show this to anyone. The fact that she could not hold down a relationship was not something of which she was proud. So much for the shrinks her parents paid for.

She never had a problem getting the man she wanted, that was easy. She genuinely felt desire and passion for them. But as soon as the relationship progressed beyond the initial stages into what she termed "cosiness": a certain level of intimacy and familiarity, she would go cold. It was the courting she enjoyed, the courting and the seduction. It was the only time she remained faithful.

Tim may be hurt now but he was lucky to be rid of her. She had lost count of how many times she had betrayed him. The last diving holiday, in the Red Sea with the club, was typical. The owner of the dive boat they had used for the week was a hunk from Yorkshire. As soon as they had set eyes on each other they knew they would be having sex. Every evening after supper, while the group was busy drinking, she would slip away to the boat and meet Hugh. That was what did it for her, being unfaithful, and the danger of being caught. That was when sex was at its best.

But she knew she had a problem and it was beginning to hurt her. She wanted to fall in love and know what it was like to be committed.

After the incident of a few years ago, her parents insisted she sought help. That was the most embarrassing chapter in her life. It started so innocently. During the day she was working as a translator for a local firm, as she was fluent in both French and Italian. She had bought her terraced cottage in Newham and needed help with the mortgage payments when interest rates rose relentlessly. Her parents, who lived in Exeter, did not like the idea of her having a lodger and instead suggested she offer private language tuition in the evenings. The demand was in Exeter so, after work, she would go to her parents' home to teach. The house was empty in the late afternoons, as her parents ran an Italian restaurant and both her sisters were married. Most of the students were from the Italian community.

Some of the seventeen and eighteen year old boys drooled over her. This was not a problem as she was not attracted to them. However, one boy was more mature for his age and Alex had to be careful not to show any interest.

When the exam results came out in August, this young man did particularly well and his mother insisted he take her a present. He had recently learnt to drive and one evening he knocked on her door, just as she had come out of the shower and was wearing her skimpy bathrobe.

When she shook his hand it was warm and dry and not damp and clammy like most teenagers. She'd had no choice but to invite him in, seeing how he had driven all that way. He'd accepted her offer of coffee, and while she was making it she'd asked after his family. While this conversation was taking place he was looking at her legs and bottom with a hunger that he could not hide.

'Enzo, are you all right?' she had asked him playfully.

'No,' he had replied, looking at his feet. 'I think I ought to leave.'

'You want me, don't you?' she'd ventured.

He temporarily lost the ability to talk. 'Yes, of course, Miss Palermo,' he had finally said, looking at her guiltily. 'You must think I'm pathetic.'

She thought he was sweet. 'How do you know I don't like you too?' This was too much for him and he could not reply. 'What are you afraid of?' she asked.

'I don't know what to do, and I'm afraid that if I keep looking at you, I'll embarrass myself.'

'Well, as far as knowledge is concerned, I know enough for both of us and, as I wouldn't want you to be embarrassed, I think you ought to come with me.' She led him to her bed.

Their affair had lasted until the end of September. He came to her most evenings. The poor boy lost a stone in weight. When the time came for him to leave for university, he refused to do so. In the end his parents forced the truth out of him and by the end of that day the church and community also knew.

171

Her parents, in dramatic Italian fashion, blamed her near-death experience for giving her brain damage. She barely remembered anything of that incident. It had happened one Easter when she was a toddler and they were having a picnic barbeque at a park by Dartmoor. She had choked on a piece of meat, or something, and had lost consciousness. Fortunately there was someone there who knew first aid and had managed to dislodge the obstruction and resuscitate her.

After the thing with Enzo, her parents gave her an ultimatum, conform or be disowned. Considering she could not teach any more and they now had to help her with her mortgage, she could not protest. The first therapist she saw was nice but ineffective. After her behaviour last Easter in the Red Sea, he referred her to someone else who was a hypnotherapist. With him she was making progress.

Other things were looking up as well. She had recently landed a job with an estate agent, which meant she no longer needed to work at her parents' restaurant nor required their financial support.

Eventually she pulled up outside her cottage, which was on high ground and within three streets of the water-front. There was a view of the harbour and sea from her bedroom and on warm days, with the windows open, the sounds and smells of the port permeated the house.

She was tired and could not wait to get to bed. This reminded her of something else that had changed. Before the latest therapist she never used to dream, or rather, as he explained, she would dream but suppress the memory. Now she remembered one or more dreams every night. The therapist told her to keep paper and pen by her bedside so she could write them down and then relate them to him.

These dreams were dark and anxious, involving people she had never met, places she had never been to and times she had not lived in. In some she was being chased. More often, she was doing the chasing. In others she was flying or floating. Things were certainly being stirred up.

She kept her bedtime routine short. When she slipped between the sheets it was past midnight. It was a calm evening and the curtain hardly moved in front of the open window. She remembered her evening at the pub and how nice it was to be with friends. There were also the two new men talking to the membership secretary. One of them could not keep his eyes off her; he looked vaguely familiar. But there was something else in his stare, apart from mischievous desire. There was compassion and tenderness as well. She did not see him leave, so could not tell how tall he was, but he looked athletic with dark brown hair and eyes, an angular face, prominent jaw, giving him a rugged look. His skin tone hinted that he could be Mediterranean, like her. Otherwise he appeared ordinary. If anything his friend was more physically attractive. He was slightly darker, almost Near Eastern, with a wonderful moustache, definitely older, more mature. She wondered what they were like.

Chapter 22: The Storm

Friday, 30th July 1982

Zen timed his return from running with the opening of the harbour office so that he could park his car back in their bay. The morning was humid and the newly risen sun hazy.

He returned with the papers, which he left in the mess before going up to shower and dress. When he came back down he was pleased to see that the others were also running late.

Steph had taken their orders and, while they waited, Harry and Zen dipped into the papers, while Andy read one of his magazines.

'Did you say you go for a dip when you reach that cove?' Harry asked.

'Yeah, why?'

'It says in here that due to the warm weather there are sharks about and bathers should be careful.'

'Mmm, don't go in that deep, nor do I stay long.'

They continued reading until Steph brought the breakfasts in.

'I've made the arrangements,' Andy announced.

'What arrangements?' Harry asked.

'You know, going out with these girls tonight,' Andy replied.

'We never agreed to that,' Zen reminded him.

'Don't be stuffy,' Andy said. 'All I want you to do is distract her friends so that I can have a private conversation with her.'

'I don't understand why you can't do that anyway,' Harry said.

'It's embarrassing, when you can't speak English, to have her friends eavesdropping.'

'How old is she?' Steph asked.

'Nineteen.'

'Jesus,' Harry said. 'It's obvious they're chaperones.'

'The three are inseparable; they do everything together. I need to find out if she'll meet me alone. You don't have to go out with her friends again.'

'I'm not dating a teenager,' Harry said.

'Neither am I,' Zen said. 'Where are you meeting them?'

'At that pub you didn't like,' Andy said.

'I wouldn't be seen dead there,' Harry said.

'You know, it's actually very nice,' Andy said. 'Upstairs there's another bar with tables and chairs.'

Zen thought for a minute; he would not have minded going out. 'I've an idea. If it's as you say and Harry agrees, we could sit upstairs and have a drink while you stay downstairs with these girls. Then, at some point, you come up with your girl and introduce her to us. That's it. That's your chance.'

'What if the others follow?' Harry said.

'Well, in that case we'll distract them for long enough,' Zen said. 'But then you must leave.'

'And it's the best offer you're going to get,' Harry added.

Andy had no choice but to agree.

Afterwards they went about their work with lethargy. Later, over lunch, they had the TV on, as they often did, and heard the one o'clock news and weather. A humid airflow had moved up from the Azores and a weather front packed with thunderstorms was crossing the Bay of Biscay, heading their way. It was due to hit the West Country and south coast that night.

In the afternoon, when Zen went ashore, he bought a tarpaulin for the boat and called one of the doctors in Plymouth to arrange Harry's medical. The earliest he could fit him in was Wednesday afternoon. While he was going about his business, the humidity and haziness increased until the sun was obscured. By the time he returned to the *Amber*, the sky was a steely grey. At seven o'clock it was so dark that they had to switch on the generator. They had an early supper of corned beef sandwiches, followed by cheese and biscuits, before getting ready to go out.

They left the *Amber* at a quarter past eight and were in the pub at half past. Andy waited downstairs for his friends while Harry and Zen went up to the first floor. It was nicer than they had imagined, with good views of the estuary towards the castle. They found a table by a window and Harry went to buy drinks.

Meanwhile Zen surveyed the clientele. It was a different age group to those downstairs, probably mid-twenties and above, mostly couples, with one group of three men at another table, and three women, sitting on stools, at the bar. When Harry returned he had bought Zen a pint of Tinner's ale and himself a Guinness.

'I didn't realise you liked Guinness,' Zen said.

'Had it in Ireland.'

'That's right; the ship was there over Easter,' Zen recalled. 'Somewhere up the Shannon. Can't remember the port.'

'Foynes, they had some great seafood and whiskey.'

'By the way, I forgot to tell you that I booked your appointment with the doctor for Wednesday afternoon.'

'Great, it'll give us something to do.'

'Tell me, did you also surf in California or just dive?'

'Both.'

'You were going to tell me what the diving was like.'

Harry described some of his adventures as they came to the end of their drinks. 'Another?' Zen asked.

'Shall we stick to halves?'

At the bar he stepped into the gap between the three women on his left and a couple on the right. He ordered the drinks and while he was waiting he looked round at the girls. The one furthest from him smiled. He smiled back.

'You don't know me,' she said, 'but I work upstairs at the harbour master's.'

'Glad to meet you,' Zen said, extending his hand across the other women. He did not recall seeing her. 'I'm Zen.'

'I'm Kim,' she said. She was medium height, slim and athletic, with a round, ruddy face and straight, dyed-blonde, shoulder-length hair. She was wearing a dark blue tracksuit. 'This is Ann and Linda.'

'Hi,' Zen said. Ann was pear-shaped with narrow shoulders, broad hips and chunky thighs. Her dark, wavy hair, almost raven-coloured, was combed back with an assortment of scrunchies and combs. She had a narrow face with small, delicate features and dark eyes. Her petit ears had pendant earrings which matched her necklace. She wore a navy, knee-length skirt and jacket with shoulder pads. Under it was a white blouse. Linda was slim, almost gaunt, with shoulder-length brown hair, held back with a headband, and a fringe that came down to her brown eyes. She wore a brown suit and jacket and cream blouse.

'We've been hearing about you,' Linda said.

'Can I buy you drinks then?' Zen offered hopefully. They look inquisitively at each other. 'In fact, why don't you join us?'

'Do you want to?' Kim asked the other two. 'We're not staying long.'

'Doesn't matter,' Zen said.

'Why not?' Ann replied.

'What are you drinking?' Zen asked.

'We're having the house white, I think,' Kim said, surveying her friends.

'Why don't you introduce yourselves to Harry and I'll bring them over.'

Zen returned with the drinks on a tray and sat between Ann and Kim. Ann took out a packet of cigarettes and offered one to Zen.

'I don't smoke,' he said. She did likewise to Harry, who also declined.

'You mind if I do?' Ann asked.

'Not at all,' Zen said. He watched her light up and decided she was rather pretty in a girlish sort of way and had a sweet smile. Meanwhile, he could overhear Kim explaining to Harry who she was and what she did at the harbour office. 'Do you live locally?' Zen asked Ann. Her light pink lipstick had left an imprint of her lips on the cigarette butt.

'This side of Plymouth.'

'How far is it? We have to go there Wednesday afternoon.'

'You need to allow an hour.'

'That's further than I thought. Do you work there?'

'Yes, Linda and I work together,' she said, looking over at her friend, 'for a charity.'

'What? Voluntary work?' Harry asked, having overheard.

'No, they're normal jobs, we get paid like everyone else,' Linda said.

'What does the charity do?' Zen asked.

'Provides assistance and refuge to abused women and their children,' Linda replied.

'Must be great to do something like that,' Harry said, impressed.

'To a certain extent,' Ann said. 'We're not in the front line. It's the local social workers and our helpline that do that. Linda works in the legal department and I'm PA to the boss.'

'What does the legal department do?' Harry asked.

'We give free advice and recommend solicitors if there needs to be litigation,' Linda replied.

'I think the girls are downplaying the work they do,' Kim said. 'There are a couple of local women I know who are the better for the charity's help.'

At this point, Andy arrived with the girls, Clare, Mandy and Zoë. They were nothing like Zen was expecting, which was silly, giggly teenagers in heels, short skirts and heavy makeup. Instead they looked quite sensible. Kim seemed to know them and, while she was talking to Mandy and Zoë, Andy had a few minutes, away from the table, with Clare. After no more than five minutes, they left.

Zen told them the story behind Andy's brief appearance. Then Kim explained that the three girls were students at Exeter University and were working the summer at the hotel.

'You have to admire him,' Kim said. 'He hasn't wasted time. They've only been here since the nineteenth,' she told her friends.

'But we only went out for the first time last Saturday,' Harry added.

'Kim says you're from London,' Ann said, turning to Zen.

'That's right,' Zen confirmed.

'Have you left anyone behind?'

'Actually, I've left a lot behind,' Zen said. He explained about his engagement, leaving out the reason why it failed. 'What about you? Is there someone?'

'Yes, I'm engaged to a merchant seaman, funnily enough.'

'Oh,' Zen said. He was disappointed as he was sure Ann was flirting with him.

'He goes away for six months and then comes back for one,' she said. 'He's four and a half months into his next cycle.'

'You live together?'

'No, I live with my mother.'

'So where does he stay when he's at home?'

'His parents. We've been engaged for seven years.'

'Seven years! Wow.'

Ann looked over at Kim and Linda. They were listening to Harry, who was telling them about the *Amber* and what it was like on board. She shuffled closer to Zen and in a lowered voice said, 'Edward's a bit old-fashioned.'

'It must be awkward, though, not to have somewhere to be alone.'

'Edward doesn't believe in sex before marriage.'

'Right, I see what you mean by *old-fashioned*, Zen said, surprised by the blunt revelation.

'He got it from his parents,' she continued. 'He's very ethical. He doesn't even talk about things like that. I suppose you're the opposite.'

'I do have some ethics, I hope.'

'No, I didn't mean that,' she said, embarrassed. 'I mean able to talk about things. You seem more open.'

'So I've been told.'

'Look, I've got to go soon,' she said, looking at her watch. 'I'm driving Linda home and promised to see Mum before she goes to bed. We only met for a drink.'

'All the way from Plymouth?'

'Actually we were both working in Exeter today and Linda lives in Tonemouth.'

'It's been a pleasure.'

'You know,' Ann said, leaning forward and lowering her voice again, 'your friend's just invited Linda to your ship for a meal.'

'Really?' Zen said, also keeping his voice down, although he could not help glancing over at them. 'I suppose you also overheard her reply?'

'I think she's going for Sunday lunch and bringing her son.'

'Her son! She's not with someone too, is she?'

'Linda doesn't have anyone.'

'Right, well, would you like to come too?'

'Very much. I've never been on a freighter'.

'Is it anything like the ones you fiancé's on?'

'He works on chemical tankers,' Ann said, looking over at Kim and giving her a knowing look.

'Is it time?' Kim asked. Ann nodded. 'Sorry, I have to leave too. I've got to let Ann's car out.'

They stood as they said goodbye and the girls headed for the stairs.

'Gosh! It's only ten,' Zen said looking at his watch. 'I suppose we'll have to wait till closing time.'

'When's that?'

'Eleven. Do you want another half?'

'Go on.'

'So what did you and Kim talk about?' Zen asked when he returned. 'It seemed technical.'

'Not really, she asked me what I did on board. She sails competitively you know.'

'Really? She has that weathered look.'

'She'll be racing in the regatta at the end of August.'

'And Linda?'

'She's very interesting,' Harry said. 'She has a young son, but she's on her own and I get the impression she's had to bring him up herself. I've asked them to come for Sunday lunch. Hope you don't mind?'

'Not at all. Ann overheard and told me.'

'She seems nice.'

'She's engaged to a merchant seaman, but I asked her to come too.'

'That's really good of you. It'll make Linda feel at ease. I'd like another chance to talk to her.'

'It could be interesting then,' Zen said. 'How old do you think they are?'

'I'd say early to mid-thirties.'

'They look younger.'

'They seem too mature to be in their twenties.'

'You're probably right. What's this?' Andy was approaching on his own. He had a half-finished pint of lager and sat at their table. 'Is there a problem?'

'The girls have left,' Andy said.

'Why so early?' Harry asked.

'They have to get up at six to serve breakfast. It catches up with them by the end of the week.'

'Did you do what you needed to do?' Harry asked.

'Oh yes, it turned out okay,' Andy replied. 'Just the two of us meeting tomorrow.'

'So why were the others stringing along?' Zen said.

'It seems they wanted free drinks and Clare was too embarrassed to tell them to go away.'

'At least it's been sorted,' Harry laughed, shaking his head.

'And it seems you both had a positive night too.'

'It's early days,' Harry said.

'Shall we finish these and go?' Andy asked. 'I'm tired.'

'It's this damn weather,' Zen said, looking out the window. 'It's murky out there. We'd better move before the rain starts.'

During the early hours the first rolls of thunder echo up the estuary. At the seaward end lightning flashes can be seen; each one closer to shore than the last; each one heralding a louder rumble. At the water's edge, not far from the *Amber*, the Black Beast stands on the mud and shingle beach where it was a few nights before. It watches the storm approaching and feels energised by it. It transforms itself into the black-backed gull and soars into the humid, restless air. It circles high above the ship's forward flagstaff before gliding onto the fo'castle. It returns to its earlier form.

It begins sniffing around the area, recording each smell, feeling the texture of the metal deck, observing every feature. All details are important, for when it can imagine this place clearly, it can materialise here directly.

Satisfied with its exploration of the fo'castle, it bounds down the flight of stairs onto the main deck and continues its progress aft.

Zen falls asleep quickly, getting into bed before midnight and feeling relaxed. A violent clap of thunder wakes him with a start and he feels the surrounding metal resonate. When the vibration subsides he hears the rain lashing the surrounding bulkheads. Picking up the torch from the bedside table he looks at the clock. It is nearly one thirty.

There is a gust of wind and he can hear the rain coming in through the portholes in the next room. The one above the bedside table is already shut because it caused too much draught. He gets up reluctantly. As he enters the day room he sees the wet curtains flapping against the bulkhead and there are already wet patches on the vinyl floor behind the desk. Avoiding these he shuts the portholes in turn and tightens the stainless steel bolts.

Pausing at the last one he looks out into the night. The rain is peppering the glass, blurring visibility. The lights of Tonemouth can be seen to the right and the fainter ones of Castlewear to the left. Both are partially obscured by the sheeting rain and no detail of the *Amber* can be seen for the darkness. Then lightning illuminates the scene and he has a brief image of the ship, the estuary and the surrounding hills. A clap of thunder immediately follows. The storm is practically overhead.

More lightning, and what impresses him this time is how agitated the surrounding waters are. He waits for the next strike, looking down at the deck to protect his eyes. When it comes, everything is momentarily lit up again.

It is then that he notices the dark shape. It is on the port side of hatch number two. His first thought is that it's an empty sack blowing in the wind. Harry must have used it to take waste wood from one of the holds to use as kindling for his makeshift incinerator. He looks in that direction but can see nothing through the wet glass and dark. He waits for the next strike.

When it comes it is as if the current has passed through his body, for the impression that burns itself onto the back of his eyes is of a large, shaggy, black dog standing on the deck. He remains staring at the same place. When the next flash comes, it is still there, but this time he has the feeling that it is looking at him. He thinks he can see its eyes glowing green. A chill goes through his body and he feels his skin erupt with goose pimples.

The next flash comes after what seems an interminable interval, but the animal has gone. He waits through two more flashes, but nothing. Has it moved on or is it hiding? After his experience with the gull, he remembers the bathroom porthole, which is still open. He tears himself away, nearly slipping on a patch of wetness, strides into the bathroom and slams the porthole shut, tightening each bolt until he can turn it no more. He wonders if anyone else is awake.

He goes back to the day room and looks back out on to the deck through several more flashes, but sees nothing. He draws the curtains and starts pacing the room in the dark. He is wide awake and his stomach is churning. He is certain all the exterior doors were locked, having checked them before going ashore, but a porthole might be open in the galley. Surely none was large enough for something that big to crawl through.

He stays awake for another half hour until the worst of the storm and his anxiety have subsided.

Eventually, the rain stops, the wind drops and it turns quiet again. He gingerly gets into bed and falls asleep.

Saturday, 31st July 1982

The alarm stirred him at seven thirty, but he ignored it; to hell with jogging. He was not going to be the first up this morning.

The generator woke him again at nine. This time he did get up. There was a damp smell in the air, which was probably caused by the wet floor in the day room. He drew the soggy curtains and opened the portholes. At first he thought that the glass had misted up, but then realised they were surrounded by dense fog. Looking out, he could only see as far as the lockers of the fo'castle. He shaved, showered and dressed.

When he went down to the mess, the others were sitting at breakfast. They were laughing at something as he entered. Andy was the first to speak. 'I was just telling Steph that, thanks to you both, I made progress with Clare.'

'Glad we could be of service,' Harry said.

'And thanks to me, you also made friends,' Andy pointed out.

'And we're grateful too,' Zen said. 'Anyway, were any of you woken by the storm?'

Each acknowledged that they had been.

'I had to shut my portholes to stop the rain coming in,' Zen said, knowing that both Harry and Andy also faced forward. 'I watched it for ages'.

'Mine's under cover,' Steph commented.

'I pulled the sheet over my head,' Andy said. 'Unfortunately, the magazines that my friend sent were on the desk and got soaked.'

'I only needed to shut the porthole in my bathroom,' Harry added, studying Zen. 'I take it the fog stopped you going out this morning?'

'I'm a fair weather runner. Any excuse to stay in bed.'

By now the others had finished eating and had left. The fog had cleared, so after breakfast Zen went out, taking the rubbish that could not be burnt. The harbour master had allowed them to use the bins in their car park. He collected the mail, only a letter for Steph, and did some shopping before returning on board.

Later, he went upstairs to help Andy on the boat deck, but they could not work on it as it was still too wet from the storm. Instead Andy went to the paint locker to get more supplies for the week ahead.

Zen decided to see if Harry needed a hand. He descended to the poop deck and passed through the engine room casing at the start of the passage that led to the crew's mess. He stepped onto the scaffold above the engine room.

It was brighter here. A surprising amount of natural light filtered through the skylight two decks above. The bulkheads were painted a cream colour. The exhaust gas pipes from the generators, the main engine and the boiler, coated in aluminium paint, ran up past him to the funnel. Whereas most of what Zen had so far seen of the ship cried of neglect, here, superficially at least, care had been taken.

The system of multi-storied, metal scaffolding, railings and stairs on which he stood had, over the years, become covered in grease. Bins of rags were placed at the entrances and landings. He took a handful before proceeding further.

He descended two levels to a lattice-patterned deck that spanned the floor area. The sound of the generator was now very pervasive and the smell a mixture of oil and diesel.

Rising through the middle of this platform was the top of the main engine. The six cylinder heads dwarfed him and everything else; and the sump was still two decks below. Aft of this, in a space narrowed by two settling tanks for lubricating oil, were the three diesel generators positioned in a row. Each was as large as a mini-bus. The middle one was being worked and, as he approached, the noise became deafening.

Zen found Harry oiling the rocker heads. When Harry saw him he indicated he should follow. They walked back, past the main engine block, either side of which were storerooms for spares and a fully equipped machine shop, past the two starting air cylinders and the top of the boiler, while heading for the forward, starboard corner and the glazed, soundproofed control room.

Once inside, and with the door shut, it was possible to talk normally. It was set out like a conference room. There was a six-seater rectangular table in the middle, at the head of which was set into the table top the automatic controls for the main engine from which compressed air, diesel, fuel oil, and speed could be adjusted.

'I see you're using the middle generator,' Zen said.

'It's the smallest of the three, so uses less diesel. Whenever I need to top up on compressed air, I'll run a cycle with one of the others.'

The wall behind the head of the table contained the electrical control panel with its ammeters, voltmeters, rheostats and switches. From here the electricity produced was distributed.

'What happens when you switch off?' Zen asked.

'I have to come in here and disengage the power first, then the reverse to switch on.'

'Can I help you with anything?

'Not really.'

'About last night…'

'You want to know if I saw anything?'

'It was a dog, wasn't it?' Zen asked.

'I saw it on the deck when I was securing my porthole. Then I think I heard it bound up the stairs and run down the poop deck passage.'

'How did it get here? Did it fall off a boat in the storm and somehow manage to find its way on board?'

'Okay, so how did it get onto the platform of the ladder, which is a good two feet from the water?'

'Maybe it climbed onto the boat first.'

'Possible, but where's it now? I'm no expert but can't imagine it would've climbed back down and jumped into the sea again.'

'I don't know, perhaps if we looked…'

'I already have. It's not on the *Amber*.'

'Maybe, if it fell off a boat, its owner followed and rescued it.'

'I suppose so,' Harry said, as he started walking back out. 'What else could explain it?'

'Why didn't you mention anything in front of the others?'

'They may have got spooked.'

'Good point,' Zen said, wondering why he had got so worked up about it. Then he remembered those eyes and the way they had looked at him.

'C'mon, about time I showed you how this generator works.'

Chapter 23: Ann

Sunday, 1st August 1982

Zen slept well that night. When he got up in the early hours to use the bathroom he saw that the fog had returned. It made it so eerily dark and quiet, so disconnected from the shore that they could be anywhere, the middle of the ocean, suspended in time or space, a ghost ship passing from one dimension to another.

He would have gone running first thing but the fog was too dense. He was not going to risk an accident and he knew that none of the ferries operated in such conditions.

After breakfast, Harry went to his engine room and Andy stayed to help Steph with lunch. Zen went upstairs to close the accounts for the previous month. He would post them tomorrow.

When he had finished, he visited the fo'castle store room where he had seen some wooden stools. He chose one and put it outside on his balcony, as he referred to this bit of deck. On his way he stopped off at the pantry and made himself a coffee. He could hear Andy and Steph in the galley, at work, so he did not disturb them. Then he sat outside to read yesterday's paper as he watched the fog disperse and the shoreline come back into view. It was turning into another warm and sunny day.

At one point Andy went ashore for an hour. At breakfast he had mentioned he needed to make a phone call and Zen had asked him to get the papers. These he brought up on his return.

Later, when Zen was on his way out to pick up the girls, he stopped off in the mess to find that the table had a centrepiece of flowers. Andy must have heard him because he came out of the kitchen smiling. 'You know how difficult it is to find flowers on a Sunday? I had to go to the petrol station,' he said.

'Has Harry seen them?'

'No, he's still dressing and tidying his cabin. You two have no idea how to treat women, do you?'

Ann was early. She appeared before him as he sat on a bench close by the steps to the pontoon, gazing across the water at Castlewear with the sun on his face. She looked different today, having her dark hair swept up instead of back. She was wearing a white, open-necked blouse, which showed the top of her white lace bra, and a blue denim skirt, which came just above her knee. On her feet she had plain canvas wedges and she was carrying a canvas holdall.

'You'd better sit, Linda hasn't come yet,' Zen said, sliding along to give her more space.

'No need, I can see them.'

When he stood and looked towards the park, he spotted them approaching. 'How old's the lad?' he asked of the slim, good-looking, fair-haired youth.

'Stephen's twelve.'

'Nearly as tall as his mum,' Zen observed. He estimated Linda's height to be five foot six, whereas Ann was slightly shorter.

When they arrived and had greeted each other, he led them down the steps to the pontoon and boat. The girls were as excited as Stephen to get into it and, as they made their crossing, he pretended to give them the tourist-speak that he had heard from the guided tour boats, which made them laugh.

'I wouldn't leave the day job,' Linda said.

'That bad?' Zen asked.

'Worse than you can imagine,' Ann replied.

When they arrived, Andy came down the ladder to help them up. Harry was waiting at the top. Once on board they went into the mess where they met Steph and to whom Linda presented a bottle of red wine, Ann one of white and Stephen a box of chocolates. The table was loaded with dips, salads and other dishes arranged around the flowers. There was Greek music playing from a small tape deck on the sideboard. All four portholes were open, letting in the warm summer air, the shrieking of gulls, as well as the sounds of the day's activities on the water.

'Lunch is ready whenever you want it,' Steph announced.

'Can we freshen up?' Linda asked.

'You can use the WC on this deck,' Zen said, taking them back into the poop deck passage and showing them the way.

Afterwards they sat to have their starters, Zen between Ann and Andy. The latter was next to Stephen who had Steph on his other side. Steph was quizzing the boy about his school. Next to Steph were Linda and then Harry. They helped themselves to the various dishes.

'Well, cheers,' Zen said, as the adults had a sip of white wine. He turned to Ann. 'How was the drive?'

'Pretty good.'

'Have you always lived in Plymouth?'

'And my parents before me,' she replied. She held a basket of lightly toasted pitta breads, which she handed to Zen after taking one herself.

'Any brothers or sisters?'

'One older sister. She's married with three children. Lives with her husband in Bristol.'

'What about work?'

'I've always worked locally. I'm afraid my life's rather boring. I've never even been abroad.'

'You don't say. What do you do when you've time off?'

'I've been to South Wales, Scotland and Cornwall. Always with Mum, though, and sometimes with Edward too.'

'I'm surprised, thought you'd be more independent.'

'I'm from a small community and so is Edward. We've known each other since we were at school.'

'Apart from Edward, has there been anyone else?'

'Well, although we've been engaged for seven years, we've been going out since our teens.'

'Is that a no then?'

'More a way of avoiding the question,' Ann said, as she bit off half a stuffed vine leaf. 'But I'll admit that I've been out for drinks with other men.'

'When Edward's been away?'

'Yes, do you think I'm awful?'

'I'm in no position to judge.'

'Besides, I'd like to find someone I can talk to, a friend. I feel I could tell you anything,' Ann said, flirting with him again.

'I'm flattered. But you must have girlfriends?'

'Yes, lots, but Linda's the only one who's close,' Ann said, looking over at her.

'What about your sister?' Zen asked. He had followed her gaze and noticed that Harry and Linda were in a world of their own. Further over, Steph and Andy were talking with Stephen who was looking about him as if he was aboard an alien spaceship and not just a freighter.

'We get on fine, but you can't discuss personal things with your own blood. You never know when you might regret it.'

'I suppose,' Zen said, although he could not imagine Ann keeping much to herself.

'You mentioned you also have a sister.'

'Yes, younger than me. We hardly speak though.'

'Really? Why's that?'

'We weren't close to begin with, but ever since I moved out she's even more distant, for some reason.'

'Probably envy,' Ann suggested. 'Probably wishes she also had the opportunity to assert her independence.'

'You might have a point.'

'You're lucky to live on your own. My father died years ago and I couldn't leave Mum.'

Zen explained how he had always yearned to do so and what he'd had to do to buy his flat.

'I like men who know what they want and pursue it. Unfortunately, I couldn't leave home because Mum, bless her, has arthritis and needs caring.'

'Sorry to hear that.'

'Both her husband and father were fishermen and, from a girl right up till my father passed away, she repaired nets, which is men's work really. I suppose that's what damaged her joints.'

'Sounds like it. When did he die?'

195

'It's been five years.'

'What from?'

'Started as lung cancer, then spread to his liver. He smoked and drank a lot.'

'You'd think you'd have stopped.'

'I don't smoke more than ten a day,' Ann said, defensively. 'The only good thing about my mother's hands is that it stopped her smoking as she can't hold a cigarette. Out of respect I don't smoke at home, so I can sometimes go a whole day.'

'That's good. Did you know Linda before you worked at the charity?'

'Yes, she's responsible for my getting the job.'

'How so?'

'She used to do a few afternoons at the Citizen's Advice Bureau in Plymouth, when Ruth discovered her?'

'Ruth?'

'Our boss. At the time that Linda was at the CAB, Ruth was having problems of her own. She'd just moved down from London and was looking for accommodation, a job, that sort of thing. Eventually she started working for the Woman's Refuge, and when she began managing the Plymouth branch, she remembered Linda and asked her if she wanted to do such work full-time and be paid.'

'So she went for it.'

'Considering she wasn't working at the time, yes. I joined a year later.'

'You mentioned you're Ruth's PA.'

'I was in a similar job before.'

'You get on?'

196

'In an arms-length sort of way,' Ann said. 'As it probably should be.' She seemed to be thinking about this as she took a sip of wine. She carefully dabbed her mouth with the serviette. Then she lowered her voice and leant towards Zen. 'She's closer to Linda and her son and she's very nice, superficially, but there's something about her that's…'

'That's what?' Zen asked, glancing over to Linda. She seemed too absorbed in Harry to overhear anything and Stephen was concentrating on something Steph was telling him.

'I don't know what to say. I've no evidence, so call it woman's intuition, but there's something about her that's unsettling, like you don't want to get on the wrong side of her.'

'Interesting. We shan't be meeting her in a dark alley then.'

'I didn't mean it to sound extreme,' Ann said, looking guilty. 'She's fair and I like my job.'

'Still, it's a lot of driving.'

'Linda and I are in Exeter for the summer and then not every day. We're helping to fill in for those on holiday. I'll be back in Plymouth full-time by the end of August.'

'When Edward's back.'

'That's right. What about you? Do you think your parents will try to find you another bride?'

'If they don't disown me first.'

'I don't understand how people can do that.'

Zen spoke about his parents and their backgrounds and what it was like to be part of the Greek shipping community in London. Ann was fascinated. 'It's like hearing about a family saga,' she observed.

The starters were followed by garlic roast lamb with potatoes and rosemary. Everyone agreed it was delicious. Both Ann and Linda were interested to hear about the different parts of Greece that Andy, Steph and Harry were from. Like most non-Greeks, they had only heard of the islands and had no idea of the attractions of the mainland.

'Would our guests like a tour before dessert?' Steph asked. 'It's not quite ready.'

'I think we need some exercise,' Harry said, feeling his sides.

It took them an hour and a half, mainly because Stephen asked so many questions, particularly in the engine room. He wanted to know what every machine did and, when on the deck, Harry had to promise him that one day he could come on board and watch the derricks and cranes remove the hatch covers. He was disappointed when he was not allowed in any of the holds.

It was nearly three thirty before they sat down again to biscuits, fruit and cheese and, at the end, Steph brought out a freshly-baked *galactoboureko*, a semolina-based, creamy custard pie made with filo pastry. It was impressive. Afterwards, they had Greek coffee and it was the first time the girls had tried that too.

'Yours is different to everyone else's,' Ann observed.

'I have mine with evaporated milk,' Zen explained. 'I had a job convincing Steph to make it.'

'He claims it's popular in Crete,' Steph said.

'I've never heard of it,' Andy commented.

'If anyone wants to use the bathroom, they should do so in the next twenty minutes,' Harry said. 'I'll be switching off the generator. You can come with me and do it yourself, young man,' he said to Stephen, whose eyes widened noticeably.

Ann looked puzzled, so Zen explained about the pressure in the pipes. She said she did want to use the bathroom and, as Linda had gone to the one nearby, he took her up the stairs to the bridge deck. 'Let me show you my balcony first,' he said, taking her out on his bit of deck. 'I sit here and read when I've nothing to do. As you can see I get the afternoon sun.'

'What a beautiful view; we're so high.'

He showed her round his day room and cabin, and left her in the bathroom.

He sat at the table to wait and continued reading the papers. Five minutes later she came out and sat next to him. 'Thanks for making lunch so nice,' she said. 'Even the bread was tasty. Where do you buy it?'

'We usually get it from the supermarket, but what you had today was baked on board.'

She moved close to him, putting her hand on his thigh. 'You've got nice friends and you seem to get on.'

'And it's not been two weeks,' Zen reflected. He felt the warmth of her body next to his.

Against his better judgment, he put his left arm around her back and held her hand with his right. They were about to kiss when the lights went out, accompanied by the piercing siren. Zen went to reset the alarm. He returned as the generator died away. 'We should go downstairs, the others will be wondering what we're up to,' he said.

When they got to the poop deck there was no one in the mess. 'I think I hear voices,' Ann said. They were coming from the direction of the galley. When they went through it was empty, so they stepped out onto the stern. They found Harry and Linda sitting on bollards enjoying the sunshine, while Stephen was transfixed by the windlass.

'I was just about to take them ashore,' Harry said.

'We have things to do,' Linda explained, 'but we've had a wonderful time, thank you.'

'Don't mention it,' Zen said.

'You coming too?' Linda asked Ann.

'Ought to. I always have Sunday dinner with Mum, although I don't think I'll be eating again.'

Harry took them ashore while Zen watched. It was five o'clock before he returned, having walked Linda and Stephen home. Zen was standing at the top of the ladder, enjoying the sun and feeling too lazy to move.

'Are you seeing Linda again?' Zen asked when Harry was beside him.

'Definitely,' Harry said, looking out across towards Tonemouth as if trying to spot her. He had his left hand above his eyes to shield them from the glare.

'Surprised such a good-looking woman's still single.'

'It's been three years since she was abandoned by her partner. Times were hard at first. They only got better when her boss offered her a job with flexible hours enabling her to work and look after Stephen.'

'Ann's told me about this Ruth. I believe she was returning a favour.'

'So I've been told.'

'I guess she needed time to get used to the idea of seeing men again.'

'That's partly so.'

'But you're not so sure?' Zen said, catching the scepticism in his voice. Harry looked distracted.

'Of course, Linda's admiring about Ruth, you know, like she's her saviour, but she also seems overly protective.'

'I don't understand.'

'Linda's told me about her work and it appears that this Ruth arranges things so that they're always working together.'

'Maybe Linda's good at her job.'

'Maybe, but then she calls her during weekends and evenings. Sometimes, she turns up and invites herself in.'

'What does Linda say about it?'

'She thinks it's the behaviour of a caring friend and that when it was Ruth who was in trouble, years ago, Linda also kept in touch on a regular basis.'

'So there you have it, there doesn't have to be an ulterior motive.'

'It's not the same thing. Linda's no longer in a crisis. This seems somehow intrusive, as if Ruth's keeping tabs.'

'Do we know Ruth's story?'

'If Linda knows, she hasn't told me, but I get the impression it was traumatic.'

'Gosh. Still, it's early days, and you've got to be careful. This could be quite innocent and you could appear to be the one who's possessive.'

'I know. It's idle talk. It doesn't worry me. On the positive side, Ruth's been good with Stephen. She's taken him out at weekends, to give Linda a break, that sort of thing. Stephen calls her "Auntie Ruth".'

'She's very fond of them,' Zen said, although he had in mind the unease Ann had expressed.

'Hey, it's a shame to waste such an afternoon. Feel like a walk to the castle?'

'Good idea. What about the others?'

'If they're in their cabins, I wouldn't like to disturb them,' Harry said, looking back through the poop deck entrance. 'We'll only be an hour.'

'Let's go.'

After they came back, Zen went to his cabin. The generator was back on at seven, earlier than usual. When he came down he found the others watching football. It turned out Andy was a West Ham fan. Later, when Steph got up to prepare supper, Zen offered to help.

'I'm not interested in football,' Zen said, once they were in the galley, 'but I'm surprised Andy knows so much about the English teams.'

'Our league football's weak,' Steph explained. 'We're only a small country, so we know about the European teams, not just the English ones.'

'What shall we eat?'

'After the lunch we had, I think we'll stick to fruit and cheese. I'll make up some platters that we can have with bread.'

'Should I get the cheeses?'

'No, I'd better go, I know which ones to use first. Besides, I want to take out what we're having tomorrow. Why don't you fetch me two platters and two bowls from the sideboard?'

When the food was ready, they put out a low table in front of the TV and feasted for the rest of the game.

Chapter 24: The Visitors

Monday, 2nd August 1982

In the afternoon, Zen went ashore. Having been to the post office and done some shopping, he called George Pittas at the office. After bringing him up-to-date with the status of the ship, George informed Zen that his twenty year old son would be coming the next day, with a friend, to stay on board until the weekend. They would probably be arriving in time for lunch.

'It's no problem George, just a bit sudden.'

'Actually, it's my idea. I'm fed up watching Theo go out all night and sleep most of the day.'

'You probably did the same.'

'I know, its envy, but at least if he does it down there he might learn something about ships.'

Back on board he informed Steph about the visitors and told him to prepare a couple of cabins. After lunch he helped Andy on the boat deck until they decided it was too hot to carry on.

The fine weather continued the next day. Zen spent the morning down in the engine room. Once every few weeks Harry wanted to inspect the machinery, test that it worked and effect repairs if necessary. It was an opportunity for Zen to learn something, as well as lend a hand.

At twelve he came back up, intending to go ashore to meet their expected guests, only to find that they were in the mess. They had arrived earlier than expected and hired someone to bring them on board. Steph had showed them their cabins, and they were now enjoying a pre-lunch beer and smoke.

John and Theo were both tall and slim. They wore long-sleeved, collarless, off-white shirts, navy jeans with broad leather belts and trainers. Both sported long, brushed-back hair. John had a fair complexion with straight brown hair, while Theo was darker skinned with black wavy locks, much like his father. After greeting them and thinking they would want to explore the ship, Zen suggested a tour after lunch, but Theo made it clear that their intention during the week was to familiarize themselves with the local beaches and clubs. Andy volunteered to be their nocturnal guide and they debated the merits of Exeter, Torquay, Paignton and Plymouth. It seemed that Andy was already well acquainted with the local nightlife. Zen concluded that he would not be seeing much of them for the rest of the week.

After lunch Andy took the boys ashore and, upon his return, worked with Zen and Harry on the cargo deck. They started spreading the fish oil, that Andy had spoken about, which was supposed to loosen the rust from the deck and protect it from further corrosion. Anything to improve its appearance for a prospective buyer, Zen thought. However, not only did it smell bad, like fish that had been rotting for weeks, but it was to have other undesirable consequences.

Wednesday, 4th August 1982

The day started with rain, so any outside work was impossible. This was just as well as their guests were still in bed, which precluded using the electric grinder. Over breakfast Andy admitted that they had not got back until two that morning.

John and Theo managed to get up for lunch and the discussion around the table was mainly about the night before. It seemed that, despite their best efforts, they had nothing to show for it, girl-wise, so they planned to visit a different club in Torquay. Andy spoke as one who had taken it upon himself, as a matter of honour, to see to it that both boys scored.

After eating, Zen allowed Andy a nap, while he drove Harry to Plymouth for his medical. This he passed without a problem.

It was not until after lunch the next day that the rain finally stopped and left them with a problem. The starboard side of the cargo deck had flooded from the accommodation bulkhead all the way to hatch number three. They realised that this was caused by the fish oil they had applied a few days earlier. It had had the desired effect of loosening the rust, but when it had rained, all the debris had been washed down the drains and blocked them. Not only that, but the dark, murky water stank.

With Zen's help, Andy attempted to free the scuppers with wires, with no success. They tried to enter the upper wing tanks through which the drain pipes passed, but could not undo the nuts of the manholes. Harry would try to loosen them the next day, but the task was the more odious because the tank tops were immersed in the disgusting puddle they were trying to clear.

They switched on at six, before Harry and Zen left for the diving club for their pool test. This also went without a hitch and later in the pub Harry was given a list of dive shops from which he could purchase or hire new and second hand gear. They calculated they would have at least two months of diving left in the season so it was worth the expense. On Sunday, the club was planning a day at a local site. It sounded interesting so they would have to get Harry's equipment organised tomorrow. It meant another trip to Plymouth.

Friday, 6th August 1982

In the morning the sanitary pump packed up. This was not a problem because there was a back-up, but it had to be repaired in case the standby also failed.

The consequence of not having one in use was that they would not be able to flush their toilets, which would be a disaster with guests on board and the weekend looming. Unfortunately, with Harry working on this, it meant they could not free the scuppers, so they would have to endure the lake and worsening smell for another day.

Harry seemed to know what to do with the pump but needed Zen's help in order to fix it promptly. It was typical therefore that of all the days that they could come, the Customs and Excise chose that morning to pay a visit. They wanted to check the bonded stores and so opened the store room and counted every packet of cigarettes and every bottle of whiskey. They performed this with a zeal that betrayed their eagerness to find a discrepancy and then appeared disappointed when all was in order. At the end, as consolation, they expected a cup of coffee and a chat.

Fortunately, Theo and John were there to help with the conversation as one of the Customs' officers had a son who was about to go to university and was interested in knowing about the application process.

The officials only decided to leave when Steph announced lunch. During the meal Zen discovered there was more happening that weekend than he had anticipated. Andy and the boys were planning a party on Saturday night to entertain their new friends. Zen said it was fine with him as long as it did not involve the generator being on too long, triggering complaints from the locals.

After lunch Zen took Harry to Plymouth to buy diving equipment. On the way to the car Zen called the office to give George Pittas an update and was informed that they should expect him for lunch on Monday. He also checked the post and was surprised to find a message from Ann. She asked if he could meet her at seven thirty in the pub and, unless he called her, she would assume he would be there.

They bought everything Harry needed and Zen recharged his cylinders. They also bought a guide to the local dive sights. They decided that, irrespective of whether they dived with the club or not, and because they had a suitable boat, they could organize their own excursions.

Back on board, it was a rush to get ready before going out again. At seven, the boat with Andy, Zen, John and Theo was on its way to shore. Harry stayed behind to try to finish the repairs to the sanitary pump, this time with Steph's help.

The upstairs lounge was busy and there was nowhere to sit, so Zen waited for Ann while standing at the bar. She did not arrive until eight thirty, apologising for being late, which was due to an accident on the main road.

'I don't want to stand,' she said, when he offered her a drink. 'Can we go somewhere else?'

'Sure,' Zen agreed, draining his glass.

'How's your week been?' she asked, as they walked through the back streets, slipping her hand into the crook of his arm.

Zen brought her up-to-date, telling her about the visitors and party.

'Weren't you going to invite me?' Ann said, sounding hurt.

'Of course you're invited.'

They came to a cobbled square where there was a pub with seating at the front. They found a free table and Ann sat while Zen went inside to buy drinks. He came back to find her smoking. 'You seem tense,' Zen observed when he sat down.

'Am I? Sorry,' she said, relaxing her shoulders. 'I was ages getting here. I wanted more time with you. Now we've only got an hour before I have to leave.'

'Your mum?'

'There are some things she can do and some she can't. She can feed herself if I make a meal and she can manage to place it in the oven to reheat. But she can't handle buttons, so I have to help her dress and undress.'

'What about more private functions?'

'She can do those all right, as well as wash herself.'

'How are you going to manage tomorrow night?'

'If it's something like that, I can get a neighbour to put her to bed,' Anne said, stubbing out her cigarette in the plastic ashtray.

'Still, it can't be easy having to get up and get your mother dressed first thing.'

'You have to do what you have to do.'

'Tell me about your work.'

'I take Ruth's calls, run her diary, arrange her meetings, some of which I also attend, prepare agendas, take minutes, write her correspondence and more.'

'Sounds busy.'

'She runs the South West division.'

'And who are these meetings with?'

'Potential donors and benefactors mainly, then there are other complimentary organisations like the social services.'

'I see; so are you the only one who attends these meetings?' Zen asked, remembering something Harry had told him the other day.

'And Linda.'

'Why Linda?'

'She's Ruth's legal adviser, remember. She tries to have her there as often as possible.'

'Is that necessary?'

'I'm no expert, but my feeling's not always.'

Zen wanted to know more. This Ruth was stimulating his curiosity, but he did not want Ann to feel she was being interrogated. 'When you were explaining what you did for Ruth, you said "and more".'

'Well, I shouldn't be telling you this, but she's a busy lady. Apart from her daytime work, she also gets invited by organisations, such as the Women's Institute, to dinners, to give talks promoting the work, and so on. This is unofficial but necessary to grease the wheels. What I'm trying to say is that I also run her social diary, unofficially.'

'You must be in touch every day.'

'During working hours.'

'So what was it that happened to Ruth, you know, to cause her to need the CAB, all those years ago?'

'I don't know, but it doesn't have to be anything dramatic. It could've been a divorce or redundancy. Maybe she was looking for accommodation.'

'Does Linda know?'

'She might, but hasn't said anything, nor have I asked.' Ann said, looking a bit vacant, as if trying to remember something.

Zen decided he had probed enough. 'You must enjoy your work, though.'

'I love it; we travel all over Devon and Cornwall for meetings.'

'What about Edward, does he enjoy his job?'

'He hates it.'

'Interesting choice of career then.'

'It pays well.'

By the time they left it was ten-thirty. Zen walked Ann to her car.

'What about tomorrow?'

'You have to be at the pontoon by seven thirty,' Zen replied.

'I have it,' she called out as he began to walk away.

'Have what?' Zen asked, turning back round to face her.

'What's been pestering me.'

'Tell me.'

'Well, I shouldn't have taken this long to remember. It's something that happened shortly after I joined.'

'I'm listening.'

'We had a woman come in with her baby, both battered as it turned out. She was hysterical and talking a language none of us understood. She was making such a noise that Ruth came in from the meeting room; she was interviewing someone, I think. Anyway, as soon as she joined us, me and this other lady, as we were trying to communicate with the client, she started speaking her language. And I don't mean in a broken sort of way, it was fluent. She calmed her down and dealt with her herself.

'You're joking,' Zen said, realizing what she was going to say.

'Yes, it was Greek. That's an unusual language to learn.'

'Few would choose to do so unless they've lived there. No explanation followed?'

'I told Linda and she asked Ruth about it, as you would in conversation, and apparently Ruth got angry and stonewalled her.'

'Extreme.'

'Got to go,' she panicked, looking at her watch. 'Remember, I haven't said anything.'

'Don't worry.'

While walking to the pub to meet Andy, he reflected on Ruth. Weird how she knew Greek. Weirder still that she did not want to say how she came to speak it. What was interesting was her reaction when Linda asked her about it, suggesting she had something to hide. Did she live there once? Although it was not only in Greece she could have learnt the language. There was a slim possibility she could have picked it up from one of the Hellenic communities in Australia, North America or South Africa.

It was a miracle he found Andy and the boys in the crowded, smoky pub. Andy took Zen to the ship before returning to his friends, who were moving on somewhere else.

Saturday, 7th August 1982

At breakfast Harry confirmed that they had repaired the sanitary pump. Today he would try and get the wing tanks open so they could clear the scuppers. The smell of the stagnant water was dreadful and Zen had noticed it was permeating through the portholes of his cabin that morning.

In the meantime, Steph, John and Theo were in the galley preparing a buffet, while Zen and Andy went shopping for the food, beer and wine. They had all put money in to cover the expenses for the alcohol.

As far as music was concerned, the ship had an intercom system. Theo had tapes in his car and one of those invited was bringing a battery-powered sound system for when the generator was off.

The shopping took most of the morning. On their return Harry had both good and bad news. He had managed to get to the drains, which he had cleared by heating them with a blow torch, and the smell had gone, but the inside of the wing tank was badly corroded, probably worse than George and his father suspected.

After lunch they left the generator running for longer so Steph could wash down the decks of the mess, poop deck landing and galley. After shut-off they spent the afternoon decorating these areas with party streamers.

Their visitors gathered at the embankment at seven thirty and Andy ferried them across. There were eighteen in all, so it took five trips.

In the end they decided to leave the generator off from the beginning. Not only were the florescent lights too harsh and not conducive to a party ambiance but the sound and vibration interfered with the sound system. They put out candles in bottles together with their gas-lights, which was much cosier.

Their guests were able to take drinks and food onto the stern and watch the sunset. As it grew darker it became even more atmospheric. There was ample light in the mess for people to see, but subdued enough for intimate dancing. There was sufficient glow coming from the street lamps of Tonemouth and Castlewear for those who wanted to go for a walk on the decks and, as a precaution, Andy had put an oil lamp on each hatch. Apart from the bathroom, on the port side of the poop deck landing, also lit by candles, the other decks were off-limits.

Ann really enjoyed herself. To Zen's surprise, she was a seriously good mover and barely sat down all night, so much so, that she must have danced with every male on board, apart from Steph.

Harry also impressed him on the dance floor. Linda had come with her son and Steph had prepared the guest cabin opposite Zen's for them. Stephen was so excited to be spending the night on a cargo ship.

Steph produced some wonderful finger-food, all made from their own supplies with the minimum contribution from the shore. He had bought in lots of vol-au-vent cases and stuffed them with tinned crab, tuna, salmon, ham and cheeses; the variety seemed

213

endless. There was also an assortment of sandwiches made with cold meats. Then afterwards he produced a selection of mouthful-sized Greek sweets that he had also made himself. When not serving, he sat out on the stern, on a bollard, smoking and sipping a bottle of beer, freely talking to whoever else was within reach. Most of the time it was Stephen, whom Steph entertained by pointing out the constellations and explaining the Greek myths that were behind them.

Andy was with Clare and John and Theo with two attractive girls to whom they seemed glued.

Zen made sure everyone had enough to drink.

Nobody started leaving until half two and the last guest disembarked at four. Andy and Harry shared the trips, with Zen making the last one with Ann.

Zen walked her to her car. It was well into first light. She was not speaking and seemed upset, which puzzled Zen, as she was so flamboyant earlier.

'You okay?' he asked. 'You seem cheesed off.'

'You didn't care whenever I danced with someone else.'

'We danced together a few times and I was pleased you were enjoying yourself,' he said, not mentioning how she appeared to smooch with some of her partners, especially when she thought Zen was watching.

'I wanted you to sweep me off my feet.'

'I'm not a great dancer,' he revealed. 'Besides, I spent most of my time serving drinks.'

'That's not what I meant.'

'Well, I'm not interested in games that are meant to wind me up,' he said, annoyed at the implication. 'Not to mention the fact that you're engaged.' He walked away, leaving her by her car.

It was four thirty before he got to bed.

Sunday, 8th August 1982

Harry had the generator going at seven-thirty as they had to leave by nine. Steph was also awake, clearing up from the night before.

John and Theo would be leaving after lunch, as would Linda and Stephen, so they would not be seeing any them when they returned.

After breakfast, Steph took them ashore. It was sunny and cloudless. During the transfer he revealed that, provided he could get Andy up, he planned to go to church. He had found the local Church of England and decided to give it a try, as he felt that, being in port, he should worship on Sundays.

'I see no problem with that,' Zen said.

'It's just that when I'm being taken ashore, and brought back, there won't be anybody attending the engine room, as now,' Steph pointed out.

'I'm not going to worry about that,' Harry reassured him.

For once their journey was not delayed by caravans and other holiday traffic, but it did require negotiating single track lanes, with intermittent passing places, sunk between overgrown hedgerows. In two places these were so deep, they were more like tunnels.

Haverne Cove, forty five minutes away, was smaller than they had expected. It was a long and narrow finger of sea ending at a sandy strand. A handful of wooden boats were beached above the high water mark, defined by a fringe of dry seaweed. On the right hand side was a quay carved out of the rock which, at its seaward end, formed a ramp that accessed the water or beach, depending on the tide. The sea was well out and calm, with little surf. There were already lots of families there. At the end of the ramp a jeep was reversing a trailer, cradling the club's inflatable, into the water. Here was a group of divers they recognised, surrounded by diving equipment.

Parking was behind the inn. This was at the bottom of the valley, before the road started to rise for the next headland. The only other buildings were derelict fish cellars. Gathering their gear, they headed onto the beach and made camp on a flat rock.

When they joined the group, the dive leader and coach were giving instructions. There would be two dives that day. The club inflatable was to take half the expected sixteen divers offshore while the rest embarked from the beach. This would be repeated in the afternoon. They elected to go on the boat dive first. It was always best to start with the most difficult one, Zen thought. He was looking for the dark-haired woman, but she had not arrived, if she was coming at all.

Although it was still ten-thirty and the first dive was not for another hour, they had to start preparing. They put on their wet suits, rubber boots and lifejackets, before carrying their tanks, with their spider demand valves already in place, fins, masks, weight belts and snorkels to the boat, which was in thigh-deep water. Once they had stowed their gear on board, they walked back onto the beach, where there was to be a briefing. First, everyone was paired off, Zen naturally with Harry, so that they each had a partner, whom they were expected to look after.

The dive leader erected a white board on a stainless steel, fold-up frame on which he had sketched a profile of the dive, which was to be on the wreck of the *SS Nevada*. She was bound for the US with a cargo of chalk when, on 9 December 1916, at daybreak, while nine miles out to sea, she was hit by a torpedo from a German U-Boat. Although fatally damaged, the Captain attempted to find a place on the coast to beach her, but sank well short. The crew got off on lifeboats and were rescued by a passing patrol boat. She was now sitting upright on shingle in 29 metres. Her deck was 14 metres from the seabed. The superstructure had been swept away and lay some way seaward. Apart from that she was fairly intact, but, because of her age, the hull plating was paper thin and there were several holes with jagged edges.

A line was attached to her bow and the divers would group there before proceeding, in pairs, along her starboard side, making a small detour to view the superstructure, before returning along the port side. They would assemble again at the bow and ascend in pairs when the instructor signalled. Finally, they were warned that there might be basking sharks in the area and they were to be careful not to disturb them.

With the itinerary understood, they moved off to the boat and the waiting equipment. Once the divers were in, arranged round the bulbous sides, the boat set off at a steady pace, heading out of the cove and on to a south easterly bearing. There were nine of them. Eight, including the dive leader, would go in the water, the ninth being the coxswain and watchman. Once out of the inlet, the dark hills took on a sinister air and, because they were leaving the cove at an angle, the

218

entrance blended in with the cliffs and vanished. A wide fringe of sea at their foot bore the foamy wakes of shallow reefs, but soon these were too far to be seen. Five minutes later they had reached the wreck, which was marked by a buoy, to which they tethered the inflatable. They were now a mile off-shore and that seemed a long way. Also, although the sea was calm, there was a current, caused by the incoming tide, combined with a swell. Both were coming from the west-southwest and caused them to rock. This, together with the constriction of his wetsuit, his lack of sleep and the remnants of the alcohol consumed the night before, made Zen feel queasy. Looking over at Harry, he noticed he was also looking pale.

They finished kitting up, checked each other's gear and, when ready, sat on the edge of the inflatable until, following the sign from the dive leader, they allowed themselves to fall into the water. They waited on the surface for the okay before venting the air in their lifejackets and slipping under the surface.

Zen was struck by the lack of visibility. He was used to the Red Sea, the Mediterranean and the Indian Ocean. This explained the need for a line. Indeed, descending into the murk, it was not until they were near the other end that they could see the bow of the freighter. Although some of the divers carried torches, there was sufficient light, once their eyes became accustomed to the gloom. But at that depth there were no colours, as the sea water had filtered out all but the blue.

As instructed, they made their way along one side, keeping slightly above the level of the deck. The hull was encrusted with marine growth and there were many cracks and gaps. The first hatch was a cavernous hole with nothing left of the combing. Further on they stopped abreast the second hold where the holes in the deck plating were much worse, and at the side of the ship was a gaping void surrounded by jagged edges, which the dive leader signalled was the point of the torpedo impact. Further on the deck was strewn with twisted metal where the superstructure once sat. Then there were more holds until they came to the stern. Zen was surprised by the abundance of small fish.

At this point the dive leader looked at his watch and must have decided that they had used up too much time on the first leg, so he directed them to go up the port side instead of diverting to the superstructure. There was nothing new to see. Although the holds were open it would have been too dangerous to venture inside. They would not be like those of the *Amber*, which were open spaces. These would have further decks within. He was feeling the cold now. They were not doing any vigorous finning and were stopping frequently. His wetsuit was more appropriate for warmer waters and he would have to consider a replacement.

Once they were back at the bow, they waited for everyone to assemble before ascending to the surface.

The worst part of any dive is the end, when the diver is bobbing in the water, cold, tired and impatient to get out. They had to take turns removing their tanks and weight belts, hand them to someone in the boat and then be helped on board. By the time everyone was seated and their gear stowed, Zen was shivering. Harry seemed okay, but then he had a thicker wetsuit. At least the shore dive would be in shallower, less exposed waters, with a lot more swimming. He was glad when

220

the boat moved off as he was beginning to feel queasy again.

Back on shore, they retrieved their gear and returned to their base. Sitting on various rocks were the other divers, who had just been on the shore dive. Amongst them was the dark-haired woman, talking to a blonde female. She wore a black, single piece bathing suit and had a towel wrapped round her shoulders.

Once they had completed the arduous task of removing their wetsuits, they wrapped themselves in towels to warm up.

'What did you think of that?' Zen asked when he could talk without his teeth chattering.

'Not quite the Caribbean,' Harry replied. 'It was dark. Plenty of fish though.'

'Was that a cuttlefish I saw?'

'Believe so,' Harry agreed. 'Not much life on the seabed.'

'It's a shingle bottom. There's not enough for them to eat, maybe.'

'On the other hand, I liked the wreck, particularly being aware of its history. The murk added to the atmosphere.'

'I enjoyed that too, till I froze. Weren't you cold?'

'Not really. The Pacific's cold too, you know. Say, I'm hungry and thirsty.'

So was Zen, now that he had stopped feeling sick. They had loads of sandwiches left over from last night. They also had bottles of made-up orange squash.

Zen unpacked the rucksack and laid everything out on a rug.

As they were eating and drinking, he saw the dark-haired girl and her friend, towels over their shoulders, walking up the beach towards them, probably on their way to the inn. When they were about to pass, she stopped and came over. Her friend followed.

'You're the new members, aren't you?' she said, her voice deeper than Zen expected.

'That's us,' Harry replied.

'Sorry, can't remember your names,' she said.

'This is Harry and I'm Zen.'

'I'm Alex and this is Frankie. We're going for something to eat.'

'No need for that,' Harry said, 'we've got too much.' He indicated the large container. 'Why don't you sit with us?'

'There's tuna and mayo, tinned crab and ham,' Zen added.

They nodded to each other in agreement, lay their towels down and sat cross-legged, helping themselves from the box.

'That's quite a selection for two,' Frankie said, reaching out for more.

Zen explained about their party.

'Where are you from?' Alex asked.

'Both originally from Greece,' Harry said.

'But you have an American accent,' Alex observed.

'Spent time in California.'

'And you have a Mediterranean one mixed in with your English,' Alex said, looking at Zen.

'That's because I've lived in England most of my life.'

'So what business are you in?' Alex asked.

'We work for the same shipping company,' Zen said. 'Till three weeks ago I was based in London and Harry on board a cargo ship. Due to a collapse in world trade, that ship's laid up in Tonemouth. We're caretaking, together with two others.'

'Wait a minute,' Alex said, 'that's the one that's been in the news.'

'That's right,' Harry said.

'I've seen it. What's her name?' Alex asked.

'The *Amber Trader*,' Zen replied, examining Alex closely. She had an attractive face, not sweet and pretty, like Ann, but more classical.

'People aren't too pleased,' Alex said.

'Some are,' Zen pointed out.

'Did you see the local paper on Friday?' Harry asked. 'Someone wrote a letter describing the *Amber* as "a pile of junk".'

'Missed that,' Zen replied.

'How long will you be staying?' Alex asked.

'We don't know,' Zen replied. 'Six months, a year, maybe two. Who can tell? What about you? What do you both do?'

'We work for an estate agent,' she said, turning to choose another sandwich. 'There was talk that property prices in Tonemouth and Castlewear would be affected.'

'And have they been?' Zen asked.

'Not that we've seen,' Alex said.

'Total nonsense,' Frankie remarked.

'I'm sure I've seen you in Tonemouth,' Zen said to Alex.

'It's possible,' Alex said. 'We've a branch at the end of the high street.'

They heard a whistle.

'We're being called to the briefing for the boat dive,' Alex said, looking at her watch. 'What was it like?'

223

'Good,' Zen replied. 'They haven't given you much time.'

'They want to finish before the tide turns,' Alex said. 'You'll like the shore dive. The rocks further out have cormorants and guillemots, as well as gulls.'

'Someone claimed to have spotted a seal,' Frankie added.

'We'll look out for them,' Harry said.

The girls finished their sandwiches and drink.

'Thanks for lunch, we wouldn't have had time for the pub,' Alex said, before heading off.

Their call came half an hour later. They put on their wetsuits and made their way to the foreshore with their equipment. The dive was on another wreck, also of the Second World War and also a victim of torpedoes, but this time the Captain managed to run the vessel aground on the rocks to the right of the cove and in front of the headland. The tide was still rising so they would have a strenuous swim to get to her, but then have the current with them as they returned. The wreck was strewn over a large area but no deeper than ten metres, and there would be some interesting reefs along the way.

Again they started as a group. Once away from the shallows, the water was clearer than it had been for the first dive. The wreck itself consisted of encrusted ribs and plates scattered on the pebbly sea floor with little structure left. There was more life though; they saw some flat fish on the sandy bottom near the beach and a large wrasse close to a reef. Harry found this dive just as interesting and Zen did not get as cold.

By five thirty they were dressed, had packed and were on their way home.

Andy was waiting in the café, sitting at a table, empty cup of tea in front of him, with his head on his folded hands. He was asleep.

Once they managed to wake him, they returned to a different ship, with no evidence remaining of any guests or the weekend party.

They had their main meal in the evening that day. Andy did not go out and they all struggled to stay up long enough to watch the news before switching off for the night.

Monday, 9th to Wednesday, 11th August 1982

The first half of the week was dominated by their efforts to get the boat deck ready to collect water. They were running low and rain was forecast for Wednesday. By Tuesday lunchtime the clearing and de-rusting had been completed and that afternoon Harry joined them in applying the final grey primer undercoat. They were hoping this would be dry by the morning so that they could paint on the green overcoat before lunch.

Meanwhile, at midday on Monday, Zen went out to collect George Pittas. He soon realised he had misunderstood him over the phone on Friday. He thought he was coming to stay on board, but in fact he was on holiday with his wife in nearby Barcombe and was combining this with visits to the *Amber*. Once on board he made a point of thanking them for looking after his son.

Wednesday was their busiest day. George came first thing and, after breakfast, they finished the boat deck. Harry then set up the system of two barrels, filters and hoses designed to collect the run-off from the deck. He sealed off the scuppers, apart from the two immediately aft that he attached to hoses. These ran into the barrels, passing through a fine, wire mesh to extract solids. From the bottom of each drum more hoses ran along the deck into the after peak tank feed pipe, hopefully providing enough for their washing and cooling requirements.

Later, Zen worked with Harry in the engine room. George wanted to check the machinery. Afterwards, they went on deck to work the cranes and open the holds for airing. Unfortunately, all the derrick head bearings had deteriorated and were grating from lack of lubrication. They would have to be thoroughly greased.

After lunch, Zen took George ashore. When they reached the pontoon, Zen got out first to tie up, but as George was stepping from the boat to the pontoon, he lost his footing and fell in the sea. This would have been funny had he not cut his hand. It bled badly and they agreed it would need stitches. He left George wet and dripping by his car in the harbour master's car park while he ran upstairs to find out where the nearest hospital accident and emergency was. They told him to go to Torbay and gave him some temporary bandages.

At the hospital George was seen promptly. Although he had not broken any bones he needed three stitches in his palm and his wrist was swollen. There was no way he could drive, so Zen had to go back to Tonemouth, drive George in his car to Barcombe and take a taxi back.

Thursday, 12th August 1982

During the night they had heavy rain with strong winds and awoke to the first of two unpleasant surprises. Zen rose first, glanced out the porthole to assess the weather and, seeing it was fine, put on his running gear and went downstairs. As usual he picked up the petrol can and unlocked the starboard poop deck door in order to get to the gangway. Not thinking to look down, when he stepped over the threshold, he went straight into cold, dark water up to his calves.

Several factors contributed to this second flooding. The ship had a slight list to starboard, as was apparent from the previous flood. It was, though, imperceptible as the decks were concave, and the dial on the bridge showed it to be no more than two degrees. Andy joked that it was because all but Harry slept on that side. The truth was that when the *Amber* was moored, the starboard anchor had more tension than the chain that was shackled to the buoy. And it was not only the poop deck; when they looked at the main deck that morning, it too was once again flooded on the starboard side.

The cause was the same as before: all the flaked rust and paint created by the work on the boat deck and the oiling of the main deck. Whenever it rained, the debris washed into the drains and clogged them. Harry tried to clear the cargo deck scuppers using wire and other probes but they were too solidly jammed. He tried heating them, as before, by entering the wing tanks, but this time it did not work. In the end he had to take all four pipes apart, clean them out and reassemble them.

The poop deck drains were a different matter; they ran through the crew's quarters below. It would not do to disassemble these and flood the cabins. Again he tried probes and heating but only managed to partly clear one, giving slow drainage. They would have to wait for a dry spell before they could affect permanent repairs. In the meantime they created a walkway with upturned bottle crates.

The second problem came to light after lunch when Steph went out aft to smoke; he noticed that one of the wires tied to the aft buoy was slack. Looking over the side he saw that it had snapped. The movement caused by the winds of the previous night must have caused the break. Harry and Andy replaced it immediately, using the boat, but the aft moorings would need reinforcing in preparation for winter.

In the evening they went to the diving club. At the pub after training, Zen hoped to get Alex on her own as he had heard from another member that she had recently broken up with a boyfriend and was now unencumbered. Unfortunately, the opportunity did not arise.

Friday, 13th August 1982

That night it rained heavily and this carried through to the late afternoon of the next day. The poop deck flooded again but the cargo deck drains were fine. At least the boat deck was now collecting water.

Andy spent the morning working inside, cleaning and painting crew cabins, and Zen went to the town. After doing the shopping he went for the post and found a letter from Ann.

> Dear Zen,
> I've had a terrible few days thinking about how we left things.
> Linda and Harry are having a meal out tonight. Linda says it's fine to join them, if you can bear to be with me.
> Please let's meet. If afterwards you want to stop seeing me, I'll understand.
> I'll come if you don't call.
> Love Ann xx

When he got to the pontoon, he started the boat and went back to the *Amber*. Harry had not mentioned anything about going out, but why should he? Irrespective of whether he ever saw Ann again, it would be nice to go out. During lunch he asked Harry whether he minded and he said it was fine by him.

They did little work that afternoon because of the rain, so they spent time in their cabins before Harry switched on to prepare for the evening.

They met the girls at the hotel, where they settled in the lounge for a bar meal. They were lucky to get the table in the bay window and could look out onto the square. They ordered drinks and chicken and fries in baskets. Linda and Harry were soon in their own world and there was no mistaking the body language.

'Sorry about Saturday,' Ann began. 'It was childish.' Zen shrugged his shoulders. 'I'd like another chance. I'd like to spend more time with you.'

'We'll see,' Zen said. He was aware that George Pittas was coming for lunch tomorrow and would prefer not to have Ann around. He wanted to avoid anything getting back to his parents. Ann went on to explain how she had been to the hairdresser, had a manicure and pedicure, implying that it was all for him.

'You look great,' Zen had to admit. She wore a black camisole under a lacy top, a straight, burgundy skirt, dark stockings and suede ankle boots. She had taken a lot of trouble.

'We could go shopping tomorrow,' she suggested.

'Where's the best place round here?' Zen asked, remembering he had to buy a better wetsuit.

'Plymouth probably, though I prefer Exeter.'

'We're expecting someone for lunch, so it depends how long he stays. Plymouth would be best, wouldn't it? I could come to you and you could show me where you live.'

'I suppose,' she said, looking distracted. Then she seemed to recall something. 'I've just remembered, Ruth's here tonight,' she announced.

'Really?' Linda responded. 'It explains why she couldn't look after Stephen, but she didn't say where she was going.'

'I'd forgotten because it was arranged some time ago. It's the WI's summer evening. They've got a room upstairs. She's giving the pre-dinner talk.'

'Wonder if we'll see her,' Linda said.

'Does she know you're here?' Ann asked.

'Didn't say where I was going,' Linda replied. Then, turning to Harry she added, 'though I did mention who I was going to be with and how much I wanted her to meet you.'

'Hope Auntie Ruth isn't disappointed,' Harry said.

'After the build-up Linda's given you the last two weeks…'

'I've not been that bad, have I? I wanted the telling to be special,' Linda said, putting her hand on his. 'Not matter-of-fact.'

'Ahh, that's sweet,' Ann said. 'Truth is, you have to catch Ruth in the right mood.'

'Perhaps we'll bump into her,' Harry said.

'You haven't told me how your night on board was,' Zen said.

'We didn't get much sleep,' Linda said, frowning.

'I'm sorry, were you uncomfortable?' Zen asked.

'No, it wasn't that. Stephen was so excited, he couldn't stop talking. He insisted on repeating the stories Steph had told him.'

'Couldn't it have waited for the morning?' Zen said. He was aware that Steph had aroused Stephen's interest in Greek mythology.

'He was worried he'd forget, so he was telling me so I'd remember for him. I didn't have the heart to stop him.'

'And who would?' Ann said.

'That's great. You can both come and stay whenever you like,' Harry said.

'I'll second that,' Zen added.

'You should be careful what you wish for, Harry,' Ann said. 'Look who's at the bar.'

'Who?' Harry asked.

'It's Ruth, she's probably early,' Linda said nervously.

'Maybe she won't notice,' Ann added.

'But if she did and thought we were avoiding her...' Linda said. 'I'll get her.'

'I'll find another chair,' Harry said.

While he was doing so, Zen was looking to see who Linda was approaching as she wound her way round the tables, but the bar was too crowded. Harry came back with a chair and squeezed it between Linda's and his.

The woman Linda came back with was shortish and stocky. She had a short mullet of light brown hair, streaked with grey, brown eyes and well-proportioned features, although her jaw was a touch too square, too strong. She did not wear makeup, which suited her as her complexion was good. She was handsome rather than attractive, with a well-built figure. She wore dark brown trousers, a matching jacket with shoulder pads, and flat brown brogues. She had a shoulder-slung handbag and was carrying a half pint of beer.

When they reached the table, the others rose.

'I'd like you to meet my new friends,' Linda said.

'My pleasure. How are you Ann?' Ruth said in a discernible Yorkshire accent.

'Very well,' Ann replied. She seemed embarrassed.

Linda introduced Zen and Harry. When they shook hands, Zen noticed that Ruth's was limp. This caused him to remember something his father had once told him years ago when he was sitting in his office, in that corner desk, doing his college work. Someone had just been to visit and his father had shown him out. When he came back in he had said to Zen, 'I won't be doing business with him'. 'But he sounded quite plausible,' Zen had replied. 'But you didn't shake his hand,' his father had said. 'His handshake was limp,' he had added. 'So what?' Zen had asked. 'It means he doesn't care about people,' was his father's reply.

'Will you join us?' Harry asked. 'I've found you a chair.'

'I've got some time before I go upstairs,' she said, while sitting. 'I'm giving a talk.' She looked about her as if trying to size them up.

'Linda's told me about your work,' Harry ventured. 'It's admirably purposeful.'

'Thank you,' Ruth said. 'Most men think we're meddlesome busybodies.'

Ann took out her cigarettes and offered Ruth one, which she accepted. After they lit up, Linda recounted how they had met and what Harry did aboard the *Amber*.

233

As this was going on, Zen kept his eyes on Ruth and noticed how her demeanour changed during the conversation, as it became apparent, from Linda's enthusiasm, how seriously Linda and Harry were already involved. When Linda related how much Stephen enjoyed his latest visit on board, she looked put out.

'A lot's happened in your life in a short time,' Ruth said at the end, feigning a smile. She took out her own cigarettes and lit up without offering one to Ann.

'It's been two weeks today,' Linda said.

'An anniversary,' Harry added.

'How long do you think you'll be staying?' Ruth asked, looking at Zen.

'We don't know,' Zen replied. 'Could be six months or up to two years.'

'Why are you here again?' Ruth asked in a tone too forceful to be solely inquisitive.

Zen explained about the state of world trade and the freight markets.

'I've read about you in the local news,' Ruth said. 'Two years is a long time to be desecrating a beautiful part of the country, shit, two weeks is a long time.'

'Actually, this economic depression's affecting everybody. We're providing an important source of income to the town,' Zen said, taken back by her aggressive reaction. Her quivering lower lip reminded him of his recent encounter with Spiros Alexandrou.

'No, what you rich people do is exploit the lower classes,' she said. There was venom in her voice.

Zen was about to rise to the occasion when he felt Ann's hand on his thigh. Under the table and out of sight, it was a calming squeeze, a signal to hold back. Zen bit his lip. An uncomfortable silence followed.

'I'd better go to my meeting,' Ruth said eventually, displaying a smirk of triumph as of one that had vanquished an enemy. She drained her glass and stood, ignoring Harry and Zen, saying to the girls, 'I'll see you on Monday,' before walking off.

'I think we'd better have another drink after that,' Harry said when Ruth was out of earshot. 'Shall I get everyone the same? I'll also check on our food.'

As Harry collected their empty glasses, Zen kept his eyes on Ruth. As she walked across the lounge, she encountered someone she knew, seated at a table, and paused briefly before continuing on her way. As she did so she looked back at Harry, who was now approaching the bar. The look she gave him was fleeting, a fraction of a second, maybe only Zen noticed it, but it contained spite and hate. It was creepy and he felt a shiver up his spine.

'Didn't see that coming,' Linda said, looking shaken.

'I'm sorry,' Ann said, her hand back on his leg. 'Ruth's very opinionated.'

'Nor does she like foreigners, so don't take it personally,' Linda advised. 'I'll pop to the ladies while Harry's getting the drinks.' She left the table.

'You look upset,' Ann said.

He was livid, but also worried and concerned. 'I'll be all right,' he said. 'Earlier on, you didn't look too happy either.'

'I'm sorry,' she said. 'I got jealous that Linda could spend the night on board and I've not been invited.'

'You're like a child who's jealous because their sibling gets something they don't,' Zen said, regretting

235

his words as soon as they left his mouth. He was still angry with Ruth. 'Besides, I assumed you had to go home.'

'I can wish things were different,' she said, visibly stung by his comment. 'Look I'd better go. Let me give you the money for the wasted food.'

'No, Ann, I'm sorry.' But she rose to leave, about to burst into tears. He got up too and put his hand on her shoulder. She momentarily tried to push him away, but relaxed. 'You must realise that wasn't directed at you,' he said as she sat back down. 'More pragmatically, what is it you want from me?'

'That's direct. Thought that was obvious.'

'You're engaged, so it isn't.'

'Edward's the man I'm going to marry, but I want a relationship with you.' She was looking down at her lap.

'Really? So how are you going to explain that to Linda'?

'She's my friend. She's often said I should see other men.'

Zen thought about this. Ann was probably stretching the meaning of Linda's statement, but that did not matter. The issue now was whether he should rebuff her, in which case it was probable that she would give up trying, or take things further and worry about the consequences later. There was no question he desired her in a physical way. It would be nice to enjoy the company of a woman, but Ann was an inappropriate choice. It was bad enough she was engaged and she was not worth a run-in with another disgruntled partner. In many ways she was also immature. What effect would an encounter with Zen have on her? On the other hand, he could not get that

236

look Ruth gave Harry out of his mind, not to mention some of the earlier revelations. This was a disturbed woman, Zen thought, and through Ann, her PA, he could keep tabs on her or obtain more information. For reasons he could not explain, he had a feeling that something was not right. He had also decided that by whatever means necessary, he was going to find out what it was about her past that she did not want known. Usually people were quite happy to talk about their life histories and traumas, either to attract pity or admiration.

He turned to Ann and took her hand. Perhaps he could keep their relationship as it was and avoid any increased intimacy. 'In that case, let's take things one step at a time and see what happens.' She was about to sweep her arms around him when Harry returned to the table.

'The food will be with us in five minutes,' he said as he took the glasses off the tray. 'They've been busy.'

'It's these damned tourists,' Zen said.

'How did your diving go last Sunday?' Ann asked, looking pleased with herself.

'It was okay,' Harry said. 'There wasn't anything remarkable about it.'

Soon after Linda returned their food came and they spoke of mundane things without mentioning the earlier encounter with Ruth. Then, after eating and more drinks, Linda had to excuse herself. 'I'd better relieve the baby-sitter,' she said.

'I'll walk you,' Harry offered, then to Zen and Ann, 'will you wait for me?'

'Sure,' Zen replied. He got up and gave Linda a kiss before Ann did the same.

'Be back in half an hour,' Harry said.

'They look good together,' Zen said, watching them leave the bar.

'Keep it to yourself, but Linda's completely smitten.'

'I think Harry might be too.'

'Stephen's still a worry though.'

'Really? Why?'

'Hasn't Harry said anything?'

'Tell me.'

'I don't know whether I …' Ann hesitated.

'He's my friend, so you should.'

'He's been getting depressed and not sleeping, since they started going out.'

'He's fine when they're together.'

'I know, he adores Harry and yet…'

'It could be a coincidence, something totally unrelated, that's troubling him.'

'That's what Linda hopes.'

'What does Stephen say?'

'That he's having bad dreams and feelings of despair.'

'Any trouble at school?'

'Not that Linda's heard.'

'Could it be hormonal? Has he been to the doctor?'

'Linda thinks it's too soon to make a thing of it.'

'I see her point.'

'Anyway, what time will you come to me tomorrow?' she said, taking his hand in both of hers and moving closer. 'And what shall we do?'

'It depends on our visitor.'

'Who's coming?'

Zen told her about George. 'But if he's got his wife with him, he won't stay long. And on Sunday, we could go to the beach, weather permitting. Have I told you that I have a dip in the sea when I go running?'

Later, when Harry was back, they walked Ann to her car. Zen promised to call her as soon as he knew what was happening.

Saturday, 14th August 1982

During the night the rain came back and lasted all day.

At eleven thirty, after a late breakfast, Zen went to collect George. Not seeing him near the embankment, he went to the harbour master's office for the post and found a message saying that, due to the weather, he had decided to postpone his visit until Monday when they would be on their way back to London.

Ann was overjoyed when he called, and after lunch he drove to her house on the outskirts of Plymouth. As soon as he had pulled up, she was out of the door and into his car. Zen rated it as one of the most boring and irritating days in his life. He bought a newspaper just to have something to read while he hung around waiting for her. He had never met anyone so indecisive. In the end he was saved by closing time and she did not even allow him the opportunity to look for a wet suit. He did not get back to Tonemouth until seven, and Ann had only bought a blouse!

Monday and Tuesday, 16th and 17th August 1982

The next morning, after breakfast, Zen went out to find George waiting for him. His wife had decided to tour the boutiques of the town rather than join them. Zen tried to remember when he had last seen her.

Instead of coming on board, they sat in the café for an hour and talked about their problems with the wing tanks and, of more immediate importance, the aft fastenings. If they were having problems in summer, what was going to happen during the winter storms? George promised to order two more mooring wires when he returned to London.

Before going back to the *Amber*, Zen went to the phone box and called Ann.

'This is a surprise,' Ann said, beside herself.

'Wanted to thank you for a lovely weekend.'

'Thank you, it was wonderful. I don't know whether I can wait till I see you next.'

'Would've been perfect if it wasn't for Ruth. I think it shook Harry.'

'Did it? That's Friday the thirteenth for you,' Ann said. 'Linda was certainly upset. She intends to give Ruth a piece of her mind.'

'She had it in for us, this Ms.., what's her name again?'

'Snyder.'

'That's it. Where's she from anyway? She had a northern accent.'

'Yorkshire.'

'Really? What part?'

'York, I believe.'

'Well anyway, when are you back in Exeter?'

'Hopefully tomorrow or Wednesday.'

'If so, leave a message and I'll meet you wherever you like.'

After he had finished with Ann, he called his average adjuster friend, Alan Brook. They had not caught up since their night out before he left London.

'My friend, how are you?' Alan asked, in his endearing Welsh accent.

'Absolutely fine,' Zen replied, before bringing him up to date with his news. 'When are you coming to visit?'

'I'm snowed under, mate. The only way owners can make money at present is to catch up on their claims.'

'No summer holiday this year?'

'Barely have time to sleep.'

'Then I won't detain you, but I need to ask a really big favour.'

'Go on.'

'Do you still use that detective agency?'

'Of course, more than ever, especially for the injury claims; we need to check for criminal records.'

'They're an international firm, right?'

'The best. Expensive, but the best.'

'I want a background check on someone. What's the procedure?'

'This is how it works. If you can wait a week it'll cost £200 plus expenses. If you want it in forty-eight hours, it's £350. If the enquiries move to North America or Australia you can double that again and add another twenty-four hours.'

'What about further afield?'

'Forget it, it could take months.'

'I get the idea. The name is Ruth Snyder,' Zen said, giving what details he could remember, including where she worked and her approximate age. 'I'll go with the faster option,' he added. 'My curiosity couldn't take a longer wait.'

'Call me after close of business on Wednesday.'

'Do you need me to send money?'

'No, I have thirty day terms.'

'One more thing. Remember when we had our drink together I told you about my problems finding a lay-up berth in England?'

'Vaguely.'

'Did you mention it to Spiros?'

'I may have done, he's very chatty. Should I have kept my mouth shut?'

'Not at all,' Zen reassured him. 'It just explains something. Speak to you on Wednesday.'

Zen spent the next two days fussing over the aft fastenings with Andy. One of them worked from the boat at the buoy, the other from the stern. The weather was windy with heavy showers, especially on Tuesday, and they had to have a break whenever there was a downpour. It was slow work but necessary because the movement of the ship whenever the wind gusted was worrying. They had to make sure that the load on the wires was evenly distributed.

Wednesday, 18th August 1982

The weather was very bad with heavy rain from Tuesday night straight through to the next afternoon. By then they were satisfied with their work. They were now secured by three doubled wires and a chain aft and the two chains forward. With the two additional wires George was sending they would have sufficient cover in an emergency.

Later, when he had the chance, Zen went out to buy a paper and pick up the post.

That afternoon two teams of fire fighters came on board for a training exercise. This had been pre-arranged by the harbour master and included Tonemouth's only fire tender. Zen could not help speculating that this was prompted by their profuse burning of rubbish.

Before five, with the rain having cleared, Zen went to call Alan. He took a notepad and pen.

'You know how to pick your friends, mate,' Alan said, after their initial greetings.

'That bad, is it?'

'Have you ever done anything like this?'

'Never.'

'So I should explain that what these people do is look for official traces. Usually all you find is birth and marriage certificates, where they live, maybe where they work. It's only if someone's been involved with something that's attracted the notice of the police or the courts that things get interesting.'

'Okay, I get it, so what have you got?'

'Before I start, are you phoning from a call box?'

'Yeah, why?'

'Let me call back, we could be a while.' Then, a minute later, 'You taking this down?'

'Yes, take it slowly.'

'Right, Ruth Snyder, born 10th September '38, in York. Her father, Samuel, died during the war, on D-day as a matter of fact. Her mother, June, married again in August '44. Makes you wonder. Do you want the home address? The mother still lives there.'

'Can't imagine I'll need it.'

'Anyway, education, eight 'O' levels and three 'As'. Do you need to know what they are?'

'Don't bother.'

'She then got a first in English at Hull University, awarded in August '59. Then there's nothing till September '62 when she starts teaching English to foreign students at Kingston-upon-Thames Polytechnic. Now it starts getting interesting. On 20th March '65 there's a record of a marriage entered at York Registry Office between Ruth Snyder and a Stelios Nicholas. Got that?'

'Just about.'

'She left her post that summer and doesn't turn up again till November '69, when there's the first of two arrests by the Metropolitan Police for vagrancy.'

'Gosh, high achieving teacher to tramp in four years. What happened?'

'Exactly. As there was no record of anything in England, they turned to Greece, obviously.'

'Obviously.'

'They put a lot of enquiries to their contact down there, especially on our behalf, but this one was the most..., well I don't know how to describe it.'

'I'm about to crush the receiver in anticipation.'

'These are the bullet points made by the agent and taken from the police reports. On the night of 17 January 1968 the police of the Prefecture of Sparta were called to a coastal village in the Peloponnese, whose name I can't pronounce. I can spell it for you, if you like.'

'Don't bother.'

'This call-out resulted in the investigation of the murder of twin baby boys, only seven months old, George and Samuel, the sons of Stelios Nicholas and Ruth Snyder-Nicholas.'

'Jesus!'

'There's more; they were also investigating the suicide of one Hariklia Georgiou.'

'What?'

'I'll just skip to the coroner's report. That puts the thing in a nutshell. Right, apparently Ruth married the son of Stella and George Nicholas, hotel owners in this place I can't pronounce, and they came to live in Greece to help run said hotel with his parents. They lived at a separate address, so probably had their own place. The twins were born on 5 June, which was appropriate.'

'What does that mean?'

'You know, Gemini. Don't you follow the star signs?'

'Not as much as you, obviously.'

'Never mind. Apparently this Hariklia claimed she was Stelios's former fiancée. She'd told her brother and sister that he'd promised to marry her before he went to England to study and because of this she'd consented to consummating the engagement on several occasions.'

'That's an imaginative way of putting it.'

'It seems therefore that she got pissed off when he came back from England married to Ruth.'

'Undoubtedly.'

'According to the brother and sister, the last straw was when Ruth got pregnant and gave birth to the twin boys. This Hariklia was going about the place saying they were really hers and had been stolen from her.'

'Didn't anybody realise she'd gone nuts?'

'Anyway, on that fateful night in January, she literally walked into the Nicholas' house. It says here that no one in the village locks their doors, unless there are tourists or gypsies around. She took the twins out of their cots and, before the parents noticed anything, was off up the road with them. The crying babies woke half the village and before long a whole crowd was running after her. It says she made her way to the cliff edge and everyone, including the parents, pleaded with her to give the children back. According to witnesses she said that if she couldn't have what was hers, nobody could. Then Ruth, who was hysterical by now and had to be restrained, screamed how anyone could do such a thing, to which Hariklia shouted back "Don't judge me. I condemn you to also suffer such a betrayal". Then she jumped.'

'You can understand how she ended up on the streets then. Do we know what happened next?'

'Fortunately she encounters the police again in December '71, when she's a witness to an assault in sheltered accommodation. She was also a resident, so she must've come off the streets by then. Then, two years later she reports another assault in a hostel for the homeless and this time she's the warden.'

'She's pulling herself back out of the gutter. What about her husband?'

'He seems to have stayed in Greece, but they never got divorced. She doesn't use her married name, however, but calls herself Ms Snyder.'

'That it?'

'No, I've left the really good stuff for last.'

'It gets better?'

'Listen to this. In April '74, she's mentioned in a case of suicide. The victim was a thirteen year old. The mother, a single parent, admitted to having had a relationship with Ruth. The suicide took place a few months after a man came into the woman's life. They'd gone out for a meal, the daughter, the mother, the boyfriend and Ruth. On the way back to the car, which was on the top floor of a multi-storey car park, the daughter jumped straight off in front of them. The police later found entries in her diary suggesting she was depressed because she feared her mother was going to abandon her for this man.'

'I can see how that can happen,' Zen said, looking for patterns. 'The daughter probably didn't realise what sort of relationship the mother was having with Ruth and didn't feel threatened by it. Then this macho male comes along and tries to take over.'

'And normally I'd agree with you. After all, Ruth's exposing herself to people who are vulnerable, so things will happen round her. However, when the same thing occurs again, three years later, it begins to look spooky.'

'When was that?'

'October '77.'

'Shortly before she came down to Exeter. And was there a man involved?'

'Exactly the same, except in this case they were walking along a busy road and the daughter, it was a girl again, jumped in front of a lorry. This time the police found a letter written to a friend, expressing the same abandonment anxiety. What's different here is that the man in question went on to stalk Ruth, accusing her of causing the girl's death.'

'I wonder how he thought she was able to do that?'

'I don't know, mate, sounds like Voodoo to me, but that's where it ends.'

'Do you think the police would've bothered to find out what happened in Greece?'

'They'd have had no reason to. According to them, no crimes were committed.'

'Alan, that's great. One last favour. Could you make two copies and send them to me together with the invoice? You keep the original in a safe place.' He gave him the address. 'Can you send it first class? I'd like to receive it as soon as poss.'

'No problem.'

'And I mean it when I say to come and visit.'

'It won't be for a while; you know what they say, make hay while the sun shines. But you'll be coming to London sometime?'

'Maybe, if I've a reason.'

'If so, give me a call.'

'Will do.'

Zen was back on board at six and found no one about. They were probably in their cabins. He went up to his and, getting his book, went and sat outside on his stool. He tried to read but could not concentrate. He could not take his mind off Ruth.

That night Andy was on his way back from the pub to the pontoon only to see their inflatable sailing away towards Castlewear. Fortunately for him, a passer-by, who also happened to be a fisherman, heard him shouting. His much faster boat was nearby and they managed to catch up with the thief, witnessing him disembark at the marina and run away. The fisherman, being a local, was able to identify the teenage culprit. They went back to Tonemouth with both boats and informed the police. Unfortunately, only the fisherman was able to give a statement because Andy's English was not good enough.

Thursday, 19th August 1982

The weather continued to improve, but remained showery. That morning Zen accompanied Andy to the police station to help translate. The teenager in question had already been spoken to. He worked for a local butcher and, having been waylaid by friends at the pub, had missed the last ferry. Not wanting to pay for a taxi he decided to *borrow* the boat. Andy gave his statement but Zen chose not to press charges. Afterwards, before going back on board, they did some shopping and Zen called the office.

That night Zen went to the diving club with Harry. Afterwards, in the pub they learnt that during the Bank Holiday weekend a dive was being planned for South Wales. A coach would be leaving on Friday evening. They would have two days diving or drinking, depending on the weather, and come back Monday.

Harry and Zen could not be away for that length of time and, besides, it was the weekend of the regatta. Harry then said, 'to be honest, if we wanted a dive, we could pack the car or boat and go somewhere ourselves. We've got that guide you bought.'

Alex, who was sitting nearby with Frankie, overheard this and said, 'We're not going either. If you want to make a foursome sometime, we might come.'

'Are you working that weekend?' Zen asked.

'It's one of our busiest,' Alex replied.

'It's also the regatta,' Zen said.

'I know, it's really good, especially the Red Arrows and fireworks.'

'Are you going?' Zen asked.

'Don't know. Tonemouth gets so packed that you can't get a place to park unless you arrive early.'

'Some watch from the fields on the surrounding hills,' Frankie added.

'Yeah, I did that one year. It's good but you miss the atmosphere,' Alex said.

'Why don't you join us on the *Amber* and you can watch the show from there?' Zen asked.

'That'd be great,' Alex replied, looking at Frankie, who nodded enthusiastically.

'Why don't you come on Thursday evening for supper,' Zen suggested. 'Do you want to meet at six outside the harbour café?'

'Think we can make that,' Alex replied. 'We can leave the car in a side street. Doesn't matter how far up the road we park.'

'One more thing,' Zen said, 'I don't mean to be a killjoy, but could you wear flat shoes, our accommodation ladder's awkward.'

'Hope you know what you're doing,' Harry said, once they were in the car.

'Was just being friendly.'

250

'Seeing how Ann has a fiancé, I suppose she's not entitled to better treatment.'

'I'm just being friendly,' Zen insisted. 'Besides, nothing's going to happen between Ann and me.'

'Whatever. Could we drop off at Linda's on the way back? There's something she's supposed to be arranging and she'll know about it today.'

Zen had never been to Linda's and Harry had to guide him. She lived in a terraced cottage in one of the first streets on the outskirts of the town.

When they arrived, Linda made them a cup of tea. Although late, Stephen was still up.

'When I told him you were coming he insisted on seeing you,' Linda explained.

'Any excuse,' Harry said, putting his arm round his shoulder.

'Okay, you've said hello, now off to bed,' she ordered.

'Well, any news for me?' Harry asked when Stephen had shut his bedroom door.

'Yes, I managed to find a B & B in Cawsands,' Linda replied.

'Never heard of it,' Zen said.

'It's in Cornwall, near Rame Head, just the other side of Plymouth. I've provisionally reserved Friday and Saturday nights. I need to confirm it in the morning.'

'It'll mean my leaving at seven and getting back early Sunday evening,' Harry said. 'Think you can manage?'

'Sure we can,' Zen said.

'You'll be able to call in an emergency,' Harry said. 'Linda will give you the number.'

'I tried to find somewhere closer, but it's a lost cause at this time of year,' Linda added, starting to rummage in her handbag.

'Hope you enjoy yourselves,' Zen said. 'Stephen going too?'

'No, that's the thing,' Linda said. 'After that incident in the hotel, I told Ruth how upset I was by her behaviour. She apologised and said how delighted she was that I'd found someone.'

'That's a turnaround,' Zen said.

'She offered to look after Stephen if we wanted to go away for a weekend, especially as it's my birthday Tuesday, so I jumped at it,' Linda said. She had found a pen and her note book and began scribbling on one of the pages.

'You know, we could've looked after Stephen,' Zen said, feeling uneasy. 'In fact, you could still do that. He already knows more about the engine room than we do, thanks to Harry.'

'I'd rather he stayed at home for his first time,' Linda said, amused, 'but thanks for offering.' She tore out the page and handed it to Zen.

'So Ruth's coming to stay for two nights?' Zen asked, pocketing the slip of paper.

'That's right,' Linda replied.

'Won't that be inconvenient for her?' Zen enquired.

'No, she's looking forward to getting away from Plymouth,' Linda said. 'On Saturday she's planning to take Stephen for a ride on the steam railway from Castlewear to Paignton and also visit the zoo. Then on Sunday, she's bringing him to Bigbury where we'll spend the day on the beach.'

After they had finished their tea, Harry and Zen left and drove back into the town.

'You okay?' Harry asked. 'You went quiet at the end there.'

'I'm fine,' Zen lied.

'I suggested Stephen stay on board, but Linda didn't want to in case Ann was there. She doesn't think she's a good example. Otherwise she would've been happy for you to look after him, even if it upset Auntie Ruth.'

'I understand,' Zen said. So much for Ann thinking she had Linda's approval. 'I don't even know whether I'll be seeing her.'

'Oh, I think you probably will. According to Linda she really has the hots for you.'

'Pity she can't reserve her passion for her fiancé.'

'From what Linda says, she's got strange ideas about marriage.'

'I'd say.'

'She believes she's better off marrying someone like Edward, who's more like a brother. She thinks the marriage has more chance of lasting, but at the same time feels it's okay to have a lover.'

'Really?' Zen said, remembering who else had promoted that theory. 'Wonder how many she's had.'

'Didn't ask.' Harry replied. 'Do you need to know?'

'No, and I won't be adding myself to the list.'

'So what are you doing with her?' Harry asked, but Zen did not answer.

Andy was waiting for them by the pontoon. By the time they got in it was nearly midnight.

Friday, 20th August 1982

Zen could not sleep. His mind was on Stephen and Ruth. He was trying to find a reason not to worry, not to have to do something about it. After all, Ruth and Linda were not having an affair, as in the previous cases. But even so, was she dangerous or was it an incredible coincidence? And why did that last boyfriend stalk her? What made him think Ruth was responsible for the suicide of his girlfriend's daughter? Was Stephen still having bouts of depression or had they now passed? Would Linda be leaving him if that were the case?

And if he decided that there was a risk to Stephen, what could he do about it? Should he tell Harry? He might make a fool of himself as well as cause insult and hurt feelings.

The weather was good that day. Zen went running before breakfast and felt calmer afterwards. He went shopping later and picked up the mail on his way back. There was a message from Ann to call him on her Plymouth office number.

'I was worried you wouldn't get my message,' she said when she answered.

'How are you?' he asked.

'It's been an awful week,' she replied. 'Only went to Exeter once and guess when that was?'

'Thursday.'

'Exactly, then Mum wasn't feeling well.'

'Sorry to hear that.'

'She's better now. There's more news, but I can't talk about it now. I've done something really naughty, but I did it for us.'

'Hit me with it,' Zen said, bracing himself.

'I had to find some way to be with you this weekend,' she began. 'I'll explain why later. So I lied to my mother and sister and told them that I'd won a theatre break in Stratford to see *A Midsummer Night's Dream*. My sister's coming down to stay with Mum. She should be there this afternoon. Hope you don't mind.'

'I'm not the one who lied.'

'Made the mistake of telling Linda; she's furious.'

'I'm not surprised,' Zen said. It certainly explained her reaction last night.

'The thing is, because Stratford's so far, I said I'd go by train and have left the car at home, so I'm catching the 17.23 from Plymouth after work. Can you pick me up from Tonebridge at six?'

'Sure. I'd better get the car out of the car bay. Do you want to eat out?'

'No, let's stay in. Can we have something on your boat?'

'Sure, I'll see to it. See you later.'

'Can't wait, bye.'

He had to trudge back to the harbour office and move the car to the main car park, which was a real nuisance because he had to hang around for twenty minutes for a space.

The package from Alan had also arrived with the post and, as soon as he was back on board, he went to his cabin and looked carefully through the report. There was nothing in it that added anything to what he already knew, so he filed it away.

255

Perhaps Ann's coming was a good thing. It would take his mind off Ruth. The hours spent thinking about it did not bring him closer to a conclusion. His intuition told him that something was not right, but then he'd not relied on it in the past, so how did he know he was not allowing his dislike for her to fuel his imagination? Yet here was a woman who had started off as a high achiever, until the tragedy in Greece, and after that catastrophe had somehow managed to raise herself from the gutter into a position where she was helping others in difficult situations. If you are dealing year in year out with such people, you were going to encounter the odd assault or worse, suicide. Could it not also happen that if you took interest in someone, identified with them, you could become emotionally involved, and if they had children, you could become their *auntie* as a way to satisfy the motherly instincts you were denied the opportunity to express? How would you then feel if this attachment was threatened?

He went downstairs while there was still time and helped Andy with the painting. Over lunch he informed Steph that Ann was coming for the weekend and to prepare the guest room. Then he came up with the idea that perhaps they could eat out Saturday night. He wanted to do this for Steph who had yet to go out in the evening.

According to the conditions of their lay-up and insurance, there had to be someone on board at all times. But with everything switched off and locked down, it was difficult to see what could go wrong. The only danger that they could think of was if someone trespassed.

'You need somewhere with a clear view of the *Amber*, the side with the ladder,' Harry said, retaining the look of disapproval after hearing of Ann's visit.

'Well, there's no such place,' Zen said.

'What about the other side?' Harry suggested. 'You could use the port gangway.'

'There are a couple of pubs in Castlewear; don't know how good they are. The trouble is that you have to moor at the marina and it's a long walk up to the town. In Tonemouth it only takes a minute to get to the boat.'

'If nobody steals it,' Andy said. 'But I don't agree. There's the hotel.'

'Yeah, but when you're sitting in the bar or restaurant, your view is blocked by parked cars, buses and the café,' Harry said.

'Not from the first floor,' Andy said.

'Isn't that where they have their private rooms?' Zen asked.

'They sometimes use them for the overflow from the restaurant,' Andy said. 'I'm sure if I asked Clare she could arrange it for us.'

'Will she join us?' Zen asked.

'Not if she's on shift,' Andy replied.

'See if we can go at seven thirty.'

After lunch and their shut-down, Zen went out to dispose of their rubbish, replenish their drinking water and top up the petrol for the boat. He also went to the off-license and bought a couple of bottles of the white wine Ann liked. He only had an hour back on board before he had to leave to pick her up. He took Harry with him and dropped him off at the end of Linda's road and wished him an enjoyable weekend.

The traffic was terrible: dozens of caravans jamming the narrow winding roads, seemingly going no faster than walking pace. When he arrived at the station, Ann had been waiting for fifteen minutes.

'I must look awful,' she said, once she was seated. 'I didn't have time to freshen up before I left work and couldn't get into the loo on the train.'

'Nothing a hot bath won't fix. Pity you fell out with Linda.'

'We haven't really fallen out.'

'You know they're going away?'

'Of course. That's why I thought it the ideal weekend to spend together.'

'And Ruth's looking after Stephen?'

'I heard. Least she could do, after Friday.'

'Has she done it before?'

'Not overnight, but she's had him for the day.'

'So, what do you want to do tomorrow?'

'I'm not going to suggest shopping.'

'Sorry. Let's decide at the time.'

It was after seven before they got back to the car park in Tonemouth. 'Don't let me forget to put money in the meter in the morning,' he instructed.

When they were on board, the generator was already on and Steph asked them about supper. Ann said she preferred to eat early, so the four of them sat down at eight. Steph had leftover Bolognese sauce from last week, so he boiled up spaghetti and grated some cheese.

Andy was going out at nine thirty and it was agreed that, as Steph did not want to have anything to do with the engine room and Zen and Ann were not bothered about watching television, he would switch off before leaving.

258

It was therefore nine forty-five when Ann lay soaking in the bath with a glass of Chardonnay on the stool beside her, two candles flickering on the shelf above the basin. Zen had moved what he needed into the guest cabin and to his surprise Ann was not upset by it. Now he sat on a chair, just outside the bedroom with the curtain half parted and close enough so they could talk. A gas light hissed on the bedside table. 'So what did you want to tell me that you couldn't say over the phone?'

'I spoke with Edward on Tuesday.'

'And?'

'He called from Rotterdam. They were leaving the next day for north Spain, which would take a few days. They'll probably be staying there next week, before sailing back to Rotterdam. That means I can expect him home any day after the 29th.'

'You looking forward to it?'

'Not really.'

'Explain to me how this works for you. How can you be engaged to someone you don't love?'

'I do love him, in a way,' she replied. 'He's loyal and committed to me. If I want something he'll get it or do it. He'll never let me down. I've known him since we were children.'

'That may well be so, as far as he's concerned. But what about you? What if you meet someone and fall in love, then you'll be the one leaving him.'

'I'll try and explain,' she began. 'I couldn't stop thinking about you all week, wanting to be with you, lying my way into arranging a weekend together. But, to me, that has nothing to do with marriage. You could be

259

a millionaire, you probably are, but you couldn't provide me with the type of security Edward can.'

'What happens when you do get married?'

'How do you mean?'

'Will you still see other men?'

'Of course, if the right one's available,' she said, then softly 'if you're available. I bet you're shaking your head. So let me ask you a question, and answer honestly. Now that you know that I will never marry you, but at the same time want an intimate relationship, are you still going to sleep in the next room?' There was a pause. 'I wonder why you're not answering? You see, I know you would never want to marry me either, yet at the same time you want me. That's how I feel.'

There was no denying what she said, Zen thought, as he heard her coming out of the bath and drying herself. She stepped over the threshold into the bedroom, naked. The light of the gas lamp tinged her skin with a warm glow and behind her the dancing flames from the candles gave her bountiful hair, now bunched on the top of her head, red highlights. She removed her clips and let her locks fall to her shoulders. She was beautiful. He got up and quickly undressed.

Saturday, 21st August 1982

It dawned a beautiful day. The generator did not come on until nine thirty. Andy had probably overslept. Zen had to be out early to get an all-day ticket for his car, so he went for a run as well. Fortunately there was enough hot water for them to shower when he returned. At breakfast Andy confirmed that he had booked a table in one of the private rooms of the hotel. They would leave at seven.

'Why don't we go for an excursion with the boat this afternoon?' Zen said when they were back upstairs, standing outside on the deck and in the sun. After their shared intimacy last night, he would happily get back into bed with her.

'Not out to sea?' Ann questioned, putting her arms around his waist.

'The boat's capable, but I want to go upriver. There are some nice villages along the banks, I believe.'

'I'd love to do that,' she said, kissing him. 'How long till lunch?'

Zen looked at his watch. 'Hour and a half. Why? What would you like to do?'

She gave him a long passionate kiss. 'Does that give you a clue?'

That afternoon, they explored all the way up to Tonebridge. Ann told him that there was a possibility of seeing kingfishers and herons, although they failed to spot any. The contrast between the busy waterfronts of Tonemouth and Castlewear and the peaceful, thickly wooded banks only a few hundred yards away, was startling.

Later they found somewhere to tie up and have tea before returning.

They showered and changed, and by a quarter to eight that evening they were all sitting at a table in one of the first floor function rooms of the hotel. The weather was balmy and the windows open. Andy had brought a pair of binoculars and they had a good view of the *Amber*. They had ordered drinks and were examining the menu.

'Do you think the whitebait's any good?' Steph asked.

'It'll be as fresh here as anywhere,' Zen said, 'but I don't know whether they'll prepare it the way you're used to.'

'I'll have it anyway.'

'Me too,' Andy agreed.

'Think I'll have the potted crab,' Ann said. 'It's my favourite.' She was stroking Zen's calf with her leg.

'And I'll have the Caesar salad,' Zen said. 'And to follow?'

They took their time deciding, but Ann chose salmon with new potatoes and salad, Andy and Steph the catch of the day, which was grilled lemon sole with fries and beans, and Zen the rump steak with fries, mushrooms and beans. They also ordered a bottle of red wine and one of white.

Once the waiter had taken their orders, all except Zen lit up. Steph and Andy wanted to know about Linda and Ann's work at the refuge.

'I wonder what Linda and Harry are doing right now?' Ann pondered sometime later, while they were into their main course.

'Probably sitting down to a meal like us,' Andy suggested.

'Do you two remember where you were in January '68?' Zen asked Andy and Steph.

'I was still at school,' Andy replied.

'I was back home, running my father's business,' was Steph's answer. 'Before I got married.'

'Do either of you recall a particular incident involving the death of two twin boys?'

'I do,' Steph said, while Andy shook his head. 'Was it in the Peloponnesus?'

'That's the one,' Zen confirmed.

'My sister and brother-in-law had just moved to Patras,' Steph said. 'It shocked everyone.'

'Do you remember the details?' Zen asked.

'Some,' Steph said 'How do you know about it?'

'A friend told me,' Zen said. 'A woman jumped off a cliff with someone else's twins.'

'That's right,' Steph said. 'I remember reading about it. They were the children of a foreigner.'

'An English woman,' Zen said.

'That's terrible. What's made you bring this up?' Ann asked.

'It came to mind while you were talking about your work,' Zen replied. 'Do you recall why the woman did it?'

'If I remember, she was the man's fiancée before he met the English woman,' Steph said. 'It was jealousy.'

'But how can you kill two innocents like that?' Ann asked. 'Why not kill the parents?'

'It was the best way to punish them, if you think about it,' Andy replied.

'What would that do to someone?' Ann asked.

'Well, if you had knowledge of Greek mythology, you'd know the answer,' Steph said.

'Here we go again,' Andy said. 'Leave it for another time.'

'No, I'm interested,' Zen said.

'Once upon a time there was a beautiful daughter of a king of Egypt, called Lamia, who became the queen of a certain part of Libya,' Steph began. 'Zeus, the philanderer, had an affair with her and she bore him two children. When Hera, Zeus's goddess wife found out she had a rage of jealousy and killed their offspring.'

'You Greeks are too hot-blooded,' Ann said.

'But Hera further punished Lamia by preventing her from closing her eyes and thereby never removing the vision of her children's ghosts from her sight,' Steph continued. 'This drove her insane and as a result she started killing other people's children.'

'That's pretty wild,' Zen said. 'Could it really happen?'

'People become killers or abusers for many reasons,' Ann said. 'Some a lot more benign than that.'

'Maybe it's time to change the subject,' Zen said. 'Tell me about this beach where Ruth and Stephen are meant to be meeting Harry and Linda.'

'What beach?' Ann said.

'Bigbury, I think they said.'

'Well, it's a bit further on from the one we went to. I'd imagine they're going for the surf.'

'It's a surfing beach?' Zen said, wondering if Harry had remembered to take his wetsuit.

'Yeah, Stephen's mad on it, they have boards.'

'I'd like to try it,' Zen said. 'Maybe we should go too. Let's surprise them.'

'I don't think that's a good idea,' Ann said. 'Linda might be surprised, but not pleasantly. Besides, I don't surf.'

'I'll have to go with Harry sometime. What's the beach like?'

'Tidal sands, backed by low cliffs. Very popular this time of year.'

'I guess they'd have to get there early in order to find somewhere to park.'

'Depends on the tides, but I'd say yes. Especially if they want to get into the main car park.'

'Did you realise you caused Linda a sleepless night last Saturday?' Zen asked Steph, changing the subject.

'Harry told me,' Steph replied, smiling. 'He's a bright, inquisitive boy.'

'A lot has to do with who does the telling,' Ann said, intending to imply a compliment. 'When I was young, I tried to read the Iliad and the Odyssey, but just couldn't get into it. Have any of you read it?'

They all had, but it was Steph who volunteered to tell her the tale.

Chapter 29: The Encounter

Sunday, 22nd August 1982

Zen woke with intent on his mind. Ann was stirring, reaching out for him, but he gently pulled away.

'Are you getting up already?' she asked.

'You can stay in bed as long as you like, but I remembered something I must do.' He started dressing.

'What? On Sunday?' She became more alert and propped herself up on one arm.

'Well, I made a bit of a blunder,' he said, as he busied himself with his laces. 'As I hadn't heard from you by Thursday evening when I went to the club, I said I'd go for a dive with them today. Then I forgot about it till we spoke of Bigbury; they're somewhere nearby.'

'Will you be gone all day?'

'No, I'll drive there, tell them I'm not feeling well and come back.'

'Is that necessary?'

'Can't just not turn up. They may delay the dive because of me.'

'I'll come too.'

'You can't risk being seen, remember?'

'I guess', she said in resignation. She looked down and was rubbing the sheet between her fingers.

'Would you like a cup of tea?'

'Least you could do,' Ann said, looking dejected.

'Look, I'm sorry,' he said, bending over her and kissing her cheek.

Downstairs, in the mess, Steph and Andy were having breakfast. 'What can I get you?' Steph said, getting up from his cornflakes.

'Don't worry, I'll do it myself,' Zen said. He was not particularly hungry, but thought he ought to eat nonetheless. He went into the pantry, put the kettle on, put some bread in the toaster and prepared a tray with butter, marmalade, mugs, teapot, plates and cutlery. When it was ready he went back into the mess.

'Are you going to church?' he asked Steph, who by now had finished and was smoking.

'Yes, why?'

'What time do you leave?'

'By nine thirty,' he said taking a long drag and blowing the smoke away from them.

'I'll come too. There's something I've got to do. What time do you return?'

'The service finishes just after eleven, but I stay for coffee, so I'd say twelve.'

'I'll either come back with you or someone will pick you up.'

'Is Ann leaving too?' Andy said. He had also finished his cereal and was now eating a pear.

'No, she's staying. Better take this up. Is someone getting the papers?'

'I'll get them in a minute,' Andy said. 'So you've made friends,' Zen heard him say to Steph as he headed for the stairs.

Ann was in a better mood when she saw that he had brought breakfast. 'I've been trying to think what I can do on my own,' she said. 'Do you have writing paper?'

'Sure, plenty. As you sit at the desk, it's in the bottom drawer on your left.'

'I have an aunt in Australia. As Mum can't write I do it for her. It's about time we sent her news.'

Steph and Zen left promptly and by nine forty-five he was driving out of Tonemouth. He was prepared for a slow journey and was banking on the fact that after their first weekend together, Harry and Linda were not going to be in a hurry to check out of their bed and breakfast. From his experience, one usually did not have to do so until ten or after. It would also be logical to call Ruth when they were leaving, as the latter's journey would be shorter. He considered waiting outside Linda's house but had no idea what Ruth's car looked like and did not want to risk being seen.

The weather was blustery from the west, probably good for surfing, and they predicted the occasional shower. His plan was to get to the car park and wait.

It was ten thirty when he arrived. He found a shady corner at the furthest, upper level from the beach and from where he could have a clear view of the entrance, but still not be seen. The lower level was already three-quarters full and there was a regular stream of cars continuing to come in. At the beach end there were steps that led down to the sands.

The first to arrive were Harry and Linda. They parked in one of the middle sections. He saw Harry going to the vendor, seated in his wooden hut, and buying a ticket, before returning to the car. It took them a while to remove their towels, wet suits, a body board and beach bag. They touched and looked at each other frequently and had the body language of a couple in love. He smiled to himself, happy for them. He felt his resolve weaken and he considered driving back. If Ruth and Stephen arrived now, while Harry and Linda were still in the car park, his plan would be unworkable. He wished that would happen as he considered the consequences of being mistaken.

Then he visualised a possible scenario. Sometime in the future, Harry, Linda and Stephen might come to a beach just like this to surf, or maybe they would be walking along the cliffs. And then it would happen; Stephen would walk over to the edge and fling himself on to the rocks below. Harry and the boy were bonding well, so it all seemed terribly implausible. Maybe Ruth was completely innocent, but was he willing to take that chance? He could not imagine what Ruth could do to drive a young boy or girl to despair and ultimately suicide, but that did not mean it could not happen. Zen stayed put.

After they had made their way onto the beach, it was only another fifteen minutes before Ruth arrived. She was easy to spot as she had her window rolled down. Zen got out of the car and positioned himself. Ruth parked at the far and, after a few minutes, made her way to the ticket vendor, having left Stephen in the car. Zen went up to her as she was returning. She recognised him at once.

'Hi, Ruth,' he said.

'What are you doing here?' she asked, with an expression of surprise mixed with suspicion.

'Thought we might have a natter actually,' Zen said, keeping his gaze firmly on her. 'Linda and Harry have already arrived, so I want you to take Stephen to them, then come back. Tell them you feel unwell and have decided to go home.'

'Fuck off,' she sneered, turning her back on him.

'Don't walk away from me, Mrs Nicholas, unless you want your life history to be public knowledge tomorrow.'

She stopped in her tracks and turned round. As she did so, he held up a brown envelope containing one of the photocopies Alan had sent him. 'We can have our chat either here in private or down on the beach, your choice.'

She hesitated for a few seconds. 'Meet me by the car,' she said before walking off.

When Ruth and Stephen had collected their things, climbed down the steps to the beach and were out of sight, Zen walked over to her car to wait, gazing out over the sea, thinking about what he was going to say.

Ruth was back ten minutes later, carrying her shoulder bag. When she reached the car, Zen signalled that they should get inside. She did so and leaned over to open his door. He slipped into the passenger seat. There was a combined scent of stale tobacco and the perfume meant to disguise it. He looked over to Ruth and saw that she was gripping the wheel with both hands so tightly that her knuckles had gone white. She was staring ahead with an expression of anger, bracing herself for what was to come, no doubt.

'I've never lost anyone,' Zen said, trying to sound as matter-of-fact and relaxed as possible, 'not through death at least, so I can't begin to imagine what it must be like. I've heard people say that you never get over the loss of a child.' He looked back over at her, but she had not changed her posture. 'I can, however, appreciate that the manner in which the tragedy takes place could have a bearing on the severity of the trauma.'

'What? Are you trying to analyse me?'

'I'm trying to imagine the terror of what happened, of what you went through.'

'What does this have to do with anything?' she hissed. 'Stop trying to sympathise and get to the bloody point.'

'They say losing a child's like having something ripped out of you, leaving a void.'

'It's not like that at all, actually,' she said, still staring ahead. 'It's like having something forced into you, the horror multiplies and takes hold. It fills you to bursting. You can never escape it. Not with alcohol or drugs. Even your dreams are woven round it.'

'I'm not judging. But I know what you've been doing and what you're planning to do.'

'Look, Mr. Zen, or whatever your name is, I don't know what you're talking about.'

'I know about the suicides.'

'So? They had nothing to do with me.'

'Maybe so; on the other hand, does Stephen keep a diary?'

'I don't know, so what?'

'Or maybe, sometime in the future, he'll be speaking to one of his friends or write them a letter revealing how depressed he is, how he's afraid he's going to lose his mother?' Zen said, opening the envelope. 'Do you want to read this? It might refresh your memory.'

'Can I keep it?'

'Sure, I've got plenty of copies,' he said, passing it towards her.

'It won't be necessary,' she said, waving it away.

'In that case, tell me why?' Then he remembered what Steph had told him about the Lamia. 'When you

271

see your children, how do you explain what you do?' he asked.

It was a long time before she spoke, but he felt he should remain silent and let the question hang in the air. In the distance the repetitive sound of the surf and the cries of gulls filled the passing minutes. It was getting stuffy in the car, so Zen rolled down his window. He noticed a change in Ruth. She started scanning about her, as one would do if they thought they were being watched. Then she adjusted the rear view mirror, using it to look behind her. This caused Zen to look round, but there was nothing there.

'You know who I blame?' she said finally, still staring in the mirror, as if addressing someone behind them. 'It isn't the women's fault; it's the men's, it's always the men. They promise things and then betray you or fail to protect you. These scum think they can come in and break up a relationship.'

'But you and Linda...'

'Given time we could've made it work, in some way,' Ruth said, turning to him, examining him for a reaction. 'It's not always about sex you know. Men just don't get it. I would've been a better father for the boy than any fucking man could be.'

'Yes, and after all that effort, after all you gave, some nobody picks her up in a bar.'

'Don't they see the distress they cause these children?'

'Not forgetting your own torment.'

'No wonder they're driven to take their life. When they see their mothers behaving like sluts.'

'And of course you've discussed this with Stephen.'

272

'Children have to be told the truth, they have to realise what's at stake. They have to be prepared to strike back, match hurt for hurt. We've been hurt. She must be hurt.'

'By we, you mean you and Stephen.'

'Only I can tell him what the pain of betrayal is, what he can look forward to.'

'And you've suffered this pain many times.'

'They think they can keep on screwing me over and over. But I always strike back. It's the only way they can be stopped.'

'But it doesn't stop?'

'They have to be stopped. They have to learn.'

'There are no second chances.'

'They're lost to us. They've fallen.'

'And the children? The innocents?'

They're better off where my children are, away from harm, away from abuse. Forever innocent and optimistic.' With these words she turned to look at the back seat. 'They come and tell me, so I know it's so.' As she said this she smiled at the empty space.

'So when were you planning that Stephen should join them?'

Ruth turned to look forward again. 'He's so naive. He doesn't realise how hopeless it is.'

'It's not going to happen.'

'He actually likes this man.'

'Ruth. It's not going to happen.'

'He's more gullible than the others, but he must be told, he will be told...'

'Except, it's not going to happen,' Zen said firmly. 'It just isn't.' At this she seemed to have come back to reality. She looked deflated, crumpled. 'As much as I'd like to see you locked up, I don't think there'll be enough evidence for the police to go on, but there's certainly enough here to discredit you. So all I can do is save Stephen. Are you with me?' He looked over at her; she nodded slowly. 'Tomorrow, I'm going to call Ann and I want to receive the shocking news that you've resigned. You're going to say that your mother's ill and that you're going back to Yorkshire to look after her. I want you out of the county by the end of the week. In return I give you my word never to speak of this. Remember, I have the means, due to this wealth you so despise, to keep tabs on you. I will check up on you every now and again and if I find a police report implicating you in anything, even a traffic offence, I'll turn everything I know over to the national press. Do you understand?'

'I do,' she said softly, her head bowed, almost appearing vulnerable.

'I'd suggest you seek help, for your own good, but I know you won't,' Zen said, putting his hand on the door release. 'I never want to see you or hear of you again.' Zen got out of the car and started walking back to his. A minute later he saw her drive past him and out of the car park.

By the time he arrived back in Tonemouth it was twelve thirty. As he approached the pontoon, Steph came out of the harbour side café.

'It was good of you to wait,' Zen said.

'Didn't think there was a rush for lunch.'

'Not really,' Zen said, looking at the time and then around him. 'Think we're in line for a shower.' He could see dark clouds approaching from the northwest. 'How long will it be until lunch?'

'If Andy's done what I asked, it'll be ready at half one. Did you manage to do what you had to do?'

'Think so.'

Once on board he went upstairs and found Ann with the morning papers, sitting at the table. She frowned. 'That took longer than you suggested.'

'Sorry, the traffic was diabolical.' He went over and kissed her. 'Lunch will be ready in an hour. Would you like a glass of wine?' He took the bottle out of the fridge as well as a San Miguel. When he had poured them out, he sat next to her. A heavy shower had started and he could hear the rain lashing the deck outside. 'Are you coming next Thursday evening to our 'do' on board?'

'What do?'

'It's the first day of the regatta and we're having a party to watch the fireworks. Everyone's inviting a friend or two; I believe Linda and Stephen are coming.'

'What time?'

'Six at the pontoon?'

'Any excuse to see you, but I can tell you for sure tomorrow.'

'I'll call in the afternoon. Anyway, cheers.'

'Cheers.'

After lunch they went for a walk to the castle and had a cup of tea back at the café before Zen drove Ann to Tonebridge station.

Chapter 30: The Party

Monday to Wednesday, 23rd to 25th August 1982

It was calm and warm on Monday morning. As a result of the good weather over the weekend, the poop deck had dried, and during the day Harry, Zen and Andy were able to unblock the scuppers. It meant undoing the pipes from inside the crew's cabins, which they protected from soiling by laying down tarpaulins.

Steph started to give the ship a clean for the forthcoming regatta and their expected guests. In the afternoon Zen went out and called Ann at the Plymouth office number, but she was not there, so he tried Exeter.

'You'll never guess what's happened,' Ann said.

Zen was tempted to be clever. 'Tell me.'

'Ruth's resigned. She said that, due to her mother falling ill, she's leaving immediately.'

'That's sudden.'

'She's not even doing her notice. She's literally cleared her desk.'

'This happens with ageing parents, as you know, but it's going to be a wrench; she's made friends.'

'I suppose she can always do the same work in Yorkshire.'

'What about you? Will you be meeting your friend here on Thursday?'

'Yes, I will,' she said softly. 'I would've liked to see you on my way home today, but as things are, it's chaos.'

'Be at the pontoon at six.'

The next day continued warm but showery. After his run and swim Zen went to the harbour master's to collect the post and Captain Stern asked if they could smarten up the ship. So, after breakfast on Wednesday, they took out the ship's bunting and started dressing the *Amber*.

Andy, the only one amongst them who had no fear of heights, climbed the masts to fasten the long flag rope. They used the signal flags kept in drawers on the bridge. Each represented a letter and from the shore, the few who could interpret them would see "Happy Tonemouth Regatta". Later, Steph went out with his camera to take photographs of the *Amber*.

Many events were planned. The Red Arrows were due on Friday, when there was also canoe racing culminating in a regional final on Saturday. There would be different classes of sail boat races, which included Kim's. In the town there would be marching bands, a medieval market, music, singing, road races and more. There would be an opening firework display the following evening and one on Sunday night to end the festivities.

Thursday, 26th August 1982

The first day of the regatta was fine but chilly. Over breakfast they decided to undertake only light work that day, mostly to do with helping Steph. He was planning a special meal for the evening. The fisherman who had helped Andy the other day had become their sporadic supplier. If he caught too much fish to sell on a particular occasion, he would either negotiate a price with them or store it in their freezer for another day.

He had called round earlier in the week and sold them a stone of his catch. So the mainstay would be grilled dabs and chips.

Zen sat out on the stern in the sunshine with a bucket of water between his legs happily peeling potatoes. He had much to be pleased about. They were closing their fifth week and a great deal had happened. In his conversations with George Pittas he had gathered that the freight market was continuing to worsen. He pretended to be concerned, but was secretly pleased. When George offered to forward his freight market reports and periodicals, Zen declined, saying he would find them depressing. Instead, he wanted a break from that pressurized existence and did not miss any aspect of it. Here, by contrast, life was laid back and carefree. There was also something in the air, he could sense it, a potential and a danger. It made living exciting. He had been on a high all week, after his successful encounter with Ruth. It was rewarding when it seemed like you had done the right thing.

Added to that, they all got on so well. Harry had become a friend and had his own reasons to be content after having spent a blissful weekend with Linda, if the look on his face over the last few days was anything to go by. Andy he also liked. They did not speak much and everything he knew about him he had heard from Steph, but he was gregarious and easy-going.

Steph was reserved but at the same time friendly, caring, hard-working and conscientious. Now that he was going to church on Sundays, perhaps he would make friends too, although he was not inviting anyone today. The times he did come out of himself, at their recent party and when they ate out the other night, showed how well he could engage, if he had a mind to.

After lunch, Zen went out for last minute shopping, coming back to read and have a nap before crossing over to Tonemouth with Andy before six. The town was jammed with visitors and their cars and they wondered if their guests would be able to park. Clare was waiting at the pontoon, having to come no further than the hotel, as were Linda and Stephen, who only had a slightly longer walk. Zen stayed to wait for the others while Andy took the first contingent across. Zen reflected that Linda seemed her usual warm, friendly self and Stephen just as eager to get on board. How were they taking the sudden departure of Auntie Ruth?

When Andy returned, Kim, from the harbour master's office, had arrived, together with her boyfriend, Jeff. Zen had given the staff an open invitation, but only Kim could come. Ann made it soon after, so he sent them across on the second trip.

Thinking that maybe Alex and Frankie had misunderstood where they were to meet, he walked up the embankment until he was abreast of the car park and then walked back. This time he found Alex waiting outside the harbour side café.

'Is Frankie having problems parking?' he asked.

'I'm afraid she's not coming,' Alex replied. 'She had an accident last night.'

'Is she all right?'

'She's had a whiplash injury. Unfortunately she's going to have to wear one of those collars.'

'Shall we walk to the pontoon?' he said, seeing that Andy was on his way back. 'How did it happen?'

'Well, as you know she lives in Tonebridge.'

'No, I didn't.'

'She left Newham late last night, after having drinks with friends, but when she got to the main road, it was closed due to an accident, so she had to take the back lanes, and you know what they're like. There's a part of one where it winds through woods with stone walls on both sides. Just as she rounded a bend she saw a large animal in her headlights and swerved to avoid it. Luckily, she turned into a gap with a wooden gate. She went straight through that and ploughed into a pile of branches.'

'How's the car?'

'The damage is relatively minor. Being a Beatle it has the engine at the back and she was able to reverse out and drive on, but by the time she got home her neck was stiff and painful. Her parents had to take her to A & E.'

When they reached the steps they descended to the pontoon. 'Who else has come?' Alex asked.

'The girlfriends of two of my colleagues, someone from the harbour office and her boyfriend and an acquaintance of mine. Hope you won't feel uncomfortable without your friend.' He was surprised she had bothered.

'I'm sure I won't.'

'So what kind of animal did Frankie see?'

'The police say it must've been a deer, but Frankie says it looked like a dog. Personally, I think it was a boar.'

'A boar!' Zen said as they climbed down to the pontoon and on to the boat.

At the bottom of the gangway Andy cut the engine and Zen took hold of a railing to tie the painter to. Alex was first up. She wore a blue, skin-tight denim skirt, which came half way up her thighs, and a red, short-sleeved top. Her smooth, shapely legs had a lemony-olive hue. Zen could not keep his eyes off them.

At the top of the ladder, she paused for the view. 'It's beautiful from here.'

'It's even better from the top,' Zen said. 'Come inside, but watch the step. Sorry it's dark but our generator's off. We only run it in the morning and evening.' He knew where the others would be so he led Alex up the three flights to the bridge. There Steph had laid out refreshments on the map table. Both of the glass sliding doors to the wings were open. The smell of old maps, denatured varnish and stale cigarettes still lingered, despite Steph's cleaning.

'Wow, this is the first time I've been on the bridge of anything,' Alex said as she stepped in from the landing with Andy behind her. Steph was waiting with bottles of beer, which were in buckets of ice, glasses of wine, soft drinks and finger food. Harry was showing everyone around the bridge machinery, with Stephen not far from his side. Zen introduced Alex to everyone and, when Harry asked about her friend, she related the story of the accident.

With the sun low in the sky, they gathered out on the starboard side. Here the railings were of solid metal up to chest height facing forward, as a break to the wind and weather, and a foot lower at the sides. There was a broad, wooden, varnished rail running all the way round the top, which was ideal for placing drinks and small plates of nibbles.

Ann was distant, a change from the warmth she had displayed on first meeting. She stood next to Linda and

Stephen, who were talking with Kim and Jeff, but was staring into the distance. Zen thought of asking her if there was something wrong.

'Have you been to sea like the others?' Alex asked, as she approached, holding a glass of red wine and a small plate of hors d'oeuvres.

'Yes, but only short journeys,' he replied, keeping his eye on Ann.

'What's it like?'

'It's different for everybody,' Harry replied, standing a few yards away with Andy.

'What do you mean?' Alex asked.

'Well, some see it as a means of travel, a way to see the world, others as a way to escape a mundane life. I found it claustrophobic, specially spending ten hours a day in the engine room.'

'But isn't it worth it for the places you visit?'

'These days most harbours are large, industrial centres, which are dirty and polluted,' Zen said. 'It costs money for a ship to be in port so they turn them round quickly; there's no time for sightseeing.'

'You've ruined my romantic view of being a sailor.'

'I find it exciting,' Andy said. 'I always make friends. I'm not interested in sightseeing, just the people I meet.'

'It used to be different in my father's time,' Zen said. 'Then places were smaller. Loading and discharging used to take weeks, not days. The captain and officers were celebrities and were entertained by the locals and showered with gifts.'

Zen was distracted. He was puzzled as to why Ann was avoiding him. At one point Linda and Ann had stepped away from the rest and were having a discreet word.

'We usually switch on the generator at dusk,' Zen announced when the sun was about to set behind the hills. 'Now's a good time for a tour.'

All but Linda and Ann, who had already been, followed Harry back down to the poop deck. There, by the entrance to the crew's mess, they stepped through the doorway of the engine room casing and on down till they stood by the generators. It was dark and shadowy.

Harry started explaining how the system worked. As he did so, he looked over at Stephen and nodded. The young lad undid the valve for the compressed air. They were using the middle of the three generators and Harry opened the box of the control panel and pulled a lever. There was a loud hiss as compressed air flooded the cylinders and simultaneously the generator started turning over, the sprung valves, two for each cylinder, starting to rock. As the revolutions increased, Harry opened the fuel valve. When ignition started, he turned off the compressed air and adjusted the fuel to the optimum setting. Finally, he signalled to Stephen to go over to the electrical control panel to switch on the power. At the same time as the lights came on, they heard the sound of other systems starting up, such as the sanitary and water pressure pumps.

When Stephen returned, Harry completed the tour, which included store rooms, freezers, the steering gear and rope lockers before ascending to the galley. Visitors were always the most impressed by the latter. Perhaps this was because it was something they could relate to.

Meanwhile, Steph was griddling the dabs on the oven hobs while deep frying potatoes. Andy helped while the rest went out on the stern where they were reunited with their drinks. It was nearly dark now and the air had stilled. The freshness of the day had gone and it was feeling humid. In the distance Tonemouth was bustling with a carnival atmosphere.

At eight they sat down to eat. Half hour later, everyone helped Steph clear up. He was so impressed by this that he fetched his camera and had Zen take photos of them in the galley at various sinks, washing, drying up or stowing things away.

They assembled on the bridge for the firework display. After a speech by the mayor, the urgent whoosh of a rocket heralded the start. When it reached a point between them and Tonemouth, it burst into a number of brighter lights which began to drift slowly down for a few seconds before each exploded. An *ahhh* of contentment could be heard from the shore.

The spectacle continued with a series of subdued intervals interspersed by more climactic displays. Some of the latter were so bright that the ship was lit as in daylight. In all, the show lasted fifteen minutes and ended with a multiple cloud burst, accompanied by cheers from the audience.

Afterwards they went back down and had the puddings that Steph had prepared: a selection of Greek pastries. The atmosphere continued to be lively for everyone except Ann, whom he sat next to, but from whom he received no response. Zen was becoming concerned.

At eleven thirty Linda said that they had to go. Harry rose to take them, saying that he would probably be twenty minutes before coming back as he would walk them home, so Kim and her boyfriend also chose to leave.

For the time that Harry was ashore, Clare related numerous stories of mishaps at the hotel involving customers and staff, before Steph offered to make everyone a cup of his mountain tea. Zen stood to stretch his legs and, glancing out the porthole, saw that Harry had returned and was standing on his own, looking out at Tonemouth. Zen excused himself and went out to him.

'Is something wrong?' Zen asked.

'No, not at all,' Harry replied.

'You seem pensive.'

'It's always sad saying goodbye. It gets more difficult each time.'

'It's not like you're miles away.'

'That may be so, but it makes a difference not being able to pick up a phone and call.'

'Guess so,' Zen reflected. 'When are you seeing them again?'

'I'm collecting Stephen tomorrow afternoon. He's coming on board for the Red Arrows. I'll see Linda over the weekend. By the way, did you hear about Ruth?'

'From Ann on Monday.'

'Why didn't you say?'

'I assumed you would've heard from Linda. I'm worried about Stephen though, weren't they close?'

'They're sad about it, but I wouldn't go as far as making it a cause for concern.'

'Interesting,' Zen said. Harry went back inside and into the mess. Zen followed.

Ann was sitting with Alex, while the others were in the galley. On seeing Zen, she got up.

'Hope you've enjoyed the evening,' Zen said to Alex as he watched Ann step into the pantry. Harry followed her.

'I have,' Alex said, smiling. 'Though I'm not sure everyone else did.'

'That's most perceptive.'

'It's taken me till now to realise Ann was with you.'

'You could've fooled me.'

'Ought to warn you that she's just asked me about the club dive last Sunday.'

'The one that never happened.'

'I'm afraid she caught me off guard and my answer may not have been what she wanted to hear or you wanted me to say.'

'Not your problem. I'm the one who's in the shit.'

'You don't sound too worried.'

'It's for a higher good.'

'Sounds intriguing.'

'It's a long story.'

'Even more intriguing. I'd like to hear it sometime.'

'Unfortunately, I'm not able to tell,' Zen said, hearing footsteps. The others came back in from the galley, with Steph carrying mugs of his mountain tea on a tray.

'Have you been convinced to try it too?' Zen asked.

'After he promised it would cure all my ills and make me superwoman?'

After having the tea, the next to go across with Andy were Clare and Alex. Zen asked Ann if she wanted to join them, but she said she wanted Zen to take her. While they waited for Andy's return, they sat at one of the mess tables with Steph and Harry.

'There's a lot happening in the town tomorrow,' Harry said. 'After the Red Arrows, I thought I'd take Stephen for a look round.'

'Excellent idea,' Zen said. 'We can take turns going out.'

A few minutes later, he could hear Andy coming up the gangway.

'You don't mind if I shut down now?' Harry said as Zen was about to follow Ann down the ladder.

'Not at all. See you in the morning.' He bade goodnight to Steph and Andy.

As he was taking her across, Ann was still not forthcoming. She sat on the bench in front of him with her head bowed.

'Didn't you enjoy yourself?' Zen ventured.

'Very much, in the beginning,' she said, looking up at him, 'till certain things began to dawn on me.'

'What things?'

'It started when Linda told me about Ruth's behaviour at the beach,' she said. 'And then, I didn't like the way that woman looked at you.'

'What woman?'

'You know, Alex. Well, I can talk.' She looked down sadly. 'But I wanted to know if anything was going on between you.'

'Well, there isn't.'

'So I asked her about the diving last Sunday, only because I didn't know what else to do,' Ann said, looking at him. Zen avoided her eyes and attended to where they were heading, pointing the torch past Ann and into the gloom. 'Are you going to tell me where you really went?'

'I can't.'

'What are you hiding?'

'I didn't go to see Alex, if that's what you think.'

'I don't think that at all, not any more. But what I do think is that it has something to do with Ruth.'

'That's absurd.'

'It somehow made sense after I'd spoken to Linda.'

'I hope you didn't run your ridiculous theory by her.'

'They're on cloud nine at the moment. I'm not going to spoil that. But, according to Stephen, Ruth was okay when she drove to the beach and she decided she was *ill* around about the time you could've been there.' They were pulling up to the pontoon. 'Why don't you say something?'

'It's not what you think. Why would I do what you suggest?'

'Because Ruth got up your nose that day at the hotel and that's why the following Monday you asked me to confirm her surname. You decided to find out about her, didn't you?' When Zen didn't answer she continued. 'So, little rich boy decided to get even. I wonder whether you have things you'd prefer people didn't know.'

He walked her to her car through the dispersing crowds. 'You have it wrong,' Zen said. 'I haven't done anything out of spite, but I can't tell you what I did that morning.'

'Can you at least confirm you were not responsible for Ruth's departure?' Ann said as she stood by her car. 'That's all I want to know. Tell me you haven't been using me.'

'I can't confirm anything, but would ask you to trust me.'

'I need to hear it from you,' Ann persisted.

'Then it's goodnight, Ann,' Zen said, turning away.

'Goodbye, Zen,' Ann said, before getting in her car.

Zen made his way back to the boat. He had not anticipated this turn of events and was upset by it, although falling out with Ann was not cataclysmic by any means. Even if he could have predicted this, he still would have acted as he did. He had no choice.

Wrapped up in these thoughts, he climbed down the concrete steps from the embankment. It was as he got onto the pontoon that he was brought up short. At the end of it, under the shadow of the passenger ferry landing, was their boat and there was someone sitting in it.

Chapter 31: The Intruder

His first assumption was that some drunk had decided to borrow their boat again. He considered rushing it and envisaged a confrontation where they might both end up in the murky waters, and held back. He then realised that the trespasser was sitting in the passenger seat and not at the stern as they would have to in order to pilot it. His next thought was that it was Ruth seeking to take revenge, probably with a knife in her handbag. But would she spoil the element of surprise by being so visible? He continued to approach cautiously.

The stranger, identifiable as a woman, was sitting slouched, her head down on the top of her knees with her hands wrapped round her bare legs, doubtless bracing herself against the chill. As he approached, the intruder heard him and raised her head. His heart went to his throat, recognising Alex; he stopped at the edge of the pontoon and stood over her.

'Is there a problem?' he asked, thinking her car must have broken down.

'I hope not,' she said looking up at him. 'Why don't you sit down and I'll tell you why I'm here.' He got in the boat and sat opposite her, pushing the engine throttle to the side. 'You see, when I was brought ashore earlier, I had something on my mind, so I held back and waited. In fact, I sat in the park just up there. Then you and Ann came out and, although I couldn't make out what you were saying, I got the gist of a falling out.'

'You got that right.'

'Any likelihood of a reconciliation?'

'No chance. She's engaged anyway.'

'Naughty girl, and boy,' Alex said, pointing her finger at him. 'What did you do to lead her astray?'

'I didn't actively pursue her, if that's what you mean.'

'To the point. The thing is, I don't want to go home. I want to go back with you. Is that a problem?'

'Err, no,' was the most inspired thing he could say. He felt something in his stomach that was not there before, as if the dab he had eaten earlier had come back to life.

'That's okay then, can we go? I'm freezing,' she said, rubbing her bare thighs.

He stood and pull-started the engine. While it idled, he reached under the seat and retrieved the torch. 'Do you mind turning round and pointing this ahead,' he said, handing it to her. If he was alone, he would have had to do it himself, which was awkward. The visibility was good enough to see large objects. It was the small things, like partly-submerged pieces of wood that were the real danger, especially during an outgoing tide.

'Why don't boats have headlights?' she asked, changing position and facing forward.

'Some do, they're called power boats and cost £25,000 plus.'

'Wouldn't you like one of those?'

'I'm more simple in my tastes.'

He zigzagged his usual path between yachts and moorings before coming to open water. 'The *Amber*'s looking dark,' she observed. Only the oil lamps were visible.

'The others would've gone to bed. Weren't you going out with some Australian not long ago?'

'Are they still talking about him?' she asked, sounding annoyed. 'He left to go back home a few weeks before you arrived.'

'He's not coming back?'

'Can't say for certain, but, as far as our relationship goes, it's run its course.'

'Is that why he left?'

'He got frustrated that we weren't making the progress he wanted. Why the cross-examination?'

'I'd rather not be looking over my shoulder.'

Reaching the bottom of the gangway, he cut the engine and tied the boat. He stowed the torch, disconnected the fuel supply and covered the engine with the tarpaulin. Then, holding the boat steady, he instructed Alex to go up first. He followed carrying the fuel tank.

The ladder wobbled and rattled noisily as they climbed. At the top he let her in through the poop deck door and locked it behind them. It was dark, but he had abandoned having his torch by the door as he now knew his way. 'Can I get you something?' he asked. 'More wine maybe?

'I'd prefer water. You?'

'Water's fine, Steph's cooking's great but tends to be salty. I usually have some in my fridge, but I think I've run out. Wait here and I'll get it.'

'You're not leaving me in the dark. How can you see? I'm disorientated.'

'Give me your hand,' he said. She offered it to him. It was cold and he squeezed it reassuringly. He led her down the short passage and over the threshold of the door into the mess. Here at least there was some light from the portholes facing Tonemouth.

'This is okay,' she said, so he left her and fetched a bottle from the pantry fridge. 'Don't we need glasses?' she asked when he got back to her.

'I've got plenty upstairs,' he assured her, taking her hand again, leading her back to the poop deck landing and up the stairs to his cabin. He unlocked the door, let her in and, walking past her, went to turn his gas light on. 'This is home,' he said when the yellow light bathed the room. 'This is the captain's office or day room and through there's the bedroom and bathroom.'

'After this afternoon it's so serene.'

'Not when the wind blows. But I prefer it at night, after we've switched off and I've only got the gas lamp and candles. The florescent lights are too harsh.'

'Isn't it spooky?'

'It's rather nice walking on the decks on a summer's evening. Would you like some water?'

'Please.'

He fetched the glasses from the dresser and filled them, taking them to her. She was still standing near the open door. After drinking, he took her glass and put both on the table, before taking her in his arms. He kissed her gently, but she pulled away, rubbed his cheek with her hand. 'You're a bit rough,' she said.

'I did shave this morning.'

'So what do you normally do in the evenings?' she asked, as she turned and shut the door.

'Watch telly, read, go to the diving club or out for the occasional drink,' he said. A puff of breeze flapped the curtains of the portholes.

'I love that smell of the estuary,' she said walking over to them. 'Do you know what I mean?'

'Yes, it's the brackish water,' he said, following.

'How long do you think you'll stay?'

'Who knows? Nine months, a year, maybe more. Why do you ask? You're not assessing when our relationship will end before it's started?'

She laughed. 'If you knew my record you'd understand.'

'Well, I've not had much luck either. One of the reasons I'm here is to escape from the repercussions of a failed engagement, and a few other issues.'

'That explains your comment in the boat,' she said, moving towards him. 'I want to know more.'

'It's a long story.'

'Another one. Can you tell me this one?' she asked, coming closer.

'This one's okay.'

'Good,' she said, embracing and kissing him, this time with desire. She started unbuttoning his shirt. He tried to kiss her again but she pulled away, taking his hand and leading him through to the bedroom.

He woke with an ache in his left shoulder and his arm was numb. Alex was lying on it as she faced him with her arm over his lower chest and her leg across his groin. Her dark hair covered his throat and upper chest. A few stray hairs tickled his nose whenever he breathed in. There was only a sheet covering them and his right side was cold.

He pulled away carefully so as not to wake her. She turned to her other side and continued sleeping. He got up and went to the next room rubbing his shoulder to ease the pain and numbness. He turned off the gaslight and watched as the wick went from bright yellow to dull red in a few seconds. A gentle breeze was playing with the curtains. Looking out the porthole he noticed it was overcast. Towards the south there was a faint flash of lightning. His left side, damp from contact with Alex, felt cold in the draft and, as warm blood pulsed through his veins, the sensation began to return to his arm. He observed the cycle of lightning and thunder for many minutes as it neared, and soon there were droplets of rain on the wind.

From the corner of his eye he saw Alex emerge from the bedroom, her naked body glowing like ivory in the dark. She said nothing as she embraced him and they watched the approaching storm. When she began to feel the cold, she pulled him back towards the bedroom. He shut the portholes first and they went back to bed, slipping under the sheet and pulling up the single blanket. They held each other for a while. There was more thunder as they began to kiss. They started making love as the rain and wind intensified. There was not the urgency of earlier and when they had finished the deluge was at its peak. They clung to each other as the rain lashed the superstructure.

They fell asleep when the storm began to fade.

Friday, 27th August 1982

The generator woke them. They looked at each other sleepily. He took her in his arms and started kissing her but she pushed him away abruptly. 'You're not having any more cuddles till you shave,' she said, barely opening her eyes. 'You're lucky I didn't make you do so last night. What's the time?'

'Must be eight,' he said expecting her to panic. When she didn't, he added, 'What time do you have to be at work?'

'Not till ten, but I'm working till six.'

'Let me shave and shower, then you can use the bathroom.'

'I'll snooze a bit longer. Can you get me a cup of tea, when you're dressed?'

When he got up he felt the chill so he lit the oil heaters and watched her snuggle down. The bathroom was also cold so he closed the porthole and door and started shaving. He ran the shower till the water steamed. By the time he left the cabin Alex was stirring.

Downstairs the others were finishing breakfast. They were expecting the papers as he would usually have been out for a run in fine weather. He tried in a clumsy way to explain things but it was Andy who caught on and suggested Steph should have laid another place. Zen said that two cups of tea would do for now.

Steph insisted on making them, so he sat for a minute while Andy explained that last night's storm had brought their flags down. He had noticed when he'd gone to retrieve the oil lamps. He wondered whether Zen would have any time in his busy schedule to help put them back up.

'What's Ann doing here?' Harry said. 'I thought she'd left.'

'Allow me boss,' Andy said. 'I'll explain the current state of affairs.'

Glad he would not have to do it himself and wondering how Andy knew, he took the two teas and went back upstairs. When he entered the cabin Alex had already showered and dressed and was sitting on the bed waiting.

'You didn't take long,' he said.

'It occurred to me that you must have things to do. Besides, I should get going.'

'If it wasn't for the storm last night, I wouldn't.'

'What do you mean?'

'It blew our flags down so I'm helping Andy put them back,' he said looking outside the bedroom porthole. They were strewn all over the deck. At least they had not ended up in the estuary. 'Why don't you come back this evening and eat with us?'

'I can't, I'm afraid. I'm working straight through to next weekend; these are busy days.'

'Can't you go from here?'

'I normally need to be in at eight forty-five. I'm the closest to the office, so I open it most mornings. The traffic's a nightmare at that time. We'd better go,' she said, barely finishing half her tea. 'I don't want a fine,' she added. 'Sorry about that.'

'I need to get the post and papers anyway.' On their way out she bade the others, still seated in the mess, good morning.

After coming back and having breakfast, Zen assisted Andy with resetting their flags, asking him how he knew about Alex. He had apparently spotted her as he was walking Clare back to the hotel.

Later, he helped Harry grease the doors and latches. Harry had to use a blow torch on some of the hinges, they were so corroded.

During the afternoon they witnessed the Red Arrows' aerial display, for which Harry had gone out to collect Stephen. The thirty minute routine was spectacular and Zen took numerous photos.

Afterwards everybody wanted to go out, including Steph, as there was so much activity in the town and on the estuary. It was decided that Zen would stay in. He spent the evening reading, or trying to. He could not stop thinking of Alex. Her departure that morning was so abrupt. Not only did she decline his invitation to come back but she did not even suggest when they might meet again.

Saturday, 28th August 1982

After breakfast, they shut down the generator, having decided not to work that day. Andy, Harry and Steph went out to do the shopping for a change, and were meeting up with Linda in order to take in more of the regatta. Zen had nothing to do, no one to speak to and felt miserable. At least the weather was beautiful. He went and sat in the quiet solitude of his balcony, looking out on the activity of the town and estuary. Again he tried to read, but could not concentrate. Instead, despite the hard stool, he kept drifting off to sleep.

He was so far gone, he did not hear them return until Andy came up and found him. There was a telephone message for him in a sealed envelope. He opened it and found:

> Taken: 11.15
> 'If you want to have supper tonight come to my place at 7:30. If you can't make it call my office and leave a message. Alex'

The office and home numbers followed as well as her home address. He read the message six or seven times. He felt like cheering; instead he looked at his watch. He had to make sure to get the car out of the harbour authority car park by one or he would not be going anywhere.

He loved her terraced cottage. It was beautifully decorated and furnished, with a cosy feel. He made a point of telling her.

Supper was delicious: avocado vinaigrette with antipasto, tagliatelle with seafood sauce and crème brûlée to finish. While they ate he told her about his engagement to Sophia.

'You're a wonderful cook,' he said, after pudding.

'My parents run a restaurant. I'd be disowned if I was no good.'

At ten thirty he got up to leave. 'I was hoping you'd stay,' she said taking his arm. He sat back down next to her and gave her a long kiss.

'I didn't want to assume.'

'You're not letting anybody down, are you?'

'Harry and Andy also went out. I told them to meet me at eleven thirty. If I'm not there the boat will be at the pontoon at nine thirty when Steph goes to church.'

'So you won't have to leave till I do. You haven't seen my bedroom. I love it, and I want to see what you think of it. Shall we go up?'

'Should we wash up first?'

'That's the last thing on my mind.'

In the morning they arranged for Zen to come that night as well.

'Let me take you out this time,' he offered.

'I like cooking. Why don't you come earlier and we'll do it together?'

It was windy that morning as he drove back. They were predicting bad weather and, as the regatta was nearly over, they decided to take their flags down.

By the time Andy took him ashore in the early evening, the wind had picked up and it had begun to rain. However, the bad weather did not detract from it being another magical evening for Zen. It started with a wonderful meal, cooked and eaten by candlelight. The food was delicious and everything that happened seemed enhanced. All his sensual perceptions and emotions were heightened somehow. Did she feel the same way? They spoke about their parents and families. They had much in common.

Monday, 30th August 1982

On that Bank Holiday Monday, once on board, Zen spent the day in a daze and was not much good for anything, so it was fortunate there was no work planned. After lunch it turned windy again. No one wanted to go out so they played gin rummy at which Andy cleaned up on points. Later, after supper, they watched football before closing at eleven.

He locked himself in his cabin, feeling exhausted as well as depressed. He was missing Alex badly. Had he been on land they would at least have spoken on the phone, so he could empathise with how Harry felt. If it had not been so windy, he would have gone out and done so. He tried to remember when he had felt this way about anybody and so quickly.

By the light of the gas lamp he brought the diary up to date and got ready for bed. He snuggled down as the winds howled around him, and fell asleep within minutes.

He awoke with a start, but did not know why. All he was aware of, at first, as he lay in the darkness, was the buffeting of the wind. Then he heard the scratching noise. He was on his back, and froze with fear, his eyes darting around the room. The sound continued, but he realised that it was coming from the outside. Someone or something was on the bridge deck scraping at the bulkhead that separated him from the exterior.

The noise was moving, coming up his body towards his head. It sounded like someone with a metal scraper was removing flakes of paint from the bulkhead surface. He had the ridiculous notion that it was Andy sleepwalking.

When the sound was level with his head it stopped, and Zen turned to that bit of bulkhead. Long minutes passed and in his mind he tried to imagine what that quarter inch of sheet metal separated him from. Due to the wind and rain, he had closed the dayroom portholes, only leaving the one in the bathroom open.

After some minutes of no scratching, he got out of bed and pulled on his bathrobe. He stepped into the bathroom and looked out the porthole, despite the fact that its size restricted his view. Seeing nothing he went into the day room. There was nothing unusual there either.

He walked to the nearest porthole and looked out. The sky was mostly clear and starry with clouds racing before the wind. He remembered that just three days previously, he had stood on this same spot, watching the approaching thunderstorm, with Alex's warm and naked body in his embrace. He remembered the sound of her voice, how she smelt, how she looked, how she tasted, how her skin felt, and he experienced a sense of emptiness.

He raised his head again to look out the porthole. He was so engrossed in his thoughts that initially he could not understand what he was seeing. At first it seemed to be complete darkness, as if there was a blackout in Tonemouth, but he could not see any stars either. When he realised that the glow from the outside was still coming in through the other portholes, the icy grip of penetrating fear seized him. There was something in front of the porthole blocking the light. Then he saw them, faint at first: two green dots. Not the verdant colour of fertile fields and luxuriant woods, but a chalky, watery, cold green. He tried to pull his eyes away, but they were locked. He could feel his legs losing strength and about to buckle at the knees but still he could not break free. The longer he was held in the stare, the larger the eyes became, for that is what he realised they were. He had the sensation of falling, of being drawn into them, as if succumbing to a power he could not resist, an authority he could not overrule, a fate he could not avoid. The eyes had intelligence and they knew him, knew him in a way he did not. They exuded hatred and icy contempt.

Then they vanished. In a blink there was nothing there but the normal view. He went up to the glass and looked all the way round. They were gone, he was certain of it. He fell into the chair by the desk, exhausted, his body cold, wet and drained. He struggled to get back into his bed, throwing the blanket as well as the sheet over himself, convinced he would never sleep again. Mercifully, fatigue overcame him.

Tuesday, 31st August 1982

The light of morning permeated the room making the events of the night before seem implausible. The more he thought about it, the more he tried to rationalise to himself that it was a nightmare or a hallucination, brought on by fatigue and depression.

He got up and went to the bathroom. A quick glance through the porthole showed a fine day. The wind had dropped, but it was chilly. He closed the bathroom door and ran the shower while he shaved.

Downstairs the others had already finished breakfast and were off on their jobs. Steph had left the cereal, milk, fruit, some toast with marmalade and butter on the table for him. He took his time eating. After a while Steph appeared and told him he looked tired and went to make him a mug of coffee, which he took with him as he went to locate the others.

They were forward, by hatch number one, starting to grease the working parts of number one crane, which they would need that afternoon as the delivery of the spare chain that George had promised them was arriving by barge. Zen had decided that the cranes were the next thing that needed attention. They were already seizing up, as was evidenced when they tried to open the holds for their airing a few weeks ago. It was likely a prospective buyer would ask to see them in action.

'You look tired,' Andy said when he got there.

'Not you too,' Zen said. He had not thought he looked that bad when he was shaving.

'Sex drains you of energy. That's why I always come back to my bed; even if it's for a few hours, it's still better sleep. You've got to learn to pace yourself.'

'Yeah, I'll bear that in mind. I can help Harry if you want to do something else.' Zen wanted to get Harry alone.

'Actually, I need both of you,' Harry said.

So Zen worked with them straight through to lunch. Harry serviced the winches on top of their housing while Andy and Zen worked on the pulleys, bearings and crane head. During their meal they agreed that it was beginning to get cold, particularly in the mornings, so Zen promised to go out, after the barge had been, to buy a gas heater for the mess. Harry volunteered to help him carry it back.

The barge came at two and it took twenty minutes to winch the chain from its hold and down into the forward chain locker. Once ashore, Zen suggested a cup of tea, so they dropped into the harbour café. He waited until they had bought their drinks before telling Harry of the events of the previous night.

Harry weighed up whether to believe Zen or not. 'Obviously, the first time you saw the dog, I saw it too, but it was walking at the time not flying,' he said in a low voice. 'I'm not going to hide the fact that I'm sceptical and think you probably dreamt or imagined it. I mean, just the other day we were reading about this Beast of Dartmoor.'

'I didn't dream or imagine anything,' Zen asserted.

'Yes, but it's a fact that people do, and perfectly normal ones at that.'

'How would you like it if it'd happened to you and you were convinced it was real?'

'That's the whole point. People dream or imagine things all the time and are convinced they're real, otherwise we wouldn't be having this conversation.'

'There's no doubt about this,' Zen insisted.

'Okay, I admitted to you, when we went for our walk together, that when I was in California I got led astray, drank a lot, fucked a lot and maybe tried a few drugs. What about you?'

'I've only once taken a drug.'

'What was it?'

'I don't know, something I smoked.'

'What effect did it have?'

'I was with friends. It made me stay awake all night.'

'It could've had something in it that caused a change in your brain. A minority are affected in this way.'

'This was years ago.'

'Doesn't matter; it may have needed a certain series of events to trigger an effect. Like the strain of keeping two women at one time.'

'I'm not keeping two women; it was more of an abrupt changeover. I understand what you're saying, but still insist I saw what I saw.'

'Let's try another scenario. Zen Makris comes to live on board a laid-up ship to escape a failed engagement, a falling-out with his parents and being stalked by someone's jealous ex-boyfriend. He thinks he's left his problems behind, but guess what?'

'I know what you're getting at.'

'I'm not finished yet. Within days of arriving, he takes advantage of an engaged woman.'

'She threw herself at me, so it's more complicated than that.'

'It always is, Zen. I'd understand if love was involved, but she was infatuated and you were just plain greedy.'

'You're right.'

'What's going to happen when she next calls or maybe she'll turn up to surprise you?'

'Well actually, we sort of fell out.'

'Not because of Alex? Because everyone, except me apparently, could tell what was happening.'

'No, nothing to do with her, but I admit, I took advantage of Ann.'

'And you know it, which is what I'm getting at. Now you can add guilt to the other issues. And then to top it all, you and Alex fall for each other and you've both spent the last five days in an emotional and libidinous frenzy.'

'I admit, I'm really tired.'

'It's the first thing we noticed when you came down this morning, and I bet you're depressed as well.'

'I do feel hollow. But it was all so real.'

'Okay, let's assume it really did happen. What's the Beast of Dartmoor doing on the *Amber*? We don't have any sheep.'

'Who said it was the Beast of Dartmoor and whatever it is, it's not after sheep, it's after me.'

'This story of the Beast is where your subconscious took it from.'

'You forget that we saw the story after the first sighting.'

'But why could that not just be a dog? Well, why?'

'I don't know. I'm too tired to argue any more.'

'We're not arguing, Let's get what we came for and you can go and have a nap.'

They finished their teas and went to the ironmongers and bought the gas heater for the mess.

Chapter 32: Benjamin Earsop

Benjamin Earsop worked late into the night. He was preparing the hundreds of indexed references that would accompany his main manuscript. It was tedious work, but it would soon be ready for the critical eye of the publisher's editor. He was running to schedule and had no doubt that this logical extension to his previous published work would be in print by next summer, Christmas at the latest. The new concepts and evidence he was putting forward regarding his field of expertise were extensive and would appeal to the popular readership.

He had hundreds of case studies on file, a third of which had been corroborated by other professionals. Over the years he'd had many clients referred to him personally. He was the acknowledged expert of this controversial field in Europe.

This had been his work for the past twenty-five years, to the exclusion of everything else. To date he could have made more money if he had continued in his original practice as a psychotherapist, treating his affluent clients from his surgeries in Harley Street, London and the Cotswolds in Gloucestershire.

He would probably also have been married with grown-up children. He had gambled everything for this and now it was about to pay off, which was why the actions of his former colleagues irked him so.

They had helped him with his research only in so far as they had agreed that it could be done within the practice. Their motives were not altruistic but for the extra fees they received for taking on some of his patients. He had long suspected that they ridiculed him behind his back and he'd had this confirmed by Veronica, the wife of the one with whom he was having an affair.

So, now that they had wind that there was more money to be made, they wanted what they called, "payment and recognition in acknowledgement for their part in the work".

Of course he had refused and they, in turn, had started legal proceedings, stating publication of work originating during their partnership. This referred to the first book, which had made only moderate sales. They were, as yet, unaware of his latest work, which his publisher anticipated would be a best seller.

These arseholes had to be stopped, but how? This latest edition was still not the end. It did not contain any of his more recent discoveries. The case he was currently involved in, if he ever came to the end of it, would warrant a book in itself.

Apart from this one patient, it had otherwise been a quiet August.

He picked up the recorder and rewound the tape that was in it, preparing to hear the contents for the third time that day. He reflected on the implications of what was on that strip of plastic. He always taped his consultations and, as a result, had thousands of recordings, many of which were connected to his writing. He had nearly fifty of this one individual.

Never before had he spent so much time with one person, but he had never heard of such a case either. Every week there was something new, a new surprise or revelation. There was no way to predict what would happen next, how it would end.

When the treatments began there was no indication of anything unusual. After it became apparent that the orthodox methods were not working, he had turned to past life regression therapy. Very controversial, but something he knew about. The results at first were good, but still in line with the limited experience of the few who had practised this method and were prepared to admit it. Normally, the emotional problems the patient suffered seemed to be focused on an imagined past life and the treatments over time released the negative pattern. In this case the reverse was taking effect. The past life was becoming stronger, awakening in fact. It was behaving as if it were real. The results were astonishing, quite outrageous.

He could certainly claim to be responsible for initiating the process, but he was now certain that it had attained a momentum of its own, quite independent of his meddling.

This "other", as he had come to call it because it still refused to reveal either its name or gender, lived in the eighteenth century. It was aware of its own identity, knew that it inhabited another's body in the present time and was now having conversations with Earsop. The patient, on the other hand, was oblivious to the existence of "the other". To add to this, the other claimed to have supernatural powers that it had learnt in its previous life and was able to transmute into other animals. Earsop had never had time for the occult previously but it was a strange coincidence that the awakening of this entity correlated with the reappearance and nocturnal activities of the Beast of Dartmoor.

In addition, the other had a purpose, which could be useful, Earsop reflected. It wanted to evolve. Maybe there was a means by which they could help each other. There were several ways Earsop could be served by this. He had already set certain events in motion that would ultimately be of financial benefit to him, but he also saw the potential for something more radical.

These were interesting times, he thought, as he pressed to replay the tape.

Chapter 33: The Summer

As the fine summer days played themselves out, giving way to the first autumnal storms at the end of September, on board the *Amber* the day-to-day life of the crew continued as before.

Andy went out most nights, apart from the second week of the month when he stayed in every evening to follow the Pan European games, which took place in Athens. During that time Clare, as well as some other friends, came to watch with him. At the end of September, the beginning of the academic year, she returned to university in Exeter and their meetings became less frequent.

Harry saw Linda and Stephen at least three days a week. They came to lunch each Sunday and on the first weekend of September, the last of the holidays before Stephen went back to school, they spent both the Friday and Saturday nights on board.

Steph, on the other hand, hardly left the ship, apart from going to church. He kept himself insulated from relationships ashore, with the exception Stephen, with whom he not only continued to discuss Greek mythology, but also started tutoring in the skills of pen and ink sketching.

Meanwhile, Zen's relationship with Alex deepened. They spent every weekend on the *Amber* and Alex even took to leaving slippers, a dressing gown and basic toiletries on board. This was their base from which she took him to her favourite places. The foremost of these, on the fringes of Dartmoor, was the wooded valley of the river Tone. Alex related how she had come to one of the picnic areas with her parents and extended family for as long as she could remember, exploring the woods with her sisters and other children while the adults prepared lunch. She showed him the spot where she had nearly choked on a piece of meat.

She was also fond of other parts of the moor and Zen had to buy a pair of walking boots for these outings. She introduced him to wild, remote places with stone formations and burial sites. Although he appreciated their beauty and unique atmosphere, he noticed that Alex was so awed and captivated that he felt she was not quite with him at times. One place in particular stood out: a tor with flat-topped rocks surrounded by an area rich in archaeological remains such as hut circles, field systems and stone tombs. Alex said some were found to contain remains and possessions, but did not specify what. Nearby was an eerie wood, with strangely shaped dwarf trees in a heavily bouldered terrain.

When the weather was not good enough for the high moor they would visit the coast, more to Zen's liking. It also meant that Alex was less distracted.

Over the second weekend of September the weather was particularly glorious and Zen, Alex, Harry, Linda and Stephen drove to a cove where they could combine a day at the beach with a dive on an offshore wreck.

During weekdays Alex needed to be close to work as it was her responsibility to open the office in the morning. This meant that if they were to see each other he had to go to her. They had some wonderful late summer evenings, one in particular being her birthday on the sixteenth of the month. Although she did not have a back garden, there was a small patio outside her kitchen door, which could also be accessed through a

313

gated alley from the street. The surrounding houses provided shelter from chill winds and they could sit out comfortably. They did not always stay at home and occasionally visited a pub or the cinema, seeing *The Shining* on one visit and *The Thing* on another.

Irrespective of any good intentions to the contrary, it inevitably meant he stayed the night. This caused him to become overtired, not to mention feel guilty for abandoning the *Amber* and her crew.

In this respect, their work continued to consist of minor repairs and maintenance aimed at a potential buyer and, apart from the nuisance of a cockroach infestation, these went well. It was hoped that a sale would happen within the first six months of their lay-up, since after this time a dry dock survey would be required before the *Amber* could trade again.

Zen was aware, through his conversations with George, that his father had reduced the sale price considerably, but two things conspired against his efforts. The first was the continued fall in the freight market, which led to a decline in the confidence of buyers. His father reacted by continuing to lower the price, sometimes every few days, but unfortunately, he was not doing so fast enough.

The second problem was a lot more serious and it was on Sunday 12th that it first came to light.

The weather that day was sunny and warm, as it had been for the whole weekend. Alex had spent the night and Zen had taken her out early, being her turn to work that day. As he was returning to the *Amber*, and because there was a particularly strong outgoing tide, he visually checked their moorings. It was then he noticed that the prow was higher in the water than normal. This meant there was not enough ballast forward to hold the ship down by the front. Water was leaking from where it should be to where it should not.

It took three weeks to ascertain the extent of the problem, by which time it was realised that action would need to be taken. By Friday, 1st October, a local repair yard was found and it was arranged for them to come on the following Monday to inspect the damage and give an estimate of the cost of repairs. In addition, George Pittas planned to be there.

Monday, 4th October 1982

That morning Zen went out for a run and was back by eight thirty. Finding only Harry and Steph in the mess, he enquired after Andy, only to learn that the latter was recovering from a traumatic evening.

After Zen had taken Alex back to shore the night before, Andy went out. At 23:30 he was returning with the boat to the *Amber* when he ran out of fuel. This should never have happened. There were two fuel tanks by the poop deck door. The first one to use the boat in the morning, usually Zen, would take a tank down, maybe both if the first seemed likely to run out. The last one to use the boat brought the tank or tanks back up. This made it more awkward for someone to steal the boat.

On Sunday, the boat had been used frequently and by everyone at some point, but nobody had thought to check the weight of the tank to see whether it was running low. At any rate, Andy was the unlucky one. He ran out on his way back and was left powerless. He tried rowing, but the outgoing tide was too strong for

315

him to get to the *Amber*. Turning back to shore, he realised he was not going to make that either and would have ended up out to sea or on the rocks had it not been for a yacht lashed to a buoy. He had to tie on to that for two and a half hours until slack tide. Mercifully, the winds were light and he managed to get back at three in the morning, feeling fed up, cold and exhausted.

Later, Zen was reflecting on Andy's ordeal as he was about to light the bottom of the oil drum in order to burn some rubbish when in the distance he saw the short and squat figure of George Pittas emerging from the forward end of the poop deck passage. He looked at his watch in a panic. He was meant to collect him from Paignton Station at eleven thirty, but his watch showed ten thirty.

George was travelling from Paddington. He must have caught an earlier train, then a cab and decided that hiring a launch was safer than risking a ride on their boat. He wore brown casual slacks, a white shirt, brown jumper, bomber jacket and beret.

Zen climbed up the stairs to meet him. They greeted each other in the traditional Greek way. 'Welcome, George.'

'How are you, Zen? But what's this? Your tan's darker than when I last saw you. You're meant to be working, not sunbathing.'

'I hate to disappoint you, but it's only on my hands and face.'

'Mine's gone already.'

'How's the hand?'

'Sore at times, but improving.'

'Didn't you miss Rhodes this year?' Zen asked as they entered through the poop deck door, ready to climb the stairs to the captain's day room. While they were passing the mess, he called to Steph to come up.

'Not at all. It's not the same now the boys holiday on their own. All those relatives suddenly seem very tiresome, especially when they're your wife's.'

'But your father-in-law owns half the island, doesn't he?'

'He only has a hotel,' George corrected him.

'So what's the problem? Free room and board; sounds good to me.'

'The problem is that he wants me to move there and take over the business.'

'Even better.'

'I don't want to be beholden to him. One day you'll understand.'

'Still, your wife must've been disappointed not to see them?' Before entering his cabin he unlocked the guest room with his master key.

'Surprisingly not,' George replied as he threw his holdall onto the nearest bed. 'She said that the time we spent in Barcombe was the best holiday she's ever had, especially after I injured my hand and was with her all the time.'

'I think she's trying to tell you something.'

'And I'm listening.'

'Maybe you should come with her again.'

'Well, that depends on what we're going to do with the double bottom tanks.' They entered the day room and sat at the square table. 'Before we come to that, remind me what else has been happening?'

317

'Let's run through events so that you can get a picture of this and any other problems,' Zen said, picking up his diary from the desk. 'We were just finishing the boat deck when you were last here.'

'How's that going?'

'We've collected quite a bit of water, but we're still using it too fast.'

'I'm sure come winter, you'll do better.'

'True. Up to the bank holiday weekend we were occupied with improving our moorings and unblocking drains. It was afterwards we started more meaningful work.'

'Ah, Steph,' George said, as the steward arrived. He got up to shake his hand. 'How are you?'

'Fine till it started getting cold.'

'I know, it's freezing in here,' George agreed looking at Zen.

'This is warm, George; wait till you see what it's like first thing.'

'But I thought you bought heaters.'

'We did, but we can't stand the smell so we turn them off at night.'

'Even the one in here?'

'Even the one in here. The fumes permeate through the curtain and I can smell them in bed.'

'And it gets into our clothes,' Steph added.

'What are you going to do when it really gets cold?' George asked.

'We'll just have to get used to it,' Zen replied.

'Do I have one?'

'You can have one of mine,' Zen replied.

'And you better throw in a few more blankets,' George instructed Steph.

'You can have the key to the linen cupboard if it makes you feel better,' Zen said. 'Anyway, are you having coffee?' George nodded. 'Two large mediums,' he said to Steph. The steward left. 'Now let's see, on Tuesday, 31st August that is, we started on the crane and winches of number one. They were covered in rust. Also, some of the hydraulic pipes were leaking and Harry had to replace them. We didn't finish till the following Friday.'

'Do you work weekends?'

'Sometimes. That one of the 4th and 5th Harry and I went diving with our boat, as a matter of fact. On another occasion, we drove to a cove near Barcombe.'

'Was it good?'

'Very interesting. It's mostly wrecks round here. The following Monday we managed to service number two all in one day. Oh yes, and that night we had the start of the European Games. Have you been watching?'

'Of course.'

'On Tuesday we started on number three. This one was bad. All the pulleys, bearings and crane head had seized. We had to use the blow torch on them. Harry had to strip down the hydraulic pump too. Fortunately we had spares. We didn't work at all the following weekend.'

'You did well,' George said. 'That was the last weekend of the games, wasn't it? There was fantastic weather. On Sunday, we had a barbeque with friends whilst watching the marathon.'

'We were glued to the set.'

'It was also when you discovered the leak.'

'It was in the morning, to be precise, when I noticed the depth forward had decreased. The next day, after we finished number three and before starting on number four, we sounded the fore peak and realised that it was losing water.'

'You'd not noticed water in the holds before?'

'Not when we first aired them. Due to the Greek holiday on Tuesday, we didn't empty the fore peak and open it till Wednesday. We found it pretty rusty inside, but no cracks. So, on Thursday we opened the holds and it was then we found water in three and four. While in number four I noticed a crack in the port wing tank and thought that maybe that pool of water came from there, when we were trying to clear the scuppers.'

'You said that they were in bad condition too.'

'Terrible, the brackets have practically dissolved. They're paper thin.'

'Your father's definitely going to want to sell her.'

'I know, but when?'

'He's taken her off the market for now and till we sort this problem out. We're not too worried about the wing tanks at the moment, but anybody inspecting a vessel will definitely want to see the double bottoms.'

'The wing tanks would probably need scaffolding, wouldn't they?'

'Exactly, something to avoid. Another thing, when I was last here, I noticed the dire appearance of the cargo deck as compared to the fo'castle, which was done recently.'

'Yes, by Andy.'

'That, together with the work he did on the boat deck shows he's capable. We want you to get a couple of workers from shore to help him do up the hatch combings and masthouses. Try and get that started as soon as possible so that we can have the *Amber* ready to go back on the market in the spring.'

'I'll get on to it tomorrow.'

'Good. Sorry to have interrupted, you were telling me about the double bottoms.'

'It wasn't till Saturday morning that we'd finished pumping out number three double bottom and I got in to inspect it. It was in bad condition. There's one beam, which you'll see later, that has completely corroded.'

'What time's the yard coming?'

'Three o'clock.'

'I'll have time to inspect it after lunch. You say, though, that all the double bottoms are leaking.'

'What we've established is that when we fill the fore peak, it leaks into all the double bottom tanks, apart from number two. The feed pipe is full of holes. I also managed to empty number one double bottom and found cracks in the bulkhead with the fore peak on both the port and starboard sides.'

'You're sure that these are cracks and not thinning metal?'

'Pretty much.'

'So how are the holds flooding?'

'Probably through the tank tops, where that rusty beam I told you about runs and with a little help from the wing tanks.'

'But they're empty now?'

'Yes, and we've also swept the holds and the tank top manholes are open. Apart from number two, of course. They've got fuel oil in them and are all right. Harry's down there rigging up the lamps.'

'By the way, how are you managing with the cockroaches?'

'We've put down poison and are clearing out our store rooms. When we can't work outside we clean and paint inside.'

Steph arrived with their coffees. 'Do you want me to bring you any snacks?' he asked.

'No, I'll wait for lunch,' George said. 'What are we having?'

'*Stifado*,' Steph replied. They knew that this Greek beef and onion stew was one of George's favourites.

'Excellent,' George said as Steph left. 'You're doing all right for food?'

'We have massive supplies of meat. It remains to be seen what effect turning the power on and off is having on the freezers.'

George then brought Zen up to date with their other ships, the ones still trading. After more than two hours Zen had a look at his watch. 'It's one o'clock, shall we go down?'

'Yes, I'm starving.'

After lunch George changed into his boiler suit and went with Zen and Harry down into the holds and the double bottoms.

The two men from the yard, led by a foreman, came at two thirty and stayed until six. They made a thorough inspection and confirmed that both double bottoms number one port and starboard had cracks with the forward bulkhead. Also, the starboard engine intake pipe was leaking and would need replacing.

They also established that number three double bottom was okay and only needed the same engine intake to be replaced. The water in the hold must have come from a leak in the starboard upper wing tank when the drains were being cleared.

322

It was number four starboard double bottom that had the biggest problems. They found that a section of girder supporting the tank top had buckled, probably due to a heavy piece of cargo being dropped accidentally, so weakening the metal and causing holes. Here the work was extensive, requiring replacement of the girder as well as a section of floor.

As the team left, the foreman promised to call George with an estimate by close of business the next day.

That evening, George insisted on taking Zen out for a meal. They went to the hotel restaurant and, once they had sat at their table and ordered, it became apparent as to why.

'There's a reason I wanted to get you alone,' George started. 'Antigoni and Nicholas are engaged to be married.'

'What?' Zen exclaimed. He was dumbfounded. His sister engaged to Spiros Alexandrou's son? When he had left London, he had agreed with his father that he should not try to speak to his mother or sister. Unfortunately, this meant he was out of touch. 'How did this come about?'

'The announcement was made whilst they were in Halkidiki. A date wasn't set at the time and your father made me promise not to tell anyone.'

'So why has he decided you should tell me now?' Zen asked. He was amazed George had managed to hold a secret that long, but dismayed his father wanted it kept from his son.

'Because they have a wedding date, the 22nd December.'

'That's sudden.'

'Please don't quote me, but I think your sister might be pregnant.'

'Jesus.'

'Your parents would like you to go, for your sister's sake and for appearances.'

'I bet they would.'

The rest of their meal was predictably sombre.

After breakfast the following morning, Zen drove George to Paignton station. When he returned he parked in the town car park as, after the end of September, it was no longer necessary to pay for its use. Then, before doing some shopping and collecting the post, he went to the social security centre to register for two workers.

He went out again later that evening to call George at home. The estimate had been accepted and they were due to start work the following Monday. There would be much preparatory work to do.

He also called Alex and they had a long chat.

There was light rain early and late that day. The rest of the time the weather was good. Zen and Steph spent most of the time cleaning out the stores.

Chapter 34: The Three Wrecks

Friday, 8th October 1982

Alex was pleased to see the weather improve that Friday afternoon. The forecast was for a cool but settled weekend. That would make a change from what they'd been having recently. It would probably be their last opportunity to dive before the winter. She had her equipment, dive bag and weekend holdall packed in the car ready to go to Tonemouth after she finished work

Last night was the first time she had seen Zen since Sunday. She had missed him so much. The club was planning its own dive at the weekend, somewhere on the north coast, but Alex wanted Zen to herself and managed to convince him, and Harry, that they should go it alone. They had already done this twice and it proved far more fun.

It had only been six weeks since the August bank holiday weekend and the regatta, yet she felt she had known Zen longer. That was not the only paradox. On the one hand she felt serene and at peace in his company and on the other she experienced a passion that was inexhaustible.

These were new sensations. She had never been so wrapped up in a man before. When she was not with him she felt fear, fear of not seeing him again. And there was jealousy. She even resented Andy because he brought other women into contact with him. She would lie in bed at night, imagine him with them and feel rage; a rage that was a product of her imagination, of course. Perhaps this was punishment for the treatment she had meted out to other men.

For the first time she was in love, and was finding it difficult to cope. She spoke to her therapist about it and he said it was natural. One of the reasons she had avoided intimate relationships was because she did not want to be hurt. Now she could face her fears and deal with them.

Later, as she drove to Tonemouth, her anxieties receded, as they always did when she was about to see him. They had supper together at seven thirty. They were a nice bunch this crew. Steph was caring and, she bet, cultured as well, although difficult to talk to. Harry seemed gentle and compassionate, his girlfriend, Linda, was great fun, and her son, Stephen, a real sweetie. As for Andy? He was sweet too, with his boyish good looks. They went ashore after their meal, Andy to meet his friends and Harry to walk Linda and Stephen home, while Zen took her to the hotel bar for a few drinks before they all met up again to return on board.

The *Amber* was dark and silent and that always thrilled her. They told each other eerie stories, trying to see who would get spooked first. They purposefully went to see scary films. *Alien* was the worst, because the *Nostromo* was also a freighter.

In the cabin Zen lit the gas light and was about to light the paraffin heater.

'Don't light it, darling,' she told him. 'I hate the smell.'

'But you'll get cold.'

'Then let's get into bed, we can keep each other warm.' As she spoke she was undressing and leaving her clothes where they dropped. He had trouble keeping up with her. He followed her into bed and they kissed and cuddled and shivered at the same time as the bed warmed.

It was after they had made love that it happened. She was lying on top of him and for the first time she looked into the eyes of a man and said 'I love you'. He told her he loved her too, as many men before had done, but this time, his words ignited a warmth, a sweetness inside her. She felt like crying. She held his face close to hers so that he would not see her eyes. She fell asleep the happiest she had been as an adult.

When she next woke it was morning. She was alone and cold. The generator was on and she could smell paraffin. The bathroom door was closed and the curtains drawn, but there was sufficient light for her to see that it was nine thirty.

Then she remembered that she'd had one of those dreams again. She tried to recall as much as she could but, as before, it was just impressions: inklings of rivers and streams, of forests and moors, of the sea and coast. Sometimes she was aware of running, sometimes flying. There were no details of other people, just the feeling of freedom and power. Whenever she had this particular type of dream, which was happening more and more frequently, she felt that she had slept deeply.

Her therapist said that the visions reflected her feeling of being more in control. It sounded plausible. She rose to go to the bathroom before getting back into bed. She was not ready to get up quite yet. She would wait for Zen to return and for it to get warmer.

She dozed until she heard him come in. He carried two steaming mugs of tea, which he placed on the bedside table while he sat on the bed. It looked like he had been for a run.

'That was quite a sleep you had,' he said.

'I needed it. I was disappointed to wake and not find you here.'

'I need to go shopping this morning and get a few things for lunch, but you can stay in bed.'

'No, I want to come too. I'll dress after my tea. Are you having a shower?'

'Not yet. For some reason the water isn't hot. Maybe used more than usual for our laundry yesterday, so Harry's making more. We can shower later. I'll stay in my tracksuit for now.'

She studied him as they drank. He looked more Italian than she imagined a Greek to be. He was not as tall as she preferred but had a well-proportioned, athletic body.

'So, are we going for this dive tomorrow?' he asked.

'Definitely, are you both up for it?'

'We are. Are you going to tell us where?'

'Maybe sometime today. We'll have to leave by twelve in order to get the tide right, so I don't know where that'll leave everyone for lunch.'

'We'll discuss it with the others.'

'I'd better get dressed,' she said, draining her tea.

That afternoon, after a lunch of *kleftiko*, lamb cooked slowly in a parcel of vegetables and herbs, served with rice, they went for a walk along the coast on the Castlewear side. It was calm, sunny and warm for the time of year and, by the time they were back on board, it was after sunset.

They had a bath and dressed for the evening. Following supper at eight, they all went out, bar Steph.

'So, where are we diving tomorrow?' Harry asked as they settled down for a drink in the hotel bar. Linda had

328

also joined them. Andy, at a rare loose end, had offered to look after Stephen and was teaching him backgammon.

'We're crossing over to the other side and driving to Spaniard's Cove, or as close to it as we can get,' Alex replied.

'I've heard about it; isn't it a nudist beach?' Zen asked.

'Unofficially it is as there's nothing overlooking it,' Alex replied.

'I doubt there'll be many undressing this time of year,' Zen remarked.

'Probably not. As there's no car park it's usually boaters that visit,' Alex said.

'So what are we going to do?' Zen asked.

'There's a place where the road widens and there's room for about eight cars. From there, there's a steep path to the beach. The walk back will be arduous but I think it'll be worth it.'

'So why there?' Harry asked.

'Although I live only a few miles away, I've never dived it. It's inaccessible to the inflatable, so the club have never taken us. They'd have to hire a bigger boat and that's expensive. It also boasts three wrecks, one rather unusual.'

'What's that?' Zen asked.

'An intact German World War I U-boat,' she revealed.

'That is unusual,' Harry said. 'How did it get there?'

'Nobody knows. There's a list of U-boats that went missing, but there's no visible ID on the hull. Those who have inspected it say that it's standing upright with the pressure hull intact and the conning tower hatch sealed.'

'So the crew could still be inside,' Linda concluded, grimacing.

'Hasn't anybody checked?' Harry asked.

'I bet it's a protected war grave,' Zen said, looking at Alex, who nodded. 'What about the other two?'

'One's a warship of the Spanish Armada, hence the name Spaniard's Cove. She was called the *San Miguel*. There's no record of where exactly she was wrecked, but, as the sand shifts during storms, occasional timbers and coins are found.'

'We've certainly had a few blows lately,' Zen said.

'I don't think they would qualify as storms,' Alex responded, 'but you never know what's been churned up.'

'It could be interesting,' Zen said. 'I'm feeling lucky. I think the fact that we've been drinking San Miguel lager all these weeks is a good omen.'

'I hope you're right, but that's not all; I've been saving the best for last.'

'We're listening,' Zen said.

'The third's one of the more famous, or should I say infamous, wrecks of the West Country and steeped in lore. But, I'm not saying any more till we get another round.'

'My turn,' Harry said, as he got up.

'No, it's about time I bought a round,' Linda intervened. 'And don't you dare tell any of the story till I come back. This is all the more exciting since the *Mary Rose* has been in the news.'

When they had settled down again with their replenished glasses, Alex began. 'Like most good tales,

330

it's a love story. He was a young man called James, from a wealthy Devon family who owned a shipyard not far from here and a plantation in the American Colonies. She was the daughter of the foreman of the yard and her name was Elizabeth.'

'Let me guess; they fell in love,' Harry said.

'There are no flies on you,' Alex said. 'Unfortunately, they wanted to get married but there was no way James's family was going to accept that, so what his father did was rather unusual. Instead of threatening his son or disowning him, he made him a proposition. He said that he was happy for them to live together, but in order to be accepted into the family, they'd have to go to America, to their plantation, and prove themselves. If they were still together after two years or so, they could come back. So shortly afterwards they were taken to a ship, went to the Colonies and began life together.

'Meanwhile, James's father put his real agenda into action. He started reconstructing Elizabeth's past. He bribed all sorts of people, including her own family, would you believe, to swear that she was a witch and a whore. When he was satisfied with the arrangements he'd made, he sent the family solicitor together with James's cousin to America. They went to James with these *revelations* about Elizabeth. He was to come home and explain how he dared to promote her as a virtuous girl to his family.

'They returned on the *Casaba*, but as they approached Plymouth a great storm struck and blew them east to the south of Devon. There they fell on the rocks. Only the cousin and a midshipman survived.'

'That's quite a story,' Zen said.

'It's not over yet,' Alex said. 'At that time there was a village behind the beach, at the top of a low cliff, near where we'll be parking. There's a sheltered strand of sand and, on seeing the ship in distress, the villagers congregated on the beach for any booty to turn up. Along with the cargo many bodies were washed ashore. One of them was said to be Elizabeth. When the looters saw her they assumed that, like the others, she was dead and cut off her finger to remove a ring. When they realised she was still alive, they took fright and threw her back into the sea to drown. Her body never turned up, neither were the culprits identified.'

'That's really gruesome,' Linda said, taking Harry's hand and snuggling closer to him.

'But it still wasn't over, if the legend's to be believed,' Alex continued. 'From that day the village was said to be cursed and their crops wouldn't grow. Worse still, a great black dog or wolf, said to be the spirit of Elizabeth, patrolled the village at night and killed off the men, one by one, or rather, the men kept disappearing. Historians say they just drifted away, but the legend sounds better. It wasn't long before the place was deserted. You can see the remains of the houses in a field. If we have any energy left after the dive and the climb back to the car, I can show you. But to finish off, it's said that, as well as these villagers, all those complicit in slandering Elizabeth's reputation also met violent deaths.'

'What makes it spookier are the stories in the local papers about this Black Dog or Beast,' Zen said glancing at Harry, who looked thoughtful.

'That's recent,' Alex said. 'Those sightings or incidents were usually confined to Exmoor but since spring they've been occurring on Dartmoor as well.'

'Have there been any sightings further south?' Zen asked. He looked at Harry again, who this time returned his stare and gave a negative shake of his head.

'I think dead sheep have been found, but no sightings,' Alex replied. 'They're probably dog attacks.'

'This is going to be quite a dive,' Harry said, 'what with corpses of German submariners, gold coins, ghosts and the Beast of Dartmoor.'

'Perhaps you should've told us the story after the dive,' Zen said.

'That wouldn't have been as much fun, besides there's nothing much left of the wrecks, so without the story you may have found it boring.'

'True,' Zen said.

'The locals say that legends like this and the stories of the Beast are our equivalent of the Loch Ness monster and there for the tourists,' Alex said.

'What do you believe?' Harry asked her.

'The wreck and the story of James and Elizabeth are historical. The rest probably evolved as it was told.'

'I know that Stephen learned about the abandoned village at school,' Linda said. 'They went to survey the ruins.' She turned to Harry and slapped his thigh to get his attention. 'You'd better take me home, otherwise Stephen will be up half the night playing backgammon.'

'We'll miss not seeing him for lunch tomorrow,' Zen said.

'We'll have a nice mummy and son day instead.' Linda said, as she stood.

'We'll wait,' Zen told Harry. 'Would you like one for the road?' he asked Alex.

'Go on then,' she replied.

He got up and went to the bar.

Chapter 35: Spaniard's Cove

Sunday, 10th October 1982

The next morning they had their first frost, otherwise it was calm and sunny. They left the *Amber* at eleven thirty after a light breakfast, and took both cars so that Alex could go home afterwards.

After a challenging drive along narrow, undulating and sharply twisting roads, most of which had grass growing along their centre line, they parked near the start of the track that led down to the beach. There were no other cars.

Fully laden, they entered a gate and descended by a steep path along a winding gulley that cut through open fields.

Where the beach began there was a shelf of sand which did not get covered by the high tide, just as Alex had described. Behind it was a low cliff. Beyond the coastal path and a stone wall was an area of scrub and short gnarled trees, which Zen presumed was where the village used to be.

They laid their equipment in the shelter of an indent in the cliff and began the process of kitting up.

When they were ready, they picked up their combined sets of two cylinders each, together with fins, masks and snorkels, and set off across the strand towards the sea. Their weight caused them to sink in the sand, which made the walk more arduous. Alex led the way, maps encased in plastic holders around her neck. She would use these, together with her compass, to guide them to the sites.

When they reached the water's edge, they were breathless. They rested as Alex described the dive they were going to do. 'I purposefully waited for the turn of the tide to give us the easiest swim, although it meant walking across more of the beach. The water out to the last rock to the right is shallow, only two metres. We'll snorkel to it in order to save air. Immediately afterwards is a drop-off of about ten metres to a sand bank. It's in this area that sightings of cannon, timbers and coins have been found.'

'The San Miguel?' Harry asked.

'Yes. From there, I'm going to take a bearing south south-east that heads for the sub and, if we come across anything along the way, we'll stop and investigate; if not we'll keep going.

'After a while there's another drop-off to thirty metres and we start heading across the silt fan of the Tone to the sub, hopefully. I've allotted a certain amount of time to reach it. If we don't see it by then I'm turning back. Okay?'

They agreed.

'The visibility may not be good and we may pass within a few metres and miss it.'

'We understand,' Zen said.

'From the sub I'm going to take a different bearing back to the eastern end of the beach where the remains of the *Casaba* are meant to be. If you look at the cliff, you'll see a stone landmark, or in this case a seamark. It was put there by James's cousin to mark the spot below which the wrecking took place. In fact, this cousin later bought the land that goes back inland to what used to be his manor house. It's called The Balize and it's derived from French or Spanish, I can't remember which, for a sea beacon or seamark. It's a long swim and, once again, there's no guarantee we'll see anything. The gradual ascent of our return will take care of any decompression. Shall we get ready?'

Once they were fully kitted up, they gave each other's equipment a final check. The sea was calm, as well as it being slack tide. They inflated their lifejackets sufficiently to give them enough buoyancy so they could swim out to the rocks using only their snorkels. When they were ready, they slipped on their fins and waded into the water.

Initially the bottom was sandy, with the odd clump of sea grass, and they caught sight of flat fish grazing. Where there were rocky outcrops there was the occasional anemone, starfish or clump of brown kelp.

They swam in a V formation. Alex led the way, with Zen and Harry either side of her, their heads level with her knees. When the depth reached two metres they entered a maze of gullies with colourful growths and sea squirts on the rocks. The water was clear and they sighted a juvenile bass.

As they approached the rocky outcrop, it became shallower. They stopped at a gap between two surface-breaking rocks, beyond which was their first drop-off. The water was darker and the bottom invisible. Alex took a compass bearing and pointed in the direction they would go. Zen and Harry both gave the okay sign. Switching from their snorkels to their demand valves, they set off on a slow descent, gradually releasing the air in their life jackets.

They levelled off when they saw the sandy bottom. It was slightly darker, because of the additional depth, and the visibility was not as good. The sea bed was bland with occasional areas of weed. Zen looked at his depth gauge; it read sixteen metres. They kept to their route, swimming at a steady but comfortable pace that allowed them to cover the area within their visibility, but unfortunately, the old San Miguel was not giving up any of its treasures today. It was strange, Zen thought, how time and the elements dissolved everything physical, but the memory of things often lived on, especially if they were traumatic. So many tragic deaths occurred in these waters and nothing to show for it. Or was there? Perhaps there was an ambience. He sensed it as soon as he saw the beach. He experienced a sadness, a melancholy.

But would he have had those feelings if he had not already known the stories? He thought not. He was just rambling. Check depth gauge: eighteen metres, they were gradually descending. It was beginning to get colder. How he wished he had bought that new wetsuit. Time: seven minutes into actual dive and the air gauge was okay. Alex and Harry looked okay.

It continued getting darker with depth, and the sandy bottom was featureless. Not even the occasional flat fish here, let alone gold coins. He tried to imagine the scene at that beach over two hundred years ago when the *Casaba* met her fate. The sailing boats in those days must have been so uncomfortable. They did not have much to complain about on the *Amber*, in comparison. Check depth gauge: twenty-one metres, nine minutes into the dive. Air okay, Alex and Harry okay.

He wondered how James and Elizabeth must have felt. James thought he had been deceived by his lover. Elizabeth had been betrayed by everybody. For a

338

moment he got carried away with these emotions, as if they were his. He pulled himself together. The monotony was causing his mind to wander. They say you should have little or no alcohol the night before a dive, as well as be fully rested.

The seabed started sloping away more steeply and, as they continued to descend, it got darker and murkier, as if everything was closing in around them. The bed was darker too, being more silt than sand. Visibility was no more than two metres. The depth was twenty-five metres and they were eleven minutes into their dive. Air okay, Alex and Harry looked more like shadows.

They quickly passed through twenty-eight metres, and at thirty-one the bottom levelled off. They were now well into the silt fan of the Tone which the currents and tide would have pushed either side of the mouth of the estuary. All this dark material originated from the uplands of Dartmoor all those miles inland. Zen recalled some of the landscapes he had walked through with Alex.

He looked at his watch. Thirteen minutes into the dive. They were still at thirty-one metres. He looked at Alex and noticed that she seemed to have slowed down. Was she hesitating or did she anticipate coming across the sub? No sooner had he thought the thought than a great dark wall loomed at them. They stopped abruptly alongside the heavily encrusted hulk.

The hull was featureless with no colours to be seen until they shone their torches at it. They had to come in close to make out the densely packed crust of multi-coloured marine growths. What the sea bottom lacked in life and variety was more than made up for here.

Alex led them to the left along the sub and, after a while, it began to taper off. Zen guessed they must be heading aft. At the back end she appeared to be looking for the stern torpedo tubes, but they found nothing. There was too much encrustation and there was silt swirling around the rudder. Perhaps it was the incoming tide, or a current, or a combination of both.

Alex then continued up the port side forward. Here, with the help of their torches, they could see that parts of the outer plating had broken up, with several holes through which they could make out the equally thickly encrusted pressure hull; the final barrier to the incomprehensible horrors that probably lurked within.

From there she took them back over the top to the conning tower. They tried to find the hatch but they could not see it. Back at the prow Alex took another compass reading and they headed off on a new bearing. Zen was relieved to get away from the sub and the gloom; this was not a nice place to be. He wanted to get the thought of those bodies, locked up inside, out of his mind. He checked his gauges. Air okay, Harry and Alex appeared okay.

They were ascending again and the visibility improved. Eventually they were back on the sixteen metre level and crossing to the other side of the bay where the *Casaba* came to grief. Again the sand revealed nothing. When they reached the rocks at the far end they swam around the gullies to use up their air and then finned back the length of the cove to their starting point using their snorkels.

Despite being helped by the incoming tide, they were exhausted and cold when they came out of the water. Their diminished energy and strength meant they struggled up the beach. Alex in particular had to stop twice.

When they reached their base, in the indent beside the cliff, they removed their tanks and life jackets and sat on the sand with their backs to the rocks to rest.

The sun was out and, although weak, it started warming them in their wetsuits. The beach remained deserted. Alex and Harry had their eyes shut, the sun on their faces, either wrapped up in their thoughts or too tired to talk. Zen wondered where on the beach Elizabeth had been washed ashore. Then he also shut his eyes and began to doze.

He was awakened when Alex cried out. Looking in her direction, he saw her clutching her body, shaking with pain, looking out at the sea. They got to her at the same time. Zen held her while Harry tried to ascertain what was wrong. She continued to scream and tremble whilst looking out at the water with terror. She was trying to push them away.

'Alex, what's wrong?' they kept repeating until she stopped struggling.

'I'm okay,' she said, looking around her confused. 'I must have fallen asleep and seen a vision or a dream. It was so vivid.'

'You scared us,' Zen said. 'The way you were clutching yourself we thought you were having the bends.'

'Shall we take you back to the car?' Harry asked. 'Maybe we ought to have you checked out.'

'No, I'll be okay. Give me a minute,' she said, taking deep breaths. 'It was really weird. Suddenly this calm, peaceful beach was transformed into a raging inferno. It was night. I could feel the spray and rain-laden wind sting my body. There were men in dark clothes with dark bearded faces carrying lanterns, standing on the sand and facing the sea. I saw where they were looking, towards the rocks at the far end. Everywhere there was tortured foam and amongst it the silhouette of a ship with a few dim lights. Beneath the howling of the storm you could hear the crack of masts breaking and the hull being crushed on the rocks, and below that the sound of screaming.

'Then things started washing ashore. At first it was items of cargo or people's belongings. The men rushed forward to retrieve them. They didn't examine them but took them away immediately. Soon there was a conveyor belt of men and women taking things up the path and coming back for more. The bodies, when they arrived, were treated differently, they weren't taken away. They were pulled a short way up the beach, examined for valuables and left where they lay.

'Then a breaker, bigger than others, came in. It deposited lots of material and one lone body half-buried in the sand. Two men came forward, grabbed it roughly under the arms and dragged it up the beach. From their lanterns I could see it was a woman with long, red hair. The men examined her and one said she was dead; but I knew she wasn't. I knew it was Elizabeth.

'They started removing her necklace and the rings from her fingers and, as they did so, I could feel the pain in my fingers. But one of them was too tight and wouldn't come off. Then one of the men took a knife out of his pocket. I knew what he wanted to do so I started shouting for him to stop. I was shouting for Elizabeth because she couldn't shout for herself. Then I felt a terrible pain as the knife cut through. That's when I started screaming and you woke me.'

'You haven't been taking any drugs or medication that could've triggered this affect?' Harry asked.

'No, of course not. I know better than that, especially if I'm diving,' she replied.

'Drugs aren't the answer to everything,' Zen said.

Harry was mute.

'What did you mean by that?' Alex asked.

'I meant recreational drugs,' Harry said, before Zen could answer.

'I've never taken anything like that or even smoked. I was thinking a lot about the story during the dive though.'

'So was I,' Zen said.

'This beach does have an atmosphere,' Harry commented.

'I feel it too,' Zen agreed.

'Perhaps Alex can sense it more than us,' Harry said. 'Maybe events if traumatic enough can imprint themselves on a place and those who are sensitive will feel them.'

'Do you think I saw it as it really happened?'

'Maybe,' Harry said, looking about him. 'I think we'd better go.'

It was a long haul back to the cars. After changing into their clothes and packing their gear in their respective boots, they decided to look for the remains of the village. They went off on to the coastal path heading east until they came to a place behind the stone wall that was fenced off by barbed wire and was overgrown. Even if there was a way over the fence, the

343

undergrowth was too thick to walk through, so they gave up and turned back.

'I don't want to spend the night alone,' Alex said.

'Why don't you go home, I'll take Harry back to Tonemouth and then I'll come back to yours,' Zen suggested.

'I don't want to cook or anything,' she said.

'You don't have to. We could go out,' Zen said.

'I don't want to do that either,' Alex said. She had slowed down and had let Harry pull away. 'Tell you what we'll do. Come back to mine now. You two can have a cup of tea while I put away my equipment and get myself sorted for tomorrow. Then we'll go back to Tonemouth and, if I leave my car on the Castlewear side, you can take me across to the marina in the morning.'

'I'm not complaining,' Zen said.

Back in Tonemouth they stopped off at a pub to have a drink, boarding the *Amber* at seven. It was already dark and they were tired and hungry. Harry switched on and promised to give the hot water a boost.

Later with the paraffin heaters on in both the day room and bathroom, Alex soaked in a hot tub. The bulkheads were sweating with the condensation and Zen could see her observing, as he often did, the individual drips roll down, gaining size as the moisture accumulated. She had known about the story of Spaniard's Cove for years, so why did she react to it now? Watching the metal walls reminded him of the sub. The thought of that cold grave made him shiver.

'Darling,' she called out to him.

'What is it?'

344

'You want to use this water?'

'Yeah, okay.' He would have preferred they soaked together but the bath was too small.

Afterwards they had the roast chicken and mashed potato that Steph had prepared earlier. There was plenty left over and Andy had another helping while he heard the story of the wreck and the events of the day.

Chapter 36: On The Beach

Going back to the beach for the first time was traumatic, but it was becoming easier with each visit. She remembers everything now and is able to deal with those memories without distress. She can stand here on the sand, under the stars, look out at the sea and the reefs and accept all but one thing.

At first she was content to live again as part of another existence. Coming out when the other was asleep. She was happy to observe a life and have the freedom of the land as well. She could not explain how she came to be sharing the same vessel with another but, in the infinite existence of her soul, what did it matter?

She had settled her accounts with those who had told lies about her, irrespective of blood tie. Many who had heard the lies had also died. She had dispensed suitable punishment on the ones who had mutilated her on this beach. Those who had watched had also had to pay. Scores perished to wipe the humiliation away. All were avenged, all but one. He had not suffered enough. She'd had her opportunity but shied away from the act, and as he was beyond retribution, she was left with a gnawing hunger for revenge.

Now that man Earsop wanted something from her. She did not know what yet but she would cooperate. They could help each other. He would give her more control, more independence and she would carry through his requests, especially if it helped satisfy her need. She had been directed to connect with the man, but this had proved more troublesome than she had anticipated.

She begins to run along the sand to the path and up the slope. When she is on level ground she quickens her pace, passing by the village which she had terrorised into destruction and on towards the coast and the sea. At the cliff edge she takes a great leap and, quickly transforming, glides on wings above the water, banking sharply westward towards the mouth of the estuary.

She lands by the engine skylight at the aft part of the bridge deck. After her many examinations of the boat, she knows this is the best entry point at night. The occupants usually locked the other doors and there were no convenient portholes. She hops through the open panel and alights onto the metal walkway of the poop deck. Only then does she transform back.

She walks through the open steel door, through the engine room casing and round to the foot of the stairs. She pauses for a moment to become aware of the occupant down here. The older man is in a fitful sleep, tortured by feelings of guilt for things he is not responsible for, punishing himself for other people's deeds; a cowering victim of random fate. He would not be disturbing her this night or any time in the future. His mind is enslaved by regret.

She climbs up to the next deck. The other, younger man is in the deep sleep of one satiated by food, drink and sex. He is an uncomplicated soul, with no desire for pretence. He wants a simple life, but also holds much anger and resentment, inflamed by the festering wound of betrayal.

There is another here, at the end of the corridor. He is the one who saw her on a previous visit. There is more awareness in him. He is fond of the other. In his mind she can sense the patterns forming that could lead to him understanding. He poses a threat and would have to be watched, even though he is distracted by a blossoming love. She comes close to his door, probing into him, making a tentative connection that would allow her to influence him, should she need to.

One more deck and she is outside the door, purposefully left ajar, as she had directed. She nudges it with her head and it opens soundlessly. She steps over the threshold, moving quietly across the room. With her muzzle, she parts the curtain and enters the bedroom.

She can hear the breathing of the two as they sleep in a lovers' embrace. The woman is now under her control, thanks in some measure to Earsop. They made sure that she believed herself to be infatuated with the man. It was essential she was to him everything he dreamed of in a woman.

She moves closer to the top of the bed and lays her head in the gap between the sleeping man's shoulders and the edge of the mattress. She looks at the back of his head. Of course, she could break his neck in an instant, if that was what she was meant to do. She is here tonight for a different reason.

From within the host, she cannot see inside the man's thoughts, there is too much mind noise in the woman. It is no better when she is asleep. No, she has to be on the *outside*. Also, she cannot *come out* directly here. She has to pass through the doorway, the portal, and that is on the moor.

She concentrates on the man. He has strong feelings for the woman. The satisfaction of his lusts and the intense physical pleasure are bonding him strongly to her. He is falling in love. But there is much more of interest here. He is hiding secrets from her, as well as

348

the man downstairs. She can see a familiar pattern: privileged upbringing, rich parents, the same spoilt brat wanting to have his own way, but when it came down to it he could betray this woman, like any other, she was sure of it. Yes, this was James and Philip all over again. Whatever this man's fate was to be, she would have no problem carrying it through.

Now that she had grounded herself in him she could visit him in his sleep. The more she learnt about him the more effectively she could wound him, punish him for what he stood for, for what he represented. And he would come to know the reason why he was being hurt. This would take time and she was patient.

She comes out of him and looks once more at the back of his head. For a moment she wants to be back in the woman. She wants to have him. She wants to enjoy him. She has to admit she is enjoying him. A wave of revulsion banishes these unwelcome feelings. How alike pain and pleasure love and hate are.

It is time to retreat. Within minutes she is in the open air again, circling and rising high above the anchored ship, before heading for the moor.

Chapter 37: Elizabeth

Alex was already under and Earsop waited for Elizabeth to speak. He never called for her, having realised that it would be undiplomatic to do so; not part of the etiquette to which she was accustomed. It was a result that he had managed to learn her name.

'Mr. Earsop,' she said in her distinct voice and accent. It was his cue to talk. Elizabeth was very much in control now.

'Good evening, Miss Bartlett, how are we today?' Earsop said, addressing her in the manner he knew she preferred.

'We are fine, sir, and you?'

'As well as can be expected. I've a lot on my mind, as you know, Miss Bartlett. Have you been thinking about what we spoke of?' Elizabeth liked him coming to the point.

'I have, sir, and have made decisions in that respect.'

'That's excellent, Miss Bartlett; something must've changed for you to be able to do that.'

'As you know, sir, I have visited the scene of the defilement and have interacted with the man, as instructed. I have overcome my apprehension and feel stronger.'

'That is great news, but what has prompted this change?'

'I saw the man for what he is. My hesitation has turned to contempt.'

'So what have you decided?'

'I think, sir, that we can come to an arrangement. I will grant you what you ask, if you will secure me the freedom I need.'

'And what precisely is it that you want, Miss Bartlett?'

'I must have more command of the host. I must be able to subdue her when I choose.'

'I have explained why I am reluctant to do this, Miss Bartlett,' Earsop said. If he gave her all she wanted, it was essentially condemning Alex's personality to death, which could have negative repercussions on his reputation.

'Be assured, sir, that I would not do anything to imperil our wellbeing. I need the host to live in this world; to provide me with a haven.'

'And to what purpose would you put this freedom, should I grant it to you?' he asked. At first she seemed reluctant to talk and there was a spell of silence. 'I confided in you, Miss Bartlett,' he added.

'Revenge, sir, pure and simple,' she said, 'if that agrees with your plans.'

'May I remind you, Miss Bartlett, that the man's fate is, as yet, undecided,' Earsop said firmly. 'Although revenge is not what I would call a positive step. Not to mention the fact that he's innocent of any involvement in your demise.'

'Previously I avenged myself on those who wronged me and there was little satisfaction in that; I destroyed myself, I diseased myself. That, sir, was because punishment for the one most responsible was spared. I have carried this grudge for two centuries. The only release rests with him.'

'And you really believe the punishment of this man will bring your grudge to an end?'

'Truly, sir. It will end when he understands and pays. It will end when he feels the pain of betrayal and humiliation at the hands of the one he loves. When all he has is taken away, he will beg me to end his life.'

'And what then?'

'My resentment will be purged and I will be free. Perhaps my resolve will weaken and the host and I will merge, who can tell. Answer me, sir, will you assist me?'

'I will, Miss Bartlett,' Earsop said. This was no time for ethics or concerns of repercussions; he was desperate. 'But you do not know what I want from you. The price may be too high.'

'I doubt it, sir, but please, reveal it to me now.'

'I also desire to purge my past, although what I require is uncluttered by the need for punishment. A simple elimination will be adequate.'

'What, sir, do you wish me to do?'

'I need you to kill two men and a woman. Do you feel up to it?'

'I will do it, sir, be confident of that,' she replied, without hesitation.

'We have an agreement then, Miss Bartlett?'

'We do, sir.'

'One thing still puzzles me, Miss Bartlett.'

'What, sir?'

'About this Zen. Why has he become the focus of your anger and resentment?'

'I see represented in him that which I have grown to loathe, that twisted constitution of privileged mind and feeble moral principal which betrayed and destroyed me. I will gain pleasure in his suffering, if that should be your will.'

'As I said, Miss Bartlett, his future is uncertain.'

'I will conform to your wishes, sir, and have patience.'

'On the other hand, Miss Bartlett, my problem is quite pressing. I need to show you the victims and where they live. You will then wait till I tell you the date and time for you to act. I need to arrange an alibi. I also need them to be killed in a certain way, one that will leave no evidence of the hand of man.'

'It will be so, sir; have confidence.'

'How will you enter their homes?'

'I require an entrance where I may pass unobstructed.'

'Both these houses are old and have fireplaces with chimneys.'

'That will be sufficient, sir. I have greater resources now.'

'If you can transform yourself into any animal or any shape you wish, why do you not materialise into your original form?' Earsop asked. He had wondered about this for some time. He knew it was a sensitive issue.

'Now that we have concluded our arrangement, Mr Earsop, I require some movement on your side,' Elizabeth said, ignoring his last question.

'Then there'll be some,' Earsop assured her. 'Remind me, Miss Bartlett, what happens when Alex is conscious.'

'I remain still and observe, sir, as I have told you. I can hear her thoughts and feel her emotions and I can influence these, but I cannot experience her senses, what she sees, what she touches, what she smells or tastes.'

'Yes, but what do you think about?'

'Nothing sir, I cannot. It is dark and her thoughts are so dominant that there is no room for my own. I am an observer.'

353

'What happens when she falls asleep? Is it different to when she's in a trance?'

'When in a trance, sir, I feel as if I have entered a large room. I am free to move, to think, to expand, to travel. When she is merely asleep, I feel always under threat, as she could wake at any time. With the trance I am more at ease, more secure and, of course, I can see you if her eyes are open, as now.'

'I know I have asked you this many times, Miss Bartlett, but are you sure you do not sleep?'

'I am conscious at all times, sir.'

'What about her dreams? Are you aware of them?'

'No, sir. All I am aware of is that when she is awake I am all compressed. Her thoughts are like noise. I feel her feelings but they are not mine. When she is asleep it is as if she is not there. There is one exception.'

'What?'

'When she is in the act and reverie of passion, she moves to one side, I see what she sees. I experience both her senses and feelings, just as she does.'

'That's fascinating, Miss Bartlett,' Earsop said, wanting to ask how she felt about the man she claimed to hate making love to her. 'You said you can influence her.'

'I can give her an itch or a headache. I can affect her mood, make her depressed or elated. I can guide her feelings and emotions.'

'Okay, let's go back to when she's asleep. You suddenly have all this space. What sort of space is it?'

'It is a dark place, sir, featureless, but I am able to think and be independent. I can will myself to float out of her form and when I materialise I have all my senses, I am intact,' she said, being careful not to mention either her portal or anchorage. 'All the time, though, I am aware that I am bound to her body, not her, like a baby is attached to a mother with a cord.'

'Why, after all this time, can you not "come out", as you say, when she's conscious? You are two separate entities after all.'

'I am sure I could, and I have tried, but I do not seem to be able to concentrate, her thoughts overwhelm me. Why all these questions?'

'Well, over the months you've changed and certain things are easier than before.'

'And how is this relevant, sir?'

'There are problems with giving you the ability to put Alex in a trance. I have to be careful when suggesting to her that someone or something other than myself can have this influence. That will make her suspicious and resistant. It may prove counterproductive.'

'What do you suggest?'

'I will teach you some techniques that will allow you to calm her, to give you more space, some limited control, without the need for trances.'

'This will be most useful, sir.'

Later, after Alex had left, he reflected upon what he had spoken about with Elizabeth. He was confident their agreement was solid, even though he realised that there was much she was not telling him.

It was fortunate she felt this way about Zen. It seemed that he would be able to help his friend, when the time came. He had a feeling his intentions were not good either. There did not seem to be much going for Mr Makris at the moment.

Chapter 38: Zen & Alex

Friday, 17th December 1982

It was after five when Zen looked down from the starboard wing of the bridge as the repair team launch left with its workmen, who had finished their protracted repairs of the fore peak and double bottom tanks. At the same time, Andy was taking their two workmen ashore for the last time that year.

They'd had to use the *Amber's* crane to remove the yard's compressor and other tools and, as it was dark, they also needed the ship's mast lights while they closed the hold. Zen had come back up to the bridge to switch these off.

It had been a monotonous, seven weeks. Apart from Sundays, the men from the yard had come every day at eight in the morning and left at six in the evening. They had confined themselves to the holds, just coming up to the mess to have their lunch, which they brought with them, Steph only providing them with drinks and the occasional beer at the end of the working week.

The workers who came from the shore, on the other hand, the ones recruited from the Social Security Office, arrived at nine and left at five. They were under Andy's supervision, scraping and renewing the hatch combings if the weather was fine, or cleaning and painting the crew accommodation if wet. At first they were inexperienced, but soon got the hang of it. As far as their work on deck was concerned, they had managed to complete the whole of number one hatch and were well into refurbishing the forward masthouse.

Indoors they had redecorated most of the crew accommodation and bathroom of the cargo deck.

It had been sunny that day, although very cold. As usual, when the yard was working they had the generator on all day, which was a comfort. He recalled that when he lived in London, a time that seemed years and not months ago, he would moan, together with everyone else, about the weather, something that was, at worst, only a minor inconvenience. He did not appreciate how uncomfortable it would be living on board now it was winter. Any weather can be faced when you start the morning in a centrally heated house.

Large metal cargo ships like the *Amber* were built to withstand most conditions and provide comfortable, albeit basic, accommodation for officers and crew. But as soon as the generator was turned off, the heat loss through the metal hull was rapid.

Once they switched off at night, it was all they could do to get into bed quickly enough. Now they had taken to wearing pyjamas, socks and even jumpers in bed. Zen had also bought them a hot water bottle each. It was a blessing in that respect to have Alex. She thought it was great fun, but then she only tended to stay at the weekends.

In the mornings it was difficult to get up, especially after a clear night and frost. Sometimes Zen would wake at four or five in the morning, shivering. They had learnt that it was best to leave the paraffin heaters on in their rooms during the day with the portholes open for ventilation. If left on at night, huge amounts of condensation would pour down the walls and make their clothes smelly and damp, and the fumes would give them headaches.

357

The gas fire they used in the mess was great. Unfortunately, Steph and Andy's cabins were too small to accommodate them, and Zen did not have the heart to get ones just for himself and Harry.

Another problem was early morning frost and ice on the external metal decks and stairs. This had caught all of them out at one time or another, especially Andy who tended to come back late at night. The forecast for this weekend was cold with occasional snow showers.

He wondered how these discomforts were affecting his colleagues. Steph seemed content for reasons of his own. He'd speculated whether the Christmas holidays would tempt him to return home but so far nothing had been mentioned. Instead he'd been shopping locally and posted gifts to Greece. He had become increasingly involved in the local church, not just going to the services, but also social functions. Occasionally he had even cooked for these. Today he had spent most of the day making sweets, cakes and pastries.

Harry continued to spend time with Linda and Stephen. They still came every Sunday for lunch and occasionally Zen and Alex would meet up with them on a weekend evening. On one Saturday in November Linda had them over for dinner.

Andy would probably put up with a lot worse and still be here if the events of that dramatic night at the end of October were anything to go by.

On that evening, Andy had gone out soon after Zen had come back from taking the workmen ashore. He had not come back when they closed down at ten thirty and, as usual, they had locked up and gone to bed.

Just after midnight Zen had been woken by hysterical screaming and a man shouting. It was so blood-curdling that he did not notice the cold, instead pulling on his clothes and shoes, running out of the day room and bounding down the stairs carrying his torch. On the boat deck landing he encountered Harry emerging from his cabin.

'What is it?' Zen yelled.

'I don't know, but it sounds like there's two of them running along the poop deck,' Harry called back.

'It's Andy and a woman,' Steph shouted from below, shining a torch up the stairwell.

'What are they doing?' Zen asked.

'I don't know, they're outside and I can't find my keys,' Steph replied.

'I'll get mine,' Harry said, running back to his cabin.

A few minutes later they had the external door open and were out, nearly tripping over the boat's fuel tank, which had been left abandoned just beyond the threshold. Steph went aft and Zen and Harry forward. When they reached the hand rail they scanned the cargo deck with their torches, but saw nothing. Then they heard sobbing coming from the other side of the poop. They sprinted round, and at the aft end, outside the port entrance to the galley, they found Andy standing, holding a wooden plank. At his feet, huddled up against the bulkhead and in the foetal position was a woman crying. Steph was already there, trying to talk to Andy, who appeared agitated, his head making rapid jerking movements as he looked from side to side.

When Zen and Harry reached them, Andy was not making any sense. His speech was incoherent. Steph got him to put down the plank, which he had pulled out from beneath one of the barrels they were using to collect water, and led him inside, while Zen and Harry dealt with the woman.

Andy had moved on from Clare and the person sitting on the deck was someone they had not seen before. She wore a long-sleeved top and, despite the cold, a skirt so short that they could see her underwear. She looked up at them repeatedly asking, 'Has it gone?' Zen and Harry looked at each other knowingly. It was Zen who said it had. She looked at him again and asked, 'You promise?' Zen promised and Harry helped her up and led her inside. Looking back, Zen noticed a wet patch on the metal deck. It smelt of urine mixed with wine and cigarettes. The poor girl had wet herself.

They sat them in the mess where they lit a gas lamp and the fire. Steph went to get some glasses and the bottle of brandy.

The woman looked as though she might be in her mid-thirties. She had long, dyed blonde hair and was tall and slim. The mascara around her brown eyes had streaked. In the subdued light her skin was freckly and she was still shaking from fear, the cold or both. Zen thought her attractive and it was only when she sat down that he noticed she had no shoes. She came to her senses and realized it too.

'I dropped my handbag and lost my shoes,' she said. Her voice was hoarse.

'I'll look for them,' Zen volunteered. He unlocked the door and went back out with the torch, carefully scanning the shadows as he went, at last feeling the biting cold. He found them aft of the galley, scattered amongst their mooring ropes and wires. On his return, Steph had poured out the brandy and Andy was talking legibly.

'We were coming up the ladder,' he was saying. 'Gloria went ahead as I was detaching the fuel tank and securing the tarpaulin. When she got to the top and stepped off the platform to the deck she started screaming and running aft. I thought she was playing some game and was calling to her to be quiet. When I got to the deck I heard her running round the corner, crying for help, shouting that an animal was chasing her. I followed. At the stern I picked up the plank and found her as you did, sitting on the deck sobbing. I didn't see anything else.'

Zen pulled up a chair and sat next to Gloria, who sat with her head down, her back stooped and her knees locked together. She had drunk the brandy and Steph had poured her another. Zen handed her the handbag and put her shoes on for her. She turned her head and gave him a nod and smile. She opened the bag and reached inside. The first thing she pulled out was a ring, which she put on her wedding finger, then a packet of Marlboro. Her hands were shaking so much that Zen had to help her light up. 'Andy was recounting what you saw,' he told her.

Gloria inhaled deeply. 'When I ran round the corner I fell over on my heels, that's when I lost them and the bag. I crawled to the nearest corner. The dog was growling at my face. I shielded my eyes, thinking it was about to attack and when I looked up again, it had vanished. Next thing I knew, Andy was standing over me.'

'Can you describe this dog?' Zen asked.

'It was big and black with a woolly coat.'

'Do you have a car in Tonemouth?' Zen asked.

'Yes, it's in the car park.'

361

'I'll take you to it,' Zen said. 'When you're ready.'

'There's no way I'm going out there in the dark again,' she said, the panic returning in her voice. Then, more gently and pleading, 'Please don't make me.'

Zen looked at Andy, expecting him to say that she could stay with him. When he said nothing, he spoke to him in Greek. 'Are you going to look after her?'

'No, she's married, she can't stay with me,' he replied.

'But you must've known that when you brought her here,' Zen said.

'Didn't you see, she just put her ring on? She never told me. All these weeks she never told me.' With that he got up and went to his cabin.

'I wouldn't dream of it,' Zen said to Gloria. 'You can spend the night on board. I'll get Steph to open a room for you.'

'I'm not sleeping alone either,' she said abruptly.

'The captain's day room has a guest cabin opposite. I'll leave the doors open so I'll only be a few yards away,' Zen said. 'We'll also place some oil lamps in the corridor so that you can see your way to the loo.'

'I suppose that'll be okay,' she said.

'Everything's locked up, so nothing can get in,' Zen reassured her.

'I'd better go and make the bed,' Steph said.

'Is there any chance of having a shower?' the woman said. 'I seem to have wet myself.'

Zen looked at Harry.

'There's plenty of hot water,' Harry said. 'I'll turn the generator on and fetch those oil lamps. Then maybe we should have a quick look round the deck.'

Andy had made no mention of Gloria, or of leaving, after that incident.

During this time, since their dive at Spaniard's Cove, Zen and Alex had become closer in a dependant, possessive way. This was new for both of them. They began to share thoughts. Some notion would come into the mind of one, and before they could express it, the other would say it. Zen mentioned this to Harry who said that the phenomenon was called synchronicity and was not uncommon among lovers.

Although they spoke about most things, Zen had not mentioned anything about The Beast to Alex, it having not been encountered since Andy's experience.

The other change during the last two months was in his dreams. Previously, he experienced them as everyone else. He was aware of having them, but remembered little the next morning. Occasionally he would recall something more memorable. Now he was seeing vivid visions nearly every night, with three different themes. In the first he would be outdoors, either in woods, in a field or along the coast. It was always night and there was something after him. He never saw what it was but he knew intuitively that it was the Beast. The harder he tried to escape, the slower his progress became, as if he was trying to run through molasses.

He could think of an explanation for this himself. He had come to Tonemouth to escape his problems, so the Beast pursuing him represented them following him. But then he also had dreams where he was the pursuer, he was the monster. He felt as if he had done terrible things and was about to do them again. He feared that this secret would come to light and people would learn the truth about him.

Finally, there were the dreams where he would be running through valleys and moorland, again in the dark. There was a companion beside him. Someone he was aware of through his peripheral vision. Sometimes he thought it might be Alex, at other times it felt like a stranger.

The rattle of the accommodation ladder brought him back to the present. Andy was on his way up. He looked at his watch. It was nearly time to collect Alex. This evening they would be attending the harbour master's Christmas party. He switched off the floods and went down below.

Later, in the harbour café, he had finished his second cup of tea when she arrived. They had not seen each other for five days and he had missed her. They hugged and kissed. 'Would you like a cup?' he asked.

'I'd rather get straight on board. I don't want to rush getting ready, besides, it looks like it might snow.'

'That's the forecast,' Zen said, as he paid. There were dark clouds coming in from the north east. The freezing wind stung their faces as they went down the steps to the pontoon. Crossing the estuary, it turned blustery and began to snow. When they reached the *Amber*, it was heavy.

'Take care how you climb those stairs; there's been ice on them all day.'

When he reached the poop deck, he saw that Alex had gone. She was not in the mess where the others were playing cards, Greek music playing in the background. So he went up to the cabin. Finding the door open, he entered and closed it behind him. She was in the bedroom unpacking. She looked a bit down.

'Something wrong?' Zen asked. She came and hugged him. 'What's the matter?'

'Oh, it's so stupid really,' she said finally.

'What?'

'All week I've had the feeling that you were going to leave me.'

'Why would I do that?'

'What's going to happen when the *Amber* leaves or is sold? You said that as soon as the repair work's done, the ship would be back on the market.'

'Just because she's for sale doesn't mean a sale's inevitable. George tells me that my father's still asking too much. In the end he may prefer to hold on to her than go down much further.'

'Nonetheless, the time will come when she will either be sold or sail. What then?'

Zen took her hand and they sat down on the bed. 'Who can predict what's going to happen. All I know is that I don't want to be without you and if, when the time comes, you feel the same, then we'll stay together either here or somewhere else.'

'I think I knew you were going to say that. I just needed to hear it.'

'We've got plenty of time before we go out. Would you like a bath?'

'Sounds like a good way to start the evening.'

'I'll light the candles and put on some music,' Zen said. He had recently purchased a tape deck.

365

The party took place in the upstairs lounge of a local pub. Several tables were set and they sat at the end of one and mostly spoke with each other.

It had occurred to Zen that Ann might also have been invited, as a friend of Kim's, but only Kim was there, with her boyfriend, Jeff. Later, after the meal, when guests started circulating and Alex was talking with someone else, he approached Kim.

'By the way, how's your friend?' he asked. 'You know, the one at the bar that evening in summer; Ann, wasn't it?'

'She's married,' Kim informed him. 'Her fiancé came back sometime in August and they went to the registry office a week later.'

'That's great news.'

They arrived back at twelve thirty to a dark and frozen ship. With the three heaters still going in the day room, bedroom and bathroom, it was a tolerable temperature. After undressing, Zen turned them off and got into bed. They made love and then lay in each other's arms, as much to keep warm as for intimacy. Zen felt her body relax and her breathing change. He continued to listen to the wind whistling past the metal of the hull as he also drifted off to sleep.

He becomes aware of standing naked in a wood, surrounded by gnarled, mature trees. The ground beneath his feet is damp and cold but not uncomfortably so. With his toes he can feel the texture of the crisp, recently fallen leaves.

It is dark, but despite that, he is able to see himself as his body is surrounded by a luminous aura. There is a woman beside him. She also glistens in a similar pearly

366

light. Beneath it her features are hazy. She is somewhat shorter than him but beautifully formed with long, flowing, red hair. She has her hands on her thighs and her pubic hair is luxuriantly curly and of a darker hue than that of her head. Her skin is porcelain white with a healthy blush. He looks up to her face, past her perfect breasts and into the bluest of eyes. As he stares into them the woman puts her right hand up to her throat. He cannot tell her age at all, she seems so unblemished and perfect.

Then she speaks and her voice is mellow, not like that of a girl, but of a woman. 'You would exploit me,' is all she says. Her voice resonates through his body like the call of a siren. He feels emotionally stirred and physically stimulated. He is conscious of not being able to control this arousal and embarrassed that it should become visible.

Then she says, 'One such as you made three years seem like thirty,' and with that her appearance changes. Her healthy glow turns grey and blue, the beautiful form becomes limp and coarse, her skin wrinkled, her hair dishevelled and her beautiful face looks beaten, cut, scarred and bruised. She is revolting.

'But I took it back.' With that statement her appearance changes again. Her beauty returns but is of a different kind. Whereas before it had a purity and innocence, now it has a cynical maturity. She seems somehow more voluptuous too, more curvaceous. Her look has a certain knowingness. Her mouth has a twist of cruelty and ruthlessness.

His feelings towards her also change. The first image provoked feelings of love and a desire to protect as well as to enjoin. Now he feels a possessive lust so desperate that he would do anything to have this woman, to kiss those manipulative lips, to fall at her feet, to bury his face in the twist of red hair, to grovel on her breasts, to do anything for the pleasure of her body.

'Come closer,' she says in the same mellow voice but now carrying an irresistible authority. He feels the excitement of someone who is about to have his darkest, deepest desires and fantasies satisfied.

When he is close enough she puts up her hand for him to stop. He could have reached out and touched her if he had the will of his own to do so.

'I could have much fun with you as my pet, compelling you to do whatever I want, but I would soon get bored,' she says, pausing to eye him up and down. 'Your form is pleasing, even more so than the others were. Pity I did not have the eyes to see the weakness and corruption that lay beneath. I could desire you now and have my fill, but why should you get such pleasure from me?'

And with those words she vanishes and he is alone in the woods. The aura that surrounded him at first was green, and when a wave of anguish and despair sweeps over him, it turns a dark red. Then he wakes.

Alex was lying with her head on his shoulder, an arm and leg across his body, as she often did. Despite being cold and on the verge of shivering, he slowly disengaged from her to go to the bathroom.

He got back into bed, huddling close to her, gradually warming up. The clock on the bedside table showed the time to be two thirty. He spent a long time thinking about the dream before falling asleep.

Saturday, 18th December 1982

Alex woke him when she snuggled up against his back. It was first light. He could hear the wind and rain continue to buffet the metal sides of the ship. He got up and lit the paraffin heaters as quickly as he could and returned to bed. Alex laughed at how cold he had become just in those few minutes. They cuddled and drifted in and out of sleep.

They woke when the generator came on. He looked at the time, it was nine thirty.

'That's later than usual,' she said.

'It's holiday time now. There's no work till the New Year, and justly so. I need to go shopping later.'

'Let's not get up just yet, though I've got shopping to do as well.'

'How did you sleep last night?'

'Like a log. Nothing works like a hot bath.'

'Talking about a bath, would you like one now.'

'They're such a luxury, I only have them here; I wouldn't say no.'

'We'll wait till the cabin warms up.'

Zen was distracted all morning and Alex asked if there was anything wrong. He could not take his mind off the dream, but told her that there was nothing amiss and that he was just feeling the effects of the last two months.

After lunch and shopping, he was back to his old self and they had great fun secretly nipping in and out of shops buying each other presents and hiding them in their bags. They stopped for tea when it started to turn dark and discussed how they would spend the holidays.

Chapter 39: The First Murder

Monday, 20th December 1982

Zen spent most of the day shopping for supplies and presents, staying on board for the late afternoon while the others also went ashore. It was cloudy and cold with sleet showers.

During this time a dilapidated, rust-streaked, grey-painted Bulgarian stern trawler entered the harbour, escorted by two tugs, and moored aft of them. The harbour master had informed him that this particular vessel had come on two previous occasions and laid up over Christmas and New Year. It intended to load horse mackerel, caught by local fishermen and destined for the European market.

They stayed in that evening, huddled in the mess around the gas fire, playing cards.

That night he dreams. He is back in the woods of two nights previously. The woman is there, naked in her luminous bubble, as he is in his.

'Come closer,' she commands.

He obeys, his eyes riveted to hers. They seem to grow as he approaches, as if they are going to swallow him up. When he is next to her she takes both his hands and then a bright light surrounds them and he feels himself falling into her. Momentarily, he is deprived of his senses and is next aware of seeing the world through her eyes, as if he were a passenger in her body. They start rising upwards into the air, beyond the woods and over hills, valleys and towns. When her head turns from side to side he sees dark wings and realises they are a bird gliding on the wind.

They have risen so high that he cannot discern any details of the terrain below. All he can see about him and in the distance are lights. Some are in long yellow strips, which he recognizes as roads, others are in groups that are towns and villages.

It begins drizzling and he can feel this against his eyes, their eyes, and the lights grow dimmer and blurred. They continue flying steadily for what could have been minutes or hours, it was impossible to tell; he has no perception of the passage of time. At some point they begin descending and circling before landing on the tiled roof ridge of a house, beside a chimney stack. The rain is heavier.

Then the white light envelopes him again and, as before, he loses his vision and is disorientated. The next thing he knows he has reformed as himself, and is holding both of the woman's hands and gazing into her eyes. She breaks the gaze and lets go of one hand and he becomes conscious of his surroundings. They are in a living room. It is finely furnished in light colours, has a prominent fireplace, armchairs, settees and glass coffee tables. There are pictures hanging on the walls and shelves for books. There are opulent light fittings and a luxurious carpet.

But the woman is leading him away. All the time, the main focus of his attention is her naked body, all he can think of is how much he longs for her. He can smell her and it is tantalizing. He wants to kiss her, taste her and possess her. As if she has heard his thoughts, she turns round to him and says, 'What would you do for me?'

He can feel himself mouth, 'Anything'.

371

She laughs. 'Will you die for my pleasure? Do you think you can give me what I need?' She continues pulling him forward, out of the living area and along a corridor.

She stops at a half-open door with a light coming out of it. She pushes this fully open and steps inside. The light extinguishes her glow and she is just a naked woman. Zen, still on the threshold, can see over her shoulder. In front of them is a double bed set in the centre of the far wall, both sides of which have a table with a lamp. There is a built-in wardrobe to the left and curtained windows on the right. On the left hand half of the bed someone is sleeping, on the right a man is sitting up with a pillow supporting his back against the headboard. He has dark, greying hair and is wearing glasses. He is reading, his head bowed and angled to take advantage of his bedside light.

He does not see her at first because she does not want him to. Then, with a wave of her hand, he folds the book, places it down in front of him and looks up. Slowly he removes his glasses. Zen can see his eyes darting all over her body. While he does this the woman poses with one hand on her hip, spinning round so he can see her from all angles. He recognises the expression on his face, a hunger he also shares. But for Zen there is jealousy as well.

The stranger goes to say something but no words leave his lips. She beckons him to follow and he stands. He is wearing green pyjama shorts. The exposed parts of his body reveal a man still fit for his years, but showing signs of a belly. He turns off the light on the bedside table and comes to her.

In the corridor they are glowing again as she takes Zen's hand and leads him out of the room. The man follows, closing the door behind him. As he walks past Zen, he does not seem at all aware of his presence. He is tall, well over six feet, with the hair covering his chest even greyer than that on his head.

Zen involuntarily follows them into another room. This one is smaller than the first, more simply furnished with a free-standing pine wardrobe and chest of drawers. There is a single bed with a side table and lamp. Across the room from the foot of the bed is an upholstered armchair. The woman points at this and Zen finds himself walking to it and sitting down.

In front of him he can see the man and woman standing, facing each other. She approaches and pushes him backwards so that he first sits and then lies on his back on the bed, his head on the pillow. There is excited anticipation on his face.

Meanwhile Zen is unable to move. He can neither turn his head away nor shut his eyes. This is absurd; at the same time as he is suffering jealousy, he feels arousal.

The woman follows the man on to the bed and straddles him, sitting on his groin, which is still clothed in the pyjama shorts. They begin rubbing against each other, slowly at first, but with ever increasing momentum as his excitement grows. When it appears as if he is close to his release, the woman's back stiffens. Her red hair falls straight, covering most of her back and finishes at a point level with her elbows. She is staring forwards. Zen can sense that something is not right.

In the time that it would have taken Zen to blink, if he could have blinked, the top part of the woman's body, the part that ended below her shoulder blades, is no longer that of the woman or of any woman. There is a quick impression of something black and furry; like the back of a dog or wolf. No sooner has that impression registered in Zen's mind than the thing's head plunges down on the man, whose look of ecstasy had now turned to terror. There follows a sickening tearing and crunching sound. The man's legs and arms start flailing wildly, but the physical efforts are for nothing, having no effect on the monster. Meanwhile the animal makes slurping noises, its head moving up and down as if it is opening and closing its mouth. The flailing turns to twitching and then stops altogether as the sickening feeding continues.

Zen feels renewed panic and fear and redoubles his efforts to free himself from his paralysis. He knows he will be next, he just knows it.

When the thing eventually raises its head from the man, it is the woman again. She stands and moves away from the bed. He can see the man fully now. His body is limp and pale but his head is twisted back despite resting on the pillow. There is a dark gash below his chin; his throat has been torn open. There are dark areas on either side of his head and shoulders where blood has soaked into the pillow and sheets.

The woman turns to face Zen and once again his gaze is claimed by her. She is completely unmarked. At her beckoning, he approaches her as she takes his hands and then there is the bright light again and they are out of the house, soaring into the night sky. He is seeing through her eyes, as before. He feels nothing, no emotions, not even the longing.

They fly for a while and when they start descending it is over calm water. After a while he sees it, the *Amber*, rising up to meet him. Just when it seems close enough to land, he knows no more.

He opened his eyes. It was the dead of night and all he could see was a faint glow of light coming from the partly open door of the bathroom. He tried to move and realised that the sheets beneath him were wet. In a flash he remembered the dream and panicked. 'It's my blood' he thought and sprang up, taking hold of the torch from the bedside table.

But it was not, he had only been sweating. His body, the under sheet and his pyjamas were drenched and now he was also shivering from standing in the cold. He took his pyjamas off and went into the bathroom and dried himself with the bath towel. He tried to remember the details of the dream but he was too tired. He felt completely drained in a way that made thinking arduous.

He went back to the bedroom, pulled out his spare pyjamas from the bottom drawer under the bed. He had no energy to do anything about the wet sheets so would have to sleep on them.

He slipped into bed again, feeling the momentary cold of the wetness, and waited to feel warm again. He eventually fell asleep.

Tuesday, 21st December 1982

He woke at 8.30. The cabin felt cold and damp. He heard a gust of wind and, with it, a spattering against the superstructure. It sounded like sleet, it made a slightly sharper sound than rain. He got up and turned on the heaters before getting back under the sheets.

Then the memory of the dream flooded back. Yes, the dream. In all his years he had never had one like it. He closed his eyes and remembered the details, together with the emotions that came with it. The feelings of physical longing when he saw the woman, the feelings of elation when he, they, were flying, the feelings of both envy and arousal when she approached the stranger, the feelings of devastation and loss at the thought of her being possessed by another man, then the revulsion and fear at the slaughter that followed. Finally, he felt emptied and void of any feelings at all.

He dozed until he heard the generator. He got up, ran the shower and stood under it, letting it wash the dried sweat away before dressing and going downstairs for breakfast.

Chapter 40: The Postcard

Tuesday, 21st December 1982

Zen spent most of the sunny but cold day ashore shopping and preparing for his trip to London. He had been feeling ever more reluctant to go as the time approached. Today these feelings had been overshadowed by the memories of the dream. He did not know what to make of it. As the day wore on he felt increasingly tired and, after packing his holdall, had a nap in the afternoon, getting up when the generator came back on for the evening.

After tidying up his quarters, he brought his bag down and put it by the poop deck door.

He found Harry in the galley chopping vegetables. Zen looked quizzically at the pot boiling on the range.

'I'm throwing the leftover chicken from Sunday into the stir fry,' Harry said. 'I think rice will go well with it.'

'Where are the others? It doesn't look like you're preparing enough for them.'

'Andy's having a nap. He's eating out tonight and Steph's not feeling well.'

'Nothing serious I hope.'

'Just a head cold; he's trying to sleep it off.'

'Wish him well for me.'

'Sure.'

'Can I get you a beer?'

'Yeah, I'm in the mood.'

Zen fetched two bottles from the pantry fridge. Handing one to Harry, they toasted the holiday season.

'Offering the workmen beer and soft drinks is making them go quickly,' Harry said.

'It means we now have only one cabin full instead of two. Besides, bottled beer doesn't last long.' He watched Harry cook as he drank and considered whether to mention the dream.

'Shall I serve you some?'

'No, I'll be leaving for Alex's soon, but I'll sit with you. Have you heard from Linda?' He was aware that she had gone with Stephen to stay with her parents for Christmas.

'I called on Sunday to check they'd arrived. I'll probably call again today.'

'Where are her parents?'

'On the outskirts of a place called Warwick.'

'I know, it has a famous castle.'

'So I've heard.'

'When are they back?'

'Middle of next week, I think.'

'In time for New Year?'

'Probably,' Harry said as he plated up and took his food to the mess. 'You look tired, are you having trouble sleeping?' he asked, as he sat at the table.

'No, just a dream,' Zen said. At Harry's prompting he recounted it as accurately as he could, as well as the earlier dream of this woman with red hair. He took care to include the different emotions he experienced. 'So, what do you make of it?'

'I'll tell you in a minute,' Harry said getting up and clearing his plate and cutlery. 'I'll make tea; want some?' Zen nodded. 'Just stay where you are.'

He returned a few minutes later with two mugs of camomile. He had a concerned expression on his face. 'I have to tell you, I've a bad feeling about this,' he said sitting back down, 'a very bad feeling.'

378

'Why? It's only a dream,' Zen said hopefully

'If you believed that you wouldn't have told me. I don't know why, but the dream together with everything else that's happened is making me uneasy.'

'But surely the dream's the result of my anxieties about my family and Alex. It can't be a coincidence that it occurred just before I'm about to go to my sister's wedding.'

'Dreams are clever devices. They have many layers with different meanings and, although what you say may have a bearing, I think there's more to it.'

'I don't see it.'

'Okay, let's review the facts. A few days after we arrive here last July we're visited by a supernatural apparition. Do you agree with that?'

'Why, yes. You've changed your tune.'

'According to the papers, the latest sightings of this so called "Beast" started at the end of May and were restricted to the moor and its valleys, right?' Harry said, ignoring his last observation.

'If you say so; you've done your homework.'

'I looked up the back copies in the library,' Harry said. 'Then, as soon as we turn up it starts venturing down the Tone valley as far as the sea and before we've even had time to unpack, it turns up on our decks!'

'That could've been coincidence.'

'Coincidence? It's obviously interested in you.'

'All right, I accept that would seem to be the case, except for what happened with Andy and Gloria.'

'I think what happened to Gloria was most revealing.'

'In what way?'

379

'Well, I never told you at the time but, after the dive at Spaniard's Cove, Andy mentioned that he'd met a woman at a party who knew Alex. I think you were in the galley with Steph at the time. Anyway, when Andy told Alex who it was, she went quiet, and when he mentioned we could be meeting her, she looked put out.'

'I'm sure we all have friends we'd rather our girlfriends didn't meet. And don't forget, this woman deceived Andy into thinking she was single. Maybe Alex felt uncomfortable about that.'

'I doubt it. Andy made no mention at the time as to her marital status.'

'Maybe Alex knows her husband. Anyway, what does that have to do with the Beast scaring her?'

'It tried to frighten her off.'

'Well, it succeeded in doing that but failed in stopping me meeting her.'

'Well, maybe she didn't reveal as much as she might have done. Who knows what information she possessed.'

'I think you're being paranoid, Harry,' Zen said, thinking about it. 'But that would assume there's some connection between the Beast and Alex.'

'I believe there is. Do you remember Spaniard's Cove?'

'That's absurd. Alex had an experience brought on by the place. She was fascinated by the story, felt the atmosphere, fell asleep and had a dream.'

'Not only do I believe there's a connection but also that your coming together was intentional.'

'I agree, it was; Alex and I intended it.'

'Many people are attracted to each other, but it's not often that the attraction is consummated. I mean, look at your life; for example, how many times have you been attracted to someone and nothing happened.'

'A lot, nine out of ten.'

'And in this case you had a helping hand getting connected.'

'How?'

'Your relationship started the first night of the regatta, didn't it?'

'Yeah?'

'Have you forgotten that Alex was meant to come with her friend Frankie?'

'Yeah?'

'If she'd come with her they would've had to leave together. What happened to Frankie?'

'She had an accident when her car came off the road because she thought she saw an animal in her path.' Zen's voice slowed as he said this. He had forgotten that incident. 'But this happens all the time, Harry. The roads are covered in dead animals from rabbits to deer.' He could, however, understand Harry's point. 'I accept there is a pattern in the events that have taken place, albeit tenuous. But coincidences occur all the time. It doesn't mean there's predestination involved.'

'Neither does it mean there isn't. It's just that these coincidences keep mounting up.'

'I'm sorry, I'm not so clued into all this New Age thinking. All right, so we were meant to come together, but why?'

'I don't know, but at least now you can understand why Gloria was attacked. It didn't want to risk her interfering.'

'Correction, why she might have been attacked. We're not seeing eye to eye on this just yet.' He did realise Harry meant well. 'I think we need more hard facts. Besides, Alex warned me that her past was dubious before we started.'

'I agree, I'm sorry. You look tired, my friend, I'm worried about you.'

'I am and have a long drive tomorrow.' He looked at his watch. 'I'd better go.'

'C'mon I'll take you.'

When he was parked outside her house, he could see through the blinds that the dining room light was on. He rang the doorbell. Alex answered immediately.

'Darling,' she said, closing the door. They embraced and kissed. 'I missed you.'

'I missed you too,' he replied. 'What would you like to do tonight?'

'Why don't we go for a walk down to the harbour? There are plenty of pubs with decent food.'

'It's cold out there and I'm really tired.'

'I've got a better idea then,' Alex said. 'There's a fish and chip shop just round the corner. One of the best in the country, I hear. I'll drop round and get some. You pop a bottle of wine in the freezer and set the table.'

'No salt or vinegar on mine.'

After she had left, he put the wine to chill and set out plates, knives and forks, before sitting down to wait.

The morning post, which Alex had not had time to examine, was placed in a neat pile at the end of the table nearest the front door. There were four items: two Christmas cards, the electricity bill and a postcard, the front of which showed that it was from Vienna. He idly turned it over. The handwriting was an erratic scrawl that was barely legible.

> Dear Alex,
> Having a great time in Vienna. Arrived Sunday (13th), so I thought I'd get the postcards out of the way before the conference starts. Be back after Christmas.
> Love Ben

He had never heard of a Ben in Alex's life. He knew the names of her work colleagues, so this was a mystery.

When she had returned and was unwrapping the parcelled food and dishing out their meal, he said, 'It takes a long time for post to get here from Vienna.'

'At least it arrived before he returned.'

'Who's Ben?'

'He's my shrink. I've told you about him.'

'But you never mentioned his name,' Zen pointed out. She had said that she was seeing someone for depression, something she had suffered from for years.

'Haven't I? It's Benjamin Earsop, so now you know. He's gone to some conference and staying for Christmas. Do you want to get the vino?'

The fish and chips were still piping hot. It was also good not to feel cold for a change.

Chapter 41: Antigoni's Wedding

Wednesday, 22nd December 1982

He left Alex at six the next morning, well before any hint of dawn. When first light did come, it was to herald a dull, overcast day.

He had only one break along the route, at a motorway services, in order to stretch his legs and use the men's room. Alex had made him a couple of ham and cheese sandwiches, so he did not need to waste time stopping to eat. Otherwise the drive was uneventful and, because of the onset of the holidays, there was little traffic to delay him, and by ten thirty he was in his dedicated parking bay of the underground garage of his apartment block.

When he entered his flat, after an absence of five months, the first thing that struck him was the smell. Not a bad smell, a fresh one. The apartment was spotless. When he'd given Heather the responsibility of looking after it and collecting his post, in return for her staying the occasional night, he had not expected this degree of gratitude. Her most recent visit must have included a thorough clean because not only could he not find a speck of dust, but there was the scent of liberally used cleaning products, and his bed had been remade.

On top of it lay his tuxedo, trousers, black tie, white shirt and navy overcoat, which had been taken from his cupboard and dry cleaned, according to his instructions, a few weeks earlier. On the carpeted floor were his immaculately polished shoes.

In the fridge he found a small carton of milk with some other groceries, and he made himself a cup of tea. It was now eleven and he had little time to get ready. He set to shaving and having a shower and was ready and dressed by twelve.

He resorted to travelling by public transport as the chances of finding parking near the church were remote, especially as it was one of the final shopping days before Christmas. On the way to the train station he looked out for a taxi, but there was none in sight.

He emerged from Bayswater Station at 13:45 and started the walk to the Greek Orthodox cathedral. As he approached the stretch of road in front of the entrance, his heart sank. Crowds were gathering in numbers, as he should have expected. He regretted not coming earlier. At least he would have got to his seat before these acquaintances, who doubtless knew about his family problems and had spoken at length about them before arriving.

He had expected his father to suggest he pass by their house first, so that they could go to the church as a family. Instead, he had told him to make his own way. It was a snub, a statement to society as to his new status and meant to cause him embarrassment. He could already see heads turning in his direction and remarks would be made. He wanted to turn on his heels and retreat, but knew he could not. He was also aware that he was being paranoid. He would not be the first or the last to fall out with his parents. So there was gossip, so what?

He was so absorbed in these thoughts, that he did not notice the parked, metallic blue Volkswagen Golf Cabriolet he had just passed.

'Zen, where have you been?' Sophia's voice came from behind him.

He spun round, surprised, and saw her locking the car door. She looked stunning in her plum coloured dress. 'Shouldn't you be inside?' he said, with a sigh.

'I should, but none of mine have arrived. I was waiting for you.'

'For me?' Zen exclaimed. 'But why?'

'We'll have plenty of time to talk about it later, let's go.' She clasped her hand round the crook of his elbow and they started walking. Zen continued looking at her in disbelief. 'Don't stare,' she said prodding her elbow into his ribs. 'You had your moment of rebellion last June, now I'm having mine.'

His trepidation fell away. She must have heard or realised what had happened and come to his rescue. People would see them and think if they were walking with arms linked and were all smiles, things could not be as the rumours had made out.

'I tried to call you this morning,' she said, as they approached the entrance. 'I was planning to pick you up.'

'I didn't hear it ring. I must've been in the shower.'

'It's good to see you,' she said, squeezing his arm.

'Likewise.'

They worked their way through the crowds, both outside and in, offering and accepting greetings and good wishes on behalf of their siblings. They made their way up the centre aisle, into the forward section of seats reserved for the families. Zen's would be on the right and Sophia's on the left, but for now they sat together.

'It's a long wait till the reception,' Zen reflected, as he removed his overcoat and scarf. The background

386

smell of burning candles and incense was calming. 'What am I going to do for three hours?'

'People usually go home and change. Didn't you drive?'

'Came by train. Didn't think I'd find anywhere to park.'

'We'll work something out,' she said, looking around her, occasionally waving at someone she spotted.

The church hushed and everyone stood. The Makris and Alexandrou families were coming in through the entrance to be followed by the bride and groom. Sophia squeezed his hand reassuringly and crossed the aisle.

The ceremony lasted over an hour, but Zen did not follow it. Although his sister was the most striking he had ever seen her, the thought of that odious, smirking rat Nicholas marrying her, made him look away. He was only vaguely aware of the sonorous incantations of the priests and the melodious chanting of the choir. Instead, he was perplexed with Sophia's behaviour. She had the most cause to want to see him punished and humiliated and yet she was the only one concerned about his feelings. In contrast, his father only briefly looked his way, while his mother at least managed a smile. Only Spiros Alexandrou and his wife came up and greeted him properly.

There was much for Sophia and him to catch up on and Zen hoped there would be an opportunity to do so. He had heard no news about what was going on in London and had no idea how this wedding had come about.

After the service, the newly married couple and the two families stood together as the guests formed a queue to offer their congratulations and best wishes.

This interminably long process was also very awkward, as he had to stand next to his mother for nearly an hour, smiling and pretending that everything was as it should be.

They left the church at four. Zen walked along the Bayswater Road towards Marble Arch until he found a taxi to take him back to Crouch End, having arranged to meet Sophia at seven in the entrance hall of Claridges.

Later that evening, Zen got out of a cab and entered the lobby of the hotel five minutes late. Sophia was already there, sitting where she could not be seen by the other guests, who were arriving in a steady stream.

'This is the second time you've surprised me,' he said, referring to her promptness.

'I didn't want to be late on this occasion.'

'Do you think there've been many arrivals?'

'I'd say most have come. It's a good time to join.'

'They're not going to announce us, are they?'

'No, but a photographer will take pictures as we enter the ballroom.'

They started making their way, first stopping at the cloakroom to deposit their coats.

'When's the meal?' he asked.

'The sit-down's at eight, followed by dancing. You don't seem to know much, do you?'

'Since I left in July, I've only received family news through George Pittas.'

'That's worrying.'

'I've no idea how this wedding came about,' he said as they approached the entrance to the reception suite. 'I even got the invitation via George.' They waited for the photographer to finish with another couple, whom neither of them knew, before taking their turn. Sophia linked arms with him and insisted they be photographed together.

They entered a small lobby, which in turn led to the ballroom where the main reception was taking place. At the entrance were waiters holding trays with flutes of champagne. They joined a queue for one of them.

'I've arranged the seating so that we're at a table with some of my father's business contacts. So no one will know us too intimately.'

'Won't that be awkward for you?'

'I wasn't on the top table anyway. You're not the only one who's fallen from grace.'

'Your father hasn't found out about...you know..?'

'Nothing like that. We'll talk later.'

They picked up a glass each and entered the opulently decorated hall. It was already fairly full, with people standing and talking in groups beneath the glittering chandeliers. A pianist was playing on a black grand in the corner.

'Actually there're a lot of business associates of my father here, as well as others I can talk to,' he said. 'Why don't you go and do what you have to do and we'll meet at the table?'

'You'll be okay?'

'I'll survive the next hour or so.'

'It's table 23.'

So he went from group to group, reacquainting with people, while enjoying a bewildering array of canapés, saying more or less the same thing. 'Yes, we've laid up most of our ships... No, not all of them in Greece...

I've no idea what the market will do or when it will improve….' and 'Isn't my sister beautiful?'

He managed to avoid his family and finally came across George Pittas, who was happily sitting with his wife, Eleni. He was crunching a mouthful of nuts.

'Hello, George and Mrs Pittas,' he said.

'We saw you at the church, but thought you might not come here afterwards,' Mrs Pittas said. She was a slight woman, no more than five feet tall, with dark hair and eyes and a warm friendly smile.

'How is it?' George asked.

'Difficult,' Zen replied.

'Don't worry, Zen,' Mrs Pittas said. 'It will take time, but your mother will bring your father round.'

It was just after eight and people had started moving through the two sets of double doors into the dining room. He held back before finding his table. There were twenty eight in all, according to the notice at each entrance. These were arranged in a semi-circle of two rows around a raised dance floor, which in turn was in front of a stage on which the band had their equipment.

The head table was in the middle of the room and they were located at the far end, to the left as one faced the stage. Sophia was already seated with the other occupants; all of whom were unfamiliar, neither could he place their names when they were introduced.

As he sat, a waiter was taking orders. They could select from Parma ham with melon or pâté to start, followed by either half a roasted duck, a haunch of venison, or salmon. Afterwards, another waiter came to pour the wine.

'You've lost weight,' Sophia said.

'You think so? I'm not surprised; I'm on the move all day and cold most of the time.'

'You're eating enough?'

'More than ever. We've a good cook. So, how did all this come about?'

'You should've called, you know.'

'What if I got your mum or dad?'

'Then why didn't you write?'

'I didn't feel I could. Last time we spoke was also during a meal and that didn't end too well.'

'I know, I'm sorry. I didn't realise things would end the way they did. I didn't think you'd go to Cornwall.'

'It's Devon actually.' Zen said, trying to describe what it was like where he was.

'Sounds nice. Look, we were friends before and should continue to be so,' Sophia said as a waiter brought her the Parma ham and Zen the pâté.

'I agree, so bring me up to date.'

'It began before you left. Surely you suspected something?'

'How? The only time I spoke to my father was in the office about business. I called my mother twice and she didn't mention anything.'

'Didn't you speak to any cousins or other relatives?'

'No.'

'So, what? You've became a recluse?'

'I didn't feel like socialising. I didn't meet up with any of my friends either, well only twice. I suppose, I didn't want to have to explain what had happened.'

'So, you just call people when you feel like talking to them? What about finding out how they are or what they're doing? It's not only about you. Is there anybody you actually care about other than yourself?'

'Of course there is,' Zen said, looking around the table to see if the other occupants had overheard. 'In Tonemouth we socialise a lot.'

'That's not quite what I'm talking about. Anyway, after the end of our engagement, the talks started.'

'What, like the next day?'

'Probably. Don't look so surprised. Nicholas and Antigoni were told to start going out in order to see whether they got on. They were given a deadline, which was the holiday in Halkidiki.'

'How convenient that the result should be positive. So everyone went to Halkidiki, as planned, and the alternative engagement was announced.'

'Accept that the marriage was to take place in spring, had it not been for unforeseen circumstances; and I wasn't in Halkidiki.'

'What do you mean you weren't there?'

'My father packed me off to my aunt in New York. I was there for two months.'

'Why would he do that?'

'I didn't want to go, but he insisted. He said it was to help me recover from my disappointment.'

'And the real reason?'

'I'm afraid I didn't hide my disapproval at the new arrangement, which explains why I'm no longer in favour.'

'Anyway, getting back to my sister, I don't know when she's expecting.'

'She's five months, so it looks like the end of April. But Zen, there are other things you should be concerned about.'

'What things?'

'Think about it. The intention, were we to marry, was to merge the two businesses.'

'That's still going to happen. I realise that.'

'The rationale is that the days of the small to medium-sized owners are over. Only operations big enough to pool resources will survive.'

'I agree. It's just that our parents seem unlikely partners.'

'That doesn't matter because once the businesses merge, our fathers will retire and Nicholas will run it.'

'I realise that too. Why should you not be happy for your brother?' Zen asked.

'I have my reasons. You're not the only one who's been marginalised. You sound like you don't care.'

'I do care, but I don't mind being excluded if that's the price I have to pay for independence.'

'This is what we didn't agree about before. I suppose we could argue about it forever.'

'So let's not. Where's the honeymoon?'

'California. Bet you don't know about New Year either?'

'Don't tell me; they're going to Torquay,' Zen said. There was a hotel there popular with wealthy Greeks and his parents had gone there for New Year once before, two or three years previously.

'Worse luck, yes. Your parents, my parents and me.'

'Guess who won't be invited?'

'It would've been bearable if you had,' she said as a waiter came and removed their plates.

'Let's not dwell on it. Instead, tell me who that bald man is, with the moustache and goatee beard, two tables away, the one who looks like a weightlifter.' Zen had spotted him as soon as they had sat down as he

393

looked out of place. 'He's not an acquaintance of my father's and he's not sitting with the other business contacts, so he must be a family friend.'

'You can't tell a soul, but he's my mother's shrink.'

'I thought that was years ago.'

'It was, but he's friends with my father. They spent a weekend down where he lives at the beginning of the year, when Mum started having problems again. He's the only one she confides in.'

'An unusual choice of guest then.'

'I'm sure he's discreet. He's quite interesting actually. He used to be a wrestler and is also a writer. He came to our house for lunch yesterday.'

'Where from?'

'He's flown in from Vienna for the wedding and is flying back in the morning.'

'Is that where he lives?'

'No, he's at some conference,' she said. 'When my parents went to see him last February, they stayed somewhere near Torquay.'

'Is that so?' Zen said. 'What's his name?'

'It's Ben, Benjamin Earsop.'

He did not get home until two in the morning. He was struggling to get his head round the coincidence of finding Ben Earsop at the reception. Was he in turn aware of Zen's presence? Later in the evening, after the main course and dessert, when the lights were dimmed and the dancing had started, he had lost sight of him.

He had danced only with Sophia, while she had several other partners. He was happy to sit and keep on drinking first the wine and then the port that accompanied the cheese and biscuits.

394

Now his brain was too fatigued and anaesthetised to think clearly. For once he was relieved not to have to light paraffin heaters and gas lamps and was grateful for the central heating. He undressed, slipped under the sheets and fell into a deep sleep.

Thursday, 23rd December 1982

He woke at 11:45, later than he had planned to. He showered, dressed, threw everything in his holdall and was in his car driving by 12:30.

The traffic was light again. The great holiday exodus would not begin until tomorrow. He stopped for an hour to have a sandwich, but otherwise continued straight through.

He had many thoughts to keep him company during the four and a half hours.

He walked into the harbour café at six thirty, having made good time. He found Harry sitting at a corner table with a pile of newspapers in front of him.

'Hello, my friend,' Zen said.

'Hi, do you want a cup of tea?'

'Shouldn't we be going back?'

'There's been a change of plan. While you've been away, we've befriended our neighbours, the Bulgarians. The captain, his wife and two officers are coming for dinner tonight. Steph's been cooking all day. They're not expected till eight. Besides it's still freezing on board.'

'I'm up, I'll get them,' Zen said. He went over to the bar. 'So, what's up?' he said, sitting down with the tray. 'What's with the papers?'

Harry picked up the top one in the pile, unfolded it and placed it in front of him. It was the Western Morning News of yesterday morning. Zen scanned the headlines. What he saw made his heart miss several beats. He felt his body go weak.

PROMINENT EXETER RESIDENT
BRUTALLY MURDERED
Retired Harley Street Psychiatrist found by wife

From the photos it was difficult to tell if it was the same couple he had seen in his dream. The article dealt mainly with the man's life story. The only actual facts were that the police were treating it as suspicious and that the incident took place in the early hours of Monday morning, shortly after midnight, the same time as Zen was having the dream.

'What do the other papers say?' Zen said, looking up at Harry.

'Nothing new, just an appeal for witnesses.'

'What does it mean, Harry?'

'Did you tell me every detail?'

'As well as I could remember. But why me?'

'Look, I don't know. In the earlier dream you had of this woman, what did she say?'

'She seemed obsessed by how much I wanted her and how little she wanted me.'

'And your feelings for her?'

'That I would do anything for her, anything to have her.'

'And when you're a wake?'

'She means nothing.'

'Does she want you to feel hurt and betrayed as some sort of punishment?'

'If so, why?'

'Look, I'm going to say something that you're going to find a bit far-fetched.'

'Go for it.'

'If we take the dream literally, the Elizabeth that Alex told us about and the Beast are one and the same. What I'm suggesting is that they are either connected to or are using Alex to get to you. To make things more complicated, there's something about you that this Elizabeth doesn't like.'

'Or maybe it's just men.'

'Quite possibly. Or a particular kind of man.'

'Look Harry, I'm not saying I don't believe you. I've seen too much, so I know what you say is possible, even if remotely. So how do we find out for certain and what do we do about it?'

'I've no idea.'

'By the way, listen to this, there's a hypnotherapist in Tonemouth who Alex goes to.'

'You never told me.'

'It was sort of a secret.'

Harry was thoughtful. 'What's she being treated for?'

'Depression is what she said. She doesn't like to talk about it.'

'We'll speak of this again, but we better go back and help the others prepare for our guests.'

'There's more.'

'Go on.'

'This shrink, whatever you'd call him, was at the wedding.'

'What?'

Zen told him the story, while they walked to the pontoon and crossed over to the *Amber*.

Chapter 42: The Second Murder

That night, after the Bulgarians had left and they'd cleared up, Zen sat down at the desk of the day room and, by the light of the gas lamp, read the newspapers for himself. It was well after midnight and he'd had a good deal of wine and food. It was cold in the cabin, despite all his heaters being on.

In the end there was not much more of interest over and above what Harry had told him. Today's edition gave a simple family background and biography. The usual stuff: Harley Street practice, children went to boarding school but now grown up and in professional careers, devoted wife. The police were revealing little, only that the murder was the result of a frenzied attack, as they liked to call it.

After he had finished with the papers, he took out the diary and caught up with events on board. He entered the generator times and the work that had been carried out during his absence. Harry had made a note of all this for him.

Besides their routine chores, they had bought an artificial Christmas tree, which they had decorated with a few lights, and there were already several presents underneath it, as well as a dozen or so Christmas cards on the sideboard. Some of the gifts were from the Bulgarians.

It was an enjoyable evening. Surprisingly, it was Steph who had made the first contact. He had spotted the captain having a smoke on his prow, while he was doing the same at the stern. They'd exchanged a few words and the invitation arose from that. The Bulgarians spoke passable Greek, with strange accents, but they brought several bottles of wine and afterwards asked them round for a meal on the evening of Christmas Day.

When he had finished, he undressed and got into bed. The sheets were cold, even with the benefit of a hot water bottle, and he had to wait until he felt warm enough before falling asleep.

After a while, Zen thinks he has woken and opens his eyes. He tries to move but his body is paralysed. Then he is aware that she is standing beside the bed. In the corner of his eye he can see the glowing envelope around her. He feels both excitement and fear. Is it his turn? Has she come to murder him too? He thinks of himself being found the next morning with a torn-out throat, lying in a pool of blood. He hears her laugh as if she has read his thoughts. She raises one hand, palm facing downwards, and his body feels light and mobile. He gets up and stands in front of her. As before, he is naked, and, wondering what has happened to his pyjamas, he looks behind him to see that he is still in bed asleep with the sheet and blankets that covered him moving slowly up and down with his breathing.

He faces her, naked, as she is, the familiar longing growing inside him. Then, she takes him by the hand, there is the bright light and they are soaring through the skies, rising higher and higher, with him watching through her eyes. They are circling to gain height and he can see everything: Tonemouth, the estuary and the *Amber*. Eventually they level off and head west by north west.

As before, he can make out yellow strings of lights for the roads and groupings for villages. Visibility is excellent and he is aware of the stars overhead. In due time he sees an orange glow on the horizon, which grows as they approach.

When they are on the brink of the expanse of what he recognises as Plymouth, they bank left and begin a steep decline. They are heading for a group of lights at a cove. When they land on a roof he knows it is going to happen again and, as before, he is briefly enveloped by the white light before finding himself inside the dark house. They are in their individual forms again in a dining room, in front of a fireplace, and the woman leads him through a door and into an entrance hall. From there she goes up a flight of stairs and left down a short corridor to a half-open doorway. As she enters, Zen is made to follow, like a pet tethered to a lead. They stop at the foot of a double bed. There are two forms huddled underneath a duvet.

Elizabeth, as this is now whom he acknowledges her to be, moves to the left hand side, beside the sleeper, who Zen sees is a woman with blonde, shoulder-length hair. She is lying on her front with her head turned to face away from her partner. Her left hand is resting on the pillow beside her, in front of her face. Moving quickly, Elizabeth takes hold of the woman with both hands, one from behind the neck and one under the chin. She rests her knee on her back and in one movement twists the woman's head until she is facing the ceiling. Zen hears the sound of breaking bones and snapping ligaments. Elizabeth lets go of the head and lets it drop back on the pillow.

Beside the now dead woman a bald-headed man stirs. He has been sleeping on his side facing the other way and he is turning round towards his wife, if that is who she was, as if he has sensed and heard that there is something wrong. At the same time Elizabeth is leaning over him, while straddling the body of his wife.

When the man looks up, it is to see the countenance of the beast as it plunges its open jaws at his throat. The scream that no doubt was about to come out of his mouth is instead the muffled gurgle of someone choking on his own blood. The body flails in vain under the covers but soon falls still and, as before, the beast continues feeding after the man has died.

The head that eventually raises up is that of Elizabeth. She gets off the bed and pauses to survey her work. The man lies staring up at the ceiling his mouth open and welling with blood. Below his chin is a larger, gaping, dark crevasse.

Elizabeth comes to Zen and takes his hands and, after the flash of light, they are flying through the night again. When they are back by his bed he stands naked as she looks at him. She seems to be thinking what to do next, but in the end she turns away and vanishes. He feels himself falling on top of his inert self.

When Zen woke, his head was throbbing and he felt feverish. From the nearby porthole he could see that daylight was breaking.

He remembered the dream. He was confused at first because he thought he was recalling the first nightmare, but then he realised that this was different. He got up and lit the oil heaters before he creeping back under the covers; he would just have to put up with the smell.

He lay there cold and shaking for a while debating whether to wake Harry, but saw no point. Before long he was asleep again.

By the time the generator came on, it was warm in the cabin. Zen got up, shaved, showered and dressed.

The mess was empty. Steph informed him that Harry had already had breakfast and that Andy was not up yet. Zen settled for some toast. Later he found Harry in the engine room, sitting in the control room reading an engineering manual.

'It's happened again,' he said as he opened the door and Harry looked up.

'What's happened again?'

'Another murder dream,' Zen said, sitting down. He related it from beginning to end.

'How are you feeling? You look terrible.'

'Tired, drained, numb, perplexed, scared; I could go on.'

'I think the murders have a purpose in themselves.'

'What makes you think that?'

'What? Do you believe these killings are random? People chosen by chance and slaughtered for the fun of it? And why should you be made to watch?'

'To make me feel like I do.'

'Which is what, exactly?'

'Frightened, vulnerable, disgusted, somehow responsible.'

'That could just be a by-product. The killings seem to be too deliberate. We'll soon find out from the papers whether there's any connection between the victims. There's also the question of why the wife was killed this time.'

'In the meantime, we remain in the dark,' Zen said, unable to hide his despair.

'The purpose behind these killings is beside the point. The fact remains that you're being set up for something.'

'There's something I've remembered which, in view of recent events, has become important,' Zen said, before telling Harry about the unexplained initial contact with the harbour office to enquire about a berth, and how he had found out that the Alexandrous had stayed in the local hotel.

'It's obvious that this Spiros wanted you here.'

'Precisely. He wanted me away from London so that I wouldn't interfere with his plans.' Zen went on to explain how Sophia was exiled to New York while the arrangements were being made.

'And Alex became a convenient honey trap to make sure you stayed. And I think we'll also find that the two victims are connected to Earsop. Isn't it convenient that both murders occurred whilst he's away?'

'The perfect alibi. And Elizabeth's problem with me has nothing to do with either Spiros or Earsop.'

'Whatever her grievance, it happened two hundred years ago. That's when that particular seed was sown.'

'Do you think I'm in danger? After all, Spiros seems to have achieved his aim, which was to marry into my family.'

'I don't know. Unless the threat comes from Elizabeth and, as we have the names of those involved in the drama two centuries ago, we might be able to find out. I've got an idea, so when we go out I need to do something.'

'There's one more thing.'

'Go on.'

'You know how I said that at the beginning of the last dream I looked back at my body?'

'Yes?'

'Well, there's more to it. I had a thought, or perhaps it was a conviction. I felt there was something missing, I was aware that Alex wasn't next to me. I then reflected that it should have been so because Elizabeth was next to me, if you see what I mean.'

'Interesting,' Harry said rubbing his morning stubble. 'Reflections during dreams can be either literal or symbolic and provide intuitive insights.'

'Symbolically and subconsciously, I am associating Elizabeth and Alex as one and the same, right?'

'Right.'

'But the literal interpretation of my feeling would be that if my spirit was with Elizabeth, but my body is lying in bed, then Elizabeth's present body should be that of Alex lying in bed with me. Couldn't that be possible?'

'No, because Alex is not Elizabeth reborn or reincarnated. Alex is Alex. I believe Elizabeth is separate. She's a haunting entity, her spirit is already here.'

'I'm not following.'

'It's more likely that Alex is possessed. She seems genuinely oblivious to what's going on. Moreover, if Elizabeth survived the wrecking of the *Casaba* and exacted her revenge in the manner she did, she must've done so with knowledge of the occult or something similar.'

'She must have lived locally then. Far enough away not to be recognised, but close enough to keep an eye on her quarry. If she was associated with witchcraft there might be a record of an accusation.'

'As I suggested, leave the research to me for the time being. But you realise the implications of this?'

'Tell me.'

'Elizabeth has the power to direct Alex's emotions and feelings.'

'I do realise what that means.'

'What's more worrying is that she seems to be able to do this to you as well.'

'But only in my sleep.'

'Even so, it's important that you fight it. Perhaps we'll discover something that will help you do this.'

'I hope so.'

'Let's talk about it later, there's something I'm in the middle of,' Harry said, holding up the manual.

Zen left Harry to go about his work and, after lunch and the close-down of the generator, they went ashore. Harry went to the library and Zen to do some last minute shopping and to buy presents for the Bulgarians, which they would deliver to them later in the evening. Two hours later, they met in the café. Harry had bought the day's papers and was looking through them. Zen sat with him to wait for Alex who would be finishing work early.

'I hope your afternoon yielded some results,' Zen said.

'You will be pleased to know that it has,' Harry replied looking smug and pleased with himself.

'Well, I'm waiting.'

'The librarian was helpful. I think she took a shine to me.'

'I'm not interested in your conquests.'

'You should be because she put me on the right track.'

'Go on.'

'Well, she's not only the head librarian, but is also involved in the local museums and is well aware of this story. James's family name was Hunt and Elizabeth's was Bartlett, by the way. There's a lot written about their families, but nothing specific to them individually.'

'That's a shame.'

'However, James's cousin Philip, who you'll remember went to the Colonies with the solicitor to bring James back, subsequently inherited the family business and went on to make a fortune. He eventually bought a manor house, inland from Spaniard's Cove, which stayed in the family for generations, eventually being gifted to the National Trust in the '50s.'

'Alex mentioned that when she pointed out that monument on the cliff.'

'Three years ago,' Harry continued, 'the National Trust reached an agreement with the Devon Records Office to lend it historical documents that it had from its properties in Devon. Some came from Philip's house. My librarian friend showed me the manifest. Amongst these is a handwritten document called 'An Account of the Circumstances Surrounding the Sinking of the *Casaba*.'

'Well, can we see it?'

'It would only be available to researchers at present, but my contact said that she had the authority, as a trustee of the museum, to make a request to the Records Office, on behalf of a researcher, whereby photocopies could be made of the document and then sent to us.'

'Now I'm interested in your conquests. Of course, this account might not contain anything of any use.'

'Naturally, but if all goes well, we could know shortly after Christmas.'

Alex's arrival interrupted their conversation. She walked in with two large carrier bags laden with presents. They went on board.

As it was nearly six, they put on the news. If there was any doubt in their minds as to whether the events in last night's dream really occurred, they were dispelled by the local headlines. The second murder was the main item but, as yet, there were no useful details included in the report.

While they were watching the television, Steph wrapped the Bulgarians' presents. Zen had bought them smoked salmon, a selection of local cheeses, a box of biscuits and a bottle of fine port. Steph and Andy went over to the trawler to deliver them.

Chapter 43: Christmas

Saturday, 25th December 1982

They woke at eight to a mild and sunny Christmas morning. By half past Zen had taken Alex ashore as she had to be in Exeter in time for church. She would be back at the quayside by seven.

Zen went for a run through the deserted streets and was ready for breakfast after a shave and shower.

From the moment he stepped onto the poop deck landing he was enveloped by the tantalizing aromas of baking. When he got to the mess he found Andy and Harry sitting at the top table. This was set with plates and cutlery, butter and margarine and a selection of marmalades, jams and honey in the small glass jars that you usually find at hotels. Zen looked at Andy knowingly. 'Are you still seeing Clare?'

'This is her present,' Andy replied. 'She's working at the hotel for the holidays, so we're back together.'

'Wonderful,' Zen said. 'Will we be seeing her?'

'She's coming tonight,' Andy replied, referring to their invitation to the Bulgarians.

'Let's see if Steph needs a hand,' Zen said.

'You can't go in there,' Harry declared. 'Steph's preparing a surprise.'

'It's been driving us crazy for hours,' Andy added.

'Is that why you switched on so early?' Zen asked Harry, as he sat beside him.

'Yes, but he's not just been baking for us,' Harry answered. 'The first consignment was collected by the Bulgarians.'

'It smells like a patisserie,' Andy said. 'I bet it's Danish pastries.' He had hardly finished his sentence when Steph came in with a platter and a bowl. The former contained croissants filled with a selection of cheeses, cold ham and salamis. The latter had just plain croissants.

'Magnificent,' was all Zen could say.

It was too much for them to finish and at ten thirty they moved to the sitting area to drink coffee and open presents. The quantity under the tree had grown significantly since they had added Alex's gifts the night before.

'Shouldn't we open them this evening when Alex is back?' Harry asked.

'No, that's all right,' Zen replied. 'She'll have loads waiting for her at her parents'.'

'So you know,' Harry announced, 'there are presents for everyone under Linda's tree. She didn't have a chance to bring them before they left.'

'And we have some for her,' Steph added.

When they had finished, they were knee-deep in wrapping paper. The presents Harry, Andy and Zen bought each other reflected their situation and comprised thick socks, gloves and scarves. In addition, Zen bought Steph a bottle of whiskey, as he knew he was fond of it, Harry a pair of swimming shorts and Andy a black leather belt.

Alex bought Steph a letter writing set, Andy three ties and Harry a grooming kit. She bought Zen a chunky jumper, a tracksuit top with hood and a new pair of wool-lined slippers. She had also bought each of them an additional hot water bottle.

The presents from the Bulgarians were all edible. There was a spicy and aromatic salami, a bottle of Bulgarian raki, one of menta and, to their great surprise, a jar of fish roe similar to caviar.

After helping Steph clear up, Zen left him roasting a capon with potatoes and vegetables for lunch. He went in search of Harry. He found him in his day room, sitting at his table. He had been listening to the news on his radio and turned it off when Zen sat down.

'So, the murdered men were psychiatrists and ex-partners of Ben Earsop,' Harry said. 'The police have asked all their patients to come forward and be eliminated from their enquiries, and Earsop, who's away in Vienna, is feared to be the next victim.'

'From the police's point of view it's the logical conclusion.'

'We're both agreed that Earsop's the instigator of these crimes even though they were committed by Elizabeth.'

'And Elizabeth?'

'Well, my friend, I think this confirms our theory. Alex and Elizabeth are one and the same or, rather, share the same body, except that Alex doesn't know it.'

'Even though Earsop must be responsible for bringing her forward?'

'Unintentionally at first, I'm guessing, but yes.'

'When I'm talking to Alex, do you think Elizabeth's listening?'

'Only Earsop knows that,' Harry said, shrugging his shoulders. 'And Elizabeth, of course.'

'As none of this is her fault, is there no way to deal with the matter without hurting Alex? Can't someone undo what Earsop has done?'

411

'What's he done? Do we know? With luck we'll learn more after Christmas.'

'And then what?'

'I've no idea. I wish there was a way to put Alex on her guard, get her to resist, which would give her a chance, otherwise she's vulnerable.'

'On the other hand, the whole thing could blow over, now that Spiros has got his way.'

'Or there's another possibility you've not considered.'

'What's that?'

'You won't like it. Could it be Sophia who's behind this?'

'It's more likely pigs could fly.'

'Why do you say that? You jilted her. Just because she's gay doesn't mean she wasn't upset. She had a lot to lose.'

'And what could she offer Earsop in payment? She's got nothing of her own.'

'Didn't you say she's a beautiful woman?'

'It's a logical theory,' Zen said, remembering their conversation at the reception. 'I just can't see it happening.'

They could hear Steph climbing the stairs. 'Lunch will be ready shortly,' he said, as he entered the cabin. He was carrying a platter of toasted bread cut into squares, topped with the fish roe the Bulgarians had given them. 'Here's something to be getting on with.'

'Mmm, this is fantastic,' Zen said, with eyes closed as he took a mouthful. 'A nice smooth ouzo would've complemented this well.'

'Isn't there any on board?'

'The captain's bar may have it, but I'm sure we'll be drinking enough today.'

'True. What were we talking about?'

'I think it was Alex.'

'So once we uncover Elizabeth's past, it might be easier to deal with her and thereby get to the truth through her,' Harry continued.

'I agree,' Zen said, having another nibble. 'I've changed my mind about the ouzo.'

'Me too.'

They had the capon with roast potatoes and a selection of vegetables, sharing a bottle of red wine, thanks to the Bulgarians.

That evening at eight, with Alex and Clare on board, the Bulgarians came with their considerably larger launch, to pick them up. For only the second time, the *Amber* was left unmanned.

The trawler was down to eight men, out of a potential complement of twenty-five, the rest having gone home to their families and, although considerably smaller than the *Amber*, it was still a large vessel.

Their setup was different as well. Having a smaller generator and a better insulated hull meant that they could keep their power running all day and night without causing a nuisance to the surrounding population. This was in any case necessary as they needed to keep their freezers going, even though there was little fish stored in them at present.

As a result, their accommodation was stifling in comparison and they soon stripped off the layers they were used to wearing. The single mess, catering for the whole crew, was colourfully decorated and had one long table running down the centre.

They had a wonderful meal: cold meats, dips and salads to start, with a warming fish stew to follow. Afterwards there was a selection of pastries, goats' cheeses and yogurts. Throughout the feast, there was plenty to drink.

In the background there was ethnic music and much exuberant talking. Zen had never seen Steph so sociable and happy; he seemed at home, as if dining at his village taverna. Andy was also making friends and Zen had overheard him arranging to go out with two of the younger crew. Harry meanwhile was talking to the chief engineer.

The captain sat at the head of the table next to his wife, with Zen and Alex on either side. He was a man in his fifties and entertained them with stories of his experiences at sea in different types of vessel. He in turn was interested in what Zen had to say about shipping from the owner's point of view.

After the meal they had coffees served with raki and menta and the air became thick with cigarette smoke. It was two in the morning when they were taken back.

Wednesday, 29th December 1982

Zen took Alex ashore early as she had to return to work. She carried a small suitcase containing her clothes of the last four days. Four days during which they were so intimate and close that it made the undercurrent of events that were taking place, of which only Zen and Harry had any knowledge, seem absurdly improbable.

414

And yet a certain melancholy hung over them, one that neither was able to admit to, let alone discuss.

Apart from Sunday when there had been light rain, the rest of the time had been mild and sunny and they had been for long walks along the coast. Zen had his camera and they had taken dozens of pictures of each other in the various settings. He'd also had the idea of collecting something from each of the beaches and coves they visited and now had an interesting assortment of driftwood in his quarters, which helped to make them more homely.

Zen carried a bag with her presents, as he walked her to her car. She had received a range of toiletries and soaps from Harry and Andy and a box of chocolates from Steph. Zen had given her one of her favourite perfumes, White Linen, a cafetière for two and a pashmina.

He would not be seeing her now until Friday evening, New Year's Eve. After she had driven off, he went for his first run in several days.

No work was planned, so they pottered around during the morning, washing clothes and catching up on chores. After lunch, Zen and Harry went out, Zen to go to the post office and do some shopping and Harry to visit the library. When they met up at the harbour café, Harry had a thick brown envelope with him.

'Have you looked?' Zen asked.

'Briefly,' Harry replied. 'No wonder it cost £7, it runs to a hundred pages.'

'Is it legible?'

'Philip had good handwriting. I made a copy for myself.'

'Naturally.'

'We'd better get back and switch on, it's got dark.'

That night the crew went back to the Bulgarian ship for an evening meal, but Zen sent his apologies and stayed behind, seeing it as an opportunity to read the account. Steph made him an omelette with chips for supper before getting ready.

Harry shut down at eight and left with the others. After Zen had reset the alarm, he locked himself in his cabin and lit the oil heaters and gas lamp. He updated the day's diary and accounts, then settled on the settee with a glass of red wine, keeping the bottle nearby.

He removed the contents of the brown envelope and looked at the grainy black and white photocopies. The handwriting was indeed neat and attractive. It was carefully written in some sort of large-paged ledger, slightly smaller than A4 size. He put the stack on the table and, picking up the first page, began to read.

Chapter 44: An Account of the Circumstances Surrounding the Wrecking of the *Casaba*

(I) My Reasons for rendering this Account

Should you have the patience and inclination to read that which is here set out, may I assure you that there is nothing within these pages that is deliberately false or misleading in so far as my memory and sanity still serve. Such is the fickle nature of our minds that a more firm assurance cannot be given, nor can I provide the testimony of witnesses.

I will, however, warn that much herein will be my own opinions and observations, influenced by the varying feelings ignited by this episode. I will fully disclose these emotions as I proceed, but shall first explain why I have come to reveal this history now, in these closing months of my life and so far removed from the time when the events took place.

The revelations contained herein will no doubt expose me to much ridicule from my peers and broader society. See how the degenerations of old age bring down the finest minds, they will declare. By this, I do not mean to boast about the mental prowess of my youth, there was nothing special about it. Nor is it my intention to bring embarrassment or shame upon my family. I therefore plead for their forgiveness forthwith.

I have long been tormented by this early occurrence in my life, but successfully kept my sufferings hidden from my faithful wife and children. This was not too taxing in my earlier years as I had numerous duties to discharge with respect to the navigation of my offspring into respectful society, the progression of the family business, the monitoring and upkeep of my wife and estate and the discharge of my civic duties.

Now that my health and energies are failing, and with the recent passing of my spouse, my sons have taken on the mantel of my business affairs. I do not believe a man should cling to his authority after his powers of reasoning begin to fall off. I have, in recent years, detected in those around me a diminished respect for my opinions and commands. I therefore decided to withdraw from the battlefield of commerce and permit younger generals their opportunity.

However, as this weight of responsibility has fallen from my shoulders, so the full force of my torments has been released. Instead of proudly reflecting on my advancements in the aforementioned arenas of my life, I am deeply troubled by my conduct during this one episode, the recounting of which follows.

Last night I was revisited by the night terror, the same one that has unfailingly pursued me for decades, like a maligned dog that will not relent to the degeneration of its own flesh. It occurs thus:

I am on the moor and in the saddle of my finest steed. It is dark and I am riding into a wooded gorge, in terrain unfamiliar to me. I am feeling nothing untoward, even though in my conscious state it would be madness to be in such a place at night.

As the trees envelope me, I proceed beside the bank of a fast flowing river. I feel apprehension for the first time; I sense there is an evil dwelling in this valley. I direct my horse to take me home with all speed, but it too is frightened and, in its frantic galloping, I fall off and am left prone on the rocky ground.

I rise to my feet, sensing that the evil has taken form and is stalking me, like a wolf would a forsaken doe. As I run, I falter at every exposed tree root, dislodged stone and slippery bank, rendering my efforts to no avail as my pursuer is gaining, its reeking breath upon my exposed neck. My limbs grow weak and my left leg lame. Finally I stumble and fall, deciding not to rise again, in resignation to my destiny.

As I turn to set eyes on the dealer of my fate, I awake in a state of shaking. It is always thus and no details have changed. The meaning of this dream is no mystery to me as you shall in good time see.

I shall only concentrate on certain specific events, as already suggested. This is due to their urgent wish to be revealed as much as to the knowledge that the time remaining to me is short.

It will also be deduced, due to the voluminous nature of this account, that there is more herein than a mere shipwreck. Therefore, without further delays and speculations, I begin.

(II) My Family and its Business Affairs

My father was one of three brothers of the Hunt family. My Uncle William was the oldest, my father, Edward, the middle sibling, and Charles the youngest. Uncle Charles died at sea, and never took upon him a wife.

My father and Uncle William worked together in the family business, which was to do with shipbuilding, ship repairing and the carrying of various cargoes across the seas.

Uncle William, being the eldest, took overall command and, according to this natural order, was the first to marry and have a son, James, their only issue. My father had me, his first born, and three daughters, two of whom are still alive, in acceptable health and content with the good fortune bestowed upon them by our Lord, being with fine husbands and issue.

Our paternal grandfather, Thomas Hunt, was the establisher of the family fortune. He began as a captain and shipowner in the trade between the West of England, Newfoundland and the Mediterranean. Manufactured goods were sold to the Colonies, from which profit salted cod and seal skins were taken to southern Europe, and finally port and French wine brought back to Bristol, together with the oil from the cod and seals. This prosperous trade encouraged other services and our grandfather established the shipyard for the building, supply and repair of Tonemouth craft, while continuing his interests in trade. He used his profits to increase the size of his sailing fleet and yard and for the purchase of estates and lands.

When it came to the induction of his sons into the business, only the two eldest, my Uncle William and my father, Edward, wished to partake in the landsman's life, whilst the youngest, Charles, preferred to go to sea and experience the adventures thereof.

My grandfather, not wishing to disadvantage any of his kin, gave equal stakes to the eldest two in the yard and to the youngest such capital in land and ships so as to be identical in wealth with his siblings.

After my grandfather's death, Charles, not wanting to be burdened by the keeping of accounts and the efficient maintenance of estates, sold his holdings and invested his monies through a broker in London on such stocks and bonds as suited his temperament. This accomplished, he continued his adventures until his untimely demise on the banks he loved so much.

Meanwhile, my uncle and father stayed at home, continuing to strive over the expansion of their fortune. They had learnt the wisdom of diverse investment of monies and continued to purchase lands, including foreign plantations, and enter into other trades at sea. This included the establishment of warehouses in Bristol from which wool, iron goods, brass, guns and ammunition were sent to West Africa and used for the procurement of slaves, who were then transported to the Colonies, particularly Georgia, and the plantations of the West Indies.

The slaves destined for Georgia commanded a particularly high price if they were experienced in the cultivation of rice. The profits from the sale of these poor souls brought rum, sugar, cotton and tobacco back to Bristol.

At the time that these events took place, my cousin James and I were fully aware of the practices of trade our family took part in. To our eternal shame, we gave no thought to moralistic concepts. We had no Wilberforce to stir our conscience at that time. God forgive me for my ignorance.

The aforementioned will, I believe, serve to provide the reader with sufficient knowledge of the family business for me to proceed

.

(III) Being an Account of my Cousin James and our Relationship

I will confess a flaw in my character, before the reader becomes aware of it himself. I was jealous of my cousin, and there was much on which to base this envy.

Being the first born son of the first born son, my cousin had an advantage. Were we to inherit the family business, as was the understanding, then he would be the principal partner.

It also seemed to me that God gave him other advantages as well. This is not to say that I was inferior to James or ungrateful to God for those gifts bestowed on me. I will explain.

In the physical sphere, we were both perfectly formed and without disability of limb, reasoning, or health. By any measure we were considered handsome gentlemen and many mistook us for brothers because of the family resemblance. But James had an added sweetness and delicacy that could disarm other men and inflame the passions of women.

Taking the comparison further, we both inherited much intelligence in the fields of learning, in the realms of the natural sciences, the languages and the philosophies, but whereas I was endowed with strong analytical abilities, James had the advantage of wit and natural rhetoric, which likewise could charm at will. This was combined with a grace of movement and gesture which I also failed to possess.

My overall temperament was steady, enabling me to tame my emotions, granting me the ability to be persistent and steady in my pursuits, whereas James was mercurial. Even this managed to attract favourable attention and he was seen as being more passionate than me.

He also possessed a forward and daring disposition, which I entirely lacked, being to this day shy and retiring. The sum of these characteristics meant that in all things social, the sphere of most interest to young gentlemen, James was the leader and I the follower or accomplice, which arrangement, owing to my nature, I preferred.

As children and young adults we spent much contented time together, but it was a series of events that occurred when we were men that brought us closer still, although not always harmoniously.

As aforementioned, we had an uncle who died young. He benefitted equally from his father's fortune but, as stated, chose to have his inheritance invested through a broker in London.

After his untimely demise, it came as a surprise that he had left this wealth to his two nephews. Throughout our formative years he had great favour with us and we with him. He wished us to lead more adventurous lives and not just the mundane ones that our parents had charted. He therefore left us with this substantial sum, together with the wish that we should use it to further our knowledge and education of the world.

Our shocked parents, however, not wanting us to be led into any temptation or be in any way diverted from the path they had so meticulously planned, insisted that these monies be invested in the family business and warned of dire consequences if we failed to act thus.

We realised that we had to obey, but, at the same time, James in particular, wished to partake in some of the benefits promised by so generous a legacy. We duly handed over the majority and lied about the modest amount left unaccounted for. Having set this sum aside, we had to take care how we disposed of it so that we did not betray ourselves. We kept it in a bank in London with the intention of using it when we were at liberty and away from home.

These occasions occurred three to four times a year when our fathers, wishing for us to increase our knowledge and experience of the management of our business, sent us abroad to Liverpool, Bristol and London. The first two held few possibilities for discreet expenditure and it was in the latter metropolis where much could be done without fear of exposure.

In addition, such was the foundation of our family wealth that it established in us a certain status and both our parents were much consumed by the question of our future betrothals. I was happy to accept these manipulations for myself as being the most appropriate for my class and nature and assumed the same for James.

As may be understood by any survey of the surrounding areas, such as were equal to us in wealth were few and far between and those of the aristocracy far too high in elevation to find us acceptable, so our parents were anxious to promote us in the right company. They considered Bath unsuitable and not equal to their aspirations and instead were of a mind to insert us into London Society.

(IV) London and our Fall from Grace

It was for the purpose of business and the familiarisation of London Society that our visit to the metropolis in March 1773 was addressed, or so our parents and I believed, for my cousin had additional plans.

When my deceased uncle decreed that we spend his legacy on furthering our knowledge of the world, I am sure he did not anticipate my cousin's interpretation of his words.

I take no pride in the revelations that follow. I could have omitted them from my account, but there would be an omission of information which, to some measure, explains my cousin's future actions and my later opinions of his intentions.

I could likewise have disassociated myself from these activities, pretending I took no part in them, but I would be making a false testimony and then where would I draw the next line of contention? Is this to be a true account or is it not?

I wish to show myself in a true light, even if unflattering at times. My conscience will not tolerate discrepancies. And which young man has not had shameful thoughts and which of us would not be tempted into dishonourable deeds given the means and the opportunity?

James was entirely untroubled and prided himself on the fact that we had succeeded in mixing with the right elements of society, the privileged gentry. It was just that the setting, the bagnios of the Covent Garden area, in which we did so, was highly dubious.

I admit in taking part in these overnight adventures, but wish by my confession to illustrate that, unlike me, my cousin was obsessed with the female gender. He would fall for every harlot he met. Each new one supplanted the previous incumbent. His appetite for encounters was unquenchable. Do not suppose that these were women of great beauty. Those with physical and intellectual merit were the courtesans and beyond our ability to acquire, being reserved for the highest classes. No, these were plain, common whores.

This having now been revealed, and with the reader appreciating my lack of pride in my actions, I will say no more of these episodes.

Had it not been for James's excessive exuberance, our misadventures might have gone unnoticed. A moderate sowing of wild oats, interspersed with visits to the theatres and coffee houses, would not have concerned anyone. However, this wayward behaviour, fuelled by alcohol, eventually came to the notice of acquaintances, these social circles being exceedingly intimate, and eventually to the attention of our parents.

It was therefore that we were prematurely recalled to Devon in the days preceding Easter.

(V) The Family Bartlett and their Daughter Elizabeth

It is necessary to introduce additional participants.

The family yard, being one of several in the area, employed local people. Some were taken aboard our fleet of ships from other parts of Devon and provided their families with the necessities of life, but the yard derived labour directly from the town. There were caulkers, carpenters, joiners, sail makers, labourers, riggers, master shipwrights, rope makers and a plethora of other artisans. One hundred and forty men, all told, in our service. Many more provided materials, such as timber and metals.

Amongst the most able shipwrights was one Thomas Bartlett, who started as an apprentice and, having taken on a wife and produced issue, his own two sons were now apprenticed with us.

Mary, his wife, came from the town and it was said that her red hair suited her wild nature. As well as the two sons, she raised two daughters to maturity. The first was pleasant of nature, but plain in appearance, and already married. The second, Elizabeth, took her mother's forthright spirit, as well as being an exceptional beauty.

Whereas for my part her striking appearance was noted and put to one side, for James it was to become a challenge. This ludicrous pursuit of an unsuitable woman was accentuated, I believe, by the recent exposure of our behaviours in London and the resultant frustrations he experienced by being denied this outlet for his carnal lusts.

I must briefly explain at this point how James became exposed to Elizabeth, for under normal circumstances this would not have been possible.

As is the necessity for all families of the working and artisan classes, all members have to work and Mary Bartlett was engaged as a seamstress and had much custom in the town. This did not include our families, but many considered her to be of a high standard, particularly for her alterations to second hand clothes.

Her daughter Elizabeth, until such time as she found a husband, was employed in the assistance of her mother and in the management of the Bartlett household. This included all the chores, amongst which was the preparation and delivery of dinner at twelve o'clock to her father and brothers. This was thus the means by which James became acquainted with her existence.

(VI) Our Return from London and our Attendance at the Yard

So it was that we returned from London at the beginning of April 1773 in time for the Easter celebrations.

Imagine the greeting waiting for us. Both our families had been observing Lent with the abstinence of various foods, drink and other earthly pleasures since Ash Wednesday. In contrast, my cousin and I had just spent a month debauching ourselves in the whorehouses of London, under the mistaken illusion that we were doing so without suspicion.

This knowledge preceded our arrival by a week. Our fall from grace was meteoric with my cousin bearing the greater measure of wrath as he was correctly identified as the instigator. We were forced to confess all, including the monies we had retained from our uncle's legacy.

Although I received my reprimand with full acceptance of my guilt, I also experienced a degree of relief, as I had judged myself unsuited to such abandonment of morals and excessive lewd behaviours. My cousin, on the other hand, was, I am certain, straightaway looking about for his next adventure.

And so, shamed, saddened and much reduced in status, we returned to out duties in the family business and under such supervision as was necessary to determine our future trustworthiness.

Our place of work, the yard, was one of the largest in the area, consisting of two slipways on the waterside. Alongside the highway was a series of sheds, arranged around an open courtyard, which housed the off-vessel work. This included planing masts, shaping spars, planks and fittings, rope-making, as well as our saw pit and storage for timbers and materials. Above the sheds were lofts, offices and drawing rooms.

With this description in mind, I would ask the reader to imagine the courtyard as a crossroads and the depository of many obstacles that had to be avoided or stepped over.

As aforementioned, James had noticed Elizabeth during her daily transits through this courtyard while delivering dinner to her father and two brothers. Owing to the predictability of her visits, James was able to position himself so that he could be on hand to assist her with her burden and thereby enquire as to her wellbeing.

As I have already stated, Elizabeth was a striking beauty. This I will acknowledge. However, her lack of breeding erased any attraction I might have had, other than that of a purely carnal nature. She was to me, therefore, an object. I would have approached such a lady in the great metropolis of London, had I had the pluck, encouraged her into an arrangement and maintained her with a regular income, had I had access to such funds. In the end, when I became bored or was desirous to enter into a more proper engagement, I would have settled the matter with a final sum, as is the custom. To solicit such a liaison in Tonemouth, Devon, was madness.

However, the more I cast my reasoning upon James, the more obsessed he became with her. I might add that at this time Elizabeth did not reciprocate James's perverse interest. He pleaded with me to remain his friend and confidant and I could do nothing other than agree. I did not consider it right to disconnect with him, no matter how great my disapproval, and so once again I became an unwitting co-conspirator.

At first my assistance was benign and involved making such discreet enquiries as were necessary to establish the girl's background. This proved to be uninteresting and revealed no scandals, as I was hopeful it would do. Had Elizabeth proved to be a woman of low morals, who was preoccupied with the young men of the area, then it would have been easier for me to encourage him to withdraw his attentions and likewise I would not have been so concerned if my pleadings were ignored. After all, such a loose woman would not pose a question of honour. The worst that would happen would be a local scandal, the payment of such sums as were required and, one would hope, the tempering of future behaviours.

Alas, Elizabeth and her immediate family had a reputation amongst the local people of being upright, God-fearing, regular attendees at church and readers of the scriptures. I say immediate, because the one and only blemish was upon Mary Bartlett's sister and Elizabeth's aunt.

She was a reclusive spinster who, it was reputed, had no desire to wed and was therefore shunned to live in the way of her choosing, by her own means, at one of the villages on the fringe of the moor to the north. She made her subsistence, as did her sister, as a seamstress.

Both had learnt this craft from their mother, but the aunt far excelled even Mary in this skill and it is said that this caused rivalry between them.

Now for the blemish. An accusation that had common currency amongst those I solicited was that she was a witch. For this there was only circumstantial hearsay and not a jot of evidence. I therefore took no notice of these rumours at the time. It has been my experience that most women choosing to live alone, away from family and in remote locations, were accused of consorting with the devil as a means of explaining their behaviour.

Also, we had not long departed from the shameful persecution and execution of women for witchcraft and I would not, in good conscience, entertain or pass on such accusations myself.

I thus procured knowledge of Elizabeth for my cousin and he in turn continued his advances, to which she feigned embarrassment and distress. I believed, at the time, that this reluctance was intended to inflame his passions further, which it succeeded well in doing. My cousin pleaded with her to meet with him outside the yard, but she declined any such suggestions.

(VII) My Uncle's Suspicions

My cousin's behaviour did not go without the notice of my uncle and father. These were men of accomplishment and status in the eyes of their workers and all who knew them. So when the talk began around the town that the esteemed son of Mr. Hunt was courting the lowly shipwright's daughter, it caused an uprising of indignation.

My uncle's fury was such, I was told, that it was barely contained by the walls of their house and had their servants hiding under their beds. He forbade any further encounters and threatened to exile James to the banks rather than have a stain put on the family reputation.

I was jubilant, I confess, for I saw the end of this pathetic episode. Little did I suspect, but the daily encounters had been replaced by discreet letter writing. It seems that James had foreseen his father's prohibition and had convinced Elizabeth to at least liaise with him on paper. He even had to supply her with the relevant materials as the Bartlett household contained few such luxuries.

Along the highway that connected the Bartlett house with the yard there was an expanse of beach upon which the fishermen laid their boats. There was one derelict hulk, covered by a tarpaulin and unmoved for years, as the owner had died. It was within the body of this that my cousin and Elizabeth would plant their offerings.

This correspondence carried on for a number of weeks and it is my contention that it was through these letters that Elizabeth either was encouraged to plot to ensnare my cousin or genuinely came to be moved by him.

I became aware of this only when my cousin came to me with such an inflation of passion that I thought he would require blood-letting. He revealed all and, after having set the sorry incident aside and with no evidence that my cousin had not done so as well, I was to search for locations where the lovers could meet and act as chaperone. I say lovers because I had concluded that this was what they had now become even though physical intimacy had not yet established itself.

'You are indeed a fool, cousin,' I remember saying to him. 'Elizabeth now has letters from you in which you are declaring your unrequited love.'

'I have run out of written words,' was his reply. 'The most eloquent descriptions and proclamations are restrained when compared with what's in my heart.'

'Have you taken leave of your senses?' I said, knowing full well that he had in fact done so and was now quite irretrievable. 'I would risk a flogging as well, were I to assist you.'

I refused to have anything further to do with the matter and, as Elizabeth also declined to meet him without a chaperone, there the matter rested. I questioned the reason why my particular presence was necessary, to which my cousin blamed the complimentary description of my nature and trustworthiness he had given her.

Many days passed and on most of them, as there was no way of avoiding the man, my cousin would prostrate himself before me, begging me to help, until I became so weary that I relented. And so it came to pass that James and I would pretend to take walks together, as we often used to in the past, under the pretext of taking the airs, when in fact he would meet Elizabeth. I would be expected to stand at a tactful distance reading some publication or other while they would converse.

I ask the reader to take stock of the following. Our settlement is situated along the waterside and surrounded by steep hills. There is no highway and communication with the outside world is by horseback. This makes the town cramped with dwellings and not considered suitable for our families. Indeed our residences were on the other bank, from where there is an adequate carriage road to Exeter and from which we cross either with the ferry or with our own waterborne transport. From the yard there is a lane, through the town, to a church and castle, which is by the entrance to the sea, and it was in the apple and plum orchards nearby that James and Elizabeth met, there being few other places for secret encounters.

I thus warned my cousin that this was excessively dangerous behaviour and it was no more than two weeks later, after only a handful of meetings, that they were betrayed. It seems some mischief-maker had followed Elizabeth and, to my great fortune, had only seen her speaking and clasping hands with James but had not spied me sitting some distance away in the churchyard. I was not to be implicated this time.

The news spread from one end of the town to the other and, by the following afternoon, my uncle knew all about it. His reprimand was immediate.

The next morning, he called James into his chamber at the yard, instructing him to sit by the side of the desk and bear witness to what was to follow. Should he speak one word, he would first be flogged, then trussed up and taken to Plymouth, where he would be pressed onto one of the British Navy's warships.

Then he called in Mr. Bartlett. The gist of my uncle's address, as later recounted by my cousin, was that the meetings between his daughter and James were to cease immediately. If Bartlett did not take action to stop it happening, he would dismiss both him and his two sons from the yard and would further ensure that no member of his family would ever find work in the county again. The severity of this threat was further emphasized by the fact that our land was experiencing a slump in trade, resulting in much unemployment, poverty and disease.

Any hope that Mr Bartlett and his wife had of their elevation in society by becoming in-laws to the Hunts was soon dashed and instead they faced the prospect of destitution. Mr Bartlett's response was that the matter would be resolved by the end of the day.

I later learnt that in the evening he gave Elizabeth the whipping of her life and the next morning his daughter was taken by ferry to the other bank, where he had hired a carriage and had her taken to the cottage of her aunt on the moor. He warned that should she re-enter the parish, he would scar her for life. She would stay away until such time as she was found a husband and only allowed to return once married and visibly with child.

This arrangement was put to Mr Hunt the next morning and accepted. Elizabeth's new abode was now near Buckfastleigh, a distance by road of some twenty miles. No means of transport could take James there in less than four hours, and such a long absence would not fail to be noticed.

My uncle saw this, as I did also, as an insurmountable barrier and I once more considered the matter closed. I concluded further that some form of written communication would continue for a while, but believed that, as no further physical contact was now possible and owing to James's frivolous nature, the romance would go cold

.

435

(VIII) My Cousin's Reaction to Prohibition

My uncle considered his son to be weak in character and determination and believed that James would bend to his will. He did not expect the demonstration of defiance that took place a few weeks later.

I wager there was a degree of preparation beforehand, but on the day in question, James vanished from sunrise to sunset. Being now late June, this was a long time.

There was great agitation within the yard during this absence. Everyone was distracted. The Bartlett men were in fear of losing their jobs and my uncle in fear of losing his son. I believe my uncle came to many conclusions that afternoon, because as events unfolded, his demeanour changed.

It was an hour from sunset before my cousin finally pulled up by boat at the yard. It was later established that he had hired the craft to take him upriver to Tonebridge, to the monthly market where Elizabeth and her aunt would be to sell lace.

Upon his disembarkation from the boat he went to his father's chamber and resigned himself of his position of work as well as his inheritance and gave notice that on the morrow he would be leaving for good to go and wed Elizabeth and set up home with her.

My father, who was there at the scene, reported that my uncle was, for once lost for words, but at the same time did not display distress or surprise. It was my subsequent surmise that he expected this particular outcome and had prepared for it.

Whereas previously he had treated James as a wayward child, he was forced to acknowledge that this approach was aggravating events and that this particular problem would have to be overcome with the use of strategy rather than force. It was unrealistic, for example, to have James pressed into His Majesty's Service, as the probabilities of his returning alive were poor.

Instead, my uncle and James returned home shortly after sunset and the cessation of work. An hour of hysteria followed when the events of the day and James's plans for the future were related to my aunt. My uncle then imposed order on the household and revealed to James, with my father as witness, his own proposals.

Mr Hunt made it known to his son that he had misjudged his feelings towards Elizabeth and that he at first believed it was no more than one of those infatuations to which James was frequently prone.

If indeed their relationship was as strong and true as James claimed it to be, then it would prove worthy if put to a reasonable trial. If James and Elizabeth were willing to suffer a probationary period, during which the soundness of their bond could be tested under unusual conditions, and survive, then they would have proved themselves worthy of elevation to marriage and acceptance by the Hunt family. Mr Hunt asked his son whether, under the circumstances, this was not fair.

I doubt my cousin had any choice but to agree. What otherwise was he to do? How was he to support himself and his wife in a manner resembling that to which he was accustomed? The remaining monies of our departed uncle were too few to give anything more than a start elsewhere. Perhaps he could have found anonymity in some filthy and crime infested neighbourhood of London or another town and procured work there as well; but what prospects would he have? He could never hope to achieve the status to which he already had access. The possibility of having his heart's desire without sacrificing his birthright was too tempting to decline.

Mr Hunt then explained his proposal in more detail. James and Elizabeth could share an abode, but in secret and not in the vicinity. They would sail at the next opportunity for the Colonies where our family had a plantation. This investment had been problematic for many years, as there was no one supervising it capably. If James was successful in managing the estate to profit, he would demonstrate in his own independent capacity the ability to be leader of the family business at such time as my uncle and father were ready to stand aside. In her turn Elizabeth would be able to prove that she was worthy to be the wife of such a man.

Following such a passing of time as required to prove the success or otherwise of the plantation in Georgia, and being still in love and childless, they would be deemed to have overcome the task. They would be forbidden to marry, but could enter into an informal 'spousal' arrangement. If they met these conditions, they could then return and Elizabeth would be accepted as James's wife.

With everyone's agreement in place, events were set in motion, and so it came to pass that James and a valet, with Elizabeth presented for the time being as his housekeeper, departed from Bristol at the end of July

1774. By all accounts the weather for their crossing was affable.

Before I continue, I will take the opportunity to explain my position on this matter.

I was convinced that James was in possession of some form of madness over Elizabeth. How else to explain the raising of the desire for one woman above all reason? I was further persuaded that whatever the means at her disposal, Elizabeth was intent on profiting herself with a betrothal to James and held no other emotions for him apart from greed.

I was therefore disappointed at my uncle's seeming capitulation to his son's irresponsible whims. It was I who felt betrayed once I reflected on the fact that, barring his complete incompetence in the discharge of his duties in Georgia, he and Elizabeth would return to England to become man and wife and then lord it over me as heads of the family business.

Who was he to receive these special favours when it was I who possessed the genuine respect for the duty of my position? Yes, this seed of resentment and envy had taken hold and as the months passed it festered and grew. This made me accepting, as well as complicit, in what was to follow.

(IX) My Uncle's Mischievous Plan

I was soon to find that my misgivings were misplaced. It was during an outburst of anger towards James, for a reason now forgotten, which allowed me a clear picture of what was unfolding behind the scenes.

I was in our chamber at the yard with my father and uncle, updating our inventories, when I let slip my feelings about the unfairness of the agreement. Up to that time my father and uncle had assumed me to be an ally of James and therefore not to be trusted. The force of my resentment must have been sufficiently apparent to convince them that not only was I acting on my account, but could be a useful ally. I was there and then recruited into the real strategy at work.

I was taken back to the day of James's disappearance. My father and uncle were well prepared for what was afoot and spent hours in conversation agreeing a plan.

The option of disenfranchising James was discussed, but it was agreed that, despite my commitment and considerable business skills, it would be better for there to be two of us and every effort had to continue to be made to bring James to his senses. It was proving unfruitful to keep forbidding him to see Elizabeth. On the other hand, they could not be allowed to have their way or have it seen as so.

That was when the idea of sending them to the Colonies came to light. It permitted them to live together under one roof, albeit as master and servant. This arrangement was not new and had been tried in other cases of social unsuitability. Also, by being at such a great distance, the arrangement was unlikely to cause social disgrace to fall upon the Hunts, not to mention the fact that James would be fulfilling a business purpose as well.

It was hoped that by allowing them to cohabitate, James would satisfy his passion and in so doing begin to see the inappropriateness of Elizabeth as a future wife. But my uncle was not going to leave this revelation to chance. The final part of his plan was unfolding here at home and was very simple. While James was realizing Elizabeth's unsuitability in Georgia, we would work to remove the last leg their relationship had to stand on; their so-called love. We would set about destroying Elizabeth's reputation.

I am sickened at the relish with which we set about this task. Yet I must reveal the facts, irrespective of how vile my involvement was.

We started with Elizabeth's family. The Bartletts were offered a transfer of land, a bountiful apple and plum orchard, giving them lifetime security, if they would agree not to contradict rumours and accusations that might in future be made against their daughter. Furthermore, they were to put out and assert that Elizabeth's aunt was a witch of some authority who was consulted on spells that would be of influence to the heart. They were also to give witness that their daughter planned her ensnarement of James and boasted of it.

I was surprised at how easily they were brought into agreement. I presented this to myself as proof that there was veracity in the accusations. I now realize that the truth was simpler. I believe Mr and Mrs Bartlett also felt uncomfortable with a union that was outside their social class.

We found two local merchants with sons of a suitable age, who were being pressed by their creditors, whereupon we took upon ourselves their debts on condition that their sons made depositions to the effect that Elizabeth had tried to bewitch them into marriage. All the dates and meetings were carefully placed as to give little scope for denial.

My uncle wanted to go even further by destroying Elizabeth's modesty with fabrications of low morality

441

and practices of loose carnal behaviours, but I maintained that this was too far and would raise suspicions on James's part. Thankfully he agreed and over the months ahead we plotted in constructing a biography of Elizabeth that could be supported by acceptable evidence, namely that she was heartless, cold and scheming with no other intention but to bewitch some poor young man above her station into marriage for the sole purpose of elevating her position.

After creating this myth, as I shall call it, the next issue was how to present it. It was agreed that there was no profit in delay, as much time had passed already, and that the news should be sent forth as soon as was practical and while the story was fresh in everyone's minds. But the means? How should it be delivered?

It was at first thought to lay the task in the hands of the family solicitor. It was the intention to send him to the Colonies in any case because the troubles in that place were such that civil unrest was becoming more frequent and it had been decided to sell the family plantation as it was too risky to maintain.

I expressed the opinion that what was needed was not just an expression of the facts as we construed and constructed them, but also some compassion as to the devastating impact such revelations could have. It should be a friend, a relative, someone to plead for the family. Myself.

At first this was rejected. In those days, even more than now, travel across the seas was perilous and, upon my success, I would be returning with my cousin on the same ship. This is not to mention the strife and dangers in the Colonies themselves.

I insisted that it was the duty of a family member to do this and of those I was the most qualified. I also had the greater motivation to press the case. Moreover, I pointed out that the news from Georgia regarding my cousin's organization of the plantation was favourable and we owed our best effort on his behalf. I persisted in my stance and my terms were finally agreed.

It was therefore at the end of April, nearly twenty-two months after James's departure, that I began my own preparations before making my way to Bristol to embark on my journey.

(X) My Re-union with my Cousin

My voyage was a most tiring ordeal of nearly two months and I arrived in need of recuperation.

Upon disembarkation in Savannah our solicitor was taken to suitable lodgings in the town. My cousin, being unable to leave the estate at that time, sent his coachman. He passed me a message expressing great pleasure and happiness at the news of my landfall.

The plantation was a long way from the town, or should I say a mere village of dreary wooden houses built upon a bluff, several miles from the sea and along the same-named river. There was little habitation along the route. I had heard, during the voyage, that the Colony possessed but 50,000 souls and half of these were slaves.

The country we traversed was low and flat, and once we were inland from the river the air became so hot and damp as to make my dress unsuitable. There was no refreshing movement of air as there were many trees and I suffered under the glare of the sun. To add to my

443

distress, the highway was uneven, making our progress slow. I complained to the driver about the scandalous state of the turnpike to which he commented that by the afternoon I was to witness the instigator of these conditions. I felt too wretched to press him for further details.

We left the road for an even more rugged approach to the house. Here we were on an elevated dyke, surrounded by flooded fields with earthworks of dams and banks. I knew these to be for the provision of rice and, on some of the drier areas, hemp.

We passed through a barrier of trees and came upon the main residence. This was of modest construction and set on a raised brick foundation. It consisted of a single-storey wooden structure that was four rooms or windows wide and two deep. It was surrounded by a terrace which was sheltered by the eaves of the gently sloping roof. The wooden planking of the building was painted white, which had much decayed in appearance, being streaked with greens, browns and greys. In addition to this there was a layer of creeping weeds that in some cases surpassed the height of the roof and had thus folded back down on themselves. By the front door, to which we now pulled up, there were decrepit wooden chairs and a table, arranged randomly, without thought or order. I had yet to see an inhabitant.

I climbed down from the coach and gratefully availed myself of the shade of the porch as I waited for my host. By now I was drenched by my own sweat and grateful to be free from the constant shaking.

The coachman, without a word, pulled away and, as soon as he had rounded the corner of the house, I heard the creaking of the door behind me. I turned to see my cousin step out onto the terrace.

I was shocked by his appearance; but let me explain. After disembarking from my terrible journey at sea, I was met with an even worse climate on the land. I therefore braced myself to see my cousin ravaged by these unfavourable airs. I was not prepared for the extent to which this had taken place. He had aged ten years.

'Cousin, you are thriving in a most indecent way,' I lied, after an embrace from which I pulled gratefully away. My cousin had been neglectful of his hygiene and scant with his perfumes.

'There is a way to live in such a place,' James said. 'You sir, on the other hand, seem much drawn down.'

'I will recover, I dare say.'

'Indeed, that will be so, but you must come in immediately. Even the slaves are not in the fields at this time.'

I followed him into an entrance hall, off which were many doors. We took the first to the right and entered a medium-sized room arranged with tables and chairs in a chaotic fashion. The ceiling was disproportionately high and, on seeing me gazing upwards, my cousin explained that such an arrangement was in place in order to keep the rooms ventilated and cool.

On the walls there were books, manuals and folios. The table tops were strewn with papers and maps of the estate.

'This is the room from which I manage the plantation,' he explained.

'But James, where is everyone? You cannot be toiling on your own.' I had seen no evidence of Elizabeth.

'As I said, even the slaves are in their huts in the middle part of the day. They work their hours in the mornings and in the afternoons. The household does not live here in the summer. It is too unhealthy. I only come on certain days.'

There was a knock and, upon the invitation of James, the coachman entered. The dark skinned fellow asked if we were to take refreshment. My cousin, addressing him by the name Bentley, ordered tea and I was in much wanting of it by then.

'So cousin, to what do I owe this visit?' James asked while we waited. 'The matter must be of great seriousness for you to undertake such a hazardous journey.'

I explained that, despite his successful efforts, I had come to survey, on behalf of the family, the political and social climate in these parts as they appeared to us to be dangerous and inflammatory. It was thought best to sell the plantation now, while such an alternative was profitable. We might be able to use the proceeds for an investment in the British Indies or the Newfoundland banks trade. I acknowledged our recognition of his efforts in the past year or two in increasing the value of the family investment.

My cousin agreed that such a sale was prudent for the reasons I proposed, but questioned why it was necessary for me to travel here when the presence of the family solicitor would have sufficed. I explained that I came to discuss certain plans of the future of the family, but felt unable at present, owing to my fatigue, to enter into such a dialogue.

He accepted this and, as the servant brought the tea together with sliced ginger bread, we talked about our old adventures and so passed the time in such an agreeable way that I did not notice that the light outside had much reduced.

'Cousin, it goes dark early here,' I said.

'No, cousin, it is still the afternoon. Within the next hour it will have rained a torrent and the sun will be back out. It will also be several degrees fresher.'

And so it was. I had never experienced such a thing. Within minutes I detected lightning and heard rolls of thunder. There soon followed a twenty minute deluge of rain that would be close to our monthly allowance back home in Devon. Soon after it had stopped the sun was shining again.

This, my cousin assured me, was the order of things on most days in summer and, now that the heat had waned, we began to see the slaves entering the fields. I now also understood the reason for the treacherous roads.

At such time as was suitable, James sent for Bentley to harness the coach and we set off inland and to higher ground, the summer house being in the nearby hills and far from the marshes and swamps.

During our lengthy ride, which was most agreeable now that the humid air had cleared, James spoke about the running of the plantation and the growing of rice. There was much of interest to learn and I was impressed by his knowledge. We agreed that while the solicitor sought a buyer, I would accompany him as he went about his duties.

We arrived in due course at a great extent of forest, which my cousin assured me was part of our estate and provided much profit from timber goods, in particular the production of lumber and turpentine. I would have the leisure to explore this tomorrow, but for now, and with the sun low in the sky, we entered a clearing in the woods.

Within it were two habitations entirely of logs. One was much larger and of better substance than the other. In a separate part of the clearing were a barn and stables. James explained that these were called log cabins in these parts. The larger one was where he stayed and where I was to be the guest. The other, smaller one was for the servants. Both cabins had porches at their front entrances.

Pulling up to the main building, we climbed off the coach and stepped onto the veranda. I paused to appreciate a splendid view over a wooded valley, before stepping through the front door.

What was inside was in complete contrast to the other house. Whereas before we entered a hall with many doors, here we came into one big room that accommodated all functions save that of bedchamber.

At one side, which corresponded with the end of the building, was a stone fireplace with seating round it. In the centre of the room was a dining table and chairs. To the left of the door which we had just entered was another table, with a similar disarray of papers as in the other house, from which I assumed was where James conducted his local business. The facing side had doors leading to various other chambers.

Barely had I time to take in these surrounding than Bentley entered behind us, holding the leather straps of one end of my chest, while another man slave was supporting the other. James instructed him to show me to my bedchamber and to make available to me such resources as were necessary to refresh myself and prepare for dinner.

I was shown one of the rooms at the back which had an agreeable bed, chest of drawers, hanging rail and dressing table. The servants placed my chest on the floor at the foot of my bed and Bentley bade me to follow him. I came back out through the main room, catching sight of my cousin standing over the desk, and out the door. I followed Bentley round to the back of the cabin where, in close proximity to it, was a hut that he called the wash house and where I was to perform my ablutions. I took the opportunity of asking why there was only the one entrance to the main cabin and was told that this was a precaution for added security.

After taking time to wash and refresh myself and rest on my bed, I was later called to supper. My cousin and I sat at the dining table and enjoyed a most handsome feast of various fishes and fowls from the marshes and forests. Bentley had laid all before us and appeared from time to time in case we had need of replenishment.

James expansively described life in Georgia and the many experiences he'd had. This was most entertaining and pleasing until such time as, through excessive fatigue and considerable wine, I asked to pardon myself or else I should fall asleep at the table.

(XI) I Go Riding with my Cousin

The next morning, after a restoring breakfast of cold fowls and bread, we set out on horseback to survey the forest holdings of the estate. James showed me how the men worked in cutting down the trees, stripping the bark and then sawing the various lengths of trunk. I was taken to the isolated huts where the perilous process of turpentine production took place.

Having now been fully appraised as to the running of the family lands, feeling refreshed with good food, rest and fresh air, and having allowed an appropriate interval since my arrival, I ventured to ask how things were transpiring between him and Elizabeth.

'I wondered how long it would be before you mentioned her,' James replied. 'Perhaps now that you have been somewhat restored from your journey you will admit that she is the purpose of your visit.'

My cousin's mood had changed and he did not display the same warmth as earlier. 'I freely confess this,' I said, 'but would ask you take thought of the difficult position our fathers have put me in.' I tried to make it sound as if I had no choice in the matter and was a mere messenger. He was in thought for a while as we rode and, assuming he had accepted this view, I asked him again about Elizabeth.

He explained that at the end of their journey and after a period of adjustment, Elizabeth had assumed the role of housekeeper, taking control of both houses and the domestic accounts thereof. With the passage of time, she had shown such aptitude for the compilation of facts and figures that she had extended her management, in gradual steps, to the whole estate, including the most effective allocation of the slave labour to produce the greatest quantity of profit from the cash crops of rice, hemp and timber products.

On the days that James was in the lowlands, Elizabeth surveyed the forest. When he was in the forest, as now, she was busy on the lowland estate. She discreetly assessed efficiency and decided on improvements; he provided the authority to have her policies carried through. In order to maintain the appearance of propriety, there was a separate bed chamber for her in the house in the lowlands as well as here in the forest, where she had a room at the side of the stables.

I was shocked and at first suspected my cousin was inflating her achievements for the purpose of promoting Elizabeth's attributes as a future wife, but the manner and the details with which he delivered this report convinced me that it was accurate. The news that had come back to us in Devon attested to the fact that the running of the estate had improved beyond expectation, and now I was informed that our sworn enemy was, by the largest measure, responsible for this. My cousin's own words were, 'Elizabeth has an astounding commercial faculty'.

I reassert, I had no doubt that this was true, especially when he produced instances of her work, examples that showed much initiative. This revelation had the effect of considerably raising my respect for my adversary, but I still retained my prejudice, I still considered her a parasite, a formidable foe who was conspiring to usurp our family name and fortune.

There were further revelations to come. He said, towards the end of our day, that he had never known or heard of a woman who was more devoted to the furtherance of her man's financial interest and, as a consequence, his love for her had multiplied in the time that they had been together.

I was dismayed for I knew not from what position I was to present my false testimony. It seemed rather flimsy and pathetic. It had been assumed that by now my cousin would have grown weary of his conquest and I was to go merely to deliver a merciful *coup de grâce*. I determined to pull back from my task for now, renew our friendship and obtain a greater understanding of their affair, perhaps to find some weakness and thereby a new line of attack.

That evening, upon our return to the lodge and after suitably refreshing ourselves from the day's toils, we again sat down to supper and it was then that I met Elizabeth. Although dressed in a manner most modest and efficient, it was difficult not to acknowledge her beauty, her presence, especially in the new light in which I now beheld her. Whereas my cousin had withered in appearance, Elizabeth had blossomed.

Indeed, up to this time, I had never heard her speak, always seeing her at a distance. If I needed further confirmation of her competence in the commercial field it was provided there and then and in the days that followed, as was her grasp of local politics. She approved of the sale of the estate and had been proposing this for some time, which explained why James was so ready to accept the idea himself.

She further revealed that she had made investigations on our behalf and had prepared a list of local landowners who she believed were likely to favour such a purchase and pay the best price. She proceeded to give details of the character, family and business affairs of each and propose motivations for their interest. She then said that we must act soon as the climate was likely to change in the autumn and our opportunity for profit would diminish.

This information would naturally be passed to our solicitor who would thereafter see to the promotion of the sale but, after that evening, I fell into a deep despair, for I saw that not only was my adversary a woman of great beauty and high intelligence, but also articulate and charming.

I began to perceive a danger far greater than that which I had supposed. I was coming to believe that this was not merely someone who had found a main chance, my vulnerable cousin, to exploit for the purposes of a cosseted life. This was a woman of such magnitude of ambition that went beyond such things. James was but a stepping stone, a means to move forward. In every respect he was no match for her and this new perception was later to be confirmed.

(XII) How I Convinced My Cousin That My Lies Were True

It was through my virtue of patience, the revising of my ideas as aforementioned and constant probing that in due time I discovered two areas of weakness in this unnatural alliance. As time passed and I learnt more, my hopes of ending this liaison increased.

Their domestic arrangements were simple. They took their meals separately until my arrival, at which time we ate together, when we were all on the same site. They would then go to separate bedchambers and it was only after the servants retired for the night that they would supposedly come together. James asserted he went to her and returned to his own bed prior to the servants returning to duty.

It was whilst I was informed of this routine that I began to observe that in spite of James's fervent testimonies, all was not well. I will explain.

In our previous adventures together, no matter how depraved they were, one thing my cousin did not do in excess was to consume alcohol. This is not to say he did not get drunk occasionally; this we both did, but then he swore abstinence and might not drink again for several days. He never pursued the beverage for its own pleasure, but always in company and for occasions. In short, he never drank alone.

During our meals in the evening, he would drink heavily, which was unusual in itself. I should mention, in addition, that on such occasions as Elizabeth was also present, we would end by only speaking with each other, as James was too intoxicated to complete a sentence of his own. Then I discovered that he continued to drink in private. I therefore set all my energies into discovering the cause of my cousin's motives to seek such daily oblivion.

My opportunity occurred on an occasion when it was our turn to patrol the lowlands. That afternoon, before we were able to make our return to the house, the area was hit by such a furious rain and windstorm that any travel was impossible for the rest of the day. Bentley did his best to prepare our chambers for the night as well as an evening meal.

Afterwards we retired to the parlour, not being ready for bed as the fury of the storm had not yet abated. As we sat, James brought out a flagon of dark rum. He said it had been supplied to him by his contacts at the harbour and was imported from the Caribbean. I had already drunk sufficient wine during the meal, but decided this was an opportunity for meaningful discourse.

After we drank a while, reminiscing over past adventures and to a point where I believed he had relaxed his defences but there remained sufficient lucidity in him, I played my hand.

'Cousin, in the days since my arrival I have heard and seen much that is commendable, and yet it is evident to me that there is also a great deal that is troubling you.'

'You are right, cousin,' he replied, with a readiness that showed that he was prepared to reveal as much. 'But that which troubles me is much cause for shame.'

'You should let me be the judge of that. You have often remarked on my sense of fairness. Refill our glasses and proceed with your confession.'

I cannot remember the conversation word for word. The quantities of alcohol were increasing, but I will relate the gist of it. Everything was as earlier disclosed: Elizabeth's devotion to James, her exceptional abilities for accountancy and business, her uncanny awareness of the market. With regard to the commercial side she had so much intellectual ammunition and willpower that it seemed illogical to take any other actions other than those that she determined.

All her predictions and decisions proved unfailingly accurate and this remarkable success had the effect of castrating my cousin. Compared to her, he was useless and, from the evidence so far, I would not have fared much better.

Now I have no trouble in believing that women are the equals to men intellectually. But Elizabeth, in her naivety, was so eager to prove herself worthy, that she inadvertently destroyed my cousin's confidence. He wanted to be her man, her knight in armour, but could not fill that role. He had reached the point where he understood his feelings and felt ashamed of them. I, on the other hand, saw fertile grounds on which to sow the seeds of resentment.

This trick could not be turned in a moment but over time. I first secured myself as his confidant and during several nights of companionable drinking, I proceeded to make suggestions accompanied by morsels of supporting, albeit false, evidence.

I implanted in him the idea that there was much in Elizabeth's success that could be explained without excessive credit being given to her intellect. I had his hungry attention; who would not want to deem themselves worthy? I conceded that her mathematical capabilities were genuine, but of a type common in many women, as they are accustomed to the rendering of the accounts in most households. Did it require such extensive abilities to perform as well in business?

I then made a suggestion, to which he readily agreed, that Elizabeth's motivations would cause her to make greater efforts than could normally be expected, and her uncanny capacity to predict the future was explained by the disclosure that during the time she spent on the moor with her aunt, she had become versed in the art of witchcraft and divination.

At a time and on an occasion which I considered most appropriate, I presented, in the most articulate way, all the additional facts I claimed to have meticulously researched and confirmed. I finished with his parents' demand that, upon the termination of his business affairs here in Georgia, he should return to explain how he could allow such a scheming snake of a woman to violate his loving family.

With my arguments thus presented, I pulled away and for some days life continued as before with my cousin showing no reaction to my revelations and with me desisting from pressing the case any further. I had at that point no intuition as to what the outcome might be.

One day, as we were inspecting the forest and coming to the end of our tour, we ventured upon a clearing to watch the late sun over a valley. James invited me to dismount and sit with him on a fallen log. I knew this was the moment and, to my delight, he proclaimed exactly that which I wanted to hear.

He said how he had pondered upon my revelations and could see supporting evidence in Elizabeth's actions and deeds. He then proceeded to reveal this proof to me at length. At first much of it was plausible, particularly where it referred to matters of commerce, but then he entered the realms of fantasy and paranoia. Alas, the excessive drinking had got its grip on my cousin's mind, but at this point I was glad of this as it helped to seal my cause.

He confessed, for example, that there had been many attempted unions in her bedchamber and in each case James found himself incapable of consummating the relationship and that this was evidence of the

457

manipulation of nature through witchcraft, for when in the past had he faced such an infirmity? He then proceeded to assert that Elizabeth's expressions of encouragement and pleasure during these aborted efforts proved she was a witch that craved the impregnation of the Devil, for which decent woman gained pleasure from the anticipation of intercourse with a man? Finally, as if to confirm his argument, he admitted to prolifically availing himself of the comforts of the young negro girls, sometimes two a night, without any diminution of enthusiasm or performance.

I may have been pleased to have accomplished my task, even if achieved by shameless subterfuge, but for the rest I now looked upon my cousin as no better than a pathetic fool.

I have little to say of the rest of our stay in Georgia, but that which I do reveal is of a significance I was not capable of understanding at the time.

In my daily discourses with Elizabeth, I saw no evidence that she had any knowledge of the nature of my interventions. On the contrary, as James continued to withdraw within himself, our conversations became friendlier and intellectually more intimate. I began to value this time, particularly once James inflicted upon himself his nightly descent into unconsciousness. As he lay upon the table or slumped in a chair, I had Elizabeth effectively to myself. It was the first time in my life that I was alone with a woman who was not my mother, governess, a servant, or a whore. It was the first time I was with a woman with whom I could exchange ideas and opinions. I was awed by her presence, her character. This unsettled me greatly and it took all my capacities of willpower to keep in mind the purpose of my expedition to Georgia.

I thought it fortunate therefore that we had but a short interval to wait for a buyer to be found for the plantation, which I may add was one of those that Elizabeth had suggested. With this achieved, we began our preparations for the voyage home.

(XIII) Our Ship, Our Dispositions and Our Fellow Passengers

And so at the beginning of August 1775, on a warm and sultry morning, I found myself back at the quayside in Savannah. We arrived in two carriages. James and I led the way in the first with the lighter valises, and Elizabeth, with Bentley at the reins, accompanied the heavier cases and boxes.

As our chattels were being carried to the launch awaiting transfer to our vessel, anchored at a distance off the shore in the middle of the river, I was aware of Elizabeth's gaze upon me. Did she have suspicions of the impending betrayal? I tried not to meet her stare. I was all too conscious that the voyage ahead would be testing for us all.

We did not have long to wait before it was our turn to be rowed to the waiting barque. The *Casaba* was a handsome merchantman, a full three-masted ship, broad of beam and poised with her proud prow facing seaward, her buxom, demurely robed figurehead, with her left hand on her breast, was pointing forward with the right, towards the horizon. It was my understanding she held a cargo of sugar and rum from the West Indies

459

and had topped up here with tobacco, hemp, indigo and naval stores. A full 360 tons laden she was.

We had a choice of several ships those days, but the *Casaba* was making a journey directly back without further stops along the northern Colonies, Bermuda or Iberia. I surmised that a voyage of the shortest duration would be the most suitable.

On coming alongside her bulging flank, a reassuringly solid dark colour, we were confined within a sturdy wooden cage, tethered as it was at the end of a stout rope, and lifted one at a time over the starboard bulwark and onto the waist. With each squeaking hoist of the lifting tackle, we would be randomly twisted either to the right or left and occasionally gave the hull a rattling crack.

While we were assembled on the deck, by the open hatch, together with the three other passengers, we were assaulted by the sounds and smells of the farmyard, all emanating from below.

In due course, we were greeted by Mr Fletcher, the steward, a thin, nervous-looking man with not a hair on his head. He asked which of our luggage was for below decks and which was for our accommodation. The distinction being duly made, we were led to our cabins by the said member of the crew, with our retained chests being handled by an assortment of rough looking deckhands, most of whom were chewing tobacco.

I will describe what was to be our world for the next five weeks or so. From the waist, an area of open deck, which in my estimation measured thirty feet long and fifteen wide, we were taken aft. At the point where the main mast rose from the planking of the upper deck were two entrances with raised thresholds, one to starboard and the other on the larboard side. We entered the starboard door, into the enclosed continuation of the waist. We were in a dark space of equal magnitude to the aforementioned and along the outside of which was our accommodation. There were four cabins on each side, and by the exterior of each entrance there was an oil lamp, secured to the bulkhead, offering additional light to that coming from the doorways through which we had entered. In the deck space between, lashed with ropes, were cases of tobacco, which rose up to the deckhead, leaving just two narrow corridors. The smell of burning oil overwhelmed the soothing aromas of the cargo.

Our chests were placed outside our cabins. Elizabeth, James and I were given three on the starboard side, with Elizabeth the nearest aft, while the other three passengers occupied cabins to larboard. Before we could enter these we were invited by the steward to be guided to the rest of our accommodation. Meanwhile, our trunks were being fastened to the deck and bulkhead.

Aft of the cabins was the area through which passed the tackle for the helm, before a set of double doors into the saloon. This, we were given to understand, would be our living space. It extended back to the four stern windows, below which ran a bench for their full width and at the centre of which was secured a small stove.

On both the starboard and larboard sides were doors leading aft and, we were informed, to such areas as were suitable for the conduct of our private hygiene and washing.

Within the saloon were arrangements of tables for dining and chairs for seating, all lashed to the deck with leather straps. There was a wooden chest against the starboard bulkhead, which contained backgammon boxes and decks of cards.

Mr Fletcher drew our attention to the framed notice on the bulkhead to the side of the main door, which gave the meal times. They were 07:45 for breakfast, 12:45 for luncheon and 18:45 for dinner. One of the passengers asked why such odd hours, to which he was informed that they ran forty-five minutes after the times of the officers' and crew's mess.

Mr Fletcher invited us to read the Captain's standing orders, which were framed and displayed in the cabin corridor. Informing us on the most important of these, he said we had free access to this deck, including the waist as far as the fo'castle, but we were not to enter anywhere else without the invitation of an officer. Similarly, we were not to speak to an officer or the captain whilst they were on duty, unless it was a matter for the safety of the ship, her crew, her passengers or her cargo. We were not to wear swords or carry any other armament. We were not to enter onto the waist whilst the ship was with pilot and in the act of such manoeuvres as arriving or sailing from an anchorage or port. Likewise, on occasions of bad weather or emergencies, we would be prohibited from venturing from our cabins. Finally, whilst the tarpaulin was being used to collect rainwater, we were to avoid that area of deck. Any requests for additional goods were to be made to the steward and we were on no account to approach the purser directly.

These prohibitions having been pronounced, we were allowed to go to our cabins. I shall describe these to you as well. The length of each was no more than eight feet with a depth of five. The bed or bunk was positioned and secured against the ribs of the hull lengthways, with the head against the forward bulkhead, and was of a height that would need a jump for a woman or a short man to mount. The reason for this was because the top edge of the bed frame rose six inches above the straw mattress, so as to give security and protection in both stormy and cold weather. Below the platform of the bed were two deep drawers for storage. There was the facility, upon request, to have a hammock fitted instead, a service I sampled on my outward journey but found it did not suit me. The bed bugs, therefore, would not be denied their nightly feast.

To the side of the head of the bed was a rope, suspended from an eye bolt on the deck head, which ran outside into the corridor to a sprung bell for the purpose of summoning the steward. The agitation of this device dropped a flap so that the correct cabin could be identified.

At the foot of the bed was a six inch recess for such personal effects as books, pens and other small items, as was also the case between the ribs on the side to the hull. In the space remaining between this end of the bed and the aft bulkhead was positioned a table top, which could be lifted and secured to the hull and would then reveal a canvas basin. Below this was a chamber pot with lid, a wooden stool and sufficient space for small valises.

The entrance to the cabin was over a raised threshold and opposite the basin. The door had a retractable flap at head height, which I presumed was for the allowance of fresh air into the chamber. All the sides of the room had dowels for the hanging of coats, clothes and any such items as might be of convenience. There was a bracket in the aft corner with the hull and the bulkhead, above the table flap, which contained an oil lamp, already lit.

This light did little to dispel the gloom, much enhanced by the dark finish of the wood, and it would cause much strain on the eyes to read or write, even in close proximity to it.

As I brought my belongings in from my chest, stowing them in the appropriate places, I was reminded of another encumbrance to our spirits, brought to my attention by my outward passage. Above us was the quarterdeck and the scene of much activity for any ship. Even now, with preparations for departure being made, there was cause to know of every movement that took place within just a few inches of our heads. Were it not for the reassuring thickness of the beams supporting the deckhead, I would fear to have one of the crew break through and fall upon me as I slept. And this was the quietest time, as we stood on standby to be notified of a fair wind. I had been informed that such would be in the early hours, when there would be an inshore breeze and a slack tide.

After having stored my belongings in the stifling cabin and having an interval before our noon repast, I determined to take some air on the waist. The flat and featureless landscape did not detain me long, however. It was already excessively warm and the sun bore down oppressively, with a sultry breeze coming in from the sea, the very zephyr that was detaining us for now. It had been explained to me, by those from these parts, that when the wind changed in our favour, after midnight, we might have sufficient run to make it to the open sea before it reverted back in the morning. Otherwise we might spend another night on the sweltering river. I had also been assured that these evenings offered sufficient moonlight to make the passage safe.

I noticed that the waist was much tidied since we came on board. The two hatches in the centre were now sealed and the pervasive smells of the holds much diminished. On top of one hatch the launch was stowed, leaving our cutter still in the water alongside.

I was looking forward to the acquaintance of my fellow passengers as I did not relish a long voyage in confinement with James. I will briefly explain the state of affairs between us, upon our embarkation.

As can be seen through my earlier accounts, my relationship with my cousin had been that of close friend and confidant. I explained how I had grown to envy much in his character that I felt I did not possess. I embarked on this adventure across the seas to bring him back into the fold, not only for the purpose of defending the family fortune, but also to re-establish that companionship which I missed.

Now with my task partly accomplished I began to reassess much of what I believed about him. Before I arrived I had expected to encounter the fighting spirit I had come to know back home. Instead I found a depleted drunk. I had prepared for a battle of wits, but instead it took mere days to reveal the frailties inherent in his liaison with Elizabeth and, with the application of intelligent argument, witness the complete collapse of his intention.

With respect to the aforementioned weakness I was able to discover in their affair, I have since concluded that it was not only Elizabeth's overwhelmingly accomplished abilities that neutered my cousin's manhood. Indeed Elizabeth was supremely competent, this was evident, but her success had only come to light because of my cousin's complete uselessness in business. Were it not for Elizabeth stepping in to run the plantation, the whole enterprise would have floundered.

How could I respect a man, even if he be my blood, who would leave the woman he claimed to love to the baying pack, rather than admit his own failures? Would it be so bad to say 'Cousin, I cannot understand business, it's not for me, thank God Elizabeth was here,' I would have understood this. He would still be a man in my eyes. Instead, I would try my best to avoid him during the weeks ahead.

When it came to Elizabeth, the waters were not as clear. Surely, her opinion of James must have changed. Perhaps she was able to smother her disappointment under the incessant work of running the estate. But what now that this burden had been removed? Perhaps the only point of interest was the observing of their interactions during the voyage.

As for my assessment of Elizabeth? What would I say if you had pressed the question on that first day upon the deck? I would maintain that yes, I was respectful and grateful to her for what she had done but, in my estimation, this only partly repaid the debt for all the trouble she had caused me and my family. I had no sympathy for her plight, I would claim, as she had brought this fully upon herself. The folly of her attempt at fortune above her station had cast her in a peril of her own manufacture. Is this not so? And yet I had great trouble in maintaining this position and these resentments when with her. I do not believe in witchcraft, irrespective of my promotion of it to James, but in the presence of Elizabeth, I sometimes felt as if I was also being bewitched. Now that we were on board the *Casaba*, I was determined to keep myself aloof, at a distance, to sever the familiarity begun in Georgia and to refrain from further sentimental nonsense.

I return to our departure. Lunch was river fish and potatoes and we, the passengers, were able to become acquainted, as I had hoped. Our fellow travellers were three merchants, Messrs Little, Smith and Williams.

Mr Little was from Liverpool and was returning home after establishing the demand in the Southern Colonies for his linens and textiles. Smith was a weapons exporter from the Midlands and Williams the owners' supercargo, being especially responsible for escorting the naval stores to Plymouth.

I saw at once the opportunity for the furtherance of my mercantile relationships over the coming weeks but, at this initial encounter, our conversations were of the more every day sort. All disclosed their town and county of origin, by which route they came to be on board, the dreadfulness of the weather and the uncivilised nature of these Colonies and their inhabitants. The political background was discussed thoroughly and everyone gave their opinion as to where it would lead, bar Elizabeth, who, although I am sure was as informed, if not more so, than the rest of us, recognised that, as a woman, her opinion would not be welcomed. As for James, he said but the minimum, and was the only one amongst us to have rum instead of wine with his repast.

These unmemorable subjects were thoroughly discussed and exhausted not only at lunch but dinner as well and, after the latter, Elizabeth retired to her cabin. I stayed longer until the men set upon a bottle of rum, to which James eagerly joined, but I excused myself and retired to the waist.

The evening air was still and the watch waited in anticipation for the coming wind at which time the pilot would be called and our voyage commence. I would gladly have stayed out for many hours, anything to escape the stuffy airless conditions within, but was immediately swamped by the blood-sucking insects for which these wetlands are known. I thus made a hasty retreat to my cabin
.

(XIV) On Board

Our voyage began, as predicted, after midnight. My sleep, as I am sure that of the other passengers, was interrupted by the shouting and commotions from the deck, which were continuous and of such a magnitude as to prohibit a return to restfulness for many hours. Fatigue finally prevailed but, on awaking, I found all to be quiet and assumed that we had not made the open sea and were anchored for another day upon the wretched river.

I summoned the steward to bring me hot water with which to wash and, having thus prepared myself, went outside to take the airs before breakfast.

The morning was well advanced and the heat thereof beginning to increase. There was little movement of air. We were surrounded by a marshy, reedy landscape, much populated by fowl, and to the east the open sea was visible. Upon the waist I saw the other passengers bar James. Messrs Little, Smith and Williams were walking up and down the larboard side, in conversation while smoking their pipes. They tipped their hats on my emerging from the starboard entrance.

Before me, at the other end of the open deck, by the fo'castle, her hands resting on the rope that ran the length of the weather bulwark, was Elizabeth, looking out across the marsh. She was attending to something for she was shielding her eyes from the sun, which was rising off our starboard bow.

After a moment's hesitation, I proceeded to take my exercise and, looking over the rail, saw that to which she had set her concentration. Both the ship's cutters were out. The first and nearest contained two sailors who were obviously fishing and the other was hidden amongst the reeds.

As I approached, the sound of my footfalls on the wooden deck alerted her and she turned towards me. She betrayed no emotion as she held my stare. I on the other hand had a moment when my composure faltered. The rays of the sun had brought forth the rich colours of her hair, which in turn framed a countenance of faultless beauty. Her engaging blue eyes disclosed a far-ranging intelligence and compassion. For that brief interval the notion entered my mind that here was a woman whose splendour of appearance and character was worth any sacrifice.

The reader may ask why did I not have this revelation before. Why now? All I can say is that until that point I knew little of the inner Elizabeth, the woman. First I had seen the form, the beauty. Then I acquired additional facts, first from James and then from our direct conversations. I gradually developed the opinions already described, all the time ignoring the inner feelings that were also being stirred. But then here on the deck in that instant I saw something else, something that overwhelmed my composure. Looking back I realise that this was the moment I fell in love with her, although I still refused to acknowledge it.

But these thoughts lasted but a few seconds and I soon swept them aside with disgust. 'Good morning, Miss Bartlett,' I said, when I was close enough. 'I see you are an early riser.'

'Since a child, Mr. Hunt, I am used to seeing the sunrise.'

I acknowledged the hidden meaning in her words with a nod. 'Not all born to privilege take it for granted, Miss Bartlett.'

'And not all born to servitude accept it, Mr. Hunt' she retorted. 'Please excuse me, I believe breakfast will be served soon and I have something to attend to.'

'Miss Bartlett, I apologise therefore for detaining you, but have you seen my cousin?'

'Not since we left the dining room last night, sir.'

I let her go and took over the vigil of the ship's boats. I realised the one in the reeds was patiently stalking fowl. I thought I might go and find the steward and enquire about James when the self same man approached me.

'My pardon, sir,' Mr Fletcher said, 'but I have not heard from Mr Hunt. There is but a short time to breakfast and I have no instructions whether to rouse him or not.'

'By all means Fletcher, knock on his door and announce the fact. The rest will be for him to decide.'

'Thank you, sir.'

James did not appear at table and Elizabeth chose to have her breakfast brought to her cabin. The steward discreetly informed me that the former rebuked his approach. I therefore sat with Messrs Williams, Smith and Little to toast, marmalade and tea.

Mr Williams, the supercargo, informed us of our situation. 'We could not guarantee sufficient distance offshore to risk leaving the river,' he said. 'The pilot has left us as we are anchored in sight of the open sea. The captain says there is a good chance of a storm this afternoon, which means a good offshore tonight.'

'Will we make the Stream, sir?' Mr. Smith asked.

'Not in one day,' Williams said. 'But we should pick up the Trades.'

'I have been informed that we should not venture on the deck again,' Little said. 'There is much disease on the marshes.'

'And it will become quite intolerable within after lunch,' Williams said.

'Perhaps you gentlemen would like the distraction of a game of cards to pass the time,' Smith said.

'As long as the stakes are low, gentlemen,' I said, 'I am not a gambler.'

'I would point out, gentlemen, that the captain does not allow card games with stakes on board,' Williams said. 'It is one of his standing orders.'

'How so?' Smith asked.

'It often causes disputes amongst the passengers,' Williams replied. 'The captain has no time to chair such arbitrations.'

'Then we shall play for points,' I said. 'And the winner can be supplied with free rum tonight. Will the captain allow this?'

'I am sure he will not object,' Williams said.

'Before we begin I have a matter to attend to,' I said, and went and asked the steward for some breakfast to be brought to James's cabin, while I went ahead and knocked on his door.

'I will have you flogged for interrupting me again,' James shouted angrily.

'It is I,' I said, 'and I have every intention of entering.'

'If you must.'

I opened the door and was assaulted by the combined smell of alcohol-laced vomit, urine, insufficient personal hygiene and unwashed clothes. 'This is disgusting, cousin.' I said. The oil lamp had gone out, but from the little I could see, everything was in disarray.

'Then go away.'

'I cannot. At this rate you will not survive the day, let alone the voyage.'

'You cannot force me to anything, sir.'

'On the contrary, it is my duty to bring you home alive. As the safety and health of the crew and passengers are in the captain's hands, I will give him leave to forcibly remove you from your cabin and to attend to such hygiene as is necessary.'

'You cannot frighten me,' he said. 'I am no child.'

472

'Then you leave me no alternative. I will speak to the captain now.'

'Wait, wait'.

I sat down on the stool, leaving the door open so I could see in the dark and could be supplied with fresh air, while I waited for the steward. 'I will give you my own standing orders for the voyage.' I began. 'You will arise for breakfast and fully attend to your hygiene before sitting at table. Afterwards you will take such time on the waist, weather permitting, as will allow the crew to complete the daily clean of your cabin, for which I will pay extra if necessary. You will also attend luncheon and dinner. If afterwards you wish to drink yourself to oblivion, you may. Any transgression, apart from illness or seasickness, will result in my having appropriate words with the officers.'

'You are a bastard, sir.'

'After we reach Plymouth you are free to fall into whatever gutter you wish,' I added, finally.

When the steward arrived I directed him to leave the breakfast on the table and to fill and light the lamp. I instructed him to inform me if my cousin was not out of bed within an hour.

I went back to the saloon and sat with the other gentlemen to cards for the morning. I had no word from Fletcher and assumed my cousin had risen and, during the course of the morning, saw him visit the heads twice. Later he sat at lunch, which again consisted of a commendable abundance of fresh fish.

Afterwards, the air became so heavy and sultry that we retired to our cabins. I removed as much as I could of my clothing and sat at the table to read, but was soon fatigued and lay in the bunk.

I do not know how long I slept before being awoken by the thunder and lashing rain of the most fantastic storm. So welcome was this deluge that I fell asleep again, despite the racket, and did not wake until the early evening.

When the tempest had passed, the air was noticeably cooler, so I dressed myself for the evening. I came out upon the waist and found the passengers, including James, enjoying the refreshed air before dinner. Messrs Williams, Smith and Little were once again walking the deck together on their side, whilst on mine James and Elizabeth were standing at opposite ends to each other, with James by the rail nearest me.

I spoke to neither and took what exercise I could before we were called to the saloon. The men sat at the table, but Elizabeth once more took her meal in her cabin.

To everyone's relief and expectation, that evening we sailed.

(XV) Our Voyage Home

We were on our way and, by the end of the first day, were upon the Stream and thereafter had favourable winds and conditions for most of our journey. During this time, the weather was never worse than fresh to moderate, with equal measures of rain and sun.

The movement of the ship was considerable but such that we overcame our sickness after a few days. Otherwise we suffered the usual deprivations and inconveniences expected of such a voyage: the rats and cockroaches, the fleas and bedbugs, and the ordeal of scorpions and centipedes whenever a new pallet of wood was brought up to the saloon for the stove. There was the continuous striving to maintain bodily hygiene as well as the cleanliness of our clothing, beds and cabins, which at best were always damp. When our fresh food and water supplies ran out, we were confined to salt meat and beer or grog to drink. What rain waters were collected with the tarpaulin, when rationed out, were too meagre to be of significance.

For the first three weeks James, Elizabeth and I had little to do with each other. I greeted Elizabeth wherever and whenever etiquette dictated but, after these initial exchanges, she avoided further conversations with me. I in turn, still unable and unwilling to acknowledge my feelings for her, was reluctant to initiate anything more. Instead I watched from a distance.

It was the same with James. Although he obeyed the rules given to him on the second day, he showed no inclination for conversation with me, or Elizabeth. This was of great concern for, despite the beneficial regime forced upon him, his demeanour and health continued to deteriorate.

Any efforts on my part to shake him out of this lethargy only made matters worse and he retreated ever more into isolation, with only the steward attending his needs. As we advanced into September and our final days afloat, this state of affairs was forced to change. It came about that the ship's cook, also acting as the onboard surgeon, was called to attend James, when the steward became concerned for him. Visiting him after lunch one day, the cook declared James much diminished in all aspects of his health and this diagnosis instilled in me the sense of urgency necessary to overcome my own reluctance to approach and speak to Elizabeth concerning him.

Being early afternoon and knowing that I would, as always at this time, find her walking the waist, I went out the starboard entrance into the open. The weather that day was more moderate than fresh. We were running before the wind after a day of continuous rain and had only suffered the occasional shower with long periods of sun. We were making good speed with the only inconvenience being the occasional salty spray coming over the bows as we rhythmically plunged forward.

Elizabeth, the only one of the passengers without, was on the starboard, leeward side, walking forward with great competence on the swaying deck. I caught up with her as quickly as prudence would allow.

'Miss Bartlett, I hope you are well today,' I said in a much raised voice. This was necessary whilst on deck in order to overcome the sounds of our hull shouldering through the sea and the even greater howling, rattling and slapping of the wind through our rigging.

'Mr Hunt, to what do I owe the honour of your attention upon me?' she said, turning to face me.

'I fear, Miss Bartlett, we must put aside our animosities and speak urgently about James.'

'I wondered, sir, to what degree his spirits must decline before you would address me thus.'

'I do not recall any effort on your part to improve his wellbeing.'

'Have I then wrongly supposed that you have taken command of his moral and physical domains? You have excluded me to suit your plans and now you want to call me up to save them.'

'I admit it is so, Miss Bartlett, but kindly explain to me how it is that a woman can have intimacy with a man one day and abandon him the next?'

'Is this question of academic interest to you, sir? If so I will gladly venture my opinion.'

'I do not want your opinion, Miss Bartlett; I want to hear your reasons for abandoning my cousin at his time of need.'

'What do you believe I have abandoned, sir? No, wait, a better question. What exactly do you consider my relations to your cousin to have been?'

'Miss Bartlett, I really don't think it is necessary for me to...'

'Let me help you, sir. There have been no intimacies, as you say, between your cousin and me.'

This much I already knew and was not what I was referring to. 'I do not understand, Miss Bartlett,' I said. 'I thought you and my cousin would have arranged an informal ceremony.'

'And so it was, sir. The captain himself performed it, not one day off from Bristol. I have the certificate.'

'You must say more, Miss Bartlett.'

'Nothing occurred during the sea voyage and I supposed it was because the conditions of our cabins were so appalling. But this routine continued in Georgia. He never once entered my bedchamber or I his, despite my encouragements.'

I was astounded. It was one thing for my cousin to assert that he had attempted and failed to engage with Elizabeth and quite another to have not even made an effort. All this time I had believed fantasies. I had no doubt that Elizabeth was telling the truth. 'Did you not address this?'

'On several occasions, sir, I assure you.'

'And his response, Miss Bartlett?'

'The bottle and the slave girls, sir. We did not speak of it and I must confess that all motivations to persist soon left me.'

'Well, Miss Bartlett, you must speak to him now, or make the attempt at least. He can hardly escape from you.'

'I will do as you ask, sir.' She nodded and walked away, leaving me alone on the waist with the crew. I stood by the lifeboats, near the central hatch, swaying as I did, immersed in such thoughts as were brought about by our conversation.

Above, the tone the wind made, as it swept through the rigging, rose with every gust; beyond, the scattered clouds were overtaking us. I looked over the starboard bulwarks, across the turbulent seas and to the horizon as much to steady my nerves as my stomach. I remember not how long I stood there, but it was a considerable time and, when I felt fatigued, I returned to my cabin to rest.

The minutiae of what transpired between Elizabeth and James during her visit to his sick bed I was never able to discover. It is sufficient to acknowledge that when she emerged from that festering hovel she had for the first time received full knowledge of the conspiracies against her and my part thereof.

Would it not be true to suppose that if I came to you and made accusations against the man or woman you loved, in the normal course of events, a disclosure of these facts to them would ensue almost immediately? I had assumed this confrontation had taken place, and that this was the cause of their present lack of communication and her displeasure with me. I further assumed that Elizabeth had accepted that her strategy was at an end and was suitably resigned to this failure.

It was after our evening repast and during the final hour of the day, when I was upon the waist taking my evening exercise, that I was confronted. I had turned at the fo'castle and found her blocking my further progress.

'You sir, I now know to be a conspirator of lies,' she said.

'And you, Miss Bartlett, have connived to enter into a station in life where you do not belong or are welcome.'

'You, sir, are either stupid or delusional from your own deceits. I suffered weeks of unwelcome approaches from your cousin before I first agreed to speak with him. Think you not to judge correctly where the fault lies first.'

'The appearance may be so, but you bewitched James into his actions and have fooled no one.'

'I disagree; you have proved the consistent fool. For I suppose you blame my aunt for these lessons in witchcraft, do you not?'

'Precisely.'

'How then did I manage to learn these spells before I met my aunt for the first time?'

'So you contend.'

'Indeed, what a pity my spells cannot make your cousin into the man I wished him to be or cure him of his present malaise. I assert that it is your cousin who forced himself upon me with such energy and persuasion that it was I who was bewitched. I was fooled into believing in him and laying my trust in his hands. And I, in due course, discovered he is no more than a bag of wind, like these sails above us. Look aloft sir, you will see yourself as well. I see you do not speak. Has your eloquence left you or are you choking on your own guilt? You know well enough that it was I who raised your estate into profit. I hid my pain and disappointment with commerce, but I have heard no thanks from you and now you have corrupted my birthplace and family with your lies. How am I to live there now?'

I felt relief as she started to walk away as I saw no way to respond, but she took three steps aft and returned.

'You know, in his letters James described you as his hero, the one who was trustworthy, the incorruptible. In them he revealed his wayward ways to me, but you were his rock, as I was to be his salvation. For a time, your eloquent manipulations deceived me too. Your cousin disgusts you and you look down on him, but you are a coward and have no honour. You appear a gentleman, but in truth reside in a deeper moral gutter than him.'

She did not wait for my response, for which I was grateful. The winds and swells had increased from the south west and Elizabeth struggled to keep her balance on the treacherous deck. I too had difficulty keeping upright, but was not ready for the confines of my cabin. There was such a tempestuous confusion of thoughts in my brain as could not be contained inside that wooden box. I stayed until it was full dark and the quartermaster came to request I go inside as they were expecting foul weather.

(XVI) Our Final Words

My thoughts tormented me as I lay on my bed as much as the storm did our poor ship that night. I took little comfort in sleep when it came, but in the morning I was much refreshed and my confusion had somewhat dissipated, as had the worst of the weather. I considered my new resolutions after breakfast and throughout the morning whilst endlessly pacing the waist. Lunch was a formality and afterwards I ventured into my cousin's cabin at such time as the steward had retrieved his tray. I was within for no more than twenty minutes, but my efforts to revive his spirits were fruitless. Afterwards, much later in the afternoon, I proceeded to the waist, where I knew I would find Elizabeth.

She was holding onto the larboard bulwarks, which was now our leeward side, as she gazed over the turbulent sea, no doubt suffering the dread of her thoughts as to what disgrace awaited her upon our landfall. I approached her and spoke thus.

'Miss Bartlett, I shall not detain you from your thoughts, but please take note of mine.' She looked towards me, her emotions again unreadable. 'You spoke true about me yesterday. In my lustful pursuit of your demise, I sacrificed my integrity, exceeded my authority and interfered where I did not understand. No more than five minutes ago I went to my cousin and confessed all my manipulations and deceits. I have offered him my apology, which he accepted, in a fashion, although I do not believe this will have any effect on his spirits.'

'No sir, I do not think so either.'

'I further give you my word, Miss Bartlett, that upon our arrival I will expose our family's lies and defend and restore your reputation, no indeed, elevate it to the level it should indeed be, no matter the cost to myself, and will not offer you an apology until this has been done.'

'I see you may be a man of courage and principle after all,' she said, her stern demeanour softening. 'Although I hope you will understand if I reserve my final judgment until after the completed act.'

'I accept no less, Miss Bartlett,' I said. For a few moments, as I stared into those eyes, I lost myself again. There was so much more I wanted to say.

'And is that all, sir?'

'What more is there? Do you wish compensation? I have a small sum of my own that I will give you gladly.'

'No, sir, I do not desire to gain. Money has been the cause of this calamity, it will not resolve it. No, sir, you have disclosed much, but have missed the most important confession, one we might even share.'

'I do not understand, Miss Bartlett.'

'Then perhaps you have not considered the matter enough. It might come to you in due course. Search your heart, sir, but for now, please leave me. I have much to think on.'

It is said that each man receives a certain allotment of opportunities in his life, and he must take them at once. One such came to me then, but, alas, my courage failed.

(XVII) The Final Days

As aforementioned, we were nearing the end of our voyage and, as I left Elizabeth by the handrail and proceeded back to the aft castle, I came across the amiable Evans, the cabin boy. I asked him as to our best arrival time. He said that we would be entering Mounts Bay that night and would complete our transit to the safety of Plymouth Roads by nightfall on the morrow.

I questioned him further about the weather and he said that it was slow moving and would give us a south south-westerly and was not expected to back round to the northwest until after our disembarkation.

With such assurances I went to the dining room for supper. Despite the condition of the sea, there were high spirits amongst the passengers with our approach to landfall, with talk of first acts upon safe deliverance ashore. There followed an interval of cards and afterwards I retired to my cabin.

During the night I was aware of a prolonged period of intense rain, high winds and heavy seas to the extent that there was much yawing and pitching, attended by considerable activity on deck. For the first time in our voyage, copious quantities of water seeped down the walls of my cabin. There was no way to sleep through such turbulence and during such weathers we were confined to our quarters. They would be manning the pumps for certain during the night.

The next morning there was a moderation in our condition and at breakfast we were informed by the steward that the storm had passed sooner than expected and we were now governed by the backing and strengthening north-westerlies. Even with reduced sail we were being driven out of Mounts Bay and past Bury Head. We would have to wait for the winds to moderate and either back further to the northeast or veer to the west-southwest. Depending on our position at the time, we would either head back to Plymouth or select another port.

And so we rode with the winds that day and were fortified to find that they did indeed moderate, by the hour. By nightfall the Master estimated that we were of a latitude with Bury Head and he would see what the morning beheld.

I retired to my damp bed that night, not having seen either James or Elizabeth but had been informed that they were taking their meals in their cabins at such times as the movement of the ship afforded it. This was prudent as there was always the danger that a rogue wave would smash in the windows of our saloon. Being in higher spirits and much fatigued, I fell into a deep sleep.

I was awakened in the early hours by a most powerful swell. We seemed to rear up and fall down with great speed as well as pitch forward and back alarmingly. I surmised correctly that we were under attack from the southwest by another storm. It was later explained to us that we had no choice but to allow ourselves to be swept northeast with the anticipation of taking refuge in Tor Bay before heading for Exeter.

During that day I sat in the forward section of the lounge, a safe distance from the stern windows, with those passengers of a mind and ability to leave their bunks. There was real danger even within the ship. There was such tossing and pitching so as to be cast from one end of a passage or room to another. Indeed I had resorted to using the straps of my bed on each of the last three nights.

I kept company with Mr Williams, the supercargo, who was not of as portly a stature as Messrs Little and Smith and appeared to be as nimble and quick of foot as myself. We entered into such conversations as could be made, as a distraction from our anxieties, whilst still observing events. The rain came back in the early afternoon and all visibility of our coast was duly lost. At this time we estimated our position to be south of Tonemouth Harbour and therefore well on our way to the shelter of Tor Bay.

The ferocity of the storm and our movements had not abated when we were ordered to go to our cabins and the captain instructed us to take such precaution as to remain in our clothing. So we retired for another sleepless night, although reassured as to the accuracy of our position. However, we had not reckoned on two factors which, due to our lack of visibility for much of the day, could not be foreseen or accounted for. Firstly, the wind veered further to the south than anticipated. Secondly, the tidal currents were pulling us westward to a stronger degree than the captain had calculated. Both these factors had the effect of making our course slowly due north, rather than rapidly northeast.

(XVIII) Our Wrecking

The consequence of these miscalculations was predictable.

The experience of falling upon the rocks in a ship is never forgotten. I recount it now after many decades, and it is as if it were last night. I have never overcome the nightmare, the night sweats or the shaking. It is an assault on all the senses and fears.

It starts with the dreaded cries of the watch as out of the sightless gloom of dark skies, raging seas and lashing spray and rain comes the sight of such reefs and rocks as to be like the jaws of a monster as it is about to bite. How can I now describe the execution of this event? A ship is noisy when under sail, and more so in a storm. There is much creaking and rendering and it sounds as if every piece of timber surrounding you does so in turn, including your bed. Now, on contact with the rocks, imagine the crushing, tearing and splintering of planks of wood all around you. And this is not a single episode, but a continuous torture. For as long as there are still two planks held together, the wind, the waves and the rocks will relentlessly seek to tear them asunder.

As this happens you see, if there is still light, the movements of your cabin, by this I mean those dimensions which you have grown accustomed to for weeks, suddenly change. Will they fall in and crush you or will they break apart and cast you into the maelstrom? As well, to this is now added the deceit of motion. Whereas before you could predict the movements of the ship, even in its most violent behaviour, now such movement is entirely random of time and direction. In my case the jolt of impact was so great as to toss me upwards. My leather restraint, weakened by decay, tore itself from the boltholes and I rushed towards the deckhead at such speed that only my extended arms prevented me from striking my face on a beam.

When I fell, it was not back onto the mattress, for the ship had tipped over on its starboard side and I landed with great impact upon the deck space between the bed and the passage bulkhead. The air was expelled from my lungs and I could not get a breath back in for what seemed an eternity. In the meantime I was being rolled from side to side into one wall or another.

On regaining my breath I was aware of a pain at the back of my head. When I had such opportunity to investigate with my hand, it felt wet and I saw in the dim light of my lamp, miraculously still burning, that there was blood.

I tried to regain the use of my legs, but was still too subdued from the blow, so instead endeavoured to prevent any further damage to myself from the constant pitching and swaying of the ship.

In due course there came a crushing noise and we seemed to settle down. At the same time the door to my cabin splintered and fell open and there came an uprising of damp and cold air with the smell of sea upon it as if the bottom of the ship had been ripped out from under her.

At last I was able to brace myself from the continuing movements against the bed and find my footing. My senses were returning and I made for the doorway, looking out into the passage whilst holding onto the doorframe. Three of the eight lamps were still lit and I could see that the cargo that was stowed in the middle had stayed in place. Both forward doors were gone and the seas were washing upon the deck. With each wave there was a blow upon our starboard side and we lurched to larboard, and with each sway our angle steepened. Some of the water thus falling on the deck washed in over the threshold, drenching the passage. Two of the passengers, I think Smith and

Little, were crawling on their hands and knees towards the waist.

Their instinct was to go on deck, as would be mine. At that moment I did not question whether this was the correct course of action. But think, so you go on deck, then what? There is no boat to enter and only rocks or wild seas to jump into.

My first and only thought was of Elizabeth. I let go of the door frame and allowed myself to fall upon the stowed cargo, holding upon the rope lashings, and made my way round until I fell back upon the larboard side of the corridor. However, passing my cousin's cabin first and finding the door splintered, I pushed my way through it. I found James, in what little light there was from the passage, upon the floor trying in vain to get up. I could not tell whether he was injured, drunk, or both. I helped him to his feet and we both fell backwards out of the cabin as a wave struck and caused us to swing round and tip again to larboard. We slid on our backs until stopped by the bulkhead, upon which, without a word as to my wellbeing, James got on his hands and knees and made for the waist.

My thoughts returned to Elizabeth as the ship received yet another blow and the seas rushed through the passage. I crawled back to the opposite side and aft, to the cabin nearest the dining lounge. The door was closed and latched and I feared she had sustained injury. I stood up and shouldered the door, which duly splintered the first time.

There before me, as I stood holding onto the frame, sitting upon the bed, fully dressed was Elizabeth. Now, I have described to you the ferocity of the storm and the violence of our wrecking and could only guess from my own experience the fear and panic the crew and passengers must be feeling. Even my cousin, who had seemed to lose all spirit for life, at the imminent approach of a violent death was now striving for his survival. And yet, there was Elizabeth, maintaining her position on the bed, despite the violent swayings and lurchings of our ship, with an air of total calm and acceptance.

Seeing her thus I realised she did not have the will to save herself. What had she to look forward to? Disgrace by all, with only the promise of a scheming coward to give her hope. Did she now see the wrecking as a godsend? I resolved then that I would either rescue her or die in the attempt.

As I was about to lunge towards her and let go of the frame, we were struck again and I fell backwards into the passage and came to rest against the bulkhead of the other side of it. It was then events took a dramatic turn. I can only assume that our keel had not yet broken and we were struck sufficiently hard by the wind and sea and in such a way as to pivot us round so that we faced the wind. This had the effect of pitching us up by the bow, so that I found myself sliding backwards by the increasing slope and the rushing waters. I fell through the doors and over the thresholds to the saloon.

I retarded my progress upon one of the legs of the fixed tables. It was near pitch black, but I could tell from the sounds, smells and spray that I was near to the stern windows and that the glass of these must have gone. I had hardly the time to consider my next move when something seemed to collapse beneath me, or maybe we slid off the rocks, for we fell full onto our

489

starboard side and into the sea. The cold and numbing water rushed into the open stern and swamped me. I held on, but then the waters receded with such force and suction that I lost my grip and instead fell upon the broken frames and, with much tearing and scraping from splintered wood, was dragged out into the sea and a tumult of waves, currents and foam.

I could see nothing and, although I was frightened for my life, I had also resigned myself to my imminent death. I spent much time underwater with sufficient occasions above it to take enough breath to keep alive. I knew not where I was and fully expected to be dashed upon the rocks at any moment. In the meantime the water was so cold that I considered this a better way of death and prayed for its quick arrival.

My strength was failing and with such senses as I had left I observed that the waves had become stronger and more orderly before being rotated head over heels and landing hard on rough shingle. The outgoing wave tried to take me back, but I righted myself before the next wave struck my back and propelled me further forward and up whatever shore I had been beached upon. In due course I was able to crawl away from the influence of the sea and until the pebbles became smaller and finer. I could see no more than a few feet and progressed until I came to what appeared to be the foot of a precipice.

I continued along the base of this cliff until I found a cleft and was able to crawl into it and escape the spray and driving rain. I did not assume my safety, not knowing whether a boulder would fall upon me from above or more likely the tide would come in and drown me. With every aspect of my being tortured by misery and discomfort, I waited.

(XIX) My Salvation, My Injuries and My Recovery

I will not dwell upon the details of my survival or the risings and fallings of my spirits that night, but suffice to say that I was in much pain from the cold and many cuts and bruisings. When first light broke I found myself sheltered upon a cove to the northeast of what I was to learn was the site of the wrecking, although I could not see any remains of the ship or cargo away from the cove. The shingle beach itself, on which I stood, had much broken and splintered timber of various sizes upon it, but no chattels.

There was no escape from my location either to the east or west, but I was relieved to see a way to the top of the cliff that was within my diminished capacity to climb. After slow and painful progress, I attained the vantage point from which I had a full view of my position and of the misfortune that had befallen us.

I found myself atop a headland, to the west of which was a strand of sand. I recognised it as Spaniard's Cove, hard by to my home town. On this fringe and upon the range of the tide and waves was laid such a scattering of bodies, timbers, sails, cargo and personal possessions as cannot be imagined or described.

The winds had moderated and backed to the northeast. The sky was overcast but the rain had stopped and the waves much reduced so as to make the scene appear calm, much as I would have imagined a battlefield after the fighting has ended.

It was clear that the scene had been much manipulated. The barrels and sacks of cargo had been broken open and the contents removed for there were none strewn upon the sands. The deceased crew and passengers had lost much of their clothing, including their boots.

I was at too great a distance to recognise any of the corpses, nor did I have the desire or stomach to go upon the strand to try and identify them. Instead I made my way inland to what I knew to be the nearest friendly habitation, the manor of a local landowner familiar to my family. I took great efforts to keep myself concealed from the inhabitants of the village behind the strand, as I reasoned correctly that they were the source of much of the thieving that took place the previous night.

Such was my salvation from what should otherwise have been certain death and for a time I allowed my affairs and health to be attended to by others. My recovery was not too arduous and I was able in due time to return to society. As you shall now, however, see, this was not to be the end of the tragedy.

(XX) An Account of the Aftermath

Many investigations and inquests followed, with conflicting evidence given by many people, also much rumour and gossip. There were those things that only I knew from my unique experience and, although I gave accounts to the inquests and the coroner's courts, there is much I investigated for myself afterwards, in my discreet way.

It was established that the wrecking had come about much as I suggested. Due to poor visibility and disorientation brought about by conflicting tides, currents and winds, our vessel was not in the position it was supposed to be in. Instead of sailing into the safety of Tor Bay, we were flung on the rocks at the western end of what is locally known as Spaniard's Cove, so named on account of an earlier wrecking.

All the passengers and crew were lost apart from me, who by the grace of God and in the manner already described, came to be saved, and a midshipman, who was washed ashore on the beach to the immediate west. I will have more to say of him.

Of the fatalities, all but six of the bodies were found within a period of two weeks from the disaster and within a range from Berry Head to Tor Bay. Most fell upon the beach that first night and amongst them was my cousin. My beloved Elizabeth was of the six that remained unaccounted for.

I will now give a report of the testimony of the midshipman. He, like me, fell into the maelstrom when the ship capsized and came off the reef. He too experienced a time of confusion at the mercy of the waves and, being of a younger age and smaller stature, succumbed to the cold and fatigue and fell unconscious.

After an interval, the duration of which he could not determine, he awoke to find himself on his back, on the sands of the strand, head facing the sea and someone tugging at his foot. Upon opening his eyes he beheld two men, one holding an oil lamp and the other attempting to remove his left boot.

The midshipmen, being of nimble wit, took stock of his situation and realized his robbers had assumed him to be dead and were unprepared for any defensive action. With an energy supplied to him by his ignited anger, he pulled free and sprung to his feet to the great shock of his accosters. Furthermore, he took hold of a plank, of which the beach was awash, and was upon them before they could regain their senses.

The man with the lamp ran into the darkness, so the midshipman only managed a blow upon the other thief and felled him onto the sands groaning. Realizing that as a victim his life was in peril, he relieved the bandit of his cloak and hat. Thus it was easy to transit the sands unmolested, helped by his newly acquired disguise, the driving rain and poor visibility. The surrounding lamps, carried by the thieves, gave the midshipman sufficient orientation to make his way.

He intended to stay away from anyone with lanterns but, soon after he set off with his new attire, he heard a scream so piercing that he believed that it could only come from a woman. He was moved to hasten to her assistance and so made way for the first lamp he saw on his left.

He came close enough to witness a terrible sight. He recognised that it was indeed a woman, lying, as he had been, on her back and with her head pointing towards the sea as if she had been dragged up the beach, and surrounded by five men. She was struggling with flailing arms and legs and one man was removing her clothes whilst another was beating her around the head with his fists until she fell silent. Then he picked up her hands and examined them for rings. On finding what he was looking for he tried to remove it but, being unable to do so he took out his knife and, although not close enough to see, our witness assumed he had cut off her finger.

Our midshipman presumed the victim to be Elizabeth, being the only woman on board, and looked about him for a plank of wood or anything he could use as a weapon, but realised that not only would his attempt at rescue prove futile and at the certain expense of his existence, but that the woman's life was almost certainly now extinguished from the severe blows she had received. I cannot tell you, dear reader, how much this description has haunted me. Even now, as I render it after all these years, my eyes grow moist and shed tears.

As the midshipman further removed himself from the danger area, he reported seeing much movement of cargo and personal belongings which were loaded onto horse-drawn carts.

This is an ample summary of the events of the tragedy as the midshipman and I were able to witness. As a result of these testimonies no one was apprehended to face justice for these crimes. I will remind the reader that this was in spite of the evidence for murder and the theft of British Navy supplies amongst the stolen cargo, which engendered the most serious and prolonged investigations.

I have assumed that the reason for this was because the goods thus stolen were quickly moved far from the area and, in addition, were handled by the most corrupt people. I shudder to think of the certainty, much strengthened by the events that were to follow, that some of these men and women were amongst those with whom I lived and did business.

(XXI) The Strange Occurrences and Terrible Tragedies that Followed

As earlier explained, Elizabeth had a spinster aunt who lived near a village on the moor, who had little intercourse with the Bartlett family before their daughter was forced to live with her. After Elizabeth and James left for Georgia, steps were taken, as described, to destroy her niece's reputation. The aunt, not wishing to take part in this betrayal, was therefore also made a victim. Her life would have vanished into obscurity were it not for my investigations. These enquiries were not because of malice on my part. I was merely curious and concerned about a woman, who despite living on limited means and being offered substantial rewards, would not make false speculations about her niece. I admired her and wished to apologise to her for my own conduct. I was further motivated by my frustration at not being able to make amends to Elizabeth.

Although in disagreement with it, I understood my family's reluctance to overturn their stance. Why subject themselves to social embarrassment when the woman in question was dead? But I was shocked by the resistance put up by her parents, even after I assured them that they would not be subject to retribution or reversal of fortune. Such was their demeanour that many years later, when I became responsible for the business, I gave notice to the brothers that they no longer had a place at what was now my yard. I found them equally advantageous positions with my rivals, but I no longer wished to see them benefit from my patronage.

Returning to the aunt, I began my enquiries after I was sufficiently recovered from my ordeal. I learnt that around the time of the shipwreck - the dates were uncertain because the other villagers did not see this woman every day and besides, they would not have heard of the event until sometime afterwards, if at all - she took to herself a tenant.

This did not surprise me. The aunt had become used to having another living with her and I assumed that at the loss of her niece, she offered accommodation to an acquaintance. The identity of the lodger remained a mystery due to the fact that for several years this individual rarely left the cottage during daytime hours. The companion only came out at night and then heavily cloaked, walking with a limp.

The aunt testified, to those who enquired, that her friend, whom she called Sarah, was badly maimed and scarred by an accident with a cart and horse and wished to keep her appearance obscured. She earned her keep first as an apprentice, then as a partner with the aunt in lace-making, the products of which were offered for sale at the weekly market of Tonebridge. I will add here that their work rose to great repute.

Sarah meanwhile kept to the boundaries of the cottage by day, but it was alleged that she went for long walks, with the aid of a stick, upon the moor at night, particularly during favourable moonlight. As is the habit of peoples of poor education, it was alleged she did this in order to search for the devil, for it is believed by many that parts of the moor, in particular those with strange stone structures, are temples to him. As evidence of this they claim the increase in fortune enjoyed by the two ladies months later, which could not entirely be accounted for by the sale of their produce. Indeed it was certainly true that they soon had the funds to greatly improve their cottage and were to want for nothing from then on. At the same time their bounty did not tempt them to live elsewhere or to acquire other more visible signs of affluence. It is my belief that Sarah did discover something, but not the devil, more likely some hidden treasure.

For my part I greatly rejoiced at their good fortune but, soon after this change in their affairs, which occurred many months after the shipwreck and close on to Christmas of the following year, my attention was diverted by a series of strange and ominous events and tragedies.

It began on the moor itself with incidents and sightings of what came to be known locally as the Beast of Dartmoor. I have learnt recently that there was also at one time a Beast of Exmoor, but cannot say whether the two are the same. The extent of the actions of this beast, described to be the size of a large dog and of a breed not identified, was to kill a few sheep and scare some shepherds. There was much speculation as to the reckless owner of this animal, for the killings, all at night, were not of a frequency necessary to sustain a creature of such size if it were entirely feral.

The Black Beast story and incidents continued in this vein for a full year and provided much entertainment and distractions throughout the district. Then, in the spring of 1778, they took a sinister turn. For the first time the attacks and sightings left the confines of the moor and started moving south, towards us. At first these incidents continued in nature and frequency as before, until they passed south of

498

Tonebridge. This did not happen until the coming on of the winter of 1778 and through to spring 1779 and it was during this interval, and only during it, that the district within the area of Tonebridge to Newham to Tonemouth and back to Tonebridge experienced the most terrifying carnage of our history.

One after another, without predictability, men were being attacked, at night, as if by a savage animal, which tore their throats out. The responsibility was naturally placed upon the Beast, but whereas its attacks on sheep were followed by the consumption of the prey, the attacks on men was to cause violent death alone. When men became affeared to go out at night, the Beast found a means to attack them in their homes. The wife would awake and find her husband dead and mutilated.

It came to be established by the incremental investigations of the authorities that the victims were associated in that they were found to have been connected in some way to the plundering of the wreck and cargo, crew and passengers of the *Casaba*. Indeed some subsequently confessed to this misdeed in the hope of escaping this severe punishment, preferring time in prison instead. Not all came to be so acquitted, because there was one murder that took place in Tonebridge goal of one who so repented. Others moved away, perhaps a good indication of guilt, and it was said that only those who travelled a sufficient distance escaped violation.

The authorities, wary to place blame on an animal that had now acquired supernatural status, instead surmised that these attacks were propagated either by a survivor of the wreck who, having lived through the trauma of mutilation and robbery on the beach, had recovered and returned to wreak havoc on the offenders, or the loved one of a victim. Quite how he was able to identify these men was not explained, nor how he managed to enter houses without forceful entry. It was decided that the attacker, having found amusement in the tales of the Beast, decided to imitate its mode of killing, to lend even more fear in the hearts of those who knew themselves to be guilty and to this effect used such tools and implements as were necessary. It was pointed out that the Beast continued to kill sheep during this time, as indeed it did, and that this was proof that the two were not necessarily connected.

I was questioned, but dismissed as being of too delicate a nature and breeding to commit such atrocities. The other known survivor, the midshipman, was found to be at sea in the Pacific upon a whaler. All the relatives of the victims of the wreck were also tracked down, but to no end. I, for my part, and notwithstanding the inconsistencies mentioned above, agreed with the authority's assumptions and continued to do so until another turn of events.

The final five victims were unconnected to the wreck, three being young men from good local merchant families and two young girls from working class families. These savage murders confounded the authorities. They knew not what I knew, for all five were those who had agreed to give false testimony against Elizabeth.

The only people who knew this fact were my father, my uncle and I and it was with great trepidation that we faced each day, being certain that this great retribution would on any night reach our own thresholds. And yet, it did not, nor did it come near to the Bartlett family, but instead, in that spring of 1779, the terror came to an end.

(XXII) The Conclusion

The year following the cessation of these events, arrangements were made for me to take upon myself a wife and there followed many years of responsibilities, which I made my best efforts to discharge. As such this episode in my life receded much, but was not totally suppressed by those affairs as are normal for a gentleman in my position. But the flame that was lit in my heart on that afternoon on the waist of the *Casaba* continued to burn to this day and will only be extinguished with my last breath.

My uncle never recovered from the loss of his son and remained a broken man. He maintained a loose hold on the business and, when he passed away in 1785, my father relinquished his control to me and I went forth to put in place such ideas for expansion as had long been on my mind. I have been blessed with much success and now benefit from the ownership of my estate in the environs of Newham and leave the business of the yard and those of our vessels involved in the Newfoundland and other trades in the capable hands of my two sons and son-in-law. May they prosper as I have.

As mentioned, one of my first acts was to remove the odious Bartlett family from my sight, but I was aware of the passing of Elizabeth's father by a consumption of the body in 1786. Her mother followed soon afterwards.

Her aunt on the other hand lived many more years and passed away in the autumn of 1799. As for Sarah, she vanished in a manner as mysterious and sudden as she first appeared, occurring well before the aunt's passing and interment at the local village churchyard.

I made what enquiries I could regarding this companion, but never identified her next destination. However, there was much speculation, as well as rumours and testimonies of sightings of her at night on the moor by those who resided in those parts and, at the time of writing these words, it is common knowledge amongst these folk that the woman known variously as the Cripple or the Cloaked One lives in a secret hermitage somewhere upon this desolate and forlorn place. Perhaps one day someone will have cause to fall upon her abode, if it exists, and with this discovery have more facts to add. As for me, with the end of this account, my own investigations and speculations are concluded.

Only that love which was both unquenched and inextinguishable remains.

Philip Hunt
The Balize, March 1812

Chapter 45: The Confession

Thursday, 30th December 1982

Zen woke to a fine, sunny day and, after breakfast, went ashore to shop. Alex had left a message at the harbour office that she wanted to meet him at the quayside café at half six. This was unexpected.

He came back to a lunch of moussaka with vegetables. All that time, though, his mind was in a haze, brought on by the information he had taken in the night before. His sole conversation about it with Harry consisted of a moment alone on the poop deck landing after lunch as he was on his way down to the engine room to switch off. Zen asked him whether he had done any reading the previous night, to which he replied that, owing to the amount they'd had to drink, he had only managed to find his cabin and bed, but would tackle it during the afternoon and evening.

With the generator off and not having much to do, Zen went to his cabin to have a nap and slept for two hours. It was dark when he woke, but he felt refreshed. He went ashore and spent the best part of an hour mingling amongst the crowds, wandering the streets and embankments.

When he observed that the starry sky had clouded over and he could feel the first spots of rain, he went to the harbour café. Inside it was welcomingly warm and, after buying a cup of tea, he sat at a table by the entrance to wait for Alex.

'Hello, darling,' she said, on her arrival, giving him a hug. Her cheek felt icy against his. 'I've missed you.'

'So have I. You must've parked a long way to get so cold.'

'I did, near the top of the town. I blame the sales.'

'Really, I thought the town was busy. At least you didn't get caught in the shower we just had.'

'No, I drove through it ten minutes ago.'

'What do you want to do, go on board or stay for a cup of tea?'

She looked around as if testing the ambience of the place. 'Let's stay, I haven't much time.'

He fetched another pot, cup and saucer and they moved further inside, away from the entrance and the draught.

'We could go back to yours if you prefer,' he said in haste, not realizing that it was impractical.

'No, I'm going to my parents' later.'

'How's work?'

'Busy, lots of enquiries; yours?'

'Quiet, we've not been up to much, as you know.'

'You're probably wondering why I've come.'

'I was hoping it was because you can't stay away.'

'That too, but I've been thinking about something we talked about the other day.'

'We've spoken about many things.'

'I mean the part about what happens when the *Amber* leaves.'

'We said we'd deal with it when the time came.'

'Well, I've thought about it and it would be ridiculous for you to give up your job in London. There aren't any jobs like yours here, but I can work in an estate agent anywhere.'

'Whatever you're happy with.'

504

'I can always take the train or drive down for the weekend to see my parents.'

'Naturally.'

'What I'm trying to say is that I'm willing to come to London and live with you, if you want me to.'

'Alex, it could be a year till then, but if the *Amber* left tomorrow, I would want us to live together too.'

'I don't think I'm saying what I really want to say.'

'What's that?' he asked, taking her hand. 'There's something troubling you.'

'There are some things I need to tell you, though I don't want to,' she said, looking downwards and not at him.

'What's it about?'

'I need to tell you about my past and why I'm seeing a psychiatrist.'

'You warned me that you weren't Mother Theresa some time ago.'

'You need to know to what degree I've strayed.'

'I've also done things I'm not proud of.'

'If after I've finished you wish to make a confession of your own, I'll hear it.'

'Okay, I've braced myself.'

'I'll start with Tim.' She told him all about her infidelities with him and the other men she had been out with. She then revealed the episode involving Enzo, the young Italian boy.

'It must've been awful for your parents,' Zen said, wondering if it was anything like he was feeling at that moment. She looked at him expectantly. 'Why tell me now?' he asked.

'Two reasons really. The first is because I've fallen madly in love with you, and the second is that my

505

parents have refused to meet you unless I tell you everything.'

'I think I like them already,' he said. He had wondered why he'd not met them yet. 'But tell me about Earsop. When did you start going to him?'

'Last spring. I was referred by my previous psychiatrist who thought that hypnotherapy might help. I started seeing Ben once a week. We only talked at first; the treatments didn't start till a month later.'

'What's he like?'

'He's nice, has a soothing voice and seems to know what he's doing and, if our relationship is anything to go by, he's been successful.'

'But you still see him.'

'Well, according to him, I've made such good progress that he asked if I could become one of his research subjects. So, since October I've been seeing him twice a week for free. He comes to me and, to be honest, it's the least I can do.'

'I suppose.'

'Well? What about us? Will we spend New Year together? Do you need time to think?'

'That's an unfair question, but I'll definitely be spending New Year with you.'

She looked at her watch. 'I'll be expecting you then, but I must go. Mustn't keep my parents waiting.'

Back outside it was clear and starry again. It meant another cold and frosty night. He walked her to her car. He was frozen through by the time he was back on board, but with the generator now on, the *Amber* had warmed up.

506

He went into the mess where the others were sitting in the TV alcove. Harry and Andy were playing backgammon and Steph was criticizing their technique.

'Anyone have plans for the evening?' Zen asked.

'I think only Harry's going out,' Steph replied, looking at Andy, who did not contradict him.

'So is Linda back?' Zen asked.

'Yes, I've arranged to drop in for a few hours,' Harry replied.

'Don't forget their presents,' Steph said. 'You're sure I can go to the Bulgarians tomorrow night?'

'Absolutely,' Zen said. 'The *Amber* will be fine.' If the rest of them were going out, why not Steph? 'When and what are we eating?'

'I have the rest of the moussaka in the oven,' Steph said. 'I thought that in this weather, it's good to have it hot. I've also made a salad. I'll get it after they finish their game.'

He saw no point in going to his cabin, so he sat at the made-up table to wait, reflecting on Alex's revelations. It made him depressed. After Harry and Andy had finished, they joined him.

'So, is it just Steph and Harry sleeping here tomorrow night?' Zen asked, once they had started eating.

'As long as some drunk doesn't steal the boat again,' Harry said.

'Or end up sleeping in it,' Andy added. 'Clare and I are staying at a hotel.'

'Which one?' Zen asked.

'The one that's along the lane behind the garage. She'd rather we didn't spend the night where she works.'

507

'Understandably, but I'm surprised you found a room,' Harry said.

'It's hidden away, so easily missed,' Andy said.

'I suppose the *Amber* is no longer good enough for you,' Zen commented.

'New Year deserves something better,' Andy remarked. 'Besides, I don't want to risk another encounter with a dog.'

'I've read about it in the papers,' Steph said. 'Apparently these black dog legends occur in many parts of the country.'

'Please don't say it has anything to do with Greek Mythology,' Andy pleaded.

'As a matter of fact…'

'Spare us this once…' Andy begged.

'No, I'm interested,' Zen said.

'It's all to do with Hecate, the goddess of witches, ghosts, dreams, sailors and some other things I've forgotten. She was not welcome on Mount Olympus and roamed the world teaching witchcraft. Her familiars were black female dogs, the most famous of which was Queen Hecabe of Troy, who she transformed into a bitch as she was trying to escape when the city fell at the end of the Trojan War.'

'I thought the familiars of witches were black cats,' Zen said.

'I prefer a cat to a dog any day,' Andy added.

'Well, that's the myth, make of it what you will,' Steph said. 'There's still some moussaka in the oven, shall we finish it?'

They all wanted some more.

After supper, no one was in the mood for cards or TV, preferring to get an early night in preparation for the weekend. It was also the case that the cold had sapped their strength and made them listless. Zen went up to run a bath before Harry went down and switched off. It was still only eight thirty.

Friday, 31st December 1982

The next morning they woke to a frozen ship. Reluctantly, Zen deferred to logic and went running. He felt good afterwards, as any form of exercise raised his metabolism and helped him cope with the cold. By the time he had bought the papers and was back on board, the generator was on and the others were also up and about.

He went and had a shower before breakfast. They had bacon, eggs and hash browns, the latter being Harry's idea and one of the things he had missed since leaving California.

'God, I needed that night's sleep,' Andy said.

'How are Linda and Stephen?' Steph asked.

'Fine, but tired,' Harry replied. 'They had a long drive.'

'I bet,' Zen said.

'They said thanks to everyone for their presents,' Harry continued, 'especially Steph for the pen and ink set.'

'Will we be seeing them?' Steph asked.

'Definitely Sunday for lunch,' Harry replied, 'when they'll also bring their presents to us.'

'And what did Linda get you?' Andy asked.

'The longest scarf I've ever seen, a thick jumper and some thermal socks,' Harry replied.

'Are we having lunch as normal?' Steph asked.

'I think we ought to have it later,' Zen said. 'And I don't think we should switch off today. It's deadly cold.'

'Thank God for that,' Andy said. 'Besides we need time to get ready. I need to do some ironing.'

'And I want to do some baking for New Year's Day,' Steph said.

'When are you sending off the monthly accounts?' Harry asked Zen.

'I'll complete them over the weekend and send them Tuesday, why?'

'I have a list of spares. You might as well use the same envelope.'

'Let me have them later.'

'Why don't you come to the engine room after breakfast? I've got it down there.'

'Okay.'

They had coffee together and afterwards Andy and Steph went to clear up and Zen followed Harry down to the engine control room. After he had shut the door, muffling the sound of the machinery, he picked up a small envelope from the conference table and handed it to Zen. 'It's all in there,' he said. 'Have a seat.' They sat. 'So? What did you think?'

'To start, there's no way Elizabeth was in love with that idiot James, certainly not by the end of it. Not being a woman of the world, she was taken in by him at first, not realizing her mistake till it was too late.'

'Then in steps Philip, competent and strong. Although at first he saw Elizabeth as a scheming whore, over time he realizes that she has real substance.'

'And falls in love with her, but can't bring himself to admit it.'

510

'Not only that, but afterwards he fails to fulfil his promise to exonerate her.'

'You can't blame him for that. He tried, but faced resistance. Besides, he thought she was dead.'

'No, no, no, that makes it worse. She's not there to defend herself. It was even more important that he follow through.'

'I guess that's why Elizabeth has such a disdain for men. They don't admit what they feel or carry out their promises.'

'True. By the way, have you spoken with your father?'

'Haven't had the chance. I'll call on my way out tonight.' He was not looking forward to it. 'They would've checked in yesterday afternoon.'

Zen went back to his cabin to fetch his wallet. They all had jobs to do in preparation for the weekend and that evening.

Chapter 46: New Year

Friday, 31st December 1982

Zen, Harry and Andy set off together. Before leaving for Alex's, Zen went to the phone box to call the hotel in Torquay to speak to his parents. They wished him a Happy New Year, as he did them, but there was no sign of any warmth or any indication that the gulf between them had narrowed.

Once on his way, and with an envelope containing the photocopy of Philip's diary beside him, he reflected that, irrespective of anything else that might change due to Alex, or rather Elizabeth, seeing the contents, he had doubts about their prospects. This was only partly to do with Alex's recent revelations. If Elizabeth was guiding Alex, how serious were her feelings? And who was he having the relationship with?

He was too early to drive directly to Newham, so he decided to stop off somewhere along the way. He wanted to visit The Balize, but the property, as he suspected, was closed for the winter and, besides, it was too late in the day to be within visiting hours. He did, however, park near the church and, in the churchyard, after much searching in the dark with the aid of his torch, managed to find Philip's grave. What he saw surprised him.

Once in Newham, he parked outside Alex's house, behind her car.

Giving each other a hug, they were soon busy preparing their meal, with Zen in charge of the vegetables, while enjoying a sherry. After they had caught up with each other's news, he explained about the package he was carrying. He related how Harry had befriended the local librarian, who was also fascinated by the story of the *Casaba*, and how the account came to light. 'Knowing how interested you are in Elizabeth, I thought you'd like to read it. It's quite revealing.'

'Revealing? In what way?' she asked with a puzzling lack of enthusiasm.

'Well, you might need to revise your views. The story's more complicated than you thought.' He gave a brief outline and expressed what he thought was a likely conclusion. When he had finished, he realised that she had not been paying attention.

'Leave it on my bureau,' she said dismissively. 'I'll look at it later.'

The meal that followed was excellent. Alex had prepared homemade cannelloni, stuffed with spinach and ricotta, in a rich tomato sauce. That was followed by *osso buco* and seasonal roasted root vegetables. They drank the fine Italian dry white that went into the making of the dish, but while they were eating Alex hardly spoke and only responded briefly to any of his prompts. She was distant, appeared nervous and on three occasions he caught her looking at the time.

'Is there something wrong?' Zen asked.

'It's nothing; I was just thinking that, after dessert, we can open the champagne.'

'That'll be something to look forward to,' Zen said, enthusiastically. They cleared the plates, caught up with the washing up and afterwards Alex took two beautiful zabagliones, set in wine glasses, out of the fridge.

'Does the music need to be that loud?' he asked. He was sure it was more pervasive than when he arrived and it was beginning to irritate him.

513

'I'll turn it down in a minute,' she replied.

When they had finished, she got up and turned down the music, coming back to the table to pick up the empty dessert glasses. 'Why don't you get the flutes from the dresser, I'll get the champagne.'

He went and got them, but before he could sit down again she called out to him.

'Can you come and open it in here?' she pleaded. 'I don't want an accident in the other room.'

'Sure,' he said, walking towards the kitchen. 'Why have you got the lights...' But before he could finish the sentence, two sets of powerful arms grabbed each of his from behind, bending them backwards in one swift action. Within a few seconds he was handcuffed and a hood was pulled over his head. When he tried to shout, a hand covered his mouth.

His struggles were pointless as he was held round the chest by one attacker from behind while the other took hold of his legs round the knees and squeezed them in a vice-like grip as he was raised off the floor. He felt a rope being wound round his ankles.

Recovering from the initial shock, he realised there was no point struggling or protesting as any such efforts appeared more likely to injure him as well as proving futile. He was already exhausted and breathing heavily. This was a well thought-out manoeuvre and, at the moment at least, there was no opportunity to free himself. But from what? Captivity certainly, but to what purpose?

While he was thus lifted up, he was carried back into the dining room. He was seated on one of the dining room chairs and more trussing with rope followed, round his waist, chest and knees. Again he tried to call out, but as soon as he did so, a hand muffled the sound.

Once he was securely tied, someone held the hood over his eyes while the lower part was raised. Another pair of hands put a strip of tape over his mouth.

He resisted the temptation to test his bindings, it would count for nothing at present, while he was being watched, and he was determined to show no signs of emotion or distress. Fear could play into their hands, as well as cloud his reasoning. Many thoughts coursed through his mind. Initially he reflected on his stupidity at not suspecting something earlier and being on his guard. Was this to be Elizabeth's revenge? Was he to be tortured and mutilated as her other victims? If so, why not just attack him in his sleep on the *Amber*? Why here? He felt a cold sweat break out all over him as if every individual pore had opened and wept. He renewed his efforts to suppress his feelings, control his breathing, and tried to be aware of what was happening around him.

Over the ever present music, he heard someone going upstairs, Alex probably, followed by creaking floorboards as she moved around the upper floor. The two men, meanwhile, receded into the kitchen and he heard the back door open and close. As he waited he wriggled about, testing his fastenings; they were secure, but not overly tight. Perhaps, given enough time...

He heard the back door open again and footsteps approached, stopping behind him. He heard some rummaging, then there was a tug on his left trouser leg, half way up his thigh. It felt and sounded like someone was cutting the material with a pair of scissors. Seconds later he felt the sting of a needle entering his flesh.

515

Within minutes drowsiness overcame him. The last thing he remembered was the music being turned off.

He becomes aware of standing next to his car. The bonnet is to his right and he is facing out to sea. There is a waist-high concrete wall in front of him and he can hear the rhythm of the waves thrusting onto and receding from the rocks below. Looking round, he recognises Tor Bay and surmises he is in one of the car parks of Torquay. How he got there, he has no idea. It is certainly a calm and mild night, he reflects, as he has no sense of being cold. Then looking about him he catches sight of the fact that he is naked. As he panics he realises he cannot feel what should be the rough concrete surface of the car park with his bare feet. Then he hears laughter behind him. Spinning round, he sees Elizabeth, standing by the rear end of his car, also naked. Behind her, and in the distance above them, is the front of a hotel.

'Are you not glad to see me?' she asks.

She stands glowing, and is so indescribably beautiful that his desire for her is instantly inflamed.

'How much do you want me?' she asks. 'How does it feel? You don't have to speak, I can sense your torment.'

There is torment indeed. He is overcome by it. He is aware that she can feel his feelings and is enjoying them. Harry's words come to mind, but any attempt to ignore or resist his longings seems fruitless.

'And even though I would draw no pleasure from it, you would have me now, wouldn't you?'

He knows he would and he hopes he can. She smiles as she acknowledges his consent. 'Would you give anything for such a concession? Speak. Let me hear the words.'

'I would,' he says. The notion of resistance makes another ineffective attempt to establish itself.

'There is something I'm going to do and I want you to approve it. If you do so, you can have me once in any way you wish. You can have the pleasure of me just the one time, if you assent to this. Will you agree to whatever I wish?'

'I will,' he says, giving no thought to what he is agreeing to. Were his feelings for Elizabeth being directed in the same way as Alex's were for him?

'You understand I do not ask your approval or your permission. I can do what I please. But just say you will assent to it and I will give myself to you afterwards.'

His excitement is rising, his fledgling resistance cannot keep up with its escalation. He just wants her to get on with it so he can touch her, so he can...

'In return for your assent to take your father's life, you can have me in any way you choose.' Elizabeth smiles as she says those words. To her this acquiescence is her ultimate victory, Zen realises. It is the confirmation of his depravity, of every man's depravity. She closes her eyes as she waits for the pleasure of feeling this capitulation.

On the previous occasions when he had been with Elizabeth, in his dreams, he assumed he was under her control in every way, his feelings as well as his astral body. This was certainly the case with the latter, but those words of Elizabeth had an unexpected effect. Something within the energy of his present form was ignited, something that for the last few minutes was just

517

a fleeting thought, some aspect of self-will, of self-consciousness was awakened and asked a question.

In that instant, what seemed like a miracle occurred. The feelings of longing and lust drained out of him. 'I do not give you this assent,' he says.

He has no sooner uttered these words than her countenance changes. She looks fiercely at him as if ready to attack. Despite the rebellion of his thoughts and feelings, he still has no control over his ethereal body. She looks into the car as if thinking what to do and, as he follows her gaze he realises that it is his body, which he can see under a blanket on the back seat, that she is now staring at.

She turns to him again and, raising her arm, she draws him to her. There is malice and anger in her eyes, he is glued to them, but he is no longer afraid. As soon as she can touch him, there is the bright light and they are soaring into the sky, as on previous occasions. They do not go far and land on the roof of the hotel, before transforming back to their original forms.

'What are we doing here, Elizabeth?' he asks. 'Or do you prefer Miss Bartlett?'

Elizabeth looks shocked at the insolence of Zen addressing her without permission. 'If I remained any longer by your body, I would have torn it apart,' she says. 'We must wait here for the signal, so be silent.' She moves closer to the front parapet of the hotel. There on the ground is a small plastic bag, which she picks up.

'What signal?'

'The signal that I can proceed with the execution. Speak no more.'

'Why do you wish to murder my father, an innocent man? Kill me, torture me.'

'You think it is only about you? Earsop wants him killed.'

'Earsop? Whatever for?'

'Actually, it is his acquaintance Spiros Alexandrou who wants him dead.'

'But Spiros is my father's friend.'

'In the same way that Alex is your lover?' she asks, a triumphant smirk on her face.

'I still don't understand,' Zen says, ignoring her comment.

'It's ironic,' she says, smiling again, as if thinking of a new way to hurt him, 'that you are indirectly the cause of your father's demise.'

'I don't understand,' he pleads. 'Grant me as much as to explain the reason.'

'I need grant you nothing,' she declared. 'But will gladly torment you. It was planned that you should marry his daughter Sophia. After the wedding, Alexandrou was to announce that he was having financial difficulties. The amalgamation of the businesses would have resulted in his rescue.'

'So that explains the rushed marriage of his son to my sister,' Zen says. So this new ship Spiros was building was bringing him to his knees after all. 'But that can still happen, why murder my father?'

'Because Alexandrou can now see the possibility of having everything. You may not know this, but you have been disowned, written out of you father's will. Everything passes to your mother and sister.'

'But surely, they'll be found out.'

'You are stupid, aren't you? You will be identified, tried and punished for his murder.'

'But that's absurd.'

'Not at all. Everything's been planned, everything's been put in place.'

'What's the motive? I knew nothing about the will till now.'

'Oh, yes, you did,' she says. 'There's a record of you calling your father earlier today, your mother will confirm that. That's when it will be assumed he told you. Then, a few hours later on New Year's Eve you go to see the woman you love. The one who confessed to you the day before that she was no better than a slut. This is in Alex's diary by the way. So, you're sitting down to a meal and at the end, just when you're about to open a bottle of champagne, a man knocks unexpectedly on the door. He turns out to be the one who's currently fornicating with her behind your back. This sends you insane. They try to reason with you, but instead you grab the vegetable knife and threaten them. Realizing that you could not overcome them, you run out of the house and in your anger come here and sit in the car park brooding, knife still beside you.' As she says this she lifts the plastic bag. 'Then, not being able to take any more, you go up to your father's room and kill him.' Elizabeth is standing at the edge of the roof looking down at the entrance to the hotel, from which the signal is to be generated.

'But no one's going to see me go in or leave afterwards.'

'No one will see me either, so it'll be enough that your finger prints are on the weapon.'

Zen remembers how he handled the vegetable knife earlier in the day. 'He loved you, you know,' he says.

'Who loved me?' she asks, taken unawares.

'Philip, he loved you all his life.'

'You lie,' she spat back at him.

'He fell in love with you on the deck of the *Casaba*.'

'He betrayed and abandoned me.'

'He thought you to be dead.'

'He broke his word.'

'By the time he recovered from his injuries, those responsible were being killed off anyway.'

'Your attempt to save yourself is futile.'

'I'm not trying to save myself, just my father.'

'It will still be futile.'

'You called me stupid earlier, perhaps I am, but your own perceptions are also flawed. Or perhaps you're purposefully avoiding facing facts.' She was refusing to respond. 'Your anger and resentment are preventing you from seeing the truth, even if it means the discovery that the love of your life felt love of equal measure for you.'

'What nonsense you speak. It is from facts and acts that I draw my conclusions.'

'Then why haven't you expressed interest in his account?'

'It won't change that which was planned, because of some worthless diary that has conveniently turned up.'

'Then why after all these years have you not visited his estate or graveside?'

'I would not tread on that cursed ground.'

'I'll prove to you that your resentment has blinded you.'

'Enough of this pointless talk.'

'Do you understand the significance of The Balize?'

'Of course I do, it refers to the monument to his ego that he erected on the headland.'

521

'Has it ever occurred to you to ask yourself why he chose such an obscure name? A name of French and Spanish origin, from what I understand.'

'These people were always using such obscure words, as if to raise others' perception of their education.'

'Ponder for a minute on what other word the rearrangement of the letters for 'The Balize' produces.'

'But it's 'La Balise'.'

'Yes, but Philip was clever. If he was spelling it in French or Spanish, he should've used an 's' and not a 'z', and 'La' instead of 'The'. Again I ask you to rearrange the letters in your mind.'

She ponders for a few minutes and Zen can see the fleeting realization on her face, soon to be suppressed. 'A coincidence, nothing more.'

'I know you don't believe that, I could see it. For one second you relented, your resolve weakened. Open your mind, there's more.'

'You men are manipulators, all the same, all weak at the first difficulty or temptation,' she raved with uncontrolled fury. 'Soon you will see your own father fall on his knees for me just like the others did, before they died.'

'My father? I confess I cannot pretend to have much strength of character, but my father will not be moved by you.'

'You're an idiot.'

'My father may be many things I don't agree with, but his loyalty and strength of purpose are beyond anything I could ever have.'

'You talk nonsense.'

522

'The men or women you have killed so far, I imagine, were felons, murderers or weak in different ways. Have you ever confronted a decent man?'

'Be quiet, fool,' she says. 'You're too late.' She is looking down at the entrance of the hotel. A man comes out and walks over to a car positioned in the forecourt car park. As he looks around, he recognises Ben Earsop. 'The time has come.' She puts up her hand to draw him to her.

'I'll make a deal,' Zen says as he approaches her. 'If my father lusts after you, as you say, then I will accept our demise. But if he resists, as I know he will, then let me show you just one thing, that's all I ask. Just one...'

He falls into her as before. There is the white light and they are airborne. Again their journey is short and they alight on one of the balconies facing the sea and near the top of the building. They transform again and are separate entities.

'That's all I ask,' Zen concluded.

She ignores him. She steps across the balcony, past a table with four chairs, to the sliding glass door. The inside is obscured by curtains. She fiddles with the lock and handle and draws the door enough for them to pass through. They enter a dark bedroom. In the double bed is a single, half-covered form, his mother. Zen is relieved that Elizabeth passes her by and moves to the other room. His parents would have booked a suite. Passing through the open doorway they come to a sitting room area. There, next to the window, sitting on a settee, in front of which is a coffee table, is his father, wearing a dressing gown and slippers, reading a hardback of some sort. He has not noticed them and would not see Zen anyway.

523

They are standing in front of the door to the corridor. Elizabeth moves forward, while Zen remains rooted in his place. She stands in front of his father and raises her hand. He raises his head. He is unperturbed, at first, as he folds his book and puts it down. Zen expects the worst, maybe Elizabeth is right after all. Is he going to see him grovel at Elizabeth's feet before she plunges the knife into him?

Instead he sees first puzzlement, then shock and finally a stern expression come over his father's face. 'Young lady, I think you've made a mistake. You're in the wrong room.' Elizabeth reaches out to him with both arms, inviting him to her. 'If you don't leave right away, I'll throw you out,' he says.

Elizabeth looks at him with a mixture of fury and bewilderment. Perhaps she would tear out his throat instead. She moves quickly towards him and Zen freezes with horror, trying to shut his eyes. She puts her hand on his head and it falls forward. She turns and reaches for Zen and, opening the door to the balcony, they move outside.

'I have put your father to sleep,' she says. 'This is your only chance to show me what you want to show me, then I will be back to do what I have to do.'

'Take me to the churchyard near Philip's house.'

They join and are airborne. They fly high into the sky, heading south along the shore, across Tor Bay, past Paignton and more coast. Before coming to Newham they turn into the dark, hilly interior. They begin to descend at a small cluster of lights and come to rest beside a church.

When they are their separate forms again he is allowed to lead the way through the churchyard to

Philip's graveside. They stand there for many minutes as Elizabeth stares.

'What does this mean?' she says, in a voice barely audible.

'Here is Philip in this plot, enclosed with a railing. On the right is his grave and on the left, or to his right, is a vacant plot. And just over there are the graves of his wife and children in the maternal family plot. A clear statement made in death.'

She seems to falter at the knees and she allows herself to be supported by the railing. Then, finding some strength, she climbs over it and, falling to the ground, she starts sobbing, periodically reaching out to touch the ground.

Zen does not know how long they are there. In this state he has no conception of time. It could have been five minutes or five hours.

At last she turns and looks up at him and says, 'In my anger you were Philip to me. But the Philip that loved me is here in the ground.'

'I understand.'

'You cannot, but it does not matter. I do sense your compassion for me and your relief, but this is mistaken. There is still great danger.'

'Please explain.'

'Earsop is relentless. It does not stop here. I was just a means. He will find another way to get what he wants.'

'Then we must stop him.'

'I have to destroy him. We will go back...'

'No, there must be another way,' he says. 'No more killing. There must be a way of incriminating him.'

'He is too careful and we might not have much time.'

'Tell me how...how you...' Zen was finding it difficult to speak. Elizabeth and his surroundings were fading.

'It's already too late,' was the last thing he remembered her saying.

When he awoke, he was back in that chair again, but with no hood over his head. The lights were on and he struggled to adjust to the brightness. He was tied differently too, without handcuffs. Alex, wearing a track suit and with bare feet, sat on the settee opposite, staring unseeing into space. Either side of her sat two burly men wearing dark, short-sleeved tee-shirts and trousers. One was bald and the other had close-cropped grey hair. They had the build of wrestlers, broad, well-built with thick necks, like Earsop. One of them looked over at him and called out. 'Ere boss, the lad's come round.'

Earsop came in from the kitchen. 'That's too bad,' he said. 'I'll have to give him another dose.' He reached for his bag. 'But since you're awake, I'm curious to know how you managed to change her mind?'

'I don't know what you're talking about,' Zen replied, groggily.

'There she was on the brink of killing your father and then she stops herself. On the point of attaining the result she was anticipating for months and fantasizing about for decades and she changes her mind.'

'That's women,' Zen said, making the wrestlers giggle.

'I'm glad to see you have a sense of humour,' Earsop said. 'Of course, I had to have a contingency plan, in case she didn't deliver, I just...'

'What contingency? If you've hurt my father?' Zen struggled in vain.

'Your efforts are pointless,' Earsop said. 'Any one of us could tear your head off with one hand. Besides, your father's quite safe and will remain so. Plan 'B' doesn't require his disposal, but yours.'

A cold fear gripped Zen.

'Don't worry,' Earsop said. 'You'll be doped anyway. It'll be over quickly.'

'That's kind of you.'

'I'm just making sure things run smoothly, that's all,' he said. 'Now, last chance to answer my question before I put you under.'

'First tell me what's happened to Elizabeth?'

'As I explained, I had a contingency plan. So if Elizabeth failed me, I had to make sure I could bottle her up,' he said looking over at Alex.

'You can't keep Alex in a trance forever.'

'Oh, you don't understand. She'll be joining you in the deep.'

'And how will our deaths be explained?'

'The jealous boyfriend discovers his father has also betrayed him and decides to take his life together with that of his deceiving girlfriend,' Earsop explained. 'Your father's grief and remorse will destroy him, giving us more or less the same result, especially when the police find Alex's diary.'

'What are you talking about?'

'Alex kept a diary. It's all in there,' Earsop said. 'Your growing anger and resentment towards your

527

father, the realization that she's having an affair. It works both ways for us.'

'Won't they discover drugs in our bodies?'

'Actually, the place I had in mind, a favourite for suicides I might add, is a shallow cliff above deep water,' he said as he reached into his bag. 'You will recall there was a full moon last night, so it's a spring ebb tide, so you'll be swept out to sea. In addition, a serious storm is coming in from the Atlantic. It's already clouding over. So it's doubtful you'll ever be found and if you are, days from now, your bodies will be so badly battered and decomposed that they'll struggle to identify you.' He took out the hypodermic and walked over to him. 'But even if they do, it's logical you could've slipped Alex barbiturates in order to make her easier to handle. That's all this is and I'll make sure some pills are left on her bedside table. And at the last minute you took some yourself, to ease the pain of those final minutes. Anyway, time's up.'

Chapter 47: The Rescue

Zen came to with the shock of hitting the water.

There were two sources of excruciating pain. One was on his left side as he hit the surface, but this was superseded by the other: the piercing, stabbing cold. His initial scream was muted as his mouth and sinuses were filled with the freezing liquid, adding a crushing ache, one in which his skull seemed ready to rupture.

Being thus immersed and disorientated, he was overcome by blind panic, as he thrashed out for air, not knowing whether his efforts were bringing him closer to the surface or taking him even deeper. This was made worse by the movement of the sea, pushing him one way or pulling him another, adding the possibility of being dashed onto rocks.

His fear escalated as his urge to breath became urgent. He momentarily thought of Alex, probably within feet of him, suffering the same ordeal.

Then there followed an eternity of struggling, where he was getting nowhere and he could feel himself weakening. How long can this take? Surely it will be over soon. Please, God, can it be over soon.

He thought perhaps the time had come when he saw lights flashing before his eyes, reminding him of accounts of near-death experiences. Then the pressure on his chest increased as if he was ensnarled in something. He tried to remove it and realized he was in the grip of someone behind him. His irrational mind thought that those wrestlers had come in with him to make sure the job was done this time. Then one arm released and within seconds was trying to force something into his mouth. Why would they be trying to suffocate him if he was already drowning? It was when he was trying to push the object away that he realised it was a demand valve.

It was many lungs-full of the pressurized air before he was breathing regularly and he could not understand why he was not taken straight to the surface. Instead he was being towed. Who was this person and how did he or she know he would be here? By now the cold was so numbing he was feeling drowsy and was offering little help to his rescuer. Another eternity passed.

He recovered some of his senses when they did finally break the surface. It was pitch dark except for some hazy lights ahead; they were making for some sort of craft. When they reached the side, two pairs of hands reached down and pulled him in. He was promptly wrapped in blankets and laid at the bottom of the boat. There was someone else beside him. Was it Alex? His vision was blurred and he was too confused to try and understand anything. He just wanted to sleep. He felt the vessel tip as someone came on board, then the engine powered up and they were cutting through the water. Almost immediately someone, he thought it was Harry, straddled him, rubbing him vigorously through the blanket.

The journey was rough and now that his body was no longer numb from the cold, he could feel himself getting a bruising on his left side, while veering onto Alex on his right. She must have been okay because he could feel her pushing back.

He tried to rear himself up, but felt nauseous and some vile, fiery liquid was trying to force its way out of his stomach. He managed to swallow it back down. Then the boat entered more exposed waters. It veered into the oncoming weather, which was causing it to lift before slapping down with every drop forward. He could hear and feel the spray covering them. Harry kept him firmly covered with the blankets. At least now he was not falling onto Alex.

This part of the journey lasted a long time and over the sounds of the engine, sea and spray, he could hear their rescuers shouting instructions to each other. 'Watch this part', 'Point the torch to starboard', 'Veer to the left', 'Veer to the right' or 'Slow down'. Eventually they came into the lee of the weather and the sea calmed. When they were on smooth water, he knew they had entered the estuary.

Again he tried rearing up and Harry relaxed his grip and uncovered his head. It was raining heavily. As he sat up, he saw Harry, in his wetsuit, sitting on the centre bench. Next to him, also in a wetsuit, was Andy. He was holding Alex, wrapped in blankets, securely between his legs. She was facing forward and when she saw Zen she forced a smile. He attempted to smile back. Behind them he saw Steph at the tiller, wearing an old brown leather jacket and shining the torch ahead. He was soaked and Zen could see the water dripping down his grim set face.

They were surrounded by the lights of Tonemouth and Castlewear and it was while they were approaching the *Amber* that he realised that they were keeping too close to the Castlewear side.

Harry noticed his puzzlement. 'We can't be seen bringing you back,' he said. 'We lowered the other ladder. I'll explain later.'

When they reached the port side of the *Amber*, Steph held on to the bottom platform of the gangway while both Andy and Harry helped Alex up. She was very shaky and Andy walked in front while Harry helped her from behind. Andy came back to help Zen who, either from the experience of being in the sea or from the drug, or both, was also weak and unsteady. Every step required all his strength, his knees giving way several times, and his grip seemed to have failed him because his hands kept on slipping when trying to hold onto the side ropes. Andy had to steady him several times from behind. In the end he had to complete the climb on his hands and knees.

Once on board, they led him to the mess, replaced his wet blankets with dry ones and sat him in one of the armchairs. Andy wheeled the gas heater in front of him and turned it on. Zen could barely hold himself upright, let alone speak.

'Take it easy, boss,' Andy said.

Zen nodded and waited, enjoying the warmth. 'What's the time?' he managed to mouth.

'Six thirty,' Andy said.

Some minutes later Harry entered the mess. He came and knelt in front of Zen. He was back in his normal dress and overcoat and told Andy to get changed.

'I've put Alex to bed,' Harry said. 'She seems okay and has gone out like a light. I've left Steph with her. We have to go back to the boat. I'll drop Andy off somewhere upriver, so he can go back to the hotel and then make it look as if I've just come back from shore on my own, so I'll be a bit longer than you expect. Don't move yet. Call Steph if you need anything.'

When Andy was ready, they left him and it did seem a long time before he returned, but Zen did not mind, the warmth was making him feel drowsy again. When Harry did come back, he pulled up a chair to sit beside him. He was dripping wet.

Steph had come down. 'She seems fine,' he said before going into the galley.

'We were lucky tonight,' Harry said. 'The wind's picking up. Any later and we wouldn't have been able to go out with the boat.'

'It seemed rough enough to me.'

'It was mostly swell. It also helped that we'd made that journey before and knew the location of the reefs.'

'What happened?'

'As you know, I went to Linda's. I'd come back and had gone to bed at about half two. Almost immediately, I had an incredible dream. I was sitting on a settee somewhere. Either side of me were these huge men and in front of us you were tied to a chair. You were asleep or unconscious. There was another man floating around talking, but I couldn't hear what he was saying.'

'That's incredible.'

'Even though I couldn't hear the conversation, I knew what was going on. I knew that these guys were planning to take you and throw you off a cliff at a place called the Devil's Cauldron and that it was to be done on the outgoing tide.'

Steph came in carrying a tray of hot tea and glasses of brandy. 'Do you want to have something to eat?' he asked. 'I could make you a sandwich.'

'I'm not hungry,' Zen said. 'This will do.'

'Then I'll leave you,' Steph said. 'I need to get out of these clothes.'

'Anyway, as I was saying, I had the dream and woke,' Harry continued. 'I'd been drinking and didn't take it seriously, thinking it was just a bit weird. I went to the bathroom and then back to sleep. Then I had the dream again, almost exactly the same, except that this time I looked down at my legs and feet and saw that they weren't mine, they were a woman's. There was no mistaking what was happening.'

'So you realised you were seeing through Alex's eyes?'

'Exactly.'

'So I wonder how she did it?'

'You mean, how did Elizabeth do it?'

'Yes.'

'It must've been telepathy.'

'Must've been.'

'Well, when I woke up for the second time, I knew what I had to do. It was imprinted in my mind. I went ashore and the first thing I did was to dial Alex's number, which I had to do three times before someone answered. I was to say nothing and hang up after thirty seconds. I don't quite understand the purpose of that, but then I went and dragged Andy out of the hotel. We got back on board and organised your rescue. It was a good thing you had that Ordinance Survey map because I wouldn't have known where the Devil's Cauldron was. I also had it in my mind that we were not to be seen bringing you back, so we hand-winched the port gangway and got to you as soon as we could. We only had to stand by for half an hour.'

'I understand,' Zen said. He was feeling worse. 'I think I need to lie down.'

Harry helped him up the stairs, into the cabin and to his bedside. He waited until he removed his wet clothes, dried off and put his pyjamas on. 'I'll be okay now,' Zen said. 'I'll be okay after some sleep. I've been drugged twice you know?'

'No wonder you're so drowsy. Don't lock the door, I'll need to check up on you both from time to time. See you later.'

'One last thing before you go, Harry. Thank you.'

Harry shut the door. The oil heaters were on. Zen would not mind the smell tonight. He checked on Alex. She was sleeping soundly. He slipped in beside her warm body and fell asleep.

Chapter 48: Resolution

Saturday, 1st January 1983

He is sitting at the side of the bed. Next to him is Elizabeth. He looks back at the sleeping forms of himself and Alex, under the bedclothes. As he turns back to Elizabeth, she puts her hand on his, as it rests on his thigh. He does not experience it in the conventional way, that is, not the touch, but he senses the emotion, a warmth. She smiles at him.

'There is much I need to tell you, some of it now, more later, but first the most important thing.' She pauses for a moment, looking forward and then back at him. 'Because of you, I've come to realise the truth.' Zen tries to reply but she tenderly puts her hand on his mouth, causing it to tingle. 'There is more. Although it was I who influenced Alex into this relationship with you, I have in turn come to care for you. You do not have to say anything, I sense what you feel better than you can describe. I also know your feelings for Alex are not what they once were; this is understandable.'

'You saved our lives.'

'By now you must have heard from Harry how it was done.'

He nodded. 'What about my father, Earsop and Alexandrou?'

'Your father's safe and Earsop's dead.'

'Dead! You didn't..?'

'No, not in the way that you fear.'

'What happened?'

'I went to him when he had gone to sleep. We had a talk, just as we are doing now. I made him an offer he could not refuse, I think that is the modern expression.'

'Oh?'

'After convincing him that he was going to die whatever happened, I gave him a choice. He could either do so by a means of his choosing or he could face one that was prolonged and harrowing. He made the right decision.'

'What did you make him do?'

'After binding him, I allowed him to wake. I dictated a confessional letter and then he injected himself with the same potion he had used on you. When he fell unconscious, I untied him and put him back into bed and waited till he died. That was an hour ago.'

'I need to know what was in the letter,' he said, looking over at Alex.

'Firstly, he confesses to arranging the murders of his former colleagues and the wife and gives the reason.'

'And what was that?'

'Revenge. I don't have time to explain more. It will all come out eventually.'

'What about the wife? Why did he have her killed?'

'She was his mistress and he felt that she knew too much.'

'So, who does he say committed these acts?'

'He doesn't, but gives sufficient description of the injuries to leave no doubt. He then confesses to aiding Alexandrou's plan to murder you and Alex, with the help of his thugs, the motive being to prevent the collapse of Alexandrou's business and the financial reward he would subsequently receive. He explains how he manipulated Alex's mind, which allowed him to use

537

her both as bait and an unwilling accomplice. Finally he states that it was the guilt of taking his former mistress's life that led him, in turn, to take his own.'

'Why did you leave out the attempt on my fathers' life?'

'Because it would have been difficult to explain how it was going to be done and who was going to do it. This way Alexandrou is revealed for what he is and what he attempted to do. I think in your father's eyes, whether the attempt was on his life or yours, would make no difference.'

'True. And what about Alex?'

'She will remember nothing of the events of last night, until she hit the water. You can tell her that Earsop drugged and manipulated her with a view to killing you both and you can give her the reason why. When they find Earsop, she will have the truth confirmed.'

'Okay, I can do that.'

'As soon as you get up, you must all go to the police and tell them that at the end of your meal together, Alex unwittingly opened the back door, so letting in Earsop's thugs, who tied you both up. They waited until two in the morning, you believe, before Earsop also arrived. You know the rest.'

'How do we explain the rescue?'

'Harry's to say that he had a feeling of foreboding and called Alex's house. Alex at that moment had managed to partly free herself and, being unattended, got to the phone and dislodged the receiver, telling Harry what he needed to know to perform the rescue. There will be a record of the call and you must tell Harry that this is his story.'

'Will the police believe this? Wouldn't she have been overheard?'

'Alex will not remember and no one else will be in a position to dispute this or offer a better explanation.'

'You're a clever girl.'

'Philip knew that,' she says, looking solemn and reflective. 'He knew I would have made him a wonderful wife.'

'I'm sure of it.'

'The other thing is that it's true that Alex was having an affair with one of her parents' waiters. This was entirely my doing as was the betrayal of her other boyfriends. She would never have done so without my influence. Please forgive her, she is entirely innocent.'

'I understand.'

'This is one thing she cannot comprehend; how her feelings have changed, will change.'

'I'm prepared for that.'

'I will come to you again, very soon and explain more, but I must allow her to wake.'

'All right, I'll see you tonight, maybe.'

'Maybe.'

He was woken by Alex stirring beside him and getting up. When she came back from the bathroom he held her. She was frightened, worried and confused, but he explained everything and reassured her that as soon as they were up and ready they would go to the police. Afterwards he went down to make a cup of tea, took Harry aside for long enough to explain what it was they had to do and made sure that everyone understood their story. After something to eat, they would be going ashore.

Things were not straightforward, though, as for those first three days of the year they suffered the worst weather so far. For the whole of this time there were periods of heavy rain and gale force winds. Because these stormy conditions coincided with spring tides, the current in the estuary was particularly strong. Consequently it was too dangerous to use their boat to go ashore. Harry had to show Zen how to operate the VHF to make a call to Richard the boatman, whose number they kept in case of such emergencies, to ask him to come and pick them up.

They had to wait an hour and, when he came, they all went ashore, including Steph. After meeting up with Andy, they spent three hours in the police station, giving statements. As Alex could not remember anything of the events of that night, Zen was the only one who could give a description of Earsop's accomplices. During that time the police went round to Earsop's and, when nobody answered, forced entry and found him dead in bed with the suicide note beside him. An ambulance and extra police were brought in and eventually the press. Zen gave the police the spare keys to his car so that they could collect it and check it for prints and other evidence.

It was eight o'clock before they could call a cab for Alex, who had decided to go and stay with her parents, and get Richard to take them back on board. Elizabeth did not come to him that night or the next.

Owing to the inclement weather, nobody could go out on either the Sunday or the Bank Holiday Monday, so they got up late, prepared meals together, ate, talked, played cards, read, watched television and walked around the windswept and rain-lashed decks when they needed exercise.

They watched the shore and wondered what was going on. A policeman and two detectives came in a launch on both days at around mid-morning and asked more questions, but did not give away any information. On the local BBC News there was only a brief mention of the discovery of Earsop's body. A connection was made, in the report, to the other two killings, but it was left that the police were investigating the death.

Then, on Monday night, after falling asleep, he finds himself standing beside the bed with Elizabeth next to him.

'I was worried about you. I expected you sooner,' he says.

'I am moved by your concern, but had much to think on.'

'You know I am willing to do whatever I can to help you.' He reaches out and takes her hand.

'You are kind to say this, but you know that it must end.'

'But why?'

'There are many reasons. To begin with, Alex must have her life back. I have no place here.'

'But what will happen to you?'

'I will face dissolution, like everybody else, as I should have done long ago.'

'But you will no longer be.'

'Do not forget, I am a monster, a ruthless murderer.'

'Some of those deserved to die and you repented.'

'It was not my place to make either the judgment or to carry out the sentence.'

'But you have changed. How can you end your existence without experiencing some happiness?'

'The manner and the power by which I have come to be is such that it will predispose me to madness. It is compassion that keeps me sane for now, but this tranquillity will not prevail.' She squeezes his hand. 'I have tasted some peace and it is enough. I do not wish to lose this feeling. I know what I must do and I now need to hear, from you, that you will carry out what I ask of you.'

'It depends what it is. I don't know if I can...'

'Enough...' she says firmly. 'What you will be doing is for me alone. I need to know I can rely on you. I have no one else. Please do not make me beg. Only you can set me free. Do I have your promise?'

'I give you my word.'

'Thank you,' she says. 'Tomorrow night I will come to you and tell you everything. You must be ready to act the next day. Make no other plans.'

'I agree.'

'I will leave you now.'

Chapter 49: The Portal

Tuesday, 4th January 1983

The weather had improved considerably that morning, which was just as well as everyone had to go back to work.

On his return from running, Zen picked up their two workers for the first time that year and left them in Andy's charge. They busied themselves de-rusting and painting the cargo deck. Meanwhile Zen kept himself occupied, helping Harry service the lifeboats. Later in the afternoon he closed the previous month's accounts and got them ready to post.

At five he took the workers back out and dropped into the police station. He was pleasantly surprised to be told that he could collect his car, which was in their yard. He moved it to the nearby car park. As he was about to take the steps down to the pontoon, someone rushed down from the harbour office to give him a message. Both his father and George Pittas had rung that morning.

He might just catch George still in the office, he thought, so he went to the phone box and called. Heather answered and was excitedly saying that she had heard what had happened to him and was he all right. He said he would tell her all about it some other time and asked about his flat. Everything seemed to be okay, so she put him through to George.

'My dear Zen,' he said. 'How are you? I only just heard this morning what happened over the weekend. I think most of the community knows by now.'

'I think I've just about recovered from the drugs and the dunking.'

'The dunking? What happened to me was a dunking. Yours was a lot worse.'

'You know, down here all I've heard about is Earsop's suicide, his confession to the other murders and his conspiring with Spiros to kill me.'

'Spiros was arrested on Saturday, late afternoon and your parents were interviewed on both Saturday and Sunday. On Monday morning, the police came with a search warrant to Spiros's office and removed his files. He's still in custody in Exeter, and is appearing before the magistrate today.'

'I can't believe it.'

'On both Sunday and Monday your parents came to Tonemouth and attempted to get on board. They saw how bad the weather was and tried to hire a boat. Your father's keen to speak to you.'

'I suppose he's on his way home.'

'He left at his usual time.'

'Did my father take Mrs Alexandrou and Sophia back?'

'He did.'

'God, can you imagine what they must be feeling?'

'Everyone's sympathetic with them, although your father's instructed that his son-in-law is not to enter this office.'

'Has he got grounds for that?'

'He feels that Nicholas must have known that something was amiss.'

'But what about Antigoni?'

'Well, your father said he would support them till such time as it was determined whether any of Spiros's business can be rescued. If not, he'll have to find work elsewhere.'

'Sad, very sad.'

'You talk like you're more sorry for them than yourself.'

'I escaped. I was lucky.'

'Spooky, I'd say. Good news is that your father's asked me to find a replacement for you so you can come home. He's prepared to pay the full cost of a captain.'

'Eh, listen George, can you do me a favour and hold back on that. Wait till you hear from me.'

'Sure Zen. Listen, it's about time I left. Call your Dad, he should be home now.'

When he called, his mother answered. On hearing his voice she burst into tears, crying 'my son' between sobs. After a brief conversation, his father took over.

'My son, are you all right?'

'I'm absolutely fine, Dad.'

'Have you been to the doctor, to make sure you're okay.'

'I promise you I'm fully recovered.'

'We tried to visit.'

'George told me.'

'I've instructed him to find a replacement as soon as possible, so you can come home.'

'So he said. Look Dad, don't take this the wrong way, but I really want to stay.'

'It hasn't got anything to do with that woman, has it?' his father said, and then almost immediately, 'I'm sorry, I didn't mean it to sound the way it did.'

'Well, it doesn't actually,' Zen said, firmly, 'but I'm enjoying what I'm doing and really like the place and crew.'

'They sound like wonderful people. They risked their lives for you.'

'We work well together. Besides, I don't imagine there's much to do in the office.'

'Apart from helping to clear up the mess Spiros left.'

'I'm sorry that things turned out the way they did. You must be disappointed.'

'Well, I'm sorry about that too. But I'm more upset by the way I've treated you.'

'It wasn't your fault, Dad. How could you know?'

'Are you sure you didn't suspect anything when you were with Sophia? Something that made you decide not to marry her?'

'Nothing that related to what happened.'

'Look, I'd prefer it if you came back and we were together again, but I admire your sense of duty and loyalty to your friends. At least visit for a few days; I can send George.'

'No, don't do that. The weather would make him ill. It won't be a problem for a day or two. We can trust the crew.'

'I know we can. But come as soon as possible.'

'There are a few things I have to do first and then I'll plan my trip.'

'Okay, son, I'll wait your call,' Captain John said. 'I'll put your mother back on.'

In the evening the weather worsened again with heavy rain and strong winds. This particularly disappointed Harry as he hadn't seen Linda for days.

That night Elizabeth comes to him as she had promised. They stand facing each other beside the bed, before she takes hold of him and they fly into the stormy night sky. They travel a long time but there is no visibility and therefore no clue as to where they are going. When they start descending, he sees treetops approaching before the white light and they are standing in a waterlogged car park and picnic area within a clearing of trees. In one corner there is a sign with a map.

'Take note of this location,' she says.

From there she leads him by the hand along a distinct footpath until they come to the banks of a river, swollen by the winter rains. From that landmark they head in another direction, along a less used path that goes deep into the woods and to where the sides of the valley begin to rise. There are some distinct outcrops of rock here, on one of which are gouged out of the stone the initials of a recent visitor and his girlfriend. Close by is a clustering of trees amongst which is thick undergrowth. It is here that Elizabeth stops and surveys the ground.

'This is where you will come tomorrow after sunset,' she says. 'You must make sure there is no one around, no cars in the car park. You will come here and clear this undergrowth. You will need something for that, as well as a pick and shovel.'

'I can buy what we don't have.'

'You will need someone with you to hold a light, but only you can touch this ground.'

'Harry will come.'

'Under the growth you will see an oblong arrangement of flat stones. They will have become

547

compacted with earth after all these years, but you must remove them until you unearth a circle of small boulders. Within them will be a bronze box, the size of a chest. You will take it back to the car, but leave the ground turned over, throwing the stones randomly as far away as you can. You will make no attempt to tidy up. Do you understand?'

'I do.'

'You will drive back to Tonemouth and leave Harry. His part will be over. Then you will drive to the castle and church by the estuary and park. You will open the box and inside it you will find bones. They are my remains.'

'Your remains? How did they come to be here? Your aunt?'

'She buried them, yes. I never recovered from the injuries sustained during the wrecking, or my broken heart, and, once my anger and resentment were spent and my revenge taken, my will to live failed. I fell into ill health and died. My aunt was so distraught in her grief that she later re-interred me in a way that she hoped would keep me close, give me a chance to come back to her, in spirit at least. Little did she know what manner of return she had arranged. She had contained my soul within this precinct while I waited. Many decades and hosts passed and then one day Alex came by and, in a chance incident, nearly died. That was my opportunity to make her my habitation, to anchor myself in her.'

'But it was only recently you materialised.'

'I was able to influence Alex in many ways, negative ones unfortunately, ways in which she would not naturally behave, but it was Earsop who unlocked my prison.' Elizabeth looks back down at the ground. 'But even so, the source of my powers and abilities have always been beneath this ground.'

'But how was it done? How did you...'

'There is much danger in that knowledge. Never concern yourself with it again, it must pass with me. That which was found by chance must be destroyed. My aunt was unable to do this, but you must. Within the chest and amongst the bones will be another smaller container, the size of a ring case. This you will not open until the correct time. You will take it with you as you walk to the coast, then along the path until you come upon that cove you know so well.'

'The one I run to.'

'Oh that you should understand the significance of that place, but for now, you will sit near the water's edge and wait, keeping your eyes on the open sea. After a span of time, for which I cannot give you an estimation, a light will emerge from the water. You will have no difficulty seeing it as it will be brilliant. You will then open the case. Inside will be a stone which will by now be glowing as well. You will take it and throw it at the light. You need not be concerned about distance or accuracy, the very act of throwing will ensure it finds the mark. The light will submerge and vanish. You can then leave.'

'But Elizabeth you must tell me...'

'I cannot,' Elizabeth cuts him short again. 'I know what you wish to know. My keeping you in ignorance is an act of mercy. Please believe this.'

'I'm sorry.'

'When you take the stone out of the box, you must not hesitate. Promise you will not fail me.'

'I promise.'

'Once this is done you can return, but there's one more thing.'

'Tell me.'

'The next day, you are to light a fire. Make it hot, use lots of wood and when you are alone cremate my bones. Then you are to take the ashes and scatter them beside Philip's grave, over the ground intended for me.'

'I will do so,' he says and, before he can add anything further, she has embraced him again and they are flying back to Tonemouth. When they are standing in his cabin he asks, 'And what happens after that?'

'I think you can guess,' she says. 'Rest now.'

'Will I ever see you again?'

'Perhaps. We shall see.'

The weather was better the next morning, but still cold with rain. Zen went out to pick up the workmen. They had three that day. They painted cabins and worked in the stores. Later he went to the ironmongers and bought some robust garden shears and a pick. They had plenty of shovels on board.

That night they were invited to the Bulgarian ship. Before that, at five o'clock, after returning their workers to the quay, he drove with Harry to the car park within the woods that were on the fringes of the moor. It was deserted.

Retracing the route Elizabeth had shown him, in the dark with their torches, was easier than he had anticipated, but the cutting down of the undergrowth, the removal of the flat stones, then the earth and finally the boulders took a good hour. Harry, meanwhile, asked no questions, appreciating the solemnity of what they were doing.

It was nine o'clock when they picked Linda up from her house. Zen drove down to the embankment and took them across to the Bulgarian trawler. He promised to join them later.

Returning to the embankment and the car, he drove towards the mouth of the estuary and parked along the road. After changing his footwear, he retrieved the palm sized metal box from within the larger one and, with torch in hand, headed for the coastal path and his summer running route. Much of the way was muddy and slippery, hard going even in his Wellington boots.

Forty-five minutes later he was sitting on the damp rocks in the cove, where Elizabeth had told him to go. At least it was not raining now, but it was cold and windy and because it was overcast it was also dark. He turned off the torch to save the battery and wondered how long he would have to wait there, staring out to sea.

After no more than half an hour, out towards the horizon he saw a light approaching. He thought it might be a fisherman at first, he had often seen them passing in the early mornings when he had been running, but then he realised the source was underwater, as if some stupid diver was out there with an underwater torch. But whatever it was it moved rapidly, zigzagging through the shoals and reefs as it neared. When it came up to the entrance to the cove, this light was so bright that it illuminated the surrounding rocks and he had to shield his eyes until they adjusted. Once they did and he could look directly at it, he made out a fuzzy glowing orb of such radiant beauty that he nearly forgot what he was there to do.

Turning away, Zen took the box out of his pocket, opened it and removed the stone. It was like a smooth rounded pebble that was completely black, but as soon as he held it in his palm it too began to glow. It started as a dull red, then it lightened to orange. It became so bright that he thought it would burn his hand, but it gave off no heat.

He could not take his eyes off it, nor could he cast it away. He wavered and, as he did so, the glow of the stone increased even more. At that moment he understood many things. He realised that if he kept this stone, there was nothing on this earth he could not have or do. There would be no one he desired whom he could not possess. No harm would ever come to him and no obstacle could stand in his way.

He also understood that the price of this course of action would be paid by Elizabeth's soul, as well as his own. Then he imagined Elizabeth, standing on the deck of that barque, nearly two hundred years ago, looking into the eyes of the man she loved, praying he would say the words she wanted to hear, hoping he would undertake what he had promised to do.

He imagined how those beautiful eyes and mouth would have smiled as he threw the stone towards the open sea.

As soon as he had done so, he felt a sense of relief. As Elizabeth had said, the stone found its mark, and both it and the glowing orb were extinguished.

When he arrived back in Tonemouth, the town was quiet. The pubs and restaurants had closed and there was no one about. At the quayside he got in the boat and began his crossing. Beneath the covered prow, under the boat's tarpaulin, was the bronze box.

As he approached the dark and lifeless hulk of the *Amber*, he could hear music coming from the Bulgarian ship nearby. He looked at his watch, it was after midnight, but he bet the others were still at the party. Hopefully there might be food, as he had not eaten, and some wine.

Tomorrow there would be more to do. The cremation of the bones and the scattering of the ashes, but for now he needed to be with people, lots of people.

About the author

My ancestral home is a tiny island in the Aegean but I was born in New York City and then spent the first six years of my life on a working cargo ship with three generations of my family. My parents moved to London when I was twelve and, when I finished my education, I worked in shipping, managing my father's ships up until the time of his death, when the business was wound up. I now live in South Devon with my wife and when I'm not writing enjoy walking, travelling, photography and cooking.

Other books by Theo Lemos

The Sea People

If you would like to know about future book releases, please visit my website, www.theo-lemos.co.uk and sign the mailing list.

I do hope you enjoy my novels and, if so, please tell your friends. Also, if you would be willing to post a short review on Amazon, I'd be extremely grateful.

Theo Lemos
South Hams, England, January 2015

Made in the USA
Charleston, SC
05 March 2015